M.C. Scott was a veterinary surgeon and taught at the universities of Cambridge and Dublin before taking up writing as a full-time profession. Now founder and chair of the Historical Writers' Association, her novels have been shortlisted for the Orange Prize, nominated for an Edgar Award and translated into over twenty languages.

For more information on all aspects of the books, visit: www.mcscott.co.uk

For the Historical Writers' Association, see: www.theHWA.co.uk

By M. C. Scott

HEN'S TEETH
NIGHT MARES
STRONGER THAN DEATH
NO GOOD DEED

BOUDICA: DREAMING THE EAGLE
BOUDICA: DREAMING THE BULL
BOUDICA: DREAMING THE HOUND
BOUDICA: DREAMING THE SERPENT SPEAR

THE CRYSTAL SKULL
2012: EVERYTHING YOU NEED TO KNOW
ABOUT THE APOCALYPSE

ROME: THE EMPEROR'S SPY
ROME: THE COMING OF THE KING
ROME: THE EAGLE OF THE TWELFTH

ROME

THE COMING OF THE KING

M.C. Scott

CORGI BOOKS

TRANSWORLD PUBLISHERS
61–63 Uxbridge Road, London W5 5SA
A Random House Company
www.transworldbooks.co.uk

**ROME: THE COMING OF THE KING
A CORGI BOOK: 9780552161800**

First published in Great Britain
in 2011 by Bantam Press
an imprint of Transworld Publishers
Corgi edition published 2012

Copyright © M. C. Scott 2011

M. C. Scott has asserted the right under the Copyright, Designs and
Patents Act 1988 to be identified as the author of this work.

Photograph of Masada on p 491 © Manahem Kahana/AFP/Getty Images
Maps © Tom Coulson at Encompass Graphics

Addresses for Random House Group Ltd companies outside the UK
can be found at: www.randomhouse.co.uk
The Random House Group Ltd Reg. No. 954009

The Random House Group Limited supports the Forest Stewardship
Council (FSC®), the leading international forest-certification organization.
Our books carrying the FSC label are printed on FSC®-certified paper.
FSC is the only forest-certification scheme endorsed by the leading
environmental organizations, including Greenpeace.
Our paper-procurement policy can be found
at www.randomhouse.co.uk/environment.

Typeset in Sabon by
Kestrel Data, Exeter, Devon.
Printed in Great Britain by
Clays Ltd, St Ives plc

2 4 6 8 10 9 7 5 3 1

For Alasdair, with love

Contents

Map: the Roman Empire in the First Century AD   8

Prologue   13

I   Caesarea, Judaea, Early Summer, AD 66   23
In the Reign of the Emperor Nero

  Map: Judaea in the First Century AD   24

II   Jerusalem, Early Summer, AD 66   205
In the Reign of the Emperor Nero

  Map: Jerusalem, Early First Century AD   206

III   Masada and Jerusalem, Mid Summer, AD 66   301
In the Reign of the Emperor Nero

  Map: Masada   302

Epilogue   475

Author's Note   481

Hibernia

BRITANNIA

Germania
Inferior

*Germania
Magna*

Coriallum

Belgica

Germania
Superior

Lugdunensis

GALLIA

Rhaetia

Noricur

*Oceanus
Atlanticus*

Aquitania

Alpina

Narbonensis

ITALIA

Galatia

Corsica

Rome

Tarraconensis

Sardinia

Lusitania

Balearic Is.

Baetica

Sicil

Africa
Proconsularis

Mauretania
Caesariensis

Numidia

Mauretania
Tingitana

N

0   miles   400

0   km   400

The Roman Empire
in the 1st Century AD

Sarmatia

Tyras   Olbia

BOSPORUN
KINGDOM

Pontus Euxinus

Moesia
Superior   Moesia Inferior

llyricum   Thracia

Macedonia   Bithynia   Pontus

Armenia

Epirus   ASIA   Cappadocia

PARTHIAN
EMPIRE

Achaea   Galatia

Lycia   Cilicia   Assyria

Creta   Cyprus   SYRIA   Mesopotamia

Mare Internum

JUDAEA

Cyrenaica   Alexandria

Arabia
Petraea   Arabia Magna

Aegyptus

The Fates guide he who will. He who won't, they drag.

Seneca

'And thus will it come about in the Year of the Phoenix, on the night when the Great Hound shall gaze down from beyond the knife-edge of the world, that in his sight shall the Great Whore be wreathed in fire and those who would save her will stoke the flames.

'Only when this has come to pass shall the Kingdom of Heaven be manifest as has been promised. Then shall the Temple's veil be rent, never to be repaired, and all that was whole shall be broken, and the covenant that was made shall be completed in accord with all that is written.'

Prophecy of the Sibylline Oracle as described to Saulos prior to the Great Fire of Rome in AD 64

PROLOGUE

North Africa, Early Spring AD **66**

The sun was a scorching ball of fire, roasting the desert and everything in it, even now, barely two hours after dawn. The harsh, grey sand took wings, ready to clog a man's lungs within a dozen breaths if he didn't keep his face covered. Underfoot, it was hot as live coals, fit to burn even the healthiest of feet.

Saulos Herodion, cousin to the king of Judaea, did not have the healthiest of feet. He had lost all the skin of his right sole and half the meat of the heel in Rome's fire and for the first full year of his time in the desert, he had not been able to place his foot to the sand without screaming.

Then, sometime in the winter of the second year – such winters as they had here – news of Seneca's death had reached him. He had few details; half a sentence passed on with no more value than a handful of dried dates, but even so, what should have heartened him had instead made plain the extent to which his world was passing him by, and he not at the heart of it.

Within a month, he had learned to walk again. Now, in this second spring, he believed he could run if he had to; certainly he was fit to return to the swift-moving world beyond the sands.

There was sorrow in his parting. The slender, black-skinned women who had tended him were the same who raised the horses on which they and their menfolk hunted. They had given him a mare as a gift and offered, with many gestures to fill the gaps in his understanding of their language, to have one of their stallions cover it for him before he left, that he might carry with him a foal of worth into the worthless lands beyond the desert.

With as many gestures, he had turned down their offer: the mare was not yet in season and he could not wait until the moon did its work and made her ready for the stallion. Because he must leave soon: today; the world could perhaps be persuaded to slow in its turning while a man grew a new skin and rested his soul, but he could not expect it to tarry for ever.

It was with genuine regret that Saulos rose on his last day among the Berber tribes, broke his fast on the fermented mare's milk and rock-hard dates he had once hated and had come to love, wrapped the loose wonder of his burnous around his head and face and walked across the roasted, roasting sand to the edge of the encampment.

Everything was ready. He had no real reason to linger, except that he had a question to ask, and his plans for the future hinged on its answer.

He found whom he sought in the shade of the oasis,

tending a pair of iron-grey falcons. Without speaking, he sank to his heels, rested his forearms across his knees and let his vision grow soft, so that he looked at everything and nothing. He had thought himself a patient man until he came among these people. Fifteen months in their company had taught him the truth; he was not remotely patient, but could seem so for a very long time, which was perhaps the same thing.

Presently, the tall, lean woman he had come to see deigned to notice him. Her hair was dark, curled tight as new ram's wool, her eyes were the deep amber-ochre of her tribe and she bore the spiralled tattoos across her cheeks and over the bridge of her nose that marked her as a hunter, not one of those women whose care had kept him alive, who had bathed the burns that had stripped the skin from his back, his legs, his feet, who had applied salves against the force of his screams and held him afterwards as he wept himself to sleep.

She had not visited him, nor lent him her horse, nor taught him how to fly the falcons at living quarry. She had, in fact, ignored him entirely from the moment Philotus had carried him on camel-back to their camp and paid his king's ransom in gold to have him tended, with half of it for his care and the other half for a promise that his presence would not be revealed to the Romans who were hunting him.

He believed without question that the promise had been kept, but he had been a spy before another, greater calling had claimed his life, and he knew the calibre of the man who hunted him, the brother spy, trained by the same teacher, to the same standards: not better – never that – but good enough to be dangerous. After nearly two years, it was inconceivable that this man might not know where Saulos was, or that he was not watching, waiting for his prey to move.

Knowing this, Saulos had lain through two winters and a summer, sending out questions, drawing in the answers as they came by dove, by horse, by foot, clasping them close and using them to shape his first hazed, hate-filled dreams into a plan so well crafted, so seamlessly wrought, that it could not possibly fail. Except in this moment.

He felt cold eyes touch him and kept his gaze turned towards the ground. It was how they were here; the women had the ascendancy. He had despised the menfolk for that when he first came.

'You have come to take your leave?' In the desert's mid-morning heat, her voice had all the cold resonance of a flute made of ice. Hate informed every breath, but it was so contained, so controlled, that it sucked the warmth from the day.

Saulos said, 'I have come to ask you a question, Iksahra sur Anmer.'

He thought he had lost her, just naming her and her father in the same breath; that she would call her falcons to fist, whistle to heel the cheetah that was her familiar, and ride away. He watched her consider it and heard the halted breath when she changed her mind.

'What question?' she asked.

'How is it that you plan to avenge the deaths of your father and mother, whom you loved?'

For that, he thought she might kill him. She carried the curved long-knife at her belt, which could lift his head from his shoulders in a single strike. The cheetah

16

that sat at her heels like a trained hound could crush a man's skull in its jaws. He had seen it done, once, or thought he had: it might have been a delirium dream. He kept his soft eyes on the harsh sand and wondered what it would be to die here, away from all that he planned.

Iksahra sur Anmer, whose father had been torn apart by four of his own horses on the orders of a foreign king, took her hand away from her knife's hilt. A single lifted finger sent the cheetah to lie loll-tongued in the shade of a date palm. She loosed the falcons to sit in the branches above and came to sit opposite him, with her forearms folded across her bent knees. Her burnous was identical to his own. It flowed around her, as the folds of a breeze. Her face was black within it, and shadowed, so that her deep-ochre eyes seemed more black than brown, set off only by their whites.

'Tell me,' she said, and Saulos let out the breath he had been holding.

It was not a simple plan, but her part in it was relatively so and he had spent six months preparing for this moment.

He said, 'I am going to travel to Judaea, to the court of King Agrippa II. Wait—' He held up his hand although in truth she had not moved, only that her eyes were drilling holes in his skull. 'His father killed your father. I know this. I, too, go to obtain vengeance. But my vengeance will be slow, a thing to be savoured over months, not swallowed whole in the time it takes for a knife to still a man's heart. My vengeance will fall not on one man alone, but on the heads of the entire Hebrew people. If I succeed in my endeavour, within a handspan of years the twelve tribes of Abraham will no longer exist. I would crave your aid in this.'

'As your whore?' Her voice dripped contempt. The spiral marks on her face stood proud a little; he kept his eyes on them and was sure not to smile at the image of that.

'Assuredly not. You would be the king's favoured falconer. Also his beastmaster, the keeper of his hunting hounds, his big cats, his hounds, his horses.' *As was your father to his father.* He did not say that, but the understanding twisted in the hot air between them.

'The new king does not hunt,' said the woman, slowly. 'The whole world knows that he prefers to keep to his bed and his . . . playthings, while his sister rules the land. It is the queen who hunts.'

'But any gift must be given to the king, even if Queen Berenice is its true recipient. In any case, it matters not which of them takes you, only that you are there, with your falcons.' He hesitated, delicately. 'Would I be correct if I were to surmise that your birds could hunt and kill a message-dove, one of those that flies fast and low across the sands and carries the written word from one side of the empire to the other?'

She did not answer that, only looked at him as if even the question were an insult.

'Good.' He gave a shallow nod. 'So then, your part in this will be to intercept the message-doves that are sent to the king's loft from across the world. They come from Rome, from Damascus, from Antioch, from Athens, Corinth, Alexandria and further abroad. They come mostly at dawn and dusk, and, while the king is at Caesarea, they fly always over a particular isthmus on the sea coast, which is out of sight of the palace, but surrounded by flat, open land, so that you cannot be watched without your knowing.

'You will take these birds from the sky and bring their messages to me so that I may know what they say. Further, as the king's beastmaster, you will be tasked with the care of some message-birds in the beast compound so that they may be sent out with the journeymen who take them to far-flung cities. Therefore, once in a while, we may use them ourselves to convey messages of our own to the king – as if they came from far abroad. Then, when we know who our enemies are, and how they are ranged against us, we will act.'

'What will we do?'

'We will foment war with Rome. King Agrippa resides at Caesarea, the city founded by his grandfather, Herod the Great. That place has its own tensions and we will use them to force the entire royal family to Jerusalem. There, if the zealots of the War Party can be made to declare war against Rome, Nero will send the legions to crush them and once that happens, the whole of Judaea will rise against the armies of occupation.'

'Then they will die,' said Iksahra, with certainty. 'No one can withstand Rome's legions.'

'Exactly so; and Jerusalem will be razed to the ground, brick by ancient brick, until nothing is left and the people who live therein are dead or enslaved in foreign lands. Then you, who hate Agrippa, and I, who hate the Hebrews, will know that our vengeance is complete.'

Saulos rose smoothly; that, too, was a skill he had learned. 'I leave with the evening's cool. If you wish to join me, I would welcome your company, and that of your beasts.'

Saulos did not ride alone from the encampment; three guides came with him, but Iksahra sur Anmer, the best hunter among the Berber tribes, was not one of them.

He concealed his disappointment, and rode with the men, letting them entertain him with stories of horses and hunts and the inexplicable deeds of women. At nightfall, when they made camp in the lee of a dune, he took himself a little away from the firelight to urinate.

He was turning back when her hand caught his wrist. She was remarkably tall. The cheetah's yellow eyes regarded him from a place that had been entirely dark.

He said, 'I had hoped you might come.'

Her face was close to his. 'You know why I seek vengeance. Why do you?'

'Will you come with me to sit at the fire? The night is cold and I am still not used to the changes in temperature. We will be given privacy, I think.'

He was right; the men saw Iksahra and left, not for privacy, but out of fear. One made the sign against evil as she passed. Another hissed something, of which Saulos only heard the word ifrit and wished he had not.

Seated, fed, with a bladder of water in his hand – these people drank neither wine nor ale – Saulos felt safer. He stared into the fire and found it easier to believe she was a woman who hunted with matchless skill, not a winged demon who might feed on his soul.

He said, 'My tale is a long one, but at its shortest . . . In my youth, I was trained as a Roman agent by the late spymaster Seneca, known as the Teacher, and sent to Judaea to bring the Hebrews under Roman rule.'

'You did not succeed in that.' Her wild eyes laughed at him.

He bit his lip. It was a long time since he had been the butt of anyone's ridicule. He said, 'No. But I did burn Rome.' Flames leapt between them. 'I lit the blaze that nearly consumed it.'

'Why?'

He studied the small fire that lay between them. None of this was as he had planned. 'For a prophecy,' he said, which was true. 'The Sibyls said that if Rome burned under the eye of the dog star, then Jerusalem might be sundered and in its place . . .' With an effort, he held her gaze. 'In its place, the god they have denied will enslave them all, and rule in glory. But Judaea must fall for that to happen.'

'And if Jerusalem falls—'

'Then all of Judaea will fall with it; yes. The loss of Rome seemed a small price to pay.'

'And your own life? Was it an accident that the fire nearly killed you?'

'No. That was my enemy's doing. He is the second reason we are going to Judaea.'

'Is he there?'

'Not yet. But I will draw him there and when I have done so, I will undermine his allies until he no longer knows whom he can trust. I will remove his friends from him, one at a time, until he is alone, and friendless and lost. I will let him see what we are doing, slowly, a piece at a time, and when Jerusalem's fall is certain, I – I alone, I will kill him, slowly, by inches, by heartbeats, and he will know, each moment, why he dies and by whose hand.'

He stopped, because the crimson haze around him was real, and the flames were licking his face as his passion brought him lower and closer to the fire.

His cheeks were scorched. Iksahra had sparks on her clothing, where his hands, smashing the sand, had disturbed the fire. Thin tendrils of smoke rose to the night air and vanished.

She gazed at him, unreadable. 'What is his name, this man you hate so much?'

Saulos closed his eyes against the sweep of her stare. 'My enemy's name,' he said, evenly, 'is Sebastos Abdes Pantera. He rides with a former centurion named Appius Mergus, and with Hypatia of Alexandria, the Chosen of Isis.'

'I will remember their names.' Iksahra sur Anmer rose and stretched out a hand. He took it and she lifted him to his feet, effortlessly. 'We have things in common,' she said, and her white teeth flashed. 'I will join you. I will hunt the message-birds. But when the time comes, I will kill King Agrippa and you will not stop me.'

CAESAREA, JUDAEA
EARLY SUMMER, AD 66

IN THE REIGN OF THE
EMPEROR NERO

Judaea
in the First Century AD

Sidon

Damascus

PHOENICIA

Tyre

Caesarea Philippi

GAULANITIS

Mediterranean Sea

Ptolemais

Bethsaida

GALILEE

Sepphoris

Tiberias

Nazareth

Sea of Galilee

Bethabara

Caesarea

Gerasa

Samaria

DECAPOLIS

Joppa

River Jordan

PERÆA

Philadelphia

Lydda

Jericho

Emmaus

Jerusalem

Qumaran

Bethlehem

Machaerus

PHILISTIA

JUDAEA

Dead Sea

Gaza

IDUMAEA

NABATEA

Masada

N

0   miles   20

0   km   20

Mediterranean Sea

Area of main map

CHAPTER ONE

'Caesarea, pearl of the east. A tinderbox, waiting for the spark.'

Pantera had not spoken in half a day. His voice was dry as the desert. 'Saulos is there,' he said. 'Can you smell him? The danger that hangs around him?'

Mergus edged his horse in closer to where they could talk and the sound not carry on the desert air. He still marvelled that they were there at all, in the desert, half a day's ride east of Caesarea: when the message-birds had come to the emperor's loft in Rome, saying that their quarry was moving, that Saulos had finally left the fastness of the Berber lands, Mergus had wanted to take ship then, that night, and be after him.

It was Pantera who had said that they should wait, that they must watch, that there were things left to learn. 'He must know we're hunting him. He'll lead us a dance if he thinks we're following too close behind. Wait until he goes to ground. When he stops, we'll hear of it.'

And so they had watched the pigeon lofts at dawn each day and waited, as children for a gift, for each new cryptic line. *Your quarry has entered Mauretania. And left again. He is in Alexandria, buying gifts fit for a king.*

'Where did he get his money?' Mergus had asked.

'He has followers still,' Pantera had answered. 'Not many, but enough; men who have denied him and his god and kept hidden, so they can do this for him now. He won't stop in Alexandria. He's heading east.'

And then the messages began again. *He's taken ship, bound for Judaea, or perhaps Syria. He is in Caesarea, pearl of the east.*

And then they had ceased. No more messages, perhaps no more movement. 'He is cousin to the king of Caesarea,' Pantera had said. 'If he's going to lie up anywhere, it'll be there.'

'It's a trap,' Mergus had said. 'We can't go.'

'It's a trap,' Pantera had agreed. 'We have to go.' Hypatia had come away from the dying empress's side to support him, and Hypatia was, in Mergus' estimation, the world's most beautiful woman, and its least available. He was not terrified of her, but he had a degree of respect that bordered on the same thing.

Even so, Mergus had argued with both of them until the point when the emperor had insisted they go and thereby put an end to all debate. In times past, perhaps, men might have reasoned with Nero, but since Seneca's failed coup, and the bloodbath that had followed it, none had dared do so.

And so they were here, in the desert, riding towards the pearl of the east, outriders to a nondescript, if well-armed, camel train and Pantera had said he could smell Saulos on the wind, which was almost certainly untrue.

'Here, I would smell him only if he stank of burned sand, horse sweat and camel piss.' Mergus guided his mare with his knees, to keep both hands free for his bow. As part of his guise, he was paid to guard thirty-two pregnant camels; a fortune on the hoof and food for a desert's load of jackals. They were presently riding through a gully that ran between two rocky bluffs and was, in Mergus' estimation, too easy to attack.

He kept his eyes sharp and his arrow nocked, and gave only a part of his mind to the vision ahead, where Caesarea shimmered as a spark of textured sunlight on the line where sand met sky and both met the ocean.

It had been there since soon after dawn, but Pantera was right; here, on a nameless track through an unnamed gully half a day's ride from the city, was something different, some fold in the air where the desert's still heat met the first breeze from the sea, and it was not the balm it should have been, but a presage of danger and death.

Mergus' mare whickered and pricked her ears, and stepped out with a new eagerness. He breathed in the altered air, in and in and—

'Bandits!'

He and Pantera called the word together. Mergus' mare knew the threat of an ambush as well as he did; she had come with him from Rome, and before that from the hell-forests of Britain where painted warriors hid behind every second tree. Even as he shouted, she was plunging sideways out of the unsafe gully towards a fissure in the rocky bluff to its northern side.

An arrow sliced the dirt where he had been. A second shattered on the rock that sheltered him and splinters of ash wood skittered across his face. Ahead, a man died, screaming. The stench of fresh blood flooded the noon-dry air. Shadows moved. Mergus shot at one of them. He heard a body fall, then another, and had no idea who had died except that it wasn't him.

'Sebastos?'

Mergus called the Greek name Pantera used among the men of the camel train. He heard no answer. Five more arrows fell in the ten square feet he could see. A cow camel bellowed and toppled to the sand, hard as a felled tree. The three brothers who led the train began to whistle orders in the language only their train knew. Men began to shout: outriders and their enemies alike. The enemy called in Greek, not Aramaic, so they were not Hebrew zealots from Jerusalem come to take the camels for their holy war. A part of Mergus thought that knowledge might be useful later, if he lived.

The rock fissure offered Mergus temporary protec-tion, but after the first few frantic heartbeats it made him a sitting target. Sweating, he slid to the ground, keeping the rock to his right and his mare to his left. From there, he fired twice more but hit no one. He had trained in the bow these past eighteen months and thought himself adequate, but no more than that; he was a blade-fighter by instinct and training.

He slid the bow on to his shoulder and loosed from his belt the hooked knife that had been a gift from the three Saba tribesmen whose camels he guarded. It was longer than an eating knife and shorter than a cavalry sword, finely wrought, sharp on both edges and slightly curved along its length. He kissed the flat iron for luck and hissed again, 'Sebastos?'

'Here!'

Another fissure stood parallel to his own, a dozen dangerous paces further along the gully. To reach it, Mergus climbed to the bluff's flat top, sprinted forward and dropped down to where Pantera crouched in the sand behind the fallen body of his horse. Three arrows marked its throat and chest.

Pantera was the son of an archer; he could shoot with his eyes shut, and kill. To cover Mergus' arrival, he stood up, fired and crouched again. From a distance, he could have been one of the robed Saba tribesmen, dark of skin, hair and eyes. Then his questing, river-brown gaze turned on Mergus and he was no one but himself; a man broken and mended again, alive with the clarity of one who has been to the edge of death and not let it destroy him.

It was the quality of Pantera's gaze that had first caught Mergus' attention two years before in Rome, at a livestock market, where the spy was hauling water, to all outward appearances a farm hand of limited intelligence – until he had asked a question and in it lay the answer to the greater question that had driven Mergus' life.

For two decades, Mergus had served his emperor, rising through the ranks of the legions. But the emperor was a distant, ever-changing name, to be honoured in the mornings along with Jupiter and the legion's standards. What mattered, what Mergus had sought and never found, was a man whom he could follow without reservation, wholeheartedly, with honour and honesty and joy.

And then he had come to Rome where he served the

emperor directly and there, on the eve of the fire, he had met Pantera and had known at that first question, and in the impact of its answer, that in this man he had found everything he sought.

From that moment on, he had followed him with honour and honesty and joy through the fire that nearly destroyed Rome and out again, and now into the desert, on the trail of the man who had lit it.

They had survived this far together; Mergus did not intend to lose Pantera to bandits in a desert for the sake of a handful of camels. 'We can't stay here,' he said.

'We need to cross the gully. There's a deeper fissure on the other side. Right and then left. Go!'

They sprinted up the gully, and across to a fissure where a dead man lay – one of their outriders. Pantera fired three arrows on the run, the last as he pressed himself in beside Mergus. Other men lay dead across the trail: one of the Saba brothers, two of the outriders and three strangers. Their desert robes flowered across the sand, bright with new blood.

A second camel was dead, the remainder were careering across the sand in panic. Nobody followed them. Nobody tried to round them up.

'They're not after the train,' Mergus said.

Thirty-two pregnant camels were worth ten times that many horses or half a thousand head of sheep. No sane man would kill them; certainly they would not be allowed to stampede into the hyena-ridden hinterlands.

Another camel died, bellowing. Mergus spat. 'They're manhunting,' he said. 'They've come for someone. Us.' This was arrogance: the presumption that no one else in the train was worth the kind of silver that had bought this raid. He believed it to be true.

Pantera nodded, absently. His gaze was fixed on the hostile desert.

Mergus bit back the question that jammed his tongue; no point now in asking how anyone knew they were there, and not safe, either. The tribesmen who owned the camels said that the ghûls who stalked the desert could take unspoken thoughts and give them shape. Mergus made the sign against evil behind his back, to ward them off. He risked another look round the rock lip that guarded his head. An arrow chased him back.

'How many of them are there?' Pantera asked it as he might have asked for the price of new arrows, and not cared the number of the answer.

'Nine different voices,' Mergus said. 'Two different fletchings on the arrows, but there could be more than two archers.'

'That's what I thought: a dozen to begin and now nine. Let's suppose they know who they're after. If I attract their fire, will you mourn my death loudly?'

A shadow crossed Mergus' heart. 'Very loudly,' he said, and tried to smile.

Pantera's grip on his shoulder was quickly gone and then the man himself was gone, firing his arrows, killing some, angering the rest and making of himself a target when he could have been hidden. Mergus pressed his shoulder into the shelf of hard rock and breathed air that stank now of blood and sweat and split guts and his own fear.

'Aaaaaaah!' A high cry, not like Pantera at all, unless the wound were mortal—

'Are you hit?'

'No.' Blood ran a river down Pantera's left arm where an arrow had run too close. He slumped against the rock. 'Mourn for me,' he said. 'Loudly.'

'He's dead! Sebastos is dead!'

Mergus howled fit to draw back the dawn-hunting jackals. He drew his palm up Pantera's arm and smeared the blood along his hooked Saba knife and then across his lips and one cheek, as if he had cut the throat of a brother out of kindness, and, out of love, had kissed him.

He ran out into the gully, stabbing the air, as one mad with grief. The desert had become a charnel house. Three bodies lay where there had been one. Another horse lay dying, stiff-legged, choking on its own blood. But the death was all done by bowmen; no one had fought hand to hand yet. Mergus searched the line of the arrow-fall, saw a fissure not unlike the one he had just left and charged it, screaming.

They thought him mad, and so he was mad, and god-held, as some men are in battle, who can run into certain death and yet not die. Mergus sprinted towards the tip of an arrow that was sighted on his heart and the man holding it lost the will to loose, dropped his guard and turned and tried to scramble out of the back of a fissure. He died with Mergus' curved knife slicing past his ribs to the pumping muscles of his heart.

Out of such courage are losing battles turned to victory. Two of the Saba brothers still lived – Ibrahim and Ilias. Of the remaining ten – nine – living outriders, eight were able to fight and two of those were armed with bows. They came together in the gully, battle-mad and ready to die.

'We will avenge your brother, and ours.'

Ibrahim's heavy hand fell on Mergus' shoulder where Pantera's had lately been. Mergus did not shake him off or point out that Pantera had never been his brother and was certainly not his lover, which is what they thought.

When they joined the camel train, Mergus and Pantera had been, to all outward appearance, strangers to each other. They had joined on different days, in different languages, with different past histories to tell. But enough of those histories had been in common for it to be natural that they formed a friendship on the course of the month's journey from the Saba homelands and they had done so, until the brothers had begun to call them bedfellows, not sure if it were true or not, and Mergus had laid bets with himself as to how long it would be before Pantera found it useful to let the other men believe that line had been crossed.

It had not happened yet, and now he was supposed to be dead. Too late, Mergus regretted that he had not thought to ask Pantera what he planned to do in his new role as an undead ghûl.

'Eight are left against us.' Sanhef, the smallest, wiriest of the outriders slid back into the gully, having been sent out to spy. 'They're trying to decide whether to ride away or attack us in here. They have no bowmen left. Mergus killed the last.'

'And we have two.' Ibrahim's smile split his beard.

Let them go, Mergus said, in the cool sanity of his mind. *Let them carry news of Pantera's death to who-ever paid them. This is what they came for.*

In the insanity he must play, bereaved of his brother, his maybe-but-not-yet lover, he whistled up his mare and mounted at the run and unslung his bow and joined Ibrahim and Ilias in their charge along the gully. As one of the two living bowmen, he took the left flank. The other took the right. The remaining six men held the centre, long blades thrust out, cleaving the air with bloodied iron. They were eight against eight, but their eight thirsted for vengeance and the enemy wanted only the silver they thought they had earned.

It was a rout: horses screamed ahead as Mergus and the men about him emerged from the valley. Three of the enemy died to arrows, none of them living long enough to answer questions. The rest escaped. They were chased awhile, but not for long; it mattered more to round up the camels.

Twenty-six camels were left alive out of thirty-two, which was a miracle. Mergus saw them tethered, saw men begin to butcher those that had died, setting the meat to hang over a smoking fire, and went back to find Pantera.

Who had gone.

There was no sign of a body in the fissure, but no sign either of a living man so that Mergus wondered whether there had been another wound besides the one he had seen, and if he should begin to search for a body.

His mourning was becoming real by the time Pantera returned at dusk. By then, the dead horses had been burned, graves had been dug for the men of the camel train, and the bodies of their enemies had been mutilated beyond recognition so they could never return as undead spirits.

'You're not dead!' Mergus greeted the spy with a joy that was not exaggerated. And then, because he had lived all his life in war and battle and his eye saw some things first, 'There's blood on your hands.'

'Not mine. A man I stopped. Is that bakheer? Can we really spare it?' This last in the Saba tongue to the over-joyed brothers, doubly pleased now, at his embracing of their gift. *Bakheer*: a delicacy made from the small intestines of a cow camel calf, pickled in brine, wine vinegar and herbs to a secret recipe known only to the Saba women who made it.

Ibrahim and Ilias had brought it out of their stock to feast their dead brother and so the rest must eat with them and not vomit at the taste, which was one to endure, not to savour. At the sight of it, Pantera gave a smile so broad it lit the fire, for which Mergus, in retribution, gave him a double helping of the foul intestinal mess.

Later, when the feasting was done, and the correct words spoken in honour of the dead, and their spirits sent to the light, and not the darkness, that the ghûls and ifrit and other djinn might not harry them; when the living had bound their wounds against scorpions, which were said to suck blood in the night, and against the flies, which certainly would do so in daytime, Mergus sat with Pantera and asked the question that had stayed all evening unsaid.

'Was it Saulos who sent them?' He spoke into the flames and no one was near enough to hear. He did not ask if Pantera had downed one of the galloping men with a bowshot, nor if the shot man had hit the ground alive and had soon wished himself dead: these things were to be presumed.

Pantera finished the tail end of a poor bandage on his

arm. Flickering firelight cast his gaze more green than brown. His skin was darker than when Mergus had first met him in Rome, his hair a shade lighter, more like old straw than oak leaves; both were the product of a month under the vicious desert sun. The darkening of his skin showed the scars on his face more clearly, giving him an asymmetry that was a source of endless fascination.

The scars on the rest of his body remained hidden, which was as well, given the present company; it would have been hard to explain why he had the signifier of a legion wrought in burn marks across his torso, and the pit of a burned-out brand of Mithras on his chest.

His lame leg, where the tendons had torn, seemed not to ache so much tonight; the desert was good to him. All these things and more Mergus studied, even as Pantera spoke.

'A man with a beard paid a gold aureus to have a dozen men attack the entire train,' Pantera said. 'They were to kill all if they could, but to be certain they had slain a man named for the Leopard, who might be calling himself Sebastos.'

'Gold?' Mergus took out his knife and his scouring cloth and began to smooth the blade. A man could risk his life as an outrider for a camel train for a month and earn one silver denarius for his trouble. If he took twenty-five such journeys, and spent nothing at any point on the way, he could convert his silver to one gold aureus.

Pantera said, 'Pay to be collected on completion. Given today's thinning of their ranks, four men have just collected a quarter of a gold coin each.'

'They might think it almost worth the risk.' Mergus

tilted his knife. His own reflection gazed back at him, bearded now, as he had never been when he fought for the legions. 'Who betrayed us?'

'Perhaps no one.' Pantera found a piece of camel fat on the ground near his heel and threw it on to the fire. It blazed with blue light and sent hot, greasy smoke to the evening sky. 'Saulos knows that where he goes, we will follow. He's two months ahead of us; he's had plenty of time to set a watch on every possible route into the city.'

'But he knew you were coming now, in this train.' Mergus' gaze roamed the group that sat round the fire. 'Someone told him that.'

'Maybe.' Pantera pulled his cloak up round his shoulders. 'We can find that out when we get to Caesarea. If we get there. What matters now is that he believes I'm dead. If he doesn't, we'll be arrested as we ride through the city gates.'

'We could leave the train before morning.' Mergus looked around him. The land stretched clear for a month's ride in every direction except east, where the sea caught it, and Caesarea was the button that held it fast.

Pantera was shaking his head. 'We can't leave without advertising exactly who we are, and anyway Hypatia's ship will dock soon; we can't abandon her now.'

'Then you'll need a new name; the raiders knew your old one.'

'I thought 'Afeef' might do. It means chaste in the Arab tongue, which would fit, don't you think?'

It did fit, in all ways: since the night of the fire in Rome, when he had conceived a daughter by the woman

Hannah, Mergus had not known Pantera to bed anyone, and that was not for want of watching.

He leaned forward and poked the flames and said, 'You can't tell the brothers we were attacked because of you. What reason will you give for wanting to change?'

'That, as they know, the ifrit will be stalking us now, and it's ill luck to keep a name when men think you dead. That a distant sorcerer could use the name to attack me; that a new one will keep me safe.'

'They love you,' Mergus said, sourly. 'You ate a double helping of their foul bakheer. They'll do whatever you ask.'

'They love their camels,' Pantera said, and pulled his robes around his shoulder and lay on his saddle pack to sleep. 'They'll do what it takes to keep them safe. I'll need a new horse, too, before we ride on. Do you suppose they'll let me ride one of the ones we captured? The little bay colt has a nice look to him. Nero would have bought him as a chariot horse. We might send him to Rome, as a gift from a dead spy.'

Mergus drew breath to speak the enjoinders to keep listening spirits from taking those words and making them real, but Pantera was asleep already, his face lined even in repose, his lashes dark on his cheeks, his breathing even and slow, so Mergus offered his prayer instead to Mithras, whose brand they both bore, that they might see their venture through to the end, that Saulos might die without destroying Jerusalem in fulfilment of a prophecy, and that both he, Mergus, and Pantera might live long enough to see it happen.

CHAPTER TWO

'If your enemy lies dead of an arrow wound,' asked Iksahra sur Anmer, 'what will you do for your vengeance?' She stood in the shade of the royal mews on the eastern edge of the king's beast garden in Caesarea, feeding shreds of meat to the oldest and wildest of her falcons.

Saulos stayed in the sun, leaning against the stables at a place that allowed him to look freely up through the gardens to the palace. As far as he could tell, they were alone, and could safely talk, if one ignored the cheetah, which lay at its ease less than three long paces away, watching him with the same pitiless, hot-cold eyes as its mistress.

Saulos did his best to ignore it. He plucked a small yellow flower from the tended line along the path and buried his nose in its fragrance. 'If Pantera dies early, I will destroy the Hebrews as we planned. But he won't have died; he's better than that.'

'So you spent a gold coin to tell your enemy—'

'I told him what he already knows; that we are

enemies, that he cannot hide from me any more than I can hide from him. This is not something you and I need discuss, particularly not now when, as you see' – Saulos nodded in the direction of the palace – 'we have company.'

A figure appeared in the distance, walking down through the gardens. That he might not appear to be watching, Saulos turned his face to the grey sea.

Behind him, Caesarea's beast garden resounded with contentment, as the horses and hounds, the great cat in its cage, the elephant sent by a distant monarch, delved into their troughs, their mangers, their baskets, and fed.

The smell was of warm bread, laced through with murder. Like many things of this place, Saulos was learning not to hate it. He breathed in, and sighed out, and dispelled the unpretty image of Pantera too easily dead, lying at peace under the spring sun; in his heart, he did not believe it was so.

'Hyrcanus is on his way,' he said. 'The king's nephew. More important, son of the queen.'

'I know. On the ship before we docked, you told me to cultivate him. I have done so.'

'The whole palace knows what you've done.' Saulos allowed himself a smile. 'Still, with what you must do today, is it safe to take him with you?'

'It's safe. He sees what he wishes to see, which is, in turn, what I wish him to see.' Iksahra set down the falcon in a soothing of bells and leather and took up her mate, the tiercel; smaller, softer, easier to handle. He fed fast, bobbing his head to tear at the nugget of goat's meat she held between thumb and finger.

For all her brittle arrogance, Iksahra was better

40

than Saulos had dared to hope. The beasts that they had brought with them, the two dozen matched horses, the four grey and white falcons, the pitiless cat that followed her everywhere, each and all thrived in her care. It flowed in the blood from father to daughter and beyond; along with ochre eyes and a clear, cold skill in the hunt, Iksahra sur Anmer had inherited a knowledge of the needs of her beasts as if they were her own, and knew how they might be met even here, far from the hot, flat sands of their homeland. Even the cheetah, which had pined on the ship, had recovered enough two days after landfall to take down an antelope in sight of the king and queen.

And while the beasts bloomed, while they hunted, while they came to accept the touch of foreign – royal – hands, so did Iksahra strike ever deeper into the bosom of the royal family, and nowhere deeper than into the heart of the young prince, Hyrcanus, who was so openly in love with the strange black-skinned woman that for his uncle, his mother or any of the other royal adults to have shown interest in her would have been crass impropriety.

And he was there now, a breathless, pink-cheeked fifteen-year-old, slightly built like all his kin, with the rich, dark hair of the Herods flooding from crown to shoulder. He ran lightly down the marble steps that led from the ornamental flower beds to the beast garden. He stopped some distance away and came forward slowly, careful of the feeding bird.

'I'm sorry I'm late. My uncle sent me to look for Saulos. He needs him to— Oh! My lord . . . my uncle . . . that is, the king asked . . . he requested . . .'

'I suspect,' said Saulos mildly, 'that your uncle, the king, ordered me to attend him immediately, to discuss matters of policy. Specifically to find a solution to the problem posed by the quite unimaginably large bribe the Hebrews are about to offer him in the hope that he might preserve their synagogue from the predations of the Greeks. Am I right?'

Saulos smiled easily, as one conspirator to another. Hyrcanus, who had just learned rather more of the latest state crisis than his uncle had told him, or was likely to tell him, grinned his relief.

'You're right. That's exactly what he said. Will you go? Will you tell him that I found you and sent you? He's in a foul temper. It would . . .' Discretion came to him late. He ran out of words, and stood in the half-shade, shifting from one foot to the other.

'It would mollify him. And therefore I will do it.' Saulos was dressed for court, in costly silks the colour of sand. He took a moment to brush away the grit, giving Hyrcanus time to regain his composure. 'Your uncle enjoys my company,' Saulos said as he passed the boy by. 'There's no shame in that; you need not be afraid to say it. And you, meanwhile, will go to sea with Iksahra, there to hunt with her falcons. I am told the tiercel is flying well for you?'

'He is! Yesterday, we caught one of the shore birds, the small fast ones that dodge between the waves. He was so fast, so perfect! It was wonderful!' The boy's eyes shone bright as the sun-struck sea.

Saulos laughed and patted him on the shoulder. 'Good! You'll be a hunter by the day's end.'

His eyes met Iksahra's over the boy's head. If he had

not spent three months in her company, the hate in her gaze would have terrified him. He walked away, snapping his fingers in time to an inner rhythm. His day, however he looked at it, was perfect.

*　　*　　*

Hypatia dreamed of Saulos before she saw him and she saw him before she ever set foot on the harbour at Caesarea and those facts were, she thought, the reason her mouth was quite so dry and the usual stable rhythm of her heart unstable. Those, and that she hated the sea.

The dreams had begun long before she had left the imperial quarters in Rome and taken ship for the east.

In truth, they had begun before her eighth birthday, which was one of the reasons she was who she was; the future servants of Isis were chosen from among the children with the most vivid dreams and Hypatia's had certainly been that.

All through her training, in the deserts south of Alexandria, in Greece, in the dreaming chambers of Mona, the same dream had come. Sometimes, she slept at peace for days at a time and thought herself free of it, then it would visit her three nights in succession, prodding her to wake, sweating, with her hands cramped and her back arched tight against an imagined – or remembered – pain.

On Mona, where the dreamers trained for twenty years before they considered themselves adept, they told her to return home and become the Oracle of the Temple of Truth in Alexandria, there to await the time when the source of terror in her dreams might visit her to ask a boon.

She had over two decades from her first dream before Saulos Herodion survived the labyrinth that led to the Temple and begged the Oracle's help. There was a moment when Hypatia could have killed him, knowing what he could do, what he might do, what he wanted to do, but she was the Oracle, bound by laws stronger than her fears, and so she had spoken the words the god had sent in the moment of Saulos' asking and, as in her dreams, Saulos had taken them and wrought fire, and death and havoc, and spilled his false god out into the world.

Now, though, in the mid-afternoon, with the sea air hot from the land, she let go of the dreams for a while, and stood at the foremast with Andros, the ship's master, at her side and watched the wonder of organization that allowed him to talk to her as easily as he had in mid-ocean, while still controlling the hundred fine manoeuvres that let him slide his ship through Caesarea's outer breakwater and into the clutter of barges, skiffs, day-fishers and deep-sea trading vessels that crowded the inner harbour.

From this distance, the royal party waiting on the steps of Augustus' temple was little more than a blur of porphyry, azure blue, spring green and scarlet with a single seam of gold in the centre; too far to put a name to anyone, except that only the king might wear gold and so it must be his family who stood around him.

Beyond that, only the blistering white stone of Augustus' temple was clear to the incoming traveller, set on a slope above the harbour, looking due west, to the setting sun and to Rome.

'They build their temples in the Greek fashion here,'

Hypatia said. 'I had not thought to see such a thing in this land of the Hebrews.'

'But Caesarea is not in the land of the Hebrews.' Andros, master of the sailing ship *Krateis*, was a big bear of a man. He smiled at Hypatia but did not embrace her, an act of self-control that took an obvious effort of will.

In Alexandria, whence they had come, Andros had been afraid of her, had barely allowed her on board; Hypatia was known throughout the city as a Sibyl, an Oracle, one given since birth to Isis, and he feared the wrath of the sea-gods if she set foot on his beloved ship.

Only sight of the emperor's ring, and a letter marked with the seal of the late empress, had changed his mind, and that unwillingly. For a month, he had treated Hypatia as ill luck, so that it was a wonder she had not slipped on a dark night and gone overboard. Then a storm had truly come, black as the ravens of Zeus, full of thunder and the raging wrath of Poseidon, and, while the men hid and wept, Hypatia had lashed herself to the rails at the prow and faced down the storm, talking reason to waves tall as pyramids, singing to the lion-roaring sea.

In the morning, when the sun had broken through the cloud and the gods had sent a good tail wind, she had been greeted as a conquering hero, and every man among them would have thrown himself overboard to save her. Some of the younger ones had, in fact, offered to do exactly that in the three days after when she had lain abed with fever and could not be roused.

They had been restrained, and Hypatia had lived, and now Andros stood there, claiming her as his own, hoping he might persuade her to stay, knowing he could not.

He lifted his palm, shading his eyes against the high afternoon sun. 'The thing to remember about Caesarea,' he said, sagely, 'is that she was built by Herod the Great, a king who was neither Greek nor Hebrew but tried to be both, and she has spent the hundred years of her life trying to merge two cultures which are as oil to wine or lions to mewling infants. She has failed and will do so for ever. The Greeks are good traders, but prone to violence. While the Hebrews . . . the Hebrews are crazy.' Andros spat, throatily. 'They love death in the name of their god more than they do life under the Romans. The rest of us are happy to pay our taxes, and hail every mad Caesar as a god, but they must resist and shout about it and to hang with the consequen— Ho there! Keep a clean line or we'll crush you to tinder!'

He threw himself forward, leaning down, shouting in the gutter Greek of the sea that no one born on land could hope to understand.

Hypatia, too, leaned forward and saw a small white-sailed day-skiff cut in front of the *Krateis*, saw it sweep under the scythe of her bow and jink a dainty tack to bring it sweeping back again towards the berthing points at the wharf.

Andros was going land-crazy, working himself to a lather at a slight so small he would have barely noticed it at sea, but was blown big now because he could smell land as well as sea, incense as well as salt, meat and fruits and oils and flowers as well as fish and the sweat of unwashed men. He leaned over the bow rail, hurling ever more inventive curses at the ill-begotten sons of parasites who were piloting the skiff. They, for their part, shouted back neatly crafted threats of their own, that had to do with Andros' virility and their ability to disarm it.

They were close enough now to see the faces on the dock, to pick out the likenesses of dress, of hair, of nose and eyebrow that knitted some together and set others apart. Hypatia left the master to his ravings and leaned back against the mast where she might seem to study the harbour, while studying instead the royal party.

She began at the outer reaches, where stood the men of the city Watch, Roman in all their mail and leather, but not Roman by birth; Syrians, she thought, the local men, who spoke Greek now, rather than their natural tongue, and had done so for three hundred years since the conqueror Alexander had taken their lands for his own. They were trained to Roman standards, though. She resolved to find the name of their commander.

Within the circle they made stood the royal party of Agrippa II, grandson to Herod the Great, whose sign of the wheat sheaves flew in gold pennants above the tower and the promontory palace.

A handful of royal children hemmed him in, nieces and nephews of this wifeless, childless king. Hypatia couldn't see Hyrcanus, nephew to the king and nominated heir, but she did notice a dark-haired girl, taller than the rest, who pointed at their big two-masted ship with the emperor's pennant and kept her stiff arm outstretched for a long time as they made way towards the harbour, as if throwing a curse, or drawing the ship in to dock, or both.

Andros was losing his verbal battle. The small

day-skiff cut in front of the *Krateis* one last time, aiming for the same place at the wharf. Light and lively, it skipped ahead, hampering the bigger ship's progress. Andros became truly manic in his fury, but there was nothing to be done but slow his own ship, to set the oars to backwater and turn in more tightly to the wharf.

'Here! Dock here!'

The shout sliced the air. The king pushed to the fore of the huddle, waving his command. Agrippa was small, like all Herod's kin, with the fine, dark hair and lean nose of the Idumaeans, whom the Hebrews called Edomites and despised. Still, they ruled over Caesarea, Jerusalem and all the rest of Judaea, albeit under sufferance of Rome.

Here in Caesarea, Agrippa showed no deference to anyone, excepting that he wore a toga in the Roman manner, with purple at the hem, and a filet of gold in his hair, and the women on either side of him wore stolas in azure blue and spring green and had their hair twisted high and cross-pinned at the crown in the style that had been favoured by the Empress Poppaea before her untimely death in childbed at the year's turn. In Rome, nobody had dared yet call the style out of fashion.

Hypatia waited at the mast head. She was the Chosen of Isis; she was used to conversations with royalty and the inevitable dramas they wrought. If, to date, the kings, queens and emperors had always been the suppliants and she the one who delivered – or not – that which they sought, it was, she believed, not so different now, just less . . . controlled.

She made herself stand straighter, and set her arms by her sides as the *Krateis* turned broadside to the dock and one of the younger freemen leapt the oar's-length gap to the shore, winding ropes on to bollards to hold the ship safely to land.

The king had commanded her presence. Holding her head high, feeling her neck unnaturally stiff, Hypatia plotted a safe course around the debris on the deck: the careful coils of rope, the taut rigging, the line that held the stone that marked the depth at which the ship might safely anchor, the—

'Do you see the falcon?' a girl's voice cried in lightly accented Greek. 'See! The black woman still has it, but Hyrcanus has the male, so he must have made a kill. And look! She has the cheetah with her! I told you it followed her everywhere.'

Hypatia had gone another two carefully measured paces before the meaning of the words brought her to a halt.

She dragged her gaze from the dockside and looked at last where the girl was pointing now, not at the *Krateis*, but at the unruly day-skiff berthed so close that sandbags had been thrown between to keep the hull of the greater, ocean-going broad-ship from crushing the small, lighter, faster – and now plausibly royal – skiff.

Her ship's greater height granted Hypatia a clear view on to the deck of the skiff and thus on to the tall, lean woman who stood on its gangplank with a leashed and hooded falcon on her wrist and a sleek, long-limbed great cat, neither leashed nor hooded, at her heel. The cheetah stood with its head high and its small round ears pricked and raked its yellow eyes across the company.

The woman who commanded it was not, in fact, the

jet black of the Nubians as the girl had implied, but a shade lighter, a deep earthen brown, with a cap of short brown-black hair curled tight as a new-born lamb's, eyes the colour of deepest ochre, and high, carved cheekbones that caught the sun as if she had painted them across with powder of gold. Looking closer, Hypatia saw that each cheekbone bore three small spirals tattooed in a line; and three more crossed the bridge of her nose, linking her fine, gull-wing brows.

The tattoos defined her origin: to Hypatia's knowledge, the only tribes that marked themselves thus were those that bred horses, hunted gazelle and herded rough goat-sheep south and west of Mauretania where the desert stretched vast as an ocean and the men, it was said, could live without water for a week while the women gave birth on horseback, and perhaps conceived the same way. They called themselves the Berberai, and had sworn allegiance to no one, nor did they have any fear of Rome.

It was the Berber woman, then, whom the girl-child had seen and the Berber woman's beasts the king had called forth. The cheetah was always going to be the first focus of attention, but the falcon was no less imposing in its way. It stood on her arm, a slate-grey she-bird with a pale flecked chest of the kind the Berberai used to hunt deer, and behind her, leashed to the arm of a green-faced seasick boy of about fifteen, was the smaller tiercel that was its mate.

Nobody watched the boy; the royal party's attention rested instead on the Berber as she strode down the gangplank with the cheetah stepping loose-limbed and lethal at her side.

At the shore, the falcon roused, screaming a challenge to the land and the colour and the many staring eyes. The younger children shrieked in horrified delight. The royal women stepped back, covering their breasts with their hands. Agrippa, the king, stood his ground, white-knuckled, staring fixedly ahead.

The Berber woman made obeisance, of sorts, to the king, to the women at his side, and, in a deep, bell-toned voice that set the bars of Hypatia's chest thrumming, said, 'Iksahra sur Anmer thanks your majesties for their indulgence. Your royal nephew is a versatile hunter, if not yet quite suited to the sea. We caught a few gulls, but nothing else of worth. I beg leave to continue his training in the deserts, that he might, in time, reach the excellence of his ancestors.'

Hypatia bit her lip and made sure not to smile. She had given orders to emperors in her time, she knew the pitch of voice that acted as a command, whatever the nature of the words, and the Berber woman had just ordered King Agrippa II of Judaea to leave his nephew – his sole heir – in her care.

Agrippa showed no sign of having noticed. His gaze glanced unseeing over the assemblage before him – the men on the skiff, the boy, the falcon, even the cheetah – and came to rest, thoughtfully, on the Berber woman who, contrary to all propriety, wore a loose white robe that barely stretched to her knees and covered her arms not at all.

It was a man's dress, and she was assuredly not a man. She was, in fact, as close as Hypatia had ever seen to one of the legendary Amazons, but for the fact that she bore no bow, and had plainly not amputated her own right breast, the better to fire her arrows.

The king thought the same. Hypatia watched him say as much behind his hand to a man dressed in silk the colour of sand who stood at his left shoulder, in the place of a counsellor.

The Oracles of Isis were well versed in reading words by the form of the speaker's lips alone. From her place high up on the deck of the *Krateis*, Hypatia watched Agrippa say, 'The Amazon will make a man of my nephew yet.'

The reply came swiftly, with amusement. 'If you give her time to do so.' The man at the king's shoulder also let his eyes rest on the Berber woman, but it seemed to Hypatia that the shock of her touched him less than it had the king, and that he gazed instead into her soul, to the passions that burned in the glacial interior, and that he was pleased with what he saw.

And then he turned his head and smiled, and so she saw at last that the messages had been true: Saulos was in Caesarea.

Two month at sea, six months before in preparation, a year before in hunting, had wound her tighter than she knew. She felt the heat of his gaze pass over her and move on, and opened her fists and wiped away the sudden greasy sweat on the weather-fine wood of the mast.

In the temple, she had been cloaked and cowled. Her voice had not been her own; her body had been the hollow reed through which Truth spoke. She had said so to Pantera, to Mergus, to the ailing Empress Poppaea in her private apartments as they had planned all that might happen.

Saulos saw the Oracle, he did not see Hypatia. I will know him and will not be known. As the empress suggests, I will take ship to Caesarea and deliver her gifts while you travel overland. Whichever of us finds him first will alert the others.

Hypatia turned her gaze to the city, to the bright houses and brighter gardens, to the merchants and traders and slaves and housekeepers and ladies and courtiers and counsellors and men of the Watch who flooded the dock and the nearby streets.

It did not look like a city on the verge of riot and revolution, but Hypatia had spent half her life visiting cities and states on the verge of war; she knew the taste of the air and the sounds of men and women trying to pretend that life had not changed and would not change. A smear of black smoke somewhere in mid-city was darker and thicker than it should have been and somewhere distant, women wailed a death.

With a nod to Andros to let him know she was all right, she gathered her dignity and stepped down the plank on to the dockside and into the maelstrom that was Caesarea.

Chapter Three

Mergus counted thirteen crosses marking the eastern entry to Caesarea; seven on the south side of the path that led to the closed gates, six to the north. Old bodies hung there, desiccated, scentless bones held together by tags of tendons, too dry now for the vultures.

Before the front riders reached them, the gates opened and a detachment of the city Watch rode out; fifteen armed and armoured men on fresh horses, who spread out in a row across the sand.

Ibrahim's train halted, smoothly. Even the camels, who had smelled water, made no effort to forge through the line of polished iron.

At the rear of the column, Mergus and Pantera leaned forward on the pommels of their saddles showing every sign of weariness, hunger and thirst – all of which were genuine – and of boredom, which was not.

'If Saulos knows we're here . . .' Mergus murmured.

'He will clear one of the crosses for each of us,' Pantera said. 'Try to get one facing the sun. Death comes faster that way.'

Pantera kept his quiet gaze on the camels ahead; in this guise, he was a Nabatean archer of limited imagination and no particular fear of Rome. Mergus, who had seen the scars on his body, and had spoken to some of the men who had made them, cursed and spat and hunched his back against the dead, and made sure he knew the fastest route to freedom.

Best to go left, he thought, south, towards Jerusalem where the Hebrew zealots, however mad, might take in a renegade centurion and his half-breed friend if they could prove themselves useful with weapons.

But no shout came, no hands fell on their shoulders, no blades were thrust in their faces with threats and menace. The camels, horses and men of Ibrahim's train were inspected by a decurion, who introduced himself as Gaius Jucundus, commanding officer of the city Watch. He greeted Ibrahim affably enough and commiserated with the men for their wounds as he rode slowly down the line.

'There's still time to leave,' Mergus said, as he came closer. Just. Maybe. If their horses were not too tired. If the Watch were slow to see them go.

'Not yet,' Pantera said. 'Let your sleeve come up. See if they know who you are.'

Obediently, Mergus made as if to stifle a yawn and, in doing so, let his right sleeve rise a little. On his forearm above the centurion's baton, the twinned XX of the Twentieth legion had recently been extended by new lines to form the double Vs of the name Valeria Victrix, given after the bloodbath of Britain's rebellion. Above the legion-sign, older, a lion stood over a bull, and both were topped by a raven.

The inkwork of the god-mark was poor, blued almost to invisibility against Mergus' olive skin, but a man did not rise to the rank of Watch captain without sharp eyes and a sharper mind and a working knowledge of the gods who held the legions close.

Jucundus spun his horse neatly, bringing it to stand just in front of Mergus. His men might have been Syrian, but he was a Roman of equestrian stock, with the hooked nose and prominent brow that marked such men, as if they were all cast from the same mould. His eyes, when he raised them, held a frank, friendly curiosity.

'If I tell the men what you are,' he said, 'they'll drag you from your horse and ply you with wine and whores. Shall I?'

'Later, maybe.' Mergus shrugged a shyness that was only partly feigned. His past with the legions was the reason he had been taken on as outrider in the first place; he had no intention of hiding it. 'I've given my oath to see Ibrahim's camels safely sold and we've already lost the best to bandits. I'd hate to be carousing while the rest were stolen.'

'Camels are hard to hide,' Jucundus said. 'In Caesarea, small men steal small things; the coins and gems that can be swallowed and retrieved two days later, or denied with plausibility. If anyone steals your camels, it'll be the governor claiming them as tax.'

A brief pause held them a moment. 'He'll take a tax on the beasts before they're sold?' Mergus asked.

'It's his new way, started this spring. He's a Greek, which means he'll extort more of whatever you're trading if you're selling to the Hebrews rather than the Syrians, who count themselves almost wholly Greek. Take that as fair warning, and if you pass it to Ibrahim, don't say it came from me. But for now, you have an escort. The Watch will keep you safe until you reach your inn.'

'Are we in danger?'

Jucundus pulled a wry face. 'Take it as a sensible precaution,' he said. 'The autumn riots have started early. Nobody's safe.'

At which he raised his arm in signal and the detachment that had blocked the path split apart and rode down to join the train, half on either side so that Ibrahim and his camels passed through the city's gates to the chime of chain mail and the tread of different horses, and the crowds gathered to view them with silent awe, as if they were royalty.

Caesarea was whiter than a pearl. It gleamed bright as a diamond in the sun, with the sea a mirror of aquamarine behind, and the sky only two shades quieter above.

Pantera was mounted on the bay colt he had set his eyes on after the battle. It was a pleasure to ride, answering easily to heel and hand with a forward, fluid gait in the open desert and a solid one in the city. He set it now to follow the mare in front and, in the guise of Afeef, Nabatean archer, observed what he could of the city.

First, he studied the gangs of sullen, brooding youths who gathered on the street corners to watch their passing and decided that the Syrians were more numerous than the Hebrews, but that the latter looked more desperate and therefore more dangerous.

After, he looked about in apparent awe at the bright

white polished stone from which the whole city was fashioned; at the width and regularity of the streets – none of the haphazard twists and turns of Rome here; at the tented podiums set at each street corner for the benefit of the Watch, living testament to the fact that Caesarea had been designed to remain under constant occupation; at the rows of houses built all the same, in the Greek style with their stairs inside, but with many-coloured flower gardens on the rooftops and in vessels by the front doors.

The flowers were a riot in their own right, with scarlet vying against cerise and saffron, magenta and violet, rust, lime and midnight blue, each trying to outdo the other with the sheer violence of its hue.

Elsewhere were signs of human violence: of smoke stains and broken doors, of blood swept into gutters and the moans of the newly injured from behind shuttered windows. And one sign of fresher violence, not far in front of the train.

Pantera leaned a little towards Mergus. 'Ahead,' he murmured in Greek. 'Three streets forward on the right. Fresh blood on the road. Wait a moment before you appear to see it.'

He watched as Mergus counted nine paces then, as if seeing the gore for the first time, lifted himself high in the saddle and, swearing, threw up his hand.

'Jucundus! Ahead! The street with the green dolphin! Fresh blood!'

Jucundus had seen action in battle, Pantera would have bet his life on that. The officer swung his horse even as the first word reached him. His orders spilled out in Greek, too fast to follow, but they brought

Ibrahim's camel train to a ragged halt. A dozen men of the Watch cantered up the line in tight formation, three men across, four deep, unslinging their shields as they rode, drawing their cavalry blades.

In a block, they came to the street marked by a soaring dolphin painted on the white gable end. In itself, that marked it as a Syrian district: the god of the Hebrews did not allow images of men or animals in his domain.

They didn't dismount. After a brief flurry of horses dragged to a hard halt, of heads thrown and hooves belling on the hard stone, the leader dragged a spear from his second and, leaning down, brought something up on its tip. After a moment, on Jucundus' command, he turned, holding it high, so that the men behind could see.

'Gods alive!' Mergus sank down in his saddle. 'It's a crucified cat.'

'Of course.' Pantera glanced at the dangling mass of bloodied fur as if it were a minor novelty. 'Don't show any interest,' he said. 'We have no reason to care.'

Mergus converted his choked oath into a curse at his horse. Under his breath, he said, 'It's a spotted cat. One of those from the temples in Alexandria. It looks like a miniature leopard.'

'And I'll wager the cost of tonight's meal that the arrow pinning its chest to the upright post bears the same tip and fletchings as those of the men who hunted us in the desert.'

Mergus said, 'Were you expecting this?'

'Something like it.' Pantera let his gaze slide past the cat for a second time. The fletchings were, indeed, the

59

same as those of their attackers. 'Saulos wishes us to know that he can do what he wants.'

'What do we do?'

'What we were going to do anyway: watch, listen, learn. Do our best not to die. You might spit against bad luck as we pass. I can't, it's not a thing a Nabatean would do.'

The train moved on at a brisk pace. They passed the cat and found that, for a mercy, it was dead, and had been before it had been nailed to the wood. More men than Mergus spat for luck as they reached it and the train was uncharacteristically quiet as they rode on.

Presently, Ibrahim took a right turn and led his men into a Hebrew part of the city where the flowers were planted in other patterns and the decorations painted on the gables were of olives and vine leaves, not animals or men. Amidst the lines of quiet order, one street was in disarray: scaffolding rose along half its length and a builder's mayhem of bricks and sand and wood and iron cluttered the empty lots.

In the centre of the chaos stood a synagogue, tall, brilliant, clad in white stone, with yellow flowers all along the paved path that led to it. The scaffolding pressed it on all sides.

Jucundus had disposed of the cat and was riding up along the side of the train. Mergus caught his attention as he passed. 'Are they building the synagogue bigger?' he asked. 'It's already larger than anything in Alexandria or Rome.'

'I think you'll find it's not the synagogue that's being built,' Pantera murmured. In Jucundus' presence, he spoke Greek with a sluggish eastern accent and professed to know no Latin. 'Ask him who's building other properties so close to the house of the Hebrew god. And why. And ask him where are the worshippers. It's the Sabbath tomorrow; they should be preparing the house of god.'

Mergus asked. And nearly asked a second time when Jucundus kept his face forward and did not seem to have heard. When the decurion spoke, it was not an answer, but a question spoken in a low voice, with his eyes fixed ahead.

'How long are you planning to stay in Caesarea?'

Mergus stifled a glance towards Pantera. 'We'll leave when we next find work.'

'Make it soon.'

'You wish us to leave because of the synagogue?' Mergus asked. 'Or the gangs of youths?'

'Because of the havoc the Hebrews of all ages will wreak at the synagogue if the building work around it doesn't stop. Or what the Syrians will do if they are made to stop. Both are unsafe.'

Jucundus kicked his horse hard. He reached the front of the train as they turned a final corner and Ibrahim called a halt before a large, well-appointed inn, built in the city's white stone with a symbol of five vine rods laid side to side hanging above its door.

CHAPTER FOUR

The Inn of the Five Vines was a tavern in the Greek style in the thriving mercantile district of the Roman-occupied capital of Judaea; a place of contradictions entirely at home with itself, alive with the scent of garlic and goat stew and journey-sweat, babbling in eight or nine different languages. A dozen different gods graced the niches at the stairwell, on the landing, in the main bar and dining area beneath, in the rooms. And in those rooms . . .

'Mattresses!' Mergus threw himself down, patting the straw beneath him as if it were goose down. 'Mattresses with no lice in and a roof over our heads and a room with just two of us, not the entire bloody train. We could forget what else we came for, and just sleep here untouched for a month!'

Pantera sat on the edge of his bed and shook his head by way of answer. The scar over his right eye was white in the evening's old light and when he was tired, as now, it drew his eye up archly, so that he looked as if he was ever on the verge of a question.

A jug of cool water had been set at the head of his bed. He poured some and drank, and Mergus saw him begin to relax, not wholly – he had never seen that – but enough.

'What do we do first?' Sobering, Mergus sat up. He, too, drank the water; after a month in the desert, it was better than any wine.

'We make contact with Hypatia.'

'If she's here yet.'

'She is. Her mark was on the water trough by the Temple of Isis. She's here and she's paid a visit to the local priests.'

Mergus closed his eyes and tried to think when he had missed that; he failed. He said, 'Whoever sold us to Saulos is quite possibly still in the train. He'll follow us wherever we go.'

'Then we'll lose him.' Pantera glanced up sharply. 'You have an idea who it is?'

'Rasul of the nine fingers,' Mergus said. 'He never would look either of us in the eye. If there's a traitor in Ibrahim's train, it'll be him.'

'Or perhaps he was just too shy. We'll find out in the morning. Tonight, we sleep here with the men. Tomorrow, we'll leave a mark so that Hypatia knows we're here, then set up a meeting with Seneca's agent in Caesarea; the Teacher may be dead, but his network was always designed to live on beyond him.

'The agent takes the name Absolom; I know nothing else about him, but there's a priest at the Temple of Tyche who'll get him a message on our behalf. When that's done, we'll find Seneca's dove-keeper and send a bird back to Rome with news that we're safely here. The more the emperor knows of what we're doing, the more chance we have of asking his help if we need it. After that, we'll see where we're sent. It might be that—'

A dozen trumpets blared. Pantera spun from the bed in a smooth rush of movement that took him out of the room and down the stairs and out towards the main square and the camels.

At some point in that progress, he ceased to be Pantera, Roman citizen, veteran of Britain – for all his quiet asking, Mergus had not yet discovered in precise detail what it was that Pantera had done there, except that it had resulted in his being mistaken for a native and crucified to the point of death – and became a Nabatean fighting man with a horse to protect and two pieces of silver not yet earned and a fondness for the bow that set him in a realm apart from mortal men. Ibrahim's men had not seen him throw knives yet; that skill remained secret.

Mergus was still Mergus when he met the commotion in the square, although he slumped more than he might otherwise have done, particularly in the presence of the governor of a province.

The governor, Gessius Florus, stood on top of a small wall to give himself height. He needed to; in a land of small men, Florus was smaller than most; in a land of plenty where waistlines expanded with age, his had always been weightier than his peers'; in a land where bald men were considered repositories of wisdom on the grounds of age, he, plentifully bald, was widely known to have won his current position on the sole strength of his wife's having shared private bath time with the late empress. Less than two years in the post, he was notorious already throughout the east for the improbable feat of being more corrupt than either of his immediate predecessors.

Governor Florus ordered silence from his trumpets. The milling camels settled and returned to their hay. The crowd that ringed the market place fell to an uneasy silence in which both the Greek-speakers and the Hebrews waited to hear the governor's reasons for disrupting their afternoon.

'Who owns these camels?' A steward called the question, not Florus himself.

'I do.'

Ibrahim stepped forward to stand before the governor, who looked past his right shoulder, pressing his lips together.

The steward said, 'Who is the buyer?'

'I am contracted to sell to Demokritos of Rhodes, who trades here in the city.'

Mergus knew this not to be true. All through the desert, the Saba brothers had spoken with reverence the name of their contractor: Yusaf ben Matthias, Hebrew counsellor and merchant. Unless that man had taken a Greek name, then Ibrahim was lying.

The crowd was made of youths, and many of them, from both factions. They murmured their surprise, not yet moved to action.

Under that sound, barely moving his lips, Mergus said to Pantera, 'You told Ibrahim of the governor's new taxes?'

'When we watered the horses, yes. Demokritos owes him two talents of gold. If anyone asks, he'll swear before any god that he's buying the entire train.'

'Even so, Florus doesn't believe him.'

'No. So there is definitely a spy among us.'

'Rasul.' Mergus spat. To Pantera, he said, 'If Ibrahim fights . . . ?'

'No risk of that. He won't decorate a cross for the price of a dozen camels. Watch now, Florus has decided on a figure.'

The steward shifted on his feet. He met no man's eye. 'The governor believes you speak untruly, that the true purchaser of these beasts is a Hebrew. He therefore levies twenty of the beasts as his tax. You will cede their ownership to him.'

'*Twenty?*' The gasp rolled around the crowd. Ibrahim was the rock on which it broke. Set man on man, Mergus would have laid all his life's wealth on Ibrahim to win; he could have torn Florus' ears off and used them to choke him. But the governor owned the Watch and suddenly there were a great many watchmen around the square, sweating in their mail and helmets. Half bore javelins. The other half had drawn their swords.

Ibrahim said, 'My lord, of the twenty-six beasts who survived our journey, five are not in calf.'

'Then we shall leave you those five, plus one.' Florus' voice had the unfortunate timbre of a eunuch. Which, given that he had a wife, was impossible, or at least unlikely.

Ibrahim said, 'If my lord wishes that the Saba take their future trade to Damascus, he has only to say so. We would not have come at all had we known we were so unwelcome.'

Mergus eased his blade in his belt. He was sworn to

this man, who had just threatened a Roman governor. The Saba were the best – at times the only – camel traders east of Alexandria. Caesarea needed them more than they needed it.

Florus smiled as a toad smiles, his eyes lost in his fat face. 'You may trade where you will,' he said. 'But now we shall take all twenty-one in-calf camels as our tariff.'

'One denarius each, as we agreed.'

It was evening, and they had eaten in the inn's hall down below, feasting on fish, because they could, and bakheer because they must show how honoured they were to have been offered it. It had been made by Ibrahim's wife in her tent, and she was the most beauteous woman of the entire Saba tribe.

While the Hebrew and Syrian youths began their nightly riots outside, they had stayed in relative safety by the fire and had toasted Ibrahim's beautiful wife and each other and their horses, living and dead, and the horses they had once owned and would own in the future and the dead men whose spirits lay quiet under the sand of the desert. They had not mentioned the camels or their losses or whether any of them would make any money for the trip.

But there was money. Ibrahim doled out the small silver coins; a subdued, thoughtful Ibrahim, whose brown eyes had become hooded, that his soul might not show to his enemies, or the spirits they could have sent to hunt him.

Mergus said, 'I'm sorry. We would have killed the governor, but . . .'

'But then we would all die long deaths, and what

would our wives say to that?' Ibrahim's smile was sad and slow, but neither as slow nor as sad as it might have been. 'Take the money in peace and keep away from the unrest here as you spend it. If you find yourselves in need of employment at the moon's turn, come back here. I may have some horses – and five barren camels – to take to Damascus. Your beds are paid for this night and the next. After that, our hospitality ends and you will have to find your own. I'm told the area around the harbour is the safest: nobody yet dares to throw stones near the palace.'

Pantera's smile matched Ibrahim's. 'We will find an inn there then that serves good food, and can supply also, perhaps, a woman for Mergus?' His eyes, scanning the room, were childlike in their innocence. Mergus flushed and looked away out of the stables towards the evening's lemon light.

Ibrahim laughed and clapped Pantera on the shoulder and kissed him on both cheeks, and told him to take the bay colt as payment for the horse that had been killed in good service.

They liked Pantera for his bow skills, he had said, which was true. Mergus thought they had come to love him for all the things they could not see, but could feel in the quiet of their souls.

Men who come to love Saulos will give their lives for him. Pantera had said that in the desert. What he had not said was that he and Saulos had much in common, and the fact that men would give their lives for love of either was only the first part of it.

Mergus was thinking that later in the evening, as he settled down to sleep. For a while, he lay listening to the growing rumble of youths hurling abuse at other youths outside. He thought no stones had been thrown yet, nor sticks pounded on flesh. Inside, the few men left downstairs slurred their toasts to the remembered dead while upstairs, men on either side of their room mumbled their way towards sleep.

Mergus murmured his own prayers to the god and lay quietly, letting the night's patterns weave across the roof, patching with starlight the places the sun had left.

Inevitably, his thoughts gravitated to the man in the other bed. There was a time, in the summer after the fire, when he had desired Pantera so much his heart had ached, when he would have given all the gold sewn into his saddle pack – none of which was his to give – for a night with him in a small room such as this.

Time hadn't dulled the ache, but had instead refined it until he came to understand that his passion for Pantera was of the mind, not of the body; that he had reached the age, perhaps, where lust gave way to something more pure. More likely, he remembered too clearly the look on the face of the woman Hannah as she took ship on the day after the fire, with Pantera's child newly made within her.

He had seen women in grief before; he had caused it often enough. There was no reason why he should remember this one so clearly, except that it had been mirrored in the lines about Pantera's eyes as he had turned away from the ship, and then again, even more finely, in the face of the woman Hypatia, Sibylline Oracle and Chosen of Isis.

And there was a question Mergus did not wish to ask, or to hear answered. He was content with what he had, or believed himself so. He lay listening to the slow peace of Pantera's breath as he crossed the Lethe into sleep and if he emerged later sweating, grasping blindly at his mattress, then Mergus planned to be at his side, speaking words of comfort in the language that worked, which was neither Greek nor Latin, nor Aramaic nor Saban, but the old, wild, ensorcelled words of the Britons that the dreamers used to sing the warriors to war, and that in a land where the women were warriors as often as the men.

Mergus slept and dreamed of Britain, and when he woke in the grey ghost-light before dawn, Pantera was gone, leaving his desert robes behind him. He had taken his two slim throwing knives.

CHAPTER FIVE

A brisk south-westerly wind ushered in the dawn, delivering the ocean's salt-spray scent to the beast gardens. The falcons smelled it and screamed for freedom.

Iksahra sang back the song her father had taught her, that calmed them and brought them to hunting sharpness at the same time. Her tones were deep and resonant, made at the back of her throat, and they threaded through the high, piercing shrieks, weaving a harmony that filled the garden and woke the other beasts.

Presently, they joined in: the cheetah, the horses, the three old hounds, no longer fit for hunting; the two new ones, brought by the tall Alexandrian woman with the striking blue-black hair and the all-seeing eyes. Each added its voice one by one to make a melody that Iksahra had heard first in childhood, and not at all in adulthood, until she had come here.

Her heart soared on the sound, always. There were mornings when she came close to weeping for the sheer heart of it and today had almost the feel of that, but not yet. For now, it was enough to revel in the luxury of solitude; her gift to herself, that made the days bearable.

Loosing the cheetah from its night-time pen, she unlocked the feed store and measured out the corn and hay for the horses, with a palm's lick of salt for those that might be ridden in the day. She lifted the trapdoor to the cold cellar and brought out a goat carcass, three days dead but not yet rotting, and cut strips off the hind leg for the birds before she gave the rest to the cheetah. It took it from her with care, that its teeth might not crush her fingers.

Iksahra crouched down, buttocks to heels so that her head was level with the cat's and it could meet her gaze with its fire-amber eyes. She reached out a hand, palm down, and the beast, more hound than cat, pressed its great, high forehead up against her in greeting and rumbled low in its throat a sound that might have been a threat and was not. She stayed with it while it fed, breathing in the scents of raw meat and wildness, running her lean fingers through the heavy silk of its pelt.

They thought she loved her falcon, the men and women of the palace, and they were right, but she loved this cat more than any bird. On the nights when they hunted together, she thought it carried the spirit of her father, sent to watch over and teach her. It had never yet showed any sign that she was wrong.

Later, up in the feed room, she weighed the meat for the birds on a small balance, measuring each portion against bronze nuggets marked with the size of bird that they should feed. The scales had been her father's, locked in a store cupboard by men who didn't understand their use. Iksahra had discovered them on her third day and Saulos had found her standing with them, unmoving, hours later.

That was the day the slaves had stopped coming to the gardens for the early morning feeding time. The memory caused her to smile. Saulos, too, had walked round her more carefully since then, which was not a bad thing.

She had not killed anybody for having hidden her father's tools; before they had left the desert, she had given Saulos her word that she would stay her hand until his plans had run their course and Iksahra had never in her life broken her word. But standing there in the feed room, she had laid her hands on her father's scales and made promises that were more precise and more sure than the ones she had made by a fire in a desert in the early spring before she and her hunting beasts had left their homeland to follow a stranger overseas.

Four birds had made the journey with her from the deserts; two falcons and two tiercels, all adults, all hunting fit. She flew them on alternate days, resting between. At home, she would have fed them on the previous day's kill and she did that here when she could, except when the kill had been a message-bird with a cylinder tied to its leg and she had had to tie weights to the carcass and send it to the bottom of the ocean.

The message had been from the new spymaster, the Poet, to the agent, Absolom, asking if he had yet met the Leopard. Saulos had been delighted in his muted, half-hidden fashion.

He had taken the slip of paper as if it were a gift from his god, smoothing it over and over until it lay flat on his palm. Later, he had brought a message of his own to send and they had used one of their precious birds, stolen from the old spymaster's pigeon loft, to take the message back.

From Absolom to the Poet, greetings. The Leopard is safe in Caesarea. His enemy is in our sights. We have hopes for a swift resolution.

If bird flight were an omen, the pigeon's swift departure from her hands at dusk was the best they could have hoped for.

The two falcons Iksahra had flown yesterday bent their heads to feed. Today's pair ate only shreds of goat, thread-fine pieces designed to whet their appetite and give them the power to fly without leaving them sated. The falcon was her best: a three-year-old haggard caught in the wild and tamed at night with a stealth that would have surprised Anmer ber Ikshel, had he lived to see such patience in his so-impatient daughter.

Iksahra stroked its breast with her forefinger, crooning. 'Soon, soon, soon we will fly. Just give me time to ready the horses, and to pick up your little brother. See how ready he is? Not as strong as you, but he's keen and together we'll—'

'Iksahra?'

The call shattered her peace. A hound belled an answer, or a greeting, and in that was the hint of who came. Iksahra took time to settle her bird before deigning to turn to acknowledge the intruder who had dared risk the dangers of her company.

'I am Hypatia of Alexandria. I came on the ship *Krateis* yesterday.'

Iksahra tilted her hand and made the falcon step

back on to the leather-covered hoop that was its day perch. The bird screamed its disappointment and struck at Iksahra's gloved hand and had to be freed, claw by claw, before she was able to shed the glove and, finally, to turn and study her enemy.

This close, Hypatia was more striking even than she had seemed on the ship, and then she had been a thing to catch all eyes; the king and his queen had both made a point of looking elsewhere, not to seem to gape.

Her hair was the deep, dense blue-black of the true Egyptians but fine, so that it shone like watered silk and caught the colours of the sun. Her skin was pale as milk, her eyes were the colour of whetted iron, sharp to pare the souls of men and women.

And she was beautiful; it was said of Cleopatra Ptolemy, queen of all Egypt, that her beauty stole the souls of all the men who saw her, but that queen had been dead for a hundred years. If she had ever had a successor, Hypatia of Alexandria was that one.

In all that time, the woman did not speak. She had patience, too.

'You are the Chosen of Isis,' Iksahra said presently. 'You come from the empress of Rome and have an appointment in the palace at dawn.'

She knew these things because the slaves knew, and few others, but Hypatia nodded, pleasantly, as if her title and her appointment had always been common knowledge.

'Polyphemos, the chief steward, is precise in his timing,' she said. 'I am told that I must go to the palace gates when a particular bell is struck in summons. I have long enough, apparently, to visit my hounds, to see that they are fed and watered and have rested in the night, and return. He said it was feeding time. He didn't tell me you would be here.'

'An oversight,' Iksahra said. Polyphemos was an arrogant, self-important, interfering fool. If he had sent the Greek woman here, now, it was so that she and Iksahra might meet with no one to oversee them.

'An oversight,' agreed Hypatia. 'Unless he hopes that you might turn me to stone. Can you do that?'

Iksahra stared at her. 'The slaves talk nonsense.'

'Good. It would be hard to present myself to her majesty if I were already petrified. May I visit my hounds? They travelled well, but the first days on land can be— Ah.' A bell sounded, a silver note that hovered over the gardens and faded, slowly. Hypatia frowned in regret. 'It would appear that I don't have as long as I was led to believe. My apologies. I'm sure the hounds are thriving in your care. If time and the queen permit, I may take them out later. Will you be here?'

'No.'

'A pity.' Hypatia bowed a little, in the desert fashion, hand on heart. 'We shall meet again later, I'm sure.'

'Perhaps.' Iksahra didn't smile, then or later. The day was broken and neither the falcon, the hounds nor the horses could mend it. When Hyrcanus came shortly afterwards, she let him talk her into taking the horses and the birds to hunt along the shore.

*   *   *

A thousand colours of silk rustled in harmony as Hypatia entered the audience room of the royal palace at Caesarea. Many-branched candles flared. Torches blazed on the marble walls. A multitude of flowers perfumed the air. Not since her second meeting with the emperor in Rome had Hypatia seen so much finery, and there it had all been displayed by men.

Here, there were only women. Queen Berenice, sister to the king, sat on a high dais at the room's far side surrounded by her court. As Hypatia stood in the doorway, she heard in her mind the voice of Poppaea, Rome's dead empress, her dead friend. 'Berenice has the heart and soul of a king. She is our hope of peace in Judaea. We do hope for that . . .'

With that hope as her guide, Hypatia stepped through the vast oak doors, took three steps forward, and paused as she awaited the steward's announcement.

'May I present Hypatia of Alexandria, who bears with her the gift of Poppaea, late empress of Rome.'

Hands clasped at her sternum, Hypatia bowed and took another three paces in. Berenice held the centre of her entourage, a radiance of blue and silver, seated on a throne set with a shining rainbow of diamonds, emeralds, rubies, turquoise, amber. Her women sat around her, all in spring green pointed with copper. Under their gaze, Hypatia began the twelve measured paces to the throne's foot.

The dark-haired girl who had called out on the wharf was there; the one whose outstretched arm had seemed to banish the *Krateis*, or at least, hold her still.

Surprisingly alert for the time of morning, the girl sat on a low stool at one edge of the dais pulling faces at Hypatia as she walked. An angled mirror-wall in silver leaf behind the throne displayed each inventive grimace, made twice as large as life.

By a quirk of the room and its angles, Hypatia alone had the benefit of this insight. Berenice and the crowd of green-clad Caesarean women who formed her court sat high up with their backs to the wall, looking down along the marble floor at the woman approaching them. They would have had to turn round to see either the girl or her reflection, a breach of etiquette that defied imagination. Mesmerized, Hypatia kept walking.

The floor sighed to the sound of her slippered feet. Geometric mosaics in black and white sprayed out on either side. Painted friezes on the northern wall showed Augustus as man and god on one side, and Roma in her guise as the virgin Athena striding into battle on the other. The goddess wore blue and silver. The women who attended her, battle-maidens all, were adorned in green, paler and more pastel than that worn by the current queen's attendants, but close enough for the art to echo life.

Windows opened out on the remaining three walls. Half of them looked west over the ocean to where the moon's last edge graced the busy, restless water.

The rest looked either south over tended flower gardens, textured now in shades of moonlight and grey, with a swimming pool glassy beyond; or east, towards the theatre where men worked by the sweating hundred, completing the final preparations for an evening performance. Torches bled hazy light through the thin vellum roof, moving hither and yon jerkily, so that, from the height of the palace, the men became a host of fireflies dancing within an upturned bowl laid out for the amusement of the queen and her attendants.

Nowhere were there signs of the unrest that was apparent elsewhere in the city; the harbour, the palace and the route between them were immune to that, at least for now.

Hypatia reached the foot of the queen's high throne as the dark-haired girl pulled one last, extraordinary face, using the fingers of both hands to distort cheeks, brows, temples and hairline. Her waggling tongue was hotly pink, as if she might be tending to fever.

Fascinated, Hypatia stared for one moment too long. The woman at the queen's left followed her gaze and swooped on the culprit, hissing threats that echoed in the newly quiet room.

Without moving her head, Queen Berenice said, 'Kleopatra, you may retire. Drusilla, let Polyphemos take her. I wish you to be present when the empress's letter is read out.'

The child named Kleopatra cast a vicious glance at Hypatia, but she followed the steward out of the room without the scene that might have resulted had her mother endeavoured to remove her alone.

The door closed, solidly. In the supple silence afterwards Berenice rose in a flow of blue silk and came to stand at the foremost edge of the dais. She was older than she had seemed on the wharfside; closer to forty than thirty, but not by much, and she knew the power of her own beauty.

Diamonds hung at her ears, strung with turquoise to match her robes and emphasize the colour of her eyes. A filet of gold adorned thick hair that hung in a glossy rope down her back. She used her makeup sparingly and with true art, so that in the light of the lamps it was easy to see why men had been drawn in their dozens to Caesarea, seeking her hand.

Three had pressed their suits to completion and had married her, one after the other. The first two were dead. The last had been abandoned in favour of Caesarea, leaving him the butt of universal ridicule. None of this appeared to have left the queen discomfited, or robbed of her power.

At the foot of the throne, Hypatia began the full obeisance required by the royal line of Persia. Berenice laughed, charmingly. 'Come, in this company that is not necessary. Rise and stand for us. We saw you on the ship that berthed next to Hyrcanus' skiff yesterday and we fear his arrival stole attention that should rightfully have been yours. We are told you are in possession of a letter from the Empress Poppaea addressed to ourself. Is it so?'

The queen's eyes were a startling deep blue, echoed by the blue silk of her stola. Meeting them, Hypatia was sure that she knew exactly what was said of her, in public and in private, and that she dared her new guest to think it, much less to speak of it.

All that in a look, while her voice, not as musical as Poppaea's had been, but beautiful none the less, carried without effort from wall to wall and back again.

'It is so, majesty.' Hypatia held the scroll in her right hand, slanting crosswise across her chest; a fragile cylinder of rolled papyrus, tied with silk and sealed with lead, copper, silver and gold, her passport to the queen's presence.

'You may present it to us.'

The thrones were raised four feet from the floor. Tall

as she was, Hypatia had to stretch to place the scroll in the queen's extended hand. One of the door-guards wore a knife capable of slitting the seals. At a royal nod, he brought it to the queen.

Papyrus crackled as the silk was cut. The small balls of sealing lead caused the thread to hang down, swinging, as Berenice scanned the manuscript. Thoughtful, she raised her striking eyes.

'Is this written by Poppaea's own hand?'

'Majesty, it is not. The empress had childbed fever and was too sick to write. She dictated to a scribe in my presence. I can attest that the words are hers alone.'

'You must be flattered.' Amusement warmed the royal voice, but not completely.

'I am.'

'Why? What does it say?' asked Drusilla, younger sister to the queen. The gossips in Rome said she was the more beautiful of the two. In Hypatia's opinion, the gossips were wrong in lamplight, but might conceivably have been correct under the harsher light of the sun.

Berenice finished scanning the letter for the second time and, pensive of face, passed it to her sister. 'Read it,' she said. 'Speak the empress's words aloud for all of us.'

'As my majesty commands.' Smiling prettily, Drusilla bent her head. She read it through once in silence, her lips stumbling across the difficult constructs, then began aloud.

'*To Berenice, queen in Caesarea—*'

'A tactful woman,' Berenice murmured. The room was perfectly still now. 'Not queen of Caesarea, nor of Judaea. Which I am not, as we all know. Continue.'

'To Berenice, queen in Caesarea, from Poppaea Sabina, empress, greetings.

'By the time you read this, the message-birds will long since have brought news of my death and the gossips will have embroidered it, saying I was poisoned, or stabbed, or thrown from a high window. Listen to none of them. I die now at the will of the gods who choose that the new life I bring into the world will not flourish, and that I will wither as it does. The doctors tell me that I will live to give birth to a fine and healthy boy child. I know that they lie, and am content with my lot.

'But now, while I have my faculties, and my memories – so many good memories of you – I wish to send you that which will bring joy to your days and peace to your land and your heart. I send therefore, as my gift and my bequest, this woman Hypatia of Alexandria and that which she brings.

'She will tell you herself of the gifts she bears. Of her, I tell you that she is the Chosen of Isis, who has served until now in the temples of Alexandria. She is not commanded by royalty, only by her god, but she has served us well and continues to do so with courage and an intellect few can match. I commend her to your care, knowing you will love her as I do.

'There's a line here, written afterwards, in a different hand.' Drusilla turned the papyrus sideways and, frowning, read, 'Listen to her. There is much she knows.' And something else. I can't read it . . . I think—'

'It says, The sisters of Isis have no love of men, but will serve the greater good where they may. Trust her if you can. She will help you.' Berenice took the letter without turning her head. Her gaze held Hypatia's, unflinching. 'The extra line was in Poppaea's own hand. She was my friend; I know her writing. Did she speak this aloud too? Or did you order her to write it?'

'Neither, majesty.' Hypatia felt heat rise to her temples. 'I was present for the dictation and saw the scribe write the letter, but it wasn't given me until after the empress's death. It must be that she added those words before it was sealed, for I was not aware of them.'

'They say the Chosen of Isis cannot lie. Is that true?'

'I would not knowingly tell a falsehood, majesty. The gods would be dishonoured and to do that would be far worse than the consequences of any lie.'

'Indeed. *Listen to her. There is much she knows.*' Berenice mimicked the empress to perfection, kindly, as a sister might, or a mother of her favoured child. 'Our friend, queen of Rome, lay dying. Her thoughts will have turned to the afterlife, as all do at such times. What did she mean when she wrote this?'

'I know only that she required me to bring you the hounds, and to serve you in whatever capacity you request.'

'Perhaps she thought you might school our brother and ourself in the worship of your gods. Isis, perhaps? Would you do that, who have been a servant in her name?'

Hypatia shook her head. 'Not unless you requested it, majesty. The god of the Hebrews would not permit such a thing and it is known that the king pays homage to him alone.' Unlike his queen, who was known to favour Greek gods, Helios and Athena foremost amongst them.

83

'And yet,' said Berenice, 'we have temples of Isis in our city.'

Hypatia gave a brief nod. 'Your majesties are kind to your subjects, allowing them freedom in their worship. The world knows of your benevolence.'

Berenice tilted her head. 'The world, I believe, considers benevolence, or its lack, to be the legacy of our grandfather. Would you say the world was wrong?'

Poppaea had promised a trap, and here it was, neatly laid and quite candid. There was a relief in seeing it so soon.

Hypatia's choices were three: to agree, to disagree – or to speak the truth as she understood it.

With the colour still high in her cheeks, she chose the last of these.

'I would say the world chooses kindly to ignore the fact that the Roman governor, acting as the hand of the emperor, decides the choice of worship in the city and has done so for the past fifty years. And that the current incumbent, like his predecessors, will not lightly offend the Syrians whose taxes fill his coffers by denying them their right to worship freely whichever god or gods they choose. I notice it has not kept their youths from their annual rush of blood to the head. It seems to have come this year rather earlier than might have been expected, and to have an unusual degree of violence.'

What she had sensed as she stepped off the *Krateis* had become increasingly obvious as she had explored the city. Only here, in the palace, was there a semblance of absolute normality, as if the outer world was unable to impose itself.

There was silence. Nobody moved except Drusilla,

who turned, smiling, and said something softly to her sister, barely to be heard.

Berenice nodded her agreement. With care, she re-rolled the letter into its cylinder and wound the threads round it.

'*An intellect few can match*. Poppaea did warn us.' Superficially, her eyes held the same warm amusement as her voice. The currents beneath were as mixed and complex as those that pulled ships to their deaths in the seas outside.

'What gifts do you bring?'

'A water clock of Alexandrian design and a pair of hunting hounds for her majesty's kennels. I have taken the liberty of leaving them in the beast gardens to be fed and cared for. It is well known that the queen loves the hunt above all other pursuits.'

'Indeed. Were the hounds Poppaea's?'

'They were, majesty. They were of Egyptian hunting stock, mixed with the war-hounds of the Britons that were sent to her as a gift after Rome's fire. She believed them among the best in the world.'

'Then perhaps tomorrow morning, when today's duty is behind us, we shall discover if this is true.' Berenice rose. Her spring-clad attendants rose with her.

Thus dismissed, Hypatia drew back to let the royal party pass her. Berenice paused, still on the dais.

'We accept the gifts of our dear friend, now dead. You will be given a room in the palace. Polyphemos will see to it. You are free to spend your time as you see fit. Five days from now, however, we require your company at the theatre. The performance will be more tedious than you can imagine but what takes place before it may be worthy of your attention. We gather here at the afternoon's sixth hour. A gown will be given. Do not take this to mean that your existing garment is considered unfit, only that we require conformity in those who follow us.'

CHAPTER SIX

Pantera woke before dawn, and left the inn quietly, but with no particular effort to keep himself hidden.

Even so, nobody followed him, which meant that he had to turn back, cursing, and retrace his steps along the silent street and up the inn's shallow stairway, had to step over the four outriders who had drunk until late in the main room and slept there on bedding rolls, had to reach the door to the slaves' quarters from which he had stolen the tunic, and lift the door catch and let it fall a fraction less softly than before, and step back, less carefully, over the sleeping men and scuff his bare foot on the edge of a bedding roll and bite back a curse, before he heard a catch in one man's breathing, heard it stop and start again in a stiffer rhythm. An opened eye gleamed in the room's faint light, but he couldn't tell whose.

Leaving the inn for the second time, he felt his way forward slowly, as if the starlight were not enough to find his way along the wide, rule-straight streets.

Out here, the air was tense, as of a city holding its breath. Small fires smouldered and there were fresh signs of violence, but the gangs of youths had gone to their beds and only slaves were up now, few and sleepy, running morning errands.

To give his pursuer time to make his own way out of the sleeping room and down the stairs and out into the market square, he stubbed his toe and lost time hopping and swearing until he saw a shadow move on the lower stairs.

Still somewhat lame, Pantera led his follower, or followers, across the square and into the streets beyond. For a while, he thought there might be two of them, but it became clear that there was only one, making more noise than he should have done. Not Rasul, then; Rasul was as quiet on his feet as any man you could wish to meet; it was what made him a likely spy.

A foot scuffed on stone at the inn's corner. Pantera cut through between two tall houses, past a garden of anemones, and turned south, towards the barracks. Twice, he passed men of the morning Watch come, yawning, to take their places on the tented podiums that filled each street corner. Some replaced night watchmen although they were fewer and stood only on the major intersections; the streets around them were clear of damage.

The follower hung back when the Watch was near, and had to be induced closer, step by slow, seductive step. At a corner where a wine merchants' row crossed with some money-lenders, Pantera let himself slide too close to the night Watch lanterns and jerked away again. His shadow sliced a wide arc across the greying ground.

Dawn had come a shade closer; he and his pursuer no longer walked in the night.

Some time later, he turned left, eastwards, towards the wall and, later still, the man following him made the same turn. And stopped. And turned in a slow circle on his heel and cursed aloud, in Greek.

Pantera lay in one of the storm ditches less than fifty paces away with his face pressed to the cold stone, his chin on his balled fist. The man who was not a spy stood near the light-wash from a window nearby. The rays of a single tallow lamp bled out, muffled, through a thin muslin curtain; not a vast light, but in the grey pre-dawn it carved valleys across a creased forehead, brightened the line of cheek and chin and temple, made a scimitar of a hooked nose so that Pantera, who had spent a month in the desert riding at this man's left flank, recognized Kleitos, the big, black-bearded Cypriot who had been the outriders' second bowman.

In the quiet of his mind, he apologized to Rasul, a man he liked and did not want to have to kill. He didn't want to kill Kleitos, either; not because he liked him, but because a living spy was more useful than a dead one. He lay still in the culvert, breathing dust and old sea water and an occasional sharpness where someone had thrown a citrus rind.

Kleitos stood longer than most men, proving that he had patience to make up for his clumsiness, but he left before the sun splashed colour on the day and Pantera eased his knife back into its sheath. Standing slowly, he dusted himself off and joined the handful of slaves padding swift-footed through the morning.

Following instructions he had learned nearly thirty

years before, Pantera worked his way back north through the Hebrew quarter. In due course, he passed the besieged synagogue, caught like an island in noble solitude with the heretic scaffolding cutting it off from the city on all sides.

Here, now, at sunrise, the silence around it was less striking than it had been in the bustling day. The houses on the street opposite were empty, their families gone in haste for fear of the violence that must surely follow the synagogue's desecration.

With nobody to watch him, Pantera walked through the gate and picked his way quietly up the brick-littered path to the forecourt.

In design, the building followed the restrained Greek style of every other temple in the city; plain fluted columns surrounded a porch and the dark maw of the entrance. Only its unadorned facings set it apart: where Jupiter might have been, or Adonis, or Augustus the man-god, in the synagogue was nothing but bare stone. And the entrance faced south to Jerusalem, where all the others faced east, to the rising sun.

There was no door, only a hanging curtain of woven camel's hair so dark it was almost black. Pantera could have pushed past it, but he had never yet desecrated the temple of another man's god and this morning was no time to start.

He was leaving when he saw the thread of old blood in the far right corner, trailing down on to the broad steps. Crouching, he tested the blood with his finger, smelled it, tasted it, found it old, dried, cold. The smell of death hung around it, three days old and still fleshy in its decay.

He drew his knife and pushed one corner of the curtain away, or tried to. The tip became stuck on something solidly fleshy. He pushed harder. The obstruction rocked away and back again. Drawing a breath against the expected stink, he ripped up the curtain—

And found that the head was a pig's, not a man's as he had feared, and that the eyes had been put out and the tongue torn away and the ears cut off. A blind, deaf, speechless pig: as vile a desecration as any Hebrew could imagine.

He felt a ripple of relief that left as fast as it came. This was not a crucified cat, sent as a personal message, but an insult to a whole people, to the young men already stoked to volcanic anger, to their fathers who might restrain them, to their mothers who might caution safety. Here was the first step to a war, and he had dealt with war before.

Pantera looked around. The building plot was an anarchy of rubble and old wood with dark holes aplenty where a part-rotten pig's head might conveniently be lost. It was the work of moments to find two planks to carry it with, a place to hide it and dry sand to scour away the blood.

The marks on the curtain were harder to remove, but also harder to see. Pantera rubbed at them with the heel of his hand, and then let it drop and stood back to examine his work.

Someone made a sound behind him; a brick was nudged out of place and skin slid on stone. He heard an indrawn breath, unmistakably human.

He spun, knife drawn back to throw, but saw no one

until he dropped his gaze to the brick-littered path that led from the gates.

A naked girl-child sat there where she had fallen, wide-eyed with shock and pain. One foot had a scrape along its side where she had stumbled on a brick. Even as Pantera watched, her white face flushed to scarlet, her eyes brimmed with tears and she opened her mouth to yell.

'No, small one. No. Hush now . . . hush. It doesn't hurt. See? We'll make it better . . .' Without thinking, he dropped the knife and gathered her up in his arms, desperate for silence, for her not to draw in the Hebrews or Syrians or anyone else who might see him in this place.

He held her close, warm against his warm, and pressed his cheek to her fine gingery hair and stroked her arms and felt her grow a little less tense. He spoke in Greek at first, not thinking, and then, thinking less, began to speak in the language of Britain, in the coaxing rhymes he had crooned to his first child, his long-dead daughter, that told of oak and salmon and mountains and crashing waterfalls and the gods that bound them.

It was so long since he had held an infant like this. There had been children in Rome on the night of the fire and he had carried them across the open spaces ahead of the flames, had lifted them on to his horse, had ushered them in their pairs and dozens and half-hundreds up the hill to Caesar's palace where they might be safe from the ravening flames.

Then, the children had not been soft as this child was soft; their hair had not smelled smokily of the evening's cooking fires and salt-mustily of a night's deep sleep;

their cheeks had not felt like soft silk under his hand, wet with snot and tears; their chubby fists, just growing to hands, had not explored his face as he bent over her.

But his dead child had been and had done all of those things. She had been the love of his heart and he had killed her, drawing his knife across her throat at the battle's end, when all was lost and the only gift he had left was to keep her from the legions. He had been British then: a tribesman, a spy gone so deeply into his new role that he had become that which he sought at first to betray.

'She'll not hurt you. And she'll not scream now, either. For which you are as grateful as we are, I imagine.'

The voice was a man's, speaking Aramaic, but not as a first language. Pantera turned slowly, unarmed. His throat hurt, from the old language, caught in mid-flow.

A bear-man stood at the synagogue's gate, as naked as the child, and as easy with it. The grey morning light showed him thick of neck and broad of shoulder, with a fleece of reddish-brown hair matting his chest and upper arms and none at all on his head.

His face was round with almond eyes and had the look of one long used to battle: his nose had been broken so many times it was surprising he could breathe at all; his cheekbones, similarly, had been reshaped at some point in his past; his teeth were thick pegs that stood widely spaced in a wider mouth. Two were missing.

He stood in balance on the balls of his feet, lightly. He was a man at home in himself, for whom fighting came naturally and only the fast, the well armed or the insane might hope to beat him. He bore a short-shafted, two-headed axe in his left hand.

Pantera looked down to where his own knife lay at his feet. The second was strapped to his arm, high up in his sleeve, crushed by the child. He wondered how far the axe might be thrown and with what accuracy. And then he remembered seeing it done; an axe throw, neat and clean and perfect, into the head of a running horse.

'Are you Parthian?' he asked, in that language.

'I am.' The man's easy smile broadened. He balanced the axe across both palms and bowed, then laid it on the ground and stepped forward over it, holding out one hand.

'I am Estaph,' he said, as they grasped, hand to calloused hand. He smelled of woodsmoke and recent coitus. 'The child you hold is Eora, my daughter. She has taken to walking in the early mornings and we don't always see where she goes.'

She was a fine-boned, fragile thing, light as a bird. It was hard to imagine her growing into a woman to match this man from the far eastern mountains.

Pantera gave her into the care of her father. 'A fine and healthy child,' he said. 'Although her foot will need the salve of a mother's kiss. Do you live here?' A sweep of his head took in the whole area around the synagogue.

'At the street's end,' Estaph said, and pointed to the endmost house. By the standards of the city, it was more of a cottage, a bare two floors high, with its roof garden more herbs than flowers. The other gardens in the street had long since withered for lack of water.

Pantera said, 'You have no neighbours?'

'We did have, but they left at the last month's end,' Estaph said. 'Nobody has come to take their place. It's not safe any more for either Hebrews or Syrians to live

94

here. Only those of us who are neither, and trade in weapons that either side might wish to buy, are safe. Or we were before someone put a sow's head in the temple.'

'You saw that?'

'I saw you move it.' Estaph made a cleansing motion with his hands. 'It won't stop them.'

'Whom will it not stop?'

There was a silence in which Estaph cradled his daughter in one massive arm, stroking her fine, reddish hair with the other hand.

Presently, looking up, he met Pantera's eyes. 'Here in Caesarea, it used to be that the Syrian youths fought the Hebrews and the Hebrews fought the Syrians and neither side needed encouragement. But this year, there are men who meet in basements and quiet corners, who worship a dead Galilean rebel as if he were Israel's messiah. They eat flesh and drink blood in his name and they hate the Hebrews more than any men I have met. They put the pig's head in the synagogue. And it is they who are stoking the street fights so they are earlier, harder, more savage than before.'

Pantera closed his eyes. There were times when Saulos was so close he could smell him, taste him, feel the air shudder where he had been. He said, 'Rome was burned by such as these.'

Estaph spat. His daughter watched him with round-eyed interest. 'Sewer rats masquerading as men,' he said. 'But they will destroy Caesarea if no one stops them.'

Pantera asked, 'Will you leave?'

'Soon. When my business is done. I'm going to Jerusalem next. There, the War Party is fighting the Peace Party but at least it's all out in the open.'

Pantera looked up at the sky, at the scribble of fine cloud, burning away in the advancing morning. 'Hebrews fighting Hebrews.' He shook his head. 'If they stopped, if they came together, if they asked themselves who is the common enemy . . .'

'Hebrews will fight each other over the price of a dried date, you know this.' Estaph spread his spatulate fingers in a shrug that spoke more than any carrier-bird's message, however well crafted. 'In Jerusalem, they have a nation to fight over, its survival, the survival of their god and their people. Menachem's War Party will go to war if necessary to rid their nation of the Roman oppressor. More, they want war, they desire it, they think their god is asking for it. Gideon's Peace Party is set against violence of any kind, at least against Romans. They think the way to be rid of an emperor is through prayer and talk. And they know that if Nero sends in the legions, their people will be crushed for ever. They're right, of course. It's madness. Maybe if their messiah did come and was able to lead them all together it would be different, but Hebrews don't like one leader, they like being set one tribe against the next. It's what has kept them in slavery for a thousand years.'

Delivered of this philosophy, Estaph spat gravely on the palm of his hand and held it out. 'I'll leave in five days' time. If you are looking for employment then, I might be hiring.'

'There are two of us,' Pantera said.

'I know. I watched you ride in yesterday. And I have heard Ibrahim's tale of your battles in the desert. Your Roman brother is welcome also.'

'Thank you. If you leave early, send word to Ibrahim

96

at the Inn of the Five Vines. He'll know where to find us.' Turning to leave, Pantera delved into his waist pouch. 'For Eora,' he said, and laid a copper coin in the girl's open palm as he left.

CHAPTER SEVEN

Morning had not yet coloured the day as Pantera passed north into the neighbouring quarter where the houses were but a single storey, and no temples graced the road ends.

There, at an unmarked junction, was a house notable chiefly for the lack of flowers in the forecourt, and the soft whirr of feathers above. A chalked sign hanging over the lintel proclaimed that the doves bred therein were the greatest delicacy to be found in Caesarea, fit to grace the tables of any king, and that thirty were ready for slaughter with some squabs also available at a good price per half-dozen. Standing beneath it, Pantera gave a precise knock on a wooden door.

The youth who came to answer was not yet grown into the man his father might wish him to be. His beardless skin bore the silken sheen of a woman and his brown eyes were big as gazelles'. His face was a long oval, alive with the naïveté of youth. He frowned as he opened the door and saw a man there he did not know.

'The grey horse I bought at market yesterday is

lame.' Pantera spoke in Greek, enunciating carefully.

The boy stared at him a moment, uncomprehending, then his eyes flew wide. 'Father isn't here,' he said, which was not the right answer at all.

'The grey horse—' began Pantera again.

'Yes, yes! I heard. Then you should . . . you will . . . you must have it seen to immediately. I know of a man. Please come in.' The boy finished in a rush, blinking back his fear. He made no effort to step back and let Pantera in. 'Father isn't here,' he said again.

'It doesn't matter. I wished only to use your services. What's your name?'

'Ishmael.'

Syrian then, and not Hellenized like the rest. It was useful to know. 'Thank you, Ishmael. May I come in?'

The boy's eyes grew larger by the moment, but still he showed no sign of letting his unexpected visitor cross the threshold until, losing patience, Pantera shouldered his way through the doorway.

Inside, the single room was small and everything in it was white, except for the wool rugs on the floor, which were striped in all the colours of the sheep from pale sand through to wet-oak brown. It smelled of a morning's cooking layered on a night's sleep.

The door closed, jarring the quiet. The draught pushed open a door at the room's far side. Pantera walked through it, checked the small courtyard and, when he was sure there was nobody to witness, stepped back in, pulling the door shut.

'I am the Leopard,' he said. 'I believe – I sincerely hope – you may have a message for me? From Rome.'

'The Leopard!' A shy smile bloomed across Ishmael's

face. Men and women, Pantera thought, would kill for that smile, one day. 'Father said you might come. He'll curse that he missed you. Two messages wait for you. The first has been here since before I was born. The second came this year.' His smile faltered. 'The Teacher sent the first, but he is dead now. The second came with one of his red roan doves and the message was in his code, but the hand that wrote it was different.'

'The Poet has stepped into the Teacher's shoes,' Pantera said. 'That is who will have sent it.' And then, because the boy was still waiting, 'We who served Seneca until his death are loyal to the emperor, and to the memory of our Teacher. It is possible to be both.'

'Yes!' All doubt dissolved, the boy's white teeth shone. He tapped Pantera lightly on the arm. 'Wait here and I will get the scrolls.'

Mercifully, the papers were not secreted in a chamber beneath the cooking fire which was the first place a competent search team would have looked, but hidden in a concealed compartment within the water tank that sat atop the roof of the house.

Steps led up from the outer walled courtyard in which stood the dovecote, source of the household's legitimate income. Pantera sat guard on the bottom step and watched half a hundred buff-rose doves coo and preen and flit in feathery leaps from cote to roof to wall and back again.

The birds were well handled, with no fear of men, so that he was able to stand among them and search out those of different colours; the six or seven whose feathers shimmered in an oily turtle green, the black pair with white flashes that looked like magpies, the pure white singleton with the pink eyes. None of them was the red roan and white of Seneca's Roman carrier-birds, but it was clear that in this flock such a bird would readily be lost in the multitude of colours.

Ishmael came back presently, beaming his success. The family had a precise and efficient system of classifying the messages that passed through their hands, for the boy did not bring the entire year's collection, but only two short, slim cylinders, carried with the awe of a novitiate bearing sacred writings.

'For the Leopard,' he said, leading Pantera back into the house. 'You may sit?'

Pantera sat on one of the two bedding rolls pushed up against the wall. Unrolled from their containers, the messages were revealed on two square sheets of finest papyrus, no thicker than spring's first leaves, no larger than them either; each side was half the length of his smallest finger. The writing in both was finer than gossamer, one achingly familiar, old, faded with age, one new in all senses, still alien to his eye.

But both used the same code, the first one that Pantera had ever learned; he could parse it now as if it were in the original Greek. He read the older first.

To the Leopard from his Teacher, greetings. Solomon is safe and sends you his thanks. I have sent gold which will reach you by other routes. I send also my congratulations; pushed to the edges of your being, you earned your name in all ways.

Scribbled at the bottom, unencoded, was a last sentence. *I send also my earnest gratitude, as from a father to his son, that you are safe.*

Pantera laid the paper leaf on his knee, where it

shivered in the sway of his breath. In the morning's half-light, it wasn't hard to conjure an image of Seneca – the Seneca of his youth – sitting at his desk in Alexandria, condemned to exile by Claudius and lucky to be alive, yet still running the most comprehensive, efficient and broad-reaching spy network in the empire.

And into that network Seneca had drawn a runaway archer's son found thieving on the streets of Alexandria. Throughout those early years, he had driven Pantera harder than even a boy who loathed himself might have done. He had asked for more and never settled for less. He had set tasks that made the threats and conspiracies of real life seem trivial by comparison. He gave praise rarely, and always salted it liberally with criticism. To a boy who had abandoned his father in disgust, he had never once in seven years suggested that he considered himself in that role.

Except that he had. *As from a father to his son . . .*

Pantera could have read that, if things had turned out differently. He had been travelling to Caesarea on his first mission. He had been given the pass code and the address of the pigeon loft, manned by an agent of Seneca's named Isaac.

But he had never gone. He had, in fact, been prevented from going by the order to divert to Damascus, there to aid the escape of a man who had attracted the ire of Aretas, king of Syria. It had been his first true mission, and it had nearly cost him his life, but he had come out of it with a sense of his own skill that nothing else could have given him. On leaving that city, another message had come, ordering him north and east to Parthia, an empire on the brink of war against Rome.

After that, Cappadocia, Cilicia, Gaul, Britain. Never again near Caesarea, until now, when he knew all that Seneca felt for him.

As from a father to his son . . .

Seneca had named him son on the night of Rome's fire, and loved him as such. Pantera had never said that he loved his old spymaster in return. If he let it, his regret for that could eat him away to nothing.

'Is it bad news?' Ishmael's angelic face peered at him, creased with concern.

'No.' Pantera pulled himself back to the present. 'I was thinking of who I used to be when this was written.'

'You were the Leopard. You're still the Leopard.' The name was magical to the boy, a talisman against all harm.

Pantera offered half a smile. 'I am not the Leopard I was,' he said.

'Why not?'

Only the young asked such direct questions. *Why not?* Because of a woman and child he had loved and then killed in Britain, to keep them from Roman harm? Because of a quite different woman of another race and another place he had loved in Gaul and Alexandria and Rome? Because of a boy-thief found and sent to Britain who had loved him?

All and none of these. Unexpectedly, he thought of Hypatia, who had warned him, once, to keep always to the truth.

He said, 'I got what I most wanted in life, and found that I didn't want it after all.'

'Father says that is the ruin of us all.'

'Your father is a wise man.'

'You haven't read the other message.'

He hadn't. He did so. It was brief and said nothing unexpected; except that it was old and late and didn't say what it should have said.

To the Leopard from the Poet: your prey remains in the pearl of the east. The emperor continues to support your cause, which is his cause. We await news of your success in Saba.

He read that last again, checking his decryption in his head. *We await news of your success in Saba.* The Poet was young, and frighteningly efficient; latest and greatest of Seneca's many protégés. Such a one should not still be awaiting news of the negotiations in Saba, when Pantera had sent a bird with all the necessary details as soon as he had taken the contract with Ibrahim.

He said, 'When did this message arrive?'

Frowning, Ishmael held the cylinder up to the light. 'The date's on the outside of the cylinder.' The collation of dots was not in any number system that Pantera knew. He waited while the boy's flying fingers added up time. 'It came . . . fifty-three days ago.'

'And there hasn't been another? Are you sure?'

'I'm sure. We know every bird. None have come from the spymaster's loft.'

'Nor from the emperor?'

'No. Although Father thinks . . .' Ishmael dropped his voice to a creaky whisper. 'He thinks we may be losing some of the birds.'

'Losing?'

'To storms. Or disease.'

'Or to men?'

Ishmael shook his head violently. 'No man could take

104

them. How would they do it? How would they know? We have told no one what we do, I swear it!'

'But the men who bring the new carrier-birds from Jerusalem and Damascus and Rome, the other men who take the birds from your loft back to their own coops so that they may return with a message; each of these knows where you are.'

'My father makes the trips to Jerusalem. He's there now. The rest are all Seneca's sworn men.'

'Men can be bought. It happens, Ishmael, more often than you might think. Did your father take birds with him?'

'Yes. He took a dozen to Jerusalem and will bring the same number back. He does it every fourth month in the travelling season. In between, the men come from Damascus, Antioch, Alexandria and Rome.'

'When will he leave Jerusalem?'

'Tomorrow.'

'Then I have an idea. Send a bird to Jerusalem now, with a message to him from me. That way we'll know if the birds are getting through.'

Ishmael chewed his thumbnail. 'But we have only one bird left and Father never wants to send the last one before the new ones are here.'

'This time, I think, we must make an exception. Let me write the message. If your father's there, he'll understand.'

Pantera used a newer code than the one that had been the standard among Seneca's men in the days of his youth. His message was short.

From the Leopard to the Messenger, greetings. I come hunting the enemy of Israel. It may be that he knows this. If this bird reaches you, bring word in person. I will be here until the month's end.

Leaving, Pantera took a left turn and then followed the hill down towards the Temple of Isis, richly kept, aflame with flowers in all the colours of the sun.

In the temple courtyard was a stone water trough for the use of the more distant worshippers who must ride to their devotions, and on it, a neat, swiftly scratched graffito in the shape of a wild lily with a hound alongside. The hound had one ear.

Resting on the trough, he scratched his own sign of the bull alongside Hypatia's mark of the lily, and gave the hound its second ear to show that he understood that she had seen Saulos, then turned back up the hill and made his way back to the inn to return the stolen tunic to a night-slave not yet risen and tell Mergus all he had found.

CHAPTER EIGHT

Somewhere, someone wept.

The noise hid in the sea-mist that rolled over the palace gardens, almost, but not quite, private. Hypatia caught the sound's thread and followed it along a paved path past a series of three marble fountains, on each of which a weed-clad Oceanid cavorted in bronze, spilling water from hand or hair or heel.

Beyond them, at a corner where the cyclamens and orchids wove a pastel carpet, she turned left towards the sea and passed through avenues of scarlet tulips, dripping dew fat as blood. There, at the garden's end, a set of stairs led down to a pair of iron gates and on the steps a dark-haired girl sat slumped with her head in her hands, sobbing just loudly enough to be audible throughout the gardens.

Hypatia crouched on the top step and waited a while, watching. When it was clear she was not going to be acknowledged, she said, 'Kleopatra?'

The girl's head snapped up. She had sharp features, honed by eyes that held exactly the same startling gaze as her aunt Berenice's, but that these were greener and paler now than they had seemed in the lamplight, almost the colour of the deep ocean sea. A tear slid down one cheek, sharp as a diamond.

'Is this because I caused the queen to send you out of the audience room the other night?' Three of the five days had passed until Hypatia was due to attend the theatre. Slowly, she was learning where she could and could not go.

'Oh, that.' The girl tipped her head, considering. Plain on her face was the calculation of what she might gain by agreeing with Hypatia's suggestion.

Honesty, or pragmatism, won. 'No. It's Iksahra, the black beastwoman. She promised she'd let me fly the falcon before we go to Jerusalem, and we might ride at any moment. But she's taken Hyrcanus and his tiercel out instead. She loves him – Hyrcanus, not the bird. They hide in the horse stalls and fornicate.' That last was said with all the boundless venom of a wounded girl-child.

Hypatia, who did not believe it, let her eyes grow wide. 'Does your uncle, the king, know that?'

'I've told him, so he must.' Kleopatra stood up, dragging her fingers through her mist-sodden hair. She wore a plain, undyed linen tunic, belted with leather, not silver. If Hypatia had not known her already, it would have been altogether too easy to mistake her for a well-dressed slave. In this palace, the slaves were dressed in fabric of better weave than at least half the city's population.

Kleopatra said, 'You're the Chosen of Isis.'

Hypatia had heard her title spoken in awe and hope,

in fear and horror, in longing, in grief, in love. More rarely than any of these, she had heard it said in hate, by priests of other gods who fell in the shadow of her own.

She had never heard it spoken as an insult before; even Iksahra had managed to keep the inflection from her voice. She inclined her head. 'I am.'

'Why?'

'Why what?'

'Why were you Chosen?'

No one in twenty-five years had asked that. Hypatia closed her eyes, the better to think. The better, in fact, to ask the god who sometimes gave answers.

Not today. Her mind was empty of all but the horror of the night's dream. It was coming continually, now that Saulos was close.

Opening her eyes, she said, 'I had dreams as a child.'

'True ones?'

'Dreams are rarely completely true. They show the essence of what might be; the skill is in the reading. But I had vivid dreams and they felt real to me, which was what mattered. And I acted on them, which mattered too. If you honour your dreams, they will honour you.'

'My dreams frighten me.'

A wind blew, there in the garden, shifting the scents of wild and tame flowers. A high, fine note sounded in Hypatia's ear, the warning whistle of the gods. 'Do you act on them?' she asked.

Abruptly, the girl stood, brushing her hands on her tunic. 'Why are you here?'

'I brought two hounds as a gift to Queen Berenice from the empress of Rome. I came to see they were being well cared for.'

'The empress of Rome is dead.'

'I know. But her majesty ordered me to bring them while she was still alive.'

'From Rome?'

'Yes.'

'Is it true the emperor has taken a boy to wife in place of the empress, and made him a woman?'

'It wasn't when I left.'

Strictly speaking, she spoke the truth: the boy in question had been gelded and was being groomed as Nero's wife, but had not actually been married at the time the *Krateis* sailed. Hypatia was an Oracle and Oracles never lied. Never.

To avert another silence, she said, 'I should go to the beast garden. I want to take the hounds out for a run along the shoreline. They were on board ship for a month; even now, after three days on land, they crave sea air and flat ground.'

Not only the hounds sought freedom and clean air. Hypatia thought perhaps her own craving was there to be read, had the child the necessary literacy. She made no particular effort to hide it.

Kleopatra's smile was sharply fierce. 'Can you ride a horse? A good horse?'

'Yes.'

'Then you can come riding with me and bring your hounds for exercise!' She smacked the stone step in triumph. 'Nobody will see us leave if we go before the mist rises.'

Hypatia said, 'The mist's rising now. If you look down to the sea, it's blue again.'

Kleopatra's hair sank straight to her shoulders. When,

110

as now, she shook her head, the morning's faint sun spun around her. 'We have an hour at least. The king doesn't rise early any more. Not since Saulos came.'

She was a fountain of facts. 'Are we going to look for Iksahra and her falcons?' Hypatia asked.

'What do you think?'

They were already walking through the iron gates. Beyond was the king's beast garden, stocked with hound kennels and stables and mews for the hunting birds. To one side, in an iron cage bigger than the perfectly serviceable, well-fitted room in which Hypatia had spent the night, Iksahra's cheetah lay on an elevated tree branch, left behind that the beastwoman might give the young prince, Hyrcanus, her full attention. It yawned as they approached, showing perfect, pearline teeth, long as eating knives. They walked close past it, to show they were not afraid.

At the stables, Kleopatra didn't have to give orders. As she rounded the corner, stable hands ran to make her horse ready, and then did the same for Hypatia. Both mounts were red mares, both kindly, clean-limbed, built for speed but not stupidly so.

The kennel-men loosed the two hounds Hypatia had brought and they came joyous to heel, tails beating the air, muzzles wet with the need to hunt. Long-legged, rough-coated, their heads were high as her waist, and when they stood on their hind limbs in greeting their front feet reached her shoulders. She had named them Night and Day; the bitch dark as winter wood, the dog the gold-fawn of desert sand.

Hypatia fed them the meat she had brought from the palace kitchens, not much, just a handful, to remind them that they loved her, not the Berber woman who was beastmaster.

Kleopatra had mounted lightly. On horseback, she grew in stature and fire, became a hunting cat in her own right with polished jewels for eyes. With a hound at either hand, Hypatia looked up at her.

'We need to be clear. Is this an offer from a friend, a request for the Chosen of Isis, or an order from a princess of Caesarea?'

The princess turned her brightened gaze on Hypatia. 'Just now, it's an order. If that changes, you can be sure I will let you know. The gates are open. We shall walk the first quarter-mile to the shore's edge, then we can let the horses run.'

The falcon screamed as she launched from Iksahra's fist; a high, keening note that cut the cool morning from horizon to horizon, so that Hypatia would not have been surprised to see the sky split apart and the night leak back through.

Such power to behold, such fury. From launch to height, the bird's spread wings became a bar of slate grey, lost for a moment as she streaked low across the brilliant sea, then found again as she leapt from the wavetops and spiralled upwards to become, in so short a time, a scribble, lost in the aching wilderness of the sky.

They were galloping now; Hypatia and the Princess Kleopatra, racing along the marginal land where sea met shore and harsh grasses kept the one from sweeping away the other. They were lying flat to their horses' necks, letting the reins free, trying to keep up with the bird and the Berber woman who had loosed it.

Ahead, Iksahra sur Anmer was a mosaic of black limbs and white linen tunic set against pale grey sands and a paler horse. She had seen the woman and the girl who were following her, Hypatia thought, but she had not slowed her mount. Kleopatra's cousin, the Prince Hyrcanus, had not seen them and was not likely to unless they placed themselves physically in front of him; he had eyes only for the Amazon who led their wild hunt along the shore.

He had good reason. Tall and lean, the woman sat her horse with the ease of a born rider, and hers was not a fair-limbed, kindly mare such as had been given Hypatia, but one of the fire-blooded horses the Berber tribes bred to keep their children safe from harm, that were kept in their tents and fed dates and asses' milk and the last of the water in drought, that fought with teeth and feet against wild beasts and bandits with equal ferocity but could be led by a three-year-old child, that could carry a woman in the last hours of pregnancy so smoothly her waters would not break.

Iksahra wore man's garb again, as she had at the docks – likely as she did all the time – and the fine linen weave of her robes wrapped around her in the wind of her gallop. From arrogance, or for necessity, she rode without reins, leaving her hands free for the hunting birds that rode with her, clinging on arched perches mounted on either side of the pommel.

She untied the tiercel as she rode, pulling the leash free with teeth that shone white against her skin. He raised his wings and lifted lightly, using the wind of their running to hold him a hand's breadth above her gauntleted wrist.

'Would you see him hunt along the ground, while his mate rides high in the sky?'

Even at a shout, her accent was light, dancing over the consonants, softening the vowels. Hypatia had drawn nearly level and found herself looking into a face of sculpted oak, with spirals tattooed across cheekbones and nose and ice-black eyes that threw her a challenge she did not fully understand. At least there was some humanity there, which was an improvement on the cold of their last meeting.

They drew their horses to a halt. The hounds flopped to lie on the sands, tongues a-loll.

Hypatia said, 'I would see your bird do what he does best.'

'What he does best is to fly high and kill.' The dancing voice laughed, not kindly. 'But he will hunt and return to me if I ask him. Or if Hyrcanus does. One day, the king's heir will hunt these lands. We are teaching him the skills he needs.'

We. A woman and her hunting beasts, laying claim to royal pretensions. A horse halted level with theirs.

From Hypatia's other side, Kleopatra said, 'Perhaps my cousin could wait? The falcon is stooping to her kill. Such a thing deserves to be watched alone.'

She spoke with her aunt's voice; if they had closed their eyes, they would have thought Berenice among them.

Iksahra did close her eyes, hooding them against the outer world. With a nod that was, by a hair, courteous rather than curt, she set the tiercel back on his perch again and turned her horse to the sea to watch her falcon at work.

They heard the bells first, the high whistle in the wind that was a prelude to a death. Faster than she had disappeared, the falcon grew in the sky, became a pinpoint and then a falling arrowhead, fixed in shape with the wings curved back, taut as a drawn bow, sleek slate grey.

Hypatia saw the prey-bird late, as a streak of sand-coloured movement flitting along the shore, piping reedily. Moments later, it died in a punch of talons on flesh and bone. Feathers danced high in the air, light as husks in a threshing yard.

Iksahra pursed her lips and whistled a single short note. The falcon made a tight turn, dragging the shore-bird in one yellowed foot, and brought it to hand, landing hard. Shore-webbed feet and a long, curled beak hung down, senseless in death. Three drops of blood smeared the pale doeskin glove.

A gasp came from Hypatia's left, a small noise, drawn from the soul, such as one might make at the height of love, or in extremes of pain. And that high whine again in her ear, so that she turned her head only a fraction, too little to draw attention to herself, and so saw the Princess Kleopatra as few people could have seen her, laid raw to the world, open, unguarded and uncaring, moved to a joy beyond words.

It was gone in a breath, in a heartbeat. Kleopatra turned her horse neatly on its hocks. Her eyes were flat again, the granite-sea of her aunt's.

'Teach me,' she said. 'Now. We could ride for Jerusalem at any time. Saulos said so. You might not come.'

'Kleo . . . !' Hyrcanus stared at her in horror, flicking his eyes to Hypatia and back in exaggerated horror.

Kleopatra gave a curt, scornful laugh. 'She's the Chosen of Isis. She knows everything.'

'Does she?' Iksahra asked.

'I know that the royal family will go to Jerusalem some time soon,' Hypatia said, truthfully. 'I have no idea at all if you'll go with them.'

She didn't say that she had no idea yet as to why they might go, except that it must be an emergency: no royal family travelled at night unless they were in haste and in secret.

Iksahra favoured her with the same hooded gaze as before. 'Where goes the king, so go I. The princess can learn as easily in the deserts outside Jerusalem as here.'

Kleopatra shook her head. 'There are going to be riots, maybe war. And whatever starts here will spread to Jerusalem within days, my aunt, the queen, said. The hunting might stop. You have to teach me now.'

'Kleo, you can't learn in a day. I've been learning for nearly two months and I truly don't know what I'm doing.' Hyrcanus was kind; warmth laced his voice, his eyes, his hand as he leaned over to take his cousin's arm.

She shook him off. Her fiery green gaze was locked now with the Berber woman's; green on black, hot, fierce passion locked on a gaze that was cold as loss. There was hate in the core of Iksahra's soul, but it was locked so tight that Hypatia doubted if even the woman herself could feel its fire.

Iksahra broke away first. She looked out across the sea. The falcon fed on her fist, throwing gobbets of feathered gore left and right, ripping at the flesh beneath. The tiercel tilted his hooded head, hearing, not moving.

'The falcon is sated. If we flew her now, she would

116

find a tree and not come down for three days. When we go to Jerusalem, we would lose her.'

'The tiercel then.'

Hyrcanus said, 'If she wants to fly it, I don't mind.' He was a prince and he still thought he was party to the decision.

The Berber woman stroked one dark forefinger down the rosy breast of her smaller hunting bird. 'So,' she said. 'This is the tiercel. He is the male. He is smaller. He is weaker. But still he gives his heart to us. Is that what you want?'

'Yes.'

'Will you do exactly as I say, in the moment I say it, without question?'

Kleopatra, who had been schooled in the etiquette of court, and in riding, and perhaps in the handling of falcons, but not at all in the nature of the worlds beyond the world and how they listened to an oath, said, clearly, 'I will.'

Her voice carried across the desert, here in the place where ghûls and ifrit roamed, listening for a word that might be taken hostage; where Isis and Mithras heard the tones of truth and placed them in the balance, to be weighed later, against other actions; where a future could change on the balance of a word.

Triumph sparked briefly in Iksahra's eyes, a flash of heat in the cold. 'Then we shall start. Hyrcanus, give your glove to your cousin.'

The Berber woman was gentle as she set the falcon and placed her glove behind the tiercel, pressing lightly against the yellow skin of his leg so that he must step back and up on to her fist.

117

Bells shaped like hollow beans were tied to his legs in the place the message cylinders were tied on the courier-birds. They chimed musically as he stepped from the perch to her gloved fist. Iksahra stroked his breast with her forefinger, settling one rose-blushed feather back into place. For all his small size, the tiercel was richer in colour than his mate, tinted bronze around his breast and throat where she was slate grey, stark against white.

'If you are to ask a bird to fly for you, you must give him a reason. He must trust you to hold him steady, to loose him cleanly, and always to feed him when he comes. If these three things apply, he will come back to you even when he has killed, trusting your hand as the safest place to eat. So to begin with, you shall feed him a piece of the bird his mate has caught and then you shall loose him . . .'

They were intimate as lovers, Iksahra and the girl, their two heads bent together, almost touching, startling in their contrast, white skin and black, straight hair and curled, tutor and pupil.

Hypatia felt a different gaze and looked up and caught Hyrcanus watching her. He gave a rueful smile and tilted his head a little and, seeing the grace of it, Hypatia moved her mare back a step and turned her away so that she and Hyrcanus might follow, but not be part of, the lesson that excluded them both.

When the bird flew and made its kill, she was not part of it, and did not see what it brought down, except that it had come from the city, and knew nothing of its death.

*

118

Later, in the afternoon, Hypatia excused herself from the palace, from the claustrophobia of attendants and guards and stewards and maids and slaves and minor royalty, away from the perfumed, incensed air, away from the flower garden and the fruit garden and the beast garden and the swimming pool with its views of the sea, and walked along the long, open streets to the city, to the fruit market she had passed through the previous day.

As she left, she found that Polyphemos wished her to have a guard, which was astonishing considering he had gone to such remarkable lengths to prevent her from seeing Queen Berenice when she had first arrived. Now that she had seen the queen, it seemed, he regarded her as his personal responsibility and pressed on her an escort from palace Watch.

Thus she went among the sellers of cherries and citrus, of plums and melons, dried dates and figs, of almonds and olives and oils thereof, and wove through the stalls in the suffocating company of Agathon and Amyntas, who attempted conversation in the first hour and abandoned it thereafter, growing ever more sullen as the heat baked their mail and their helms and their hands in their leather gloves.

They did not know Pantera, and so did not know to look closely as she dropped a purse of silver coins in front of a particular vendor, to buy a small glazed mug containing his speciality of roasted almonds done in honey and minted oil, with shredded marigolds sprinkled over. They did not see the pickpocket who removed her purse from the vendor's open belt pouch and returned it again shortly thereafter, nor did they notice when the pickpocket's accomplice nodded to her as she traversed the next aisle, eating the almonds, sharing them with her guards out of pity.

She returned to the stifling palace feeling elated and irritable together. There was a time when, had the god allowed, she would have hated Pantera. That time was gone; in Alexandria and then Rome, she had seen the valleys and height of his soul and had found in herself a measure of respect that was granted to few in her life. She was not yet sure if she counted Pantera a friend, but she had been genuinely glad to see him and Mergus, had met their eyes and smiled at them covertly across the sea of strangers' faces, and their smiles, covertly returned, had felt like splashes of colour in a grey winter's day.

She gave the remains of her almonds to Polyphemos, who flushed an unfetching crimson. Leaving him, Hypatia went to see to the two hounds, Night and Day, who greeted her with joy, and had never yet brought her grief.

CHAPTER NINE

'*Our enemy holds . . . has . . . the ear of the king. The royal family thinks . . . expects to leave for Jerusalem in secret by his order. Soon. I go where they go. Beware Iksahra, the king's falconer. She's signed it with the lily and the hound.*'

Mergus was proud of the speed of his decoding, done without slate or paper. 'Hypatia's gift was accepted,' he said. 'She's in.'

He and Pantera sat in a pungent fisherman's tavern three blocks inland from the harbour, far enough from the side door for the smell of newly gutted fish from the day's catch not to reach them, but not so far that the sea breeze could not keep the air clean.

They ate unleavened bread and olives and watered wine and, in their shadowed corner, with no one close enough to overhear or oversee, they ate fragments of Hypatia's papyrus softened in the wine and rolled into pellets and fitted into the hollow core of an olive.

It was a drover's dream of a meal and it was as drovers they ate and drank and talked, loudly and at length of

121

the horses they dreamed of owning, the camels they would like to buy, the likelihood of a new train's leaving Caesarea and where it might go. Never once did they look over their shoulders at Kleitos, the bearded Cypriot whose efforts to follow them had grown less subtle over the days. He had at least two accomplices in the tavern. Both had finished their meals and were sitting alone, pretending to drink wine.

Presently, as the watchers dulled towards sleep, Mergus leaned towards Pantera and murmured, 'What next, and where?'

Pantera drained his wine, tipping the last dribble on to the table, as an offering to the watching gods. 'We need to contact Seneca's agent at the Temple of Tyche. First, we have to lose Kleitos and his idiot friends.' He belched and leaned forward, planting both palms on the table so his mouth was by Mergus' ear. He grinned, loosely. 'If you could pretend affection, we might slip upstairs. There's a room with a window overlooking the stables. Saulos was always a prude. There's a reasonable chance that the men who follow him are the same.'

In so many ways, Pantera was wise. In a few, he was completely blind. Against the sudden turmoil in his chest, Mergus leaned over and kissed Pantera on the cheek, and laughed and ruffled his hair and, standing, made a slurred observation just too loudly for privacy.

He left the room with Pantera's hand on his shoulder, both of them swaying with the evident effects of drink. Nobody followed them up the stairs.

Tyche, protector-goddess to the city of Caesarea, was wealthy. Images of her in Greek and Roman form were set atop marbled plinths flanking the broad, paved pathway that led to her temple. On its porch, a flame burned in a shining bronze brazier tended by three white-clad priests who ranged in age from a sweating novice through a twitchy lay member of the city's council to a white-haired sage who leaned over the fire as if nothing else in the world was deserving of his attention.

His face was a dull liverish red from the constant heat, and the skin pulled tight about the frame of his skull. His eyes were yellowed at the whites and clouded at the centres.

Leaving Mergus at the foot of the steps, Pantera mounted with due solemnity towards the brazier. He felt in his belt pouch and found the offerings he had brought from Rome. According to a code laid down when he was a child and long before he had been recruited to the service of his emperor, he laid dried thyme, mint and sage one at a time on the flames.

Three threads of smoke sweetened the afternoon air. The novice stared at him in vapid resentment of his intrusion and the added work it might bring. The lay councillor kept his eyes on the skyline, too preoccupied with the threads of riot-smoke rising there to acknowledge his existence. But the sage stepped away from the heat, motioning for Pantera to follow him across the porch to the temple's inner cool.

A wash of pale afternoon light kept the place from true darkness. From round a corner, the brazier sent sweet smoke to freshen the air. Pantera sank to his heels with his back to the wall, closed his eyes and murmured the invocation to the god; his god, not Tyche.

'The journey was long?' The old priest's voice was

thin as his skin, a paper, sawed across a reed. Still, he spoke the words Pantera needed to hear, and waited for the right answer.

'As long as my life.'

'You will go longer still.'

'I intend to.'

Seneca had always made his greeting-tests simple: in their brevity was their accuracy, and so their assurance of safety. The priest slid his arms into his sleeves. The lines on his face softened, like old leather laid in water. He said, 'Your master is dead.'

Pantera nodded, wordless. Each man said it as if it must be news; perhaps to them it was.

'I hear he was allowed to take his own life.'

'Nero is merciful,' Pantera said, which was true. The others had not been granted such mercy. It was said that the wife of Piso, the chief conspirator, killed herself on the second day of her questioning, when she was being carried from the cells to the place of torture in a litter, her leg bones having been broken in so many places on the first day that she could not walk.

She had used her own belt, tying it to the rails of the litter to throttle herself, which must have taken some considerable courage but meant she had not been forced to give the names of those who had conspired. Thus, fewer had died than might have done, and all by their own hand. Nero was merciful because he was not sure. Certainty would have made him a monster.

Pantera said none of this, but the priest waited anyway while his thoughts ran their length, so that he might as well have spoken them out loud.

At the end, Pantera said, 'Seneca's replacement is

known as the Poet. Beyond the name, nothing has changed; we use the same codes, the same routes, the same principles.'

'Is that safe?'

'It has been thus far, and Seneca took a lifetime setting up his network. To change it now would take more time than we have got.'

'So, then, I will wait until someone else comes who throws three herbs on the brazier. In the meantime, do you have a question?'

'I do. And I have brought a gift.'

A particular gold coin had lived for the past two months in the hem of Pantera's tunic. Standing now, he pressed it into the priest's palm.

The old man tested its weight briefly, and then smoothed his thumb over the image on the surface where rested the golden head of the Emperor Caligula, as sharply defined as when the coin fell from the dies of the mint. 'Your need for succour must be great,' he said.

'I ask for your help in delivering a message.'

'So?' Failing eyes came up to search his face. 'It is many years since I earned gold for the god by running errands.'

'Fifteen years, so I was told, and now once more, which may be the last. One needs to know that the bull calf went safely to market, sent by the leopard's attention.'

'That is the message? All of it?'

'It is. Unless you have reason to believe that the ears for whom it is spoken are no longer loyal to their former master?'

'I believe no such thing. That one has been loyal for life. He remains so still.'

Pantera let himself smile. 'Then you have the weight of my gratitude already. If we succeed in our endeavour, there is another like it. You yourself may have no need of gold, being bathed in the love of the god, but Tyche herself will find a use for it, I'm sure.'

The priest's gaze drifted down at the lively spark of gold in his hand. Its shine leapt between his fingers, a small fish hunting morning flies. He blinked, as if his weak eyes were dazzled. 'Will Caesarea come to harm from this?' he asked, at length.

'It will come to harm if our quest here fails. We hunt a man who seeks nothing less than the total annihilation of Israel. With your help, we will . . . remove him before he can wreak his havoc on your city.'

'Did he kill your Teacher? Did he betray him to death and torment?'

'No. Of this one crime, he is innocent. Seneca tried his best and he failed: his death was his own creation. Saulos is rather a traitor to the Hebrew people. He claims the Galilean as the messiah, and turns people away from their faith.'

'You seek the apostate? The spewer of falsehoods?' Anger livened the priest's voice. 'We of Tyche know him well, and despise him. We may not follow the goatherd's god of the burning bush, but we know that if their promised messiah is ever to come, it will be the Galilean's grandson who holds the title, not a man long dead who failed to deliver his people from the yoke.' He tilted his head again. 'Unless your enemy wishes to wrest the kingship for himself?'

Pantera gave a small bow. 'The priests of Tyche are ever wise: that is exactly what he wants. He would rule under Rome as a vassal, and call it freedom.'

'Can you stop him?'

'With your help, I think I can.'

'Then your message will reach the ears of the one you seek: Yusaf ben Matthias, a merchant of some wealth, trained in the ways of Hebrew wisdom. He sits on the council of the Sanhedrin in both Caesarea and Jerusalem. Your Teacher picked his men wisely, all those years ago, when we were all young.' The priest smiled, lost in a haze of better times. His old, fast hands gathered past, present and future in the fire smoke and braided them to a single rope. 'Yusaf will respond tomorrow evening if he can. You know the place to meet?'

'I do.' Pantera bowed then, and took his leave. The reed-voice followed him out.

'You don't ask anything for yourself.'

'I didn't know that I could.' The steps that led down from the temple were long, the voice inescapable.

'Some men cannot. But you, who have been touched by your god, could ask of the Galilean's daughter, who is mother to your child. Both she and the infant thrive and are content in their love for each other and the man who cares for them. The boy who is not your son, but thinks of himself as such, is bored and wishes to join you. He cannot yet, but when he meets manhood he will try. If you would have freedom to teach him, you must kill your enemy. If he does not kill you first.'

Pantera had reached the bottom of the steps. He did not turn, or speak again, but left the old man standing in the still afternoon with gold light leaking from between his fingers, and went to find Mergus, to take him to the harbour, where the agent Yusaf ben Matthias might choose to appear to them on the next day's evening. If he was alive. If he chose to come. If he had not in the meantime sold news of them to Saulos.

CHAPTER TEN

The same doubts haunted Mergus throughout the following day, magnified by the fragile beauty of this place, which had lain all day in silence, without a single riot.

Come evening, he and Pantera walked down to the harbour where an old sun lay at ease in the west, draping mellow light across the ocean. Fat gulls flopped after a fishing boat late to dock. Old men in tattered tunics sat on a line of steps, mending fishing nets with nimble fingers.

Mergus and Pantera passed the Temple of Augustus, its white marble washed to citrus in the evening light. The tide was out; a line of green showed where it reached, and all below was studded with limpets and strands of seaweed. The air hung soft with salt and ripe with ready violence.

Mergus said, 'I was in Colchester, in Britain, just before the revolt broke out; it felt like this. I wish they'd fight and get it over.'

Pantera was just behind him. 'It'll happen before the

night's out. The king's taking the petition at the theatre tonight. If anything's going to spark a riot, that will.'

Mergus was about to say 'What petition?' but Pantera stumbled on a loose coil of rope and caught Mergus' elbow as he fell, swearing vocally, and blaming Mergus for all the ills the world had ever seen.

Recoiling, Mergus pushed himself away. 'Leave then, I don't care!' He dusted himself down with the exaggerated dignity of the drunkard and stormed on the last few paces to the quayside, praying that he had read aright the warning in Pantera's eyes.

He turned the corner. The fishing boat had docked and emptied. The old men had all gone home. A gaggle of dock boys was leaving, no different from the dock boys who roamed the banks of the Tiber in Rome, or the quay at Ostia, or Alexandria or any other city Mergus had been to. They stared at him, whispering, and ran past.

He walked alone along the harbour's edge, practising in his mind the pass phrase Pantera had taught him: *The moon is fine and full tonight, perfect for fishing*, and then the reply: *You are right; if we leave at the moon's height, we should have luck.*

For courage, he said it aloud: 'The moon is fine and full tonight—'

A flash of dark, where had been only white walls. A scrape of a heel on the harbour stone. A tingling in the air, as of past thunder and present lightning . . .

Mergus wrenched himself bodily away from where he had been, spun, rolled forward and over his shoulder and came up with his knife in his hand. He cursed that he had not brought a longer, legionary blade, something that might be of use against the black death in front of him, and the flashing iron that struck for his neck, his shin, his thigh, his ears – his *ears*? – one after the other in a set of moves so fast they left him breathless and bleeding and wanting to clutch at his head to see if the knife had severed the last so swiftly he had not yet felt their loss.

There was pain in his right thigh and his left shin and blood ran freely from a single wound on the top of his right wrist where the skin flapped forward every time he slashed out with his own blade, showing a shine of bone beneath the blood.

He was slicing, not making contact. He bled from a dozen points, and his opponent was whole, unblooded. Deep-set eyes studied him from under a tumble of long black hair brilliant as a raven's wing that framed in its turn a lean face, not given to laughing.

It wasn't laughing now. It was still, sober, thoughtful, assessing where next to make a cut so that Mergus feared for his ears again, that he might look like the bear-warriors of the Eceni, who lopped off their right ears and shaved their heads to show themselves wholly given to the she-bear. They were—

The blade passed by his neck. His body became elastic, sheering sideways. He slipped and fell and rolled, rug-wise, towards the harbour's edge, flung out an arm and felt his palm scrape on grit, smelled salt and weed and the slop of swaying water at the tide's turn.

A voice above him said, 'If we leave at the moon's height—' and he felt the knife's point on the inner edge of his shoulder blade, just to the left of his spine, felt his ribs part to receive it, his heart pause, ready to hug

131

the iron, to draw it in, to cease its ceaseless beat for ever.

'No!' Mergus wrenched round, scrabbling for purchase on the stone and then the oak that bounded the harbour's edge. He felt a fist crunch on the back of his head, twisted his face to save his nose, and—

And offered his soul to Mithras, for he was lying on his back at the water's edge with one arm scraping the barnacles and the knife above him, held two-handed, was coming straight for his heart. In the slow pearl of time that held him, he heard his own blade splash into the harbour, and the rippling waves it set dancing against the edge.

And then, from nowhere, an arrow struck the oak a hand's breadth from his head. It stood there, humming, while Mergus' heart clenched and unclenched and he thought he might be sick from shock.

With frozen clarity, a voice said, 'If he dies, you die. Choose.'

The knife held still. Mergus stared at it, blinking. Softly, not to him, his assailant said, 'The moon is fine and full tonight, perfect for fishing.'

'You are right,' said the other voice. 'If we leave at the moon's height, we should have luck.' Mergus thought it was Pantera. He prayed so, but he had never heard Pantera so bloodlessly calm.

'Who are you?' The knife had not moved. Mergus allowed his focus to slide sideways to the arrow. It was fletched in the Nabatean fashion, with goose and crow in white and black alternating bars. He had ridden through the desert with those arrows beside him.

'I am father to your newborn cousin,' Pantera said.

132

'I am the last left alive who saw your grandfather, the Galilean, lifted living from his tomb and carried to safety under the care of Mariamne, who was his wife, who carried in her womb his unborn daughter. That daughter's name is Hannah. She is your father's sister, although in looks, she could be your twin.'

The knife vanished, gone as surely as the sun was gone. Mergus lay where he was, studying the killer who stood over him, giving him a woman's eyes, and her healing soul, and found that with both of these, he did, indeed, look like the woman he had met in Rome.

'You are Menachem ben Yehuda,' he said, at last, when nobody else had spoken. 'Eldest grandson of the Galilean. Leader of the War Party in Jerusalem.' He tried to sit up, and lay back again, with the world swimming round him, sending scarlet streaks across the dove-grey dusk.

'He is Menachem,' agreed Pantera. 'And I am Sebastos Abdes Pantera, son of Julius Tiberius Abdes Pantera. My father was an archer in the service of the Jerusalem Guard.'

'The archer's son, I heard, gave his life to the service of the late spymaster Seneca. Has he now a new master?'

They waited, Mergus and the man Menachem, who led the War Party in Jerusalem, who led, in that case, the zealot assassins, who killed men without care or compassion, so it was said.

'I serve Seneca's successor,' Pantera said carefully, 'who is known as the Poet. The line of succession is clear, and our allegiance to it.' He did not say that the Poet was named Jocasta, nor that it was her younger brother, Publius Papinius Statius, who had the public fame for poetry he didn't write. He never said that, nobody did; it was possible nobody else knew.

A shadow passed over Mergus' face. Firm fingers wrapped his wrist, away from the skin wound. A hand slid under his shoulder. He was drawn up to sit, and then to rise. He stood, swim-headed, and looked for Pantera and found him standing in the shadows of the merchants' booths barely ten yards away. He was holding a Nabatean war-bow at full draw as if it were a child's toy.

'We came to meet Yusaf ben Matthias. You are not he.' Mergus spoke to Menachem, but his eyes were on Pantera, drawing him back to the world they shared. He saw the arrow's tip taken down, heard the sigh of the string relaxing.

'Ben Matthias has an appointment he could not avoid. He sent me in his stead, to see if you were truly sworn to Seneca, or had been sent instead by his enemy to destroy his agents now that the Teacher is dead.'

'We are here to destroy his enemy,' Pantera said, warily. 'And in doing so, to save your people. If you will help us, we will be grateful. If you would hinder us . . .'

'Then we would find out which is the faster, my knife or your arrow.' Menachem smiled now and Mergus saw that he was a decade younger than Pantera, that his smile came more readily, that his face was less lined from the sun. But his eyes held the same distant appraisal, his voice the same irony, his shoulders the same set, as of a war-hound, ready to hunt.

Menachem said, 'Yusaf ben Matthias is at the theatre, where it is illegal for anyone to bear a weapon of war. If you leave your bow where the Watch will not find it, I will take you to him.'

CHAPTER ELEVEN

From a distance, the theatre at Caesarea was a swarm of dancing fireflies, caught in the blue bowl of dusk.

Closer, the gyrating sparks resolved to torches, held by taut, wary watchmen, always in pairs, never more than a short spear's throw from the next nearest pair; between them was a festering soup of Syrians and Hebrews, of men, women and boys just old enough to carry clubs and stones and perhaps put them to good use.

Pantera reckoned their numbers in the thousands: the theatre was said to have seats for five thousand while the entire adult population of Caesarea was in excess of thirty thousand, and it seemed likely that most of them were trying to gain access. The arithmetic of that alone was explosive.

'We should enter separately,' Menachem said, when they were still on the outer fringes of the crowd. 'Once inside, it would be useful if you sat next to me, but for both our sakes you should appear not to know me: a dozen different men have agents in there, and it will

135

serve neither of us if we are thought to be in collusion.'

He was gone, ghosting through the crowds, with his head down and his shoulders hunched, as if that way he might hide the shining raven's wing of his hair, or the zealot's light in his eyes.

Pantera watched him until he was truly impossible to see any more. Nobody seemed to be following him through the throng.

'Do you trust him?' Mergus asked.

Pantera slid both hands into his sleeves and straightened the lie of his knives, slid each one out of its sheath and back in again. They moved smoothly, stayed pleasingly secure.

He said, 'No. But I don't mistrust him enough yet to be sure he's lying. Can you stay outside, near the doors? I wouldn't put it past Saulos to try to burn this place: he has an unhealthy fondness for fire.'

'How will I warn you?'

'Do you remember the bark of the hunting vixen that the legions used in Britain to warn of a possible ambush? And can you do it? Good.'

He clasped Mergus' shoulder, and knew that it didn't touch the depth of his care, that there should be more if he could think how to frame it. *I care more deeply than you know, but not as deeply as you would wish. Don't die for me. Please.* He didn't say it. He smiled, and saw Mergus smile back, worry still sharp in his eyes.

'If you can't get hold of me, call the Watch and get Jucundus; he cares for the welfare of his city.' Pantera lifted his hand and watched Mergus turn back, away from the entrance. 'Stay safe,' he said.

*

'I think not.'

Pantera caught the thin wrist that slid under his cloak, and twisted until he heard the elbow joint creak on the edge of breaking. The youth who had brushed against him gave a strangled grunt, but had the sense not to call aloud.

They were in the theatre, in the humid crush of men and women caught between the doors and the tiered seating, patiently waiting to take their places. Men on either side eyed them and decided not to intervene; they had been seen, though, and both knew it.

Pantera smiled amiably. 'You will leave now. I will return to the gentleman in the woollen coat the coins he has unaccountably mislaid. Do you understand?'

The youth nodded, green-faced. His breathing rasped in short, harsh cycles. His eyes flitted in widening orbits, never looking Pantera in the face. In Caesarea, men or boys – the council made no distinction in terms of age – had their right hands removed if they were caught thieving in a public place. 'I am not the Watch,' Pantera said. 'But I'll call them if I see you here again. Go now.'

He let go. The youth – too old to be a boy, not yet old enough to be a man – had the presence of mind to ease slowly into the oncoming crush, rather than bolting like a flushed deer, which would surely have brought the Watch on his heels. The crowd parted and came together again like the maw of some giant sea-monster and the boy was gone.

'You dropped these.' Pantera tapped on a nearby shoulder. The man's head turned, slowly. Raven hair shone with a new lustre in the lamplight. Dark, deep-set eyes stared flatly at Pantera, and Pantera gazed as flatly back.

'I dropped them?' said Menachem, leader of the War Party. He looked down, puzzled. On Pantera's palm lay five brass sestertii and a silver denarius bearing the image of Caligula, a year's wages for a boy gutting fish, or an apprentice weaver.

'If you didn't, then your pockets have just been picked.' Pantera flicked his eyes towards the door, where the youth was leaving, not looking back. 'I would think on a night with tensions such as this one, perhaps you dropped them?'

'Thank you.' Menachem bowed a little, from the waist. His gaze took in Pantera as if anew; his build, his height, his serviceable tunic, perhaps the two knives under his sleeves: they were not so hidden that a trained man might not see them. 'Our people are not wealthy, however much gold they might choose to throw away tonight. I owe you thanks. Would you care to join me?'

Pantera inclined his head. He sat. Menachem sat. Below the hum of the crowd, he murmured, 'Nicely done, but whose coins are they?'

'If you look three rows down, you'll see a Greek with a broken nose. He will find his purse has been cut. Not by me. The boy was almost good enough.'

And thus did Pantera take the place he had marked as he came in, the only seat left at the end of a row, which might afford a quick exit if one became necessary and yet still give him a clear view of the stage.

The stage . . . which was lit by a profusion of flame so startlingly bright that those coming in covered their eyes, and had to look away.

Looking at it now, Pantera counted no more than a dozen lit braziers on the platform, but behind them a bank of beaten copper took up the whole back wall of the theatre, curved to catch the pinpoints of torchlight and stir into them a thunder of scarlet and sun-fire and high-toned ambers, then multiply them a hundredfold before hurling them out across the auditorium.

Pantera sat, saturated in colour, until, presently, a priest from the Temple of Augustus emerged from behind the black-curtained wings and walked with meditative slowness across the stage, swinging a bowl of sandalwood to sweeten the sweaty air.

He was barefoot, and walked with a dancer's grace, and yet it sounded as if he stamped past in the nailed sandals of the legions, so cleanly was the sound picked up and sent out to the listening thousands. It was, Pantera thought, a product of the copper wall and the vellum roof and a particular resonance of the raised stage. Such things were known in Corinth and Athens, but Pantera had not expected it here.

From his right, softly, Menachem said, 'The stage upsets you? The light is, I agree, particularly penetrating this time.'

'I was in Rome during the fire,' Pantera said. 'To see flame this intense touches memories I would rather leave behind.'

'And the camel train? I understand there were aspects of your journey you might also like to leave behind you?'

'Nothing we didn't expect. Ibrahim had the worst of it, with the governor taking all his good camels in tax as soon as we arrived. Yusaf ben Matthias paid for

139

the whole shipment in advance. Was he happy with the results? I have a silver coin resting on the answer.'

'A silver coin is your pay for the entire journey,' Menachem said. 'You would rest it on a gamble?'

'Not a gamble. I only bet on certainties.'

Menachem turned to look fully at Pantera. His face was perfectly bland. 'Will you name for me those certainties and the nature of the wager?'

'Ibrahim brought five barren camels on a month's journey, knowing from the start they were not in calf. All through the month, they were the ones that we protected first, from jackals or bandits, from thirst or hunger. We considered what might be inserted into the womb of a camel to be retrieved later and decided it might be something that was worth more than its own weight in gold. Gemstones, therefore, or balsam. I bet that it was balsam. Mergus thought diamonds. Perhaps you could settle that for us?'

Menachem considered a moment. 'You win,' he said. 'The camels brought balsam, equal in value to three talents of gold. Yusaf paid half a talent to the camel drover for the journey, and he will send him back with the same and horses this time, of Berber breeding, which will fetch almost as much in the markets of the desert.' He looked up. Something close to a smile played on his lips. 'Does Ibrahim know of your wager?'

'Would we be alive if he did?'

'Probably not.' Menachem did smile then, and it lit his face, shedding years. 'Watch now,' he said. 'It's starting.'

A cymbal clashed at the stage-side. At its command, the entire theatre fell silent. To the high notes of a reed pipe, five well-muscled slaves drew on to the stage a set of thrones and benches, enough to seat a dozen, and set them so that the central thrones, adrape with silks, entwined with carvings of vines and olives, faced the very apex of the auditorium.

As promptly as the slaves departed, so did the royal retinue enter. King Agrippa led, clothed in tissue of gold, long-striding across the stage to stand in front of his throne. Berenice, his queen, if not his wife, followed a pace behind, then eleven men and women followed, draped in silks of alternating colours; the queen in blue, her women in green and the men in varying shades of amber, citrus and pale copper-gold.

Hypatia was among the women. Pantera saw her first as he would in any room she entered, as any man would, who had eyes to see. They had robed her in a shade of dark emerald green that brought out the faint tint in her eyes, and pinned up her blue-black hair so that her neck was exposed, smooth as alabaster, slim as a swan's, thin enough to wrap his one hand round, almost.

Seen like that, a man might have thought her fragile, which would have been a mistake. Pantera had learned not to think thus in Alexandria and then Rome, when they had seemed to be enemies. He had come to be grateful for it since.

And then Agrippa had stepped apart from the rest, and drew all eyes, for he was no longer a mere man, but had become the blistering sun; dressed from shoulder to heel and beyond in tissue of gold with a filet of gold in his dark hair and diamond-studded gold on his fingers.

To a rising trill of pipe music, he stepped up on to a wooden pedestal placed at his feet by a kneeling slave.

His flaring, dancing sun-fire robes hung down to the floor so that it seemed as if a far taller man stood there. Somewhere, a steward clapped his hands, once. The reed notes tumbled to silence.

As if released, the theatre hummed to quiet life again. Menachem leaned to Pantera and murmured, 'Agrippa's father died here in this theatre. He makes a point of dressing in gold, as did the old king, to silence those who say his death was an act of God, to punish his hubris. His sister is next to him, Berenice of Cilicia, who was married to the son of the Alabarch of Alexandria. When he died after a year of her marital bed, she married her uncle, Herod of Chalcis. When he died four years later, she married King Polemon II of Pontus, Colchis and Cilicia.'

'Lucky man,' said Pantera, drily. 'How long did he last?'

A smile split Menachem's long, lean face. He spread his palms in mock distress. 'Polemon graces the world yet with his presence, but he no longer has the pleasure of her company. Berenice left him to return here, to Caesarea. Men say she has . . . unnatural relations with her brother and that they could not bear to be parted.'

'Men often say such things of the women who rule over them,' Pantera observed. 'What do you say?'

'That she is the granddaughter of Herod the Great, whose name is for ever despised, and she will for ever bear the stain of his blood; that she worships false gods, that she is given to Rome above all else, but that even so she rules Caesarea far better than does her brother and, the riots of the last half-month notwithstanding, Caesarea is more peaceful, more prosperous and more

142

godly with her here. It is said—' On the stage, the king had raised his hand. Menachem lowered his voice still further. 'It is said that Agrippa sent to his sister four times begging her to come back and rule at his side. She came only after the start of the corn riots of ten years ago. They ceased within a day of her return and the city has known very little violence since. What happens here tonight may keep it at bay for some time longer. Watch now.' He leaned forward. 'This is what you have come here to see.'

The king's raised hand had summoned forth a string of five blue-robed men from the front row of seats. They walked at a measured pace along the ground at the front of the raised stage. From his place high in the auditorium, Pantera saw little more than their heads.

'Hebrew or Syrian?' he asked.

'Hebrew. They come to petition the king for the safety of their central synagogue, which lies now beset by scaffolding. You will have seen the harm that has fallen on it. Queen Berenice, of course, will hear them. Her response will carry more weight, but it must be given in private, and appear to come from the king.'

'Where's Florus?' Pantera asked. 'If something of import is happening, should Rome's governor not be here?'

Menachem gave an eloquent shrug. 'Our overseer doesn't choose to involve himself in disputes between Hebrews and Syrians. In his view, Rome stands above such things. But if you look closely now . . .'

Pantera looked closely; everyone did. Across the theatre, silence fell in a thick, breath-held blanket. In it, a silver pipe sang three notes. At their dying away, the foremost of the Hebrew men left his fellows and approached the stage alone.

Seen from the height of the seating, the most obvious feature of the man who mounted the set of small wooden steps was the shining length of his beard, grizzled here and there with silver, so that he seemed sombre even when, as now, he smiled.

Beyond that, what set him apart, even from the royalty on stage, was the splendour of his robes. He wore a long-coat of midnight silk so thick it took the frantic coppered fires of the theatre and soothed them to stillness. Its luxury enfolded him, screaming wealth and restraint together, a thing rarely done here, or in Rome, or even in Alexandria, which prided itself on the subtlety of its riches.

Reaching the stage, the newcomer turned to face the king. With perfect pride, and perfect humility, he knelt, pressing his face to the floor. His voice welled out across the auditorium, carried by the magnificent acoustics of the copper-backed stage.

'Yusaf ben Matthias salutes his king and his queen, and offers the salutations of his people, who are their people.'

CHAPTER TWELVE

Mergus stood still and a torchlit tide of people passed him by. He was wearing an outrider's tunic and plain sandals with a plain eating knife at his belt, given to him by Menachem to replace the one he had lost. It was sharpened along both edges to the point where he could use it as a razor, but outwardly it did not look like a soldier's weapon.

Certainly, he had no gladius with which to run an opponent through, no nailed sandals to stamp on his skull and crack it open, sudden and satisfying as a hammered nut. Even so, the breadth of his shoulders, or the tilt of his head, or the flat line of his brows, marked him as a legionary and the citizens of Caesarea, men and women, Hebrew and Syrian alike, gave him a clear berth by lifelong instinct without ever knowing they'd done it.

He was free, then, to watch as Pantera stepped into the throng and was instantly lost, swept on towards the theatre by people who did not know him, but equally did nothing to avoid him. No halo of space marked him as different. Nobody paid him any attention at all until he reached the theatre door, where he had to haggle for entry exactly as did all the other strangers from outwith the city whose names were not known to the Watch.

And then, because the tide was still flowing, Mergus was able to see the other man in the living, heaving ocean about whom there was also a halo, not because he held himself with the bearing of a legionary but because he was too big to offend, and so clearly a fighter; a bull of a man with a head fully shaved, with bear's shoulders and hams for fists and pegs for teeth, of which two were missing. He bore two short twin-headed axes, one at either side of his belt; if the passing men let their eyes rest on anything as they veered to avoid him, it was those.

Mergus hunched his shoulders, tucked his chin into his chest and cut sideways across the flow. He laid his hand on the big man's arm, ready for a swing if it came. It did not. The man turned, his face open, ready, entirely free of guile.

Mergus bowed. 'I am Appius Mergus, lately a centurion of the Twentieth,' he said. 'You, I believe, are Estaph the Parthian, whose daughter is named Eora. You helped a friend of mine to remove a pig's head from unfortunate surroundings. He would want me to thank you keeping watch for his safety tonight.'

The bear-man's face passed through a recognizable sequence from suspicion to contemplation to interest. It stuck at the last. 'May I know how you learned my name?'

'My friend spoke of a man with bear's shoulders and a bare head, and of his infant daughter, of her beauty and intelligence; of the sagacity of her father, who is a merchant, but also, he thought, a warrior of some renown.'

That was the simple version, and almost true. Pantera's description had been precise, complete and accurate but it was what he had added at the end that mattered. *He looks bored. And bored men seek entertainment. If he's with us, he will be useful. If he's against us, he will be difficult. Talk to him if you get the chance, find out which.*

On the basis of that, Mergus had made his own assumption, which was that a certain kind of individual, having met Pantera, was inclined to follow him closely, if not out of desire or admiration, then in the understanding that where he went, life was always interesting.

The tilt of Estaph's head, the open question in his eyes, was living proof of the theory. Mergus wished he'd placed a bet.

He said, 'Our friend has gone into the theatre, to learn how much the Hebrews will pay to preserve their synagogue. I am here to see that no harm befalls him when he comes out. You, however, have a wife and daughter to protect on a night when Caesarea's wrath might boil over into violence. Should you not be with them?'

Estaph shook his head. 'They went with a pack train to Damascus the evening after I met your friend. They will stay safely with my wife's father until I can return.'

'In that case . . .' Mergus made a small gesture of invitation and saw Estaph's smile spread wide. 'Our enemy is a man of skill and imagination. He is not Pantera's twin, but it is useful to assume that he knows all that we

147

know. I imagine we will not have long to wait before—'
He spun quickly on one heel, tracking a man's movements on the edge of the crowd. 'Do you see the Greek with the black beard on the crowd's furthest edge?'

'The one walking away from the theatre, towards the city centre?'

'Yes. His name is Kleitos. He has already tried to kill us once.'

'Then we should kill him?' said the big Parthian hopefully, and laughed at the look on Mergus' face.

Mergus drew his fine-honed eating knife. 'I had heard the Parthians were the most skilled men in the empire in the use of a hand axe at close quarters. It would cheer my night immensely to see you prove that true.'

* * *

In the theatre, Pantera watched Yusaf kneel before his king. The Hebrew's voice was hurled out to the audience by the beaten copper wall. Even so, four thousand men and women held their breaths, straining to hear him. For effect, the reed pipe sweetened the air. Menachem did not strain. He sat with his head in his hands, as if wishing himself elsewhere.

'We would hear your petition,' Agrippa said.

A steward in long, gilded sleeves unrolled a scroll at Yusaf's side. The merchant glanced at it, but gave no sign of reading directly. To Pantera, it looked as if he knew his words by rote. His words rang brazen through the air.

'We, the Hebrews of Caesarea, cognizant as we are of the honour done to us by our late king, Herod the Great, and all his kin in the creation of this city, wish

148

publicly to proclaim our precedence above those of other tribes and other gods. Our city is a Hebrew city, founded by a Hebrew king and ruled by his grandson. But in this, our city, foul men despoil our worship. We will not soil our king's ears with the detail, but what has been done is known in every street and avenue from the harbour to the outer walls. We are reasonable men and do not wish strife with our neighbours. Therefore we bring now to the king eight talents of gold, and respectfully request that he give us leave to buy the lands around the house of God that has been so ruinously defiled.'

Eight talents. *Eight talents?*

It was not given to speak in the presence of the king without express invitation, but the intake of breath sucked at the theatre walls with its gale.

Eight talents was a room's worth of gold. A river. An ocean. For the worth of eight talents, a man could buy every camel in the east and its progeny and its progeny's progeny for the next ten generations. If Ibrahim and his brothers had earned so much as a single talent of gold, they would have retired to their Saba villages and bought themselves as many Saba wives as they wanted, each one preparing pickled calves' intestines for the rest of their idle lives.

Even in Caesarea, where men could spin money out of straw, Pantera doubted whether they made that much. Yusaf probably didn't make a talent's clear profit in a decade, although the balsam might have tipped the scales in that direction. Eight, though . . . eight would have bled the entire Hebrew population dry of every ounce of profit.

Yusaf rose stiffly to his feet and handed to his king a small scroll, the promissory note.

Agrippa took it, slowly, as he might have taken sacred texts for safe keeping. 'Did I understand correctly: you wish to buy the land around the synagogue that you might hold it free of other buildings?'

'We do.'

'And if it is not for sale?'

'We feel that any man will sell to his majesty, if he is offered a reasonable price.'

'And with this, we could be reasonable.'

'Immensely so.'

There were stirrings in the crowd, the first warnings of shouts to come, whatever the protocol of speaking in the royal presence, the first clenched muscles of beatings and stabbings, the first wave of the violence that threatened to crest the bulwarks of civility and break into bloodshed.

A voice murmured across the stage, too quiet for those in the seating to hear, even with the copper curtain. The king cocked his head and asked a soft question, equally inaudible to those beyond him. A woman's voice rode over the answer, tuneful as a mountain spring. Its tone ended in dismissal. Bowing, Yusaf withdrew from the stage leaving the king alone on his pedestal.

Tension hung taut across the theatre. Nobody shouted yet, but the air was thick with waiting.

As if in answer, the king flung both his arms high. A cascade of high-toned silver bells rang from behind the bronze wall. On their signal, scarlet and saffron silks rained from its height to hang halfway down, casting the braziers in blood red.

Agrippa, set ablaze by the new light, brought both arms crashing down.

At which, every light within the theatre was doused; every torch, every lamp, every candle, snuffed before the king's hands reached his sides. The radiant, many-coloured theatre was struck to utter darkness as surely as if the sun had been extinguished.

The men and women of Caesarea were seasoned theatregoers, not readily impressed by pyrotechnics or displays of *deus ex machina*, but they gasped aloud then, and again when a single man's voice boomed from the stage out across the auditorium.

'A king lives for ever in the eyes of God. Mere mortals rise and die, taking four legs in the morning, two in the afternoon and three in the evening to stagger to their graves. Keep to your seats now, men of Caesarea, and witness such wonders as have never before been seen in the civilized world!'

'Should we stay to watch the play?' Pantera asked quietly.

'We should,' Menachem said. 'Whether we wish to is another question. The riots will start now. This is not a safe place to be.' He glanced sideways, past Pantera. 'By happy chance, it would seem that we are near the end of a row which is near the door. If we were to depart now – a call of nature, perhaps, that must urgently be answered – it might be that we will not cause great offence.'

Outside, vast man-high torches shed good light all around the theatre. Pantera and Menachem walked together to the place where the light ended and the dark began. And with that dark, a crowd; the two thousand men – more – who had not gained entry to the theatre stood outside it, waiting to glean what news they could from inside. They were not happy, but none of them was young.

'The youths aren't here,' Pantera said. 'But these men are angry enough to wreak havoc on their own.'

'Whatever we do now,' Menachem said, 'the fighting will start. Yusaf's efforts were laudable, but we have to acknowledge that he has failed. Perhaps if Agrippa had taken the bribe at the moment of its offering . . . But we shall never know, now, what might have been.' He held out his hand, the beginnings of a cautious friendship. 'I leave for Jerusalem tonight. If you travel there, send me word. It can be a difficult place to enter if you are not known.'

'I will remember.' Pantera had been born in Jerusalem, but now did not seem the time to say so. He shook hands with the dangerous young man who faced him. 'May your night pass in peace.'

Behind them, the theatre simmered to a boil. Noise leaked out like a great rushing tide, and the Watch stood back to let men and women flee from the coming violence.

CHAPTER THIRTEEN

Keeping ahead of the growing riot, Kleitos walked swiftly north along the wide avenue that led from the palace to the Temple of Augustus and thence to the harbour. Mergus and Estaph followed him at a distance, keeping his bulk always in view in the growing dusk. Estaph held a double-headed throwing axe in either giant hand with an ease that left Mergus feeling uncommonly cheerful.

Kleitos turned east after a tall villa with a verdigrised roof and trotted easily down progressively narrower residential streets and across a small square, past a nine-pillared fountain, whose music sang in measured tones as the water landed, past a small temple to Jupiter Dolichenos and along a wall, blind for three storeys without a single window.

Kleitos turned the corner at the wall's end. Mergus and Estaph stopped just short of it, and listened.

Inside, men spoke in Greek, with the true accent of Athens and Corinth. A torch had been lit, perhaps several torches; the air was alive with the light, peppery

153

smoke of good pitch, thickened by heavier strands of burning straw.

'A carpenter's workshop is there,' Estaph said, in Mergus' ear. 'They make furniture for half the city. The wood is aged for ten years in their sheds. Does your enemy like fire?'

'Always.'

Already the orange glow of the fire had turned to lemon and the shadow play of the men was faster and easier to watch.

'Six,' Mergus said, after a moment's counting. 'Three each. Let's go.'

Flames smothered him as he rounded the corner. Momentarily, he was lost in scorching heat and light and a dark, dense smoke that sucked the air from his lungs and brought tears to his eyes so that he faltered as he ran and the knife in his hand struck awry and the first of the arsonists did not die cleanly, but fell, choking, with blood jetting from a torn artery in his neck, and his hands scrabbling at his throat.

He heard the smack of iron on bone and a body toppled next to him, hard as a felled tree, then Estaph was at his side, tears streaming down his wide cheeks. Through smoke and fire, he croaked, 'It's a trap.'

A blurred shape moved beyond them. Mergus' knife flashed out and back, wetly dripping. A man fell, yowling like a cat. 'Three more,' Mergus said, and held up his fingers in case the big man couldn't hear clearly. 'Kill them.'

Easy to say. Not easy to do when the three were warned and Estaph had breathed in too much of the poisonous black smoke and was blundering, bear-like, swiping at random with the two-headed axe that was as dangerous to the friend who might be standing too close behind him as it was to the enemy in front.

Mergus dodged one blow that came near to breaking his skull and ducked down, and found that the air was clearer below waist height. He could see a pair of legs and knew Kleitos by the shape of his knees, having spent a month in the desert sitting opposite him at the fires.

He had one knife and he didn't need to see a whole man to know where his throat was, to feel in his bones that place just above the larynx, where a knife might pass through and the tip slide into the spinal column, bringing instant, silent death.

He crouched, pulling himself tight, ready to leap—

And rolled sideways, away from the spear that smashed the pavings where he had been. His knife clattered to the ground. He thrust down on his palms and came up into the sea of smoke, and peered forward through new tears and saw Estaph grappling the spear-bearer, holding the haft of the weapon, thrusting it back and back, keeping the point away from his own massive abdomen. Two others came at him from either side, as men at a bated bear. One of them held the Parthian's own axe.

'Estaph! Left!' Mergus grabbed a burning plank and swung it, flat, and hit no one, but forced one of the three back, and gave Estaph time to spin away from the axe and reach out and grab it with his left hand, even as his right hand held the spear, so that he was drawn out tight and wide, with the haft of a weapon in each hand, unable to let go of either in case it killed him.

Mergus tucked his head down below the smoke, bunched his fists at his side, and ran. As a human ram, he battered the side of the spear-holder. Ribs broke on the crown of his skull. He felt the jerk and rip as Estaph wrenched the spear free of the hands that gripped it, and drew it back, and smashed the hilt into the face in front of him, breaking bones and teeth and the soft tissues of the mind.

Mergus was still moving, turning, swinging himself free of the spear-bearer's corpse. He dropped down, pivoting all his weight on one palm, slid his legs out wide, and scissored them together to trap the ankles of the axe-holder. He spun on his own axis, and kept spinning away as the man fell. He rose at last, gasping, in time to see Estaph strike down into the smoke with his axe, and come up again, smiling.

'Kleitos,' said Mergus.

'That way.' Estaph doubled over, coughing, but his free hand pointed south, towards the theatre, from whence came the distant sounds of riot, like an evening's thunder.

CHAPTER FOURTEEN

Agrippa's treasury in Caesarea was a room within a room, locked and barred and windowless and altogether too much like a prison for Berenice's comfort.

With a riot brewing outside, she hadn't wanted to go there, but basic decency required that the entire royal family take a detour to examine the Hebrews' gift, and make the right noises to Polyphemos, who was blotched white and scarlet with the shock and kept hopping from one leg to the other, exclaiming that the gods – or god, he was unclear as to which – were positively beaming benevolences on the king and his family.

Polyphemos was given to displays of high emotion, but tonight even stolid Koriantos, the royal treasurer, was speechless, and that was not a thing Berenice had ever expected to see. Sometime in the recent past, he had bitten his knuckles so hard they bled and now he was walking round and round the gold like a hen who has hatched her first egg and found she has given birth to a harpy.

He had ordered extra torches brought in, and extra

guards to hold them, and so the cramped room smelled of avarice and panic and the air glittered with polished iron from the guards' mail and the bright, terrifying glamour of gold.

Berenice was a queen of the royal line; she was able, therefore, to smile, and nod, and smile again and ignore at all times the noise of the riot that was reaching its climax in the streets outside the palace.

It was no surprise, the riot. She had felt the pressure growing for days; sometimes she could taste it, rusty and sharp, like fetid iron, tinged with blood and bile. But now it was crushing her temples in a headache of fantastic proportions and the possibility that she might vomit was becoming increasingly real.

Such a thing could not be allowed to happen. Breathing the night air, she stepped out into the corridor that led to the throne room and, closing her eyes, counted down the line of the women who stood waiting in the corridor behind her. Drusilla was first, placid and compliant as ever, then Kleopatra, who was neither of these, but had bled for the first time a month ago and by rights should be found a husband.

After Kleopatra came Selene, Koriantos' cousin on his mother's side, who was sharper than she ever let on, and behind Selene . . . behind Selene stood the startling Alexandrian woman with the blue-black hair who had come as a gift from Poppaea, the friend-become-empress whom Berenice had loved, and who had loved her, and had understood more than anyone the many routes to power. Poppaea never did anything without good reason, and Hypatia, Chosen of Isis, had been her parting gift in this life.

Berenice did not believe that those given to Isis ever truly bent to the command of any other mortal. Their first meeting had been . . . disconcerting. Rarely had she felt so easily read, so readily seen. Her soul had been laid bare of its coverings and studied and it had taken a lifetime's training to stand still and endure it, and smile, and maintain a steady flow of her own questions, so that she might not seem discomfited. She had learned from it, though, and thought she knew how to use that knowledge.

From her place at the head of her train, she turned. 'We go next to the audience chamber,' she said to Hypatia. 'There, you will watch and listen to everything that takes place, but you will not speak unless asked. Afterwards, when we are alone, you will speak the truth to me, as the Oracle does.'

Hypatia inclined her head. 'Majesty.'

Berenice straightened her back and turned to face ahead. A hundred blazing torches had lit their way to the palace and continued to do so within it. She led her women down the corridor towards the audience room, sweeping at a near-trot along marble tiles beneath lamps that burned sandalwood with their oil, to keep the air perpetually sweet; past confusions of cut flowers, of blood-red tulips in gold vessels, purple irises and scented thistles in silver, yellow thorowax in white marble; past watchmen at ten-pace intervals, dressed in full chain mail, sweating in the hot, humid air.

The chamber was as it had been, but that a second dais had been raised, with a throne for the king. The two banks of seats were set opposite one another, women to the west, men to the east, with the frieze in echo behind.

Agrippa was already there, lost in all his tissue of gold, so much his father's son, and trying so hard not to be. And beside him, as ever . . . was nobody, at least nobody that mattered. Two counsellors sat, one on either side, and if she had been pushed, Berenice could probably have named them, but the third seat, which should have been occupied, was empty. As queen, she could not be seen to smile, but her heart danced, seeing an opening where none had been before.

She nodded towards her brother and saw Agrippa twitch a reply. He was tense, possibly also in pain, and for the same reasons as she was; he had always been sensitive to the mood of the city and just now it was as jagged and vicious and full of hate as it had been on the night their father died, when his three children had hidden in a palace cupboard and listened to the slaves whisper of the effigies on the rooftops that men paid good money to rape and stab and set on fire.

It was not a good thing to remember. Berenice took her seat and, after a finite pause, her courtiers did likewise: Drusilla, Selene, Kleopatra, Hypatia, those latter two not looking at each other, not making eye contact, which meant that the morning's hunt had raised tensions or secrets that must be hidden.

And then, swiftly, Yusaf ben Matthias was ushered to a seat that was apart from both the men and the women, midway between both. The man who was the Hebrews' most senior counsellor sat with his hands on his knees after the manner of the Egyptian pharaohs; with his beard and his so-costly silks, he came close to matching them for dignity.

Berenice caught his eye and nodded, fractionally,

enough for him to know he had her support. She held his gaze for a heartbeat. They were not allies, but, for tonight, his wish was hers, and she needed him to know that.

A cymbal sounded the beginning of the conference. Berenice closed her eyes and sat back against the stiff, jewel-crusted throne and prayed to three different gods that Hypatia was at least half of all that myth and rumour said she was.

'You pay us too much,' Agrippa said, with no preamble. 'The Syrians will wonder how you collected eight whole talents of gold.'

Yusaf answered evenly. 'His majesty has six thousand loyal Hebrew merchants in Caesarea, each one of whom values the sanctity of God's house above all else. If each man therefore donates a shekel here, a gold aureus there, even a handful of denarii, the amount comes to what our king holds now in his treasury. We commend it to his care, and pray that it might be used wisely.'

'There are ten thousand Syrian men in Caesarea, and as many youths,' Agrippa answered. 'Would you have us hold them back single-handed when they endeavour to tear down your synagogue? They will do that if we grant you this. You must know that.'

'I know that if his majesty orders peace,' Yusaf said, 'the peace will be kept. The Watch will see to that.'

'The Watch can do nothing in the face of ten thousand angry citizens.'

'And yet if it is known that the Watch will mount a guard on the synagogue, it may send a message to the Syrians that will cool their ardour.'

'It will tell them that their king does not love them,' Agrippa said. 'It would not be true and we cannot allow them to believe so. It would be the end of our reign.'

Berenice saw Yusaf blink, open his mouth to speak and close it again. He lowered his head.

Nobody else spoke. Polyphemos lifted his arm to strike the cymbal that closed the debate. She caught his eye and made him stop; as queen, she alone had permission to speak after the king. She softened her voice, and yet gave it power to carry.

'And yet if his majesty fails to act on so public a giving, on such a weight of generosity, if he returns the money, the Hebrews will likewise come to believe he does not love them. As will the Syrians, who may become importunate in their enthusiasm. It is well known that his majesty worships the Hebrew god. The gift was given to him. Therefore, he may use it as a pious act. None will think less of him.'

Agrippa turned his head, resting his chin on one finger, and studied her as if from a distance. She wondered then if he had been drugged; in the light of the many blazing torches, his eyes were dark dots. She thought he might accept, saw him nod, as if to an inner voice, and open his mouth and she leaned forward and forward, until Drusilla tapped her elbow and said, 'Beware,' in Latin, softly.

She had not heard Saulos enter. Soft-footed, smelling of smoke and rage, he strode past, throwing her a look of such loathing, such triumph, that she felt her heart tumble in her chest. Shock held her still as he took his seat and by the time he had turned he was still again; the consummate counsellor, all-wise and ready with an answer. His features, when he turned to Yusaf, were a portrait of restrained regret.

'The king loves all his subjects equally,' Saulos said. 'Which is why he must return the gold to the Hebrews and yet forbid the Syrians from any further action which will discommode them in their worship. In such a way, will he be seen to reign with an even hand, fairly and decently.'

Yusaf slapped his hands on the chair arms. 'But there will be chaos! The Syrians will take advantage. Our youths will not be restrained. They will—'

'They will do as their king commands. As will you.' Saulos' voice held a new bite. 'And now he commands you to silence.'

Agrippa had not spoken. He stared at Yusaf, who stared back, disgust barely veiled in his eyes.

'Then, with great regret, I must take my leave. Your majesty . . . My queen.'

He had not been dismissed, but Yusaf rose anyway, his knees cracking in the hush. Guards came forward, one on either side, to hold him still or to help him depart, whichever was commanded.

Agrippa waved him away. 'Leave the eight talents in our treasury after you are gone. If we return them to you, and so refuse your request, know that it will be in sorrow, but that we do what is best for our city.'

'Your city is in riot, majesty,' Yusaf answered. 'The Syrians bay for your blood. Know that we would have prevented it, had we been granted the power to do so.'

CHAPTER FIFTEEN

Kleitos was a large and clumsy moth, flitting haphazardly through Caesarea, along wide streets, with their flower gardens muted under the rising moon; Mergus and Estaph were fleet as wolves on his trail, silent as night owls whose wing feathers make no sound.

Here, in the mercantile quarter, everything was uneasily peaceful. The sounds of the riot were a background mumble, and if there were fires beyond the one that Kleitos and his friends had tried to light, their flames were yet to paint the horizon.

This is not Rome. Not Rome, Mergus said to himself, timing the words with each footfall. *Not Rome . . . not fire . . . not burning . . .*

He had not realized how afraid he was of fire until the smell of smoke in his nostrils had been tainted also by memories of roasting flesh, and the ears of his mind had been deafened by the screams of men and women, burning. He turned back at each corner and searched the horizon, but saw no fire, yet. The roar of the crowd grew louder though, until it was the roar of a circus crowd, a gladiators' match, heard from the far side of the city.

Kleitos was heading north towards the Hebrew quarter. Two blocks past the Temple of Tyche, he reached a crossroads and stepped back off the roadway while half a dozen watchmen ran past, heading towards the palace. Mergus raked his gaze along the line to see if Jucundus was among them – he wasn't – and when he looked back again, Kleitos was gone.

'That way,' Estaph said, and pointed.

Cursing, Mergus followed him at a run across the open street and into the road end beyond. The area had been prosperous once, with small, neat houses and lush gardens; recent neglect had left it shabby.

There was worse than neglect ahead. Making his way cautiously through the dark, Mergus saw scaffolding loom ahead and by that sign knew they had reached the beleaguered synagogue, where Pantera had met Estaph and over which men were rioting down near the palace.

'Stop.' Mergus caught Estaph's elbow. 'This is a trap. Kleitos has gone too easily and into a place that we know. If we follow him in there, we'll meet more than six against us.'

Feeling Estaph hold still at his side, Mergus took time to peer through the dusk. Night was on them now, so that grey starlight made of his hand a phantom, stole his feet that he might not see where he trod. Ahead, in the synagogue's porch, a flame was struck, and a small lamp lit. Shadows leered from either side; men waited, and something else, that fluttered and cried and then died, suddenly, with the soft noise of a bird's neck breaking.

Kleitos stepped into the lamplight. He held the bird

and laid it down with something approaching reverence on to an olive jar turned upside down.

'God of all gods . . .' Mergus touched the brand of Mithras at his chest. He turned, slowly, backing away. 'They've sacrificed a dove on an upturned vessel.' And then, at the unchanged contours of Estaph's face, 'It's what they do here to cleanse a building of leprosy; they're saying the god of the Hebrews is a leper.'

Estaph's eyes gleamed. 'When your friend and I re-moved a sow's head from the porch, I thought they could do nothing worse. I was wrong; this is a thousand times worse. If the Hebrews find this . . .'

'They won't. It must be removed.' Grimly Mergus looked back along the route they had come. 'I'll stay here. You should find Jucundus and—'

'No.' Estaph took his arm. 'I am Estaph of Parthia, axeman and son of axemen. I do not walk away from battle.'

'This is not your fight. And we are outnumbered. I counted five men, including Kleitos.'

'It is not your fight, either, but we have already killed together this night, there is no reason to stop now. How well can you throw your knife?'

'Well enough.'

'Good.' Estaph slid one of his axes into his belt. The other was shining, the colour of the moon. He raised it in salute. 'Your friend, Pantera – he draws men to him, I think, and they take risks for his sake?'

Mergus nodded, his mouth set.

'So then we will make the risks less, and we will live through it, so that he has no need to find yet others to follow him into danger.'

166

Mergus found himself smiling too tightly, with his throat hard. He reached out and grasped Estaph's forearm, up high, by the elbow, so they linked, arm to arm, as legionaries did before battle. 'Take care, my friend.'

'And you keep away from my side. The axes need room to swing.'

And thus it was that, dry-mouthed, Mergus wormed his way forward until he could see all of the porch, and the shadows of men around it, and the small pot, with the zigzag lines drawn in blue below its lip, and the maker's mark on its upturned base, half hidden by the limp body of the dove.

Men gathered about it, weapon-ready and sharp, watching out to the night. Kleitos was among them, but boxed in by others, so there was no clear space through which a knife might pass.

Frustrated in his first choice, Mergus picked instead the tallest of the men, who carried a knife in one hand and a bow in the other. In the absolute dark of the shadows, he rose to his feet, sighted and threw.

The blade was a glimmer of torchlight, flying. And then a hilt, buried under a man's chin, with thin blood spraying like spittle from his throat. It was not a clean throw, but it was good enough; and already Estaph was passing him, roaring, with his two moon-bladed axes spinning in the torchlight.

Mergus gripped his own knife and, screaming, hurled himself after.

CHAPTER SIXTEEN

They were in the queen's private apartments: Berenice, Drusilla and Hypatia. Outside the window, the ocean raged. White waves cut with moonlight smashed the rocks at the foot of the headland. Beyond, all the sea was black as silk. Almost, it was possible to forget the riots, if one concentrated on the violence of the sea.

Hypatia turned back into the room. She had been given leave to stand, to move around, to do whatever might be necessary for the wisdom of Isis to come to her chosen vessel.

The chosen vessel should have been empty, should have kept her mind clear to hear the voice of the god, but Saulos filled her mind; Saulos in the flesh, striding into the audience chamber to take control of the meeting that had nearly slipped away from him; Saulos, smelling of fire and smoke; Saulos, in her dreams, worse than any of this.

Queen Berenice had asked a question and was waiting for a reply. She was clear-skinned and clear-eyed and hiding her headache well. Yet she, too, had seen Saulos, and his triumph, and she, too, was afraid.

Hypatia said, 'If you are asking my opinion on Yusaf's dilemma, I believe there is a way that the king might give the Hebrews what they want and still keep the Syrians from destroying the synagogue in revenge. But I think it will not be permitted to happen.'

'Explain,' said the queen.

They were alone, as much as any queen can be. The slaves and servants had been dismissed but for the men who guarded the door and even they had taken up their weapons and stepped outside. Drusilla was pouring wine; a fire-coloured Caecuban, well aged and still warm from the heat of the day. The goblets were of gold so thin that a finger's pressure might dent them.

Passing one now, the queen's younger sister smiled and it seemed to Hypatia that this was Drusilla's role, to smile at visitors and keep them sweet, to laugh when the conversation might otherwise become excessively serious. She wondered what it cost her, and whether the queen despised her for it as her daughter undoubtedly did.

Kleopatra had been ordered to bed as soon as they left the audience room. Hypatia did not know where she had gone, but bed did not seem likely on this night.

Berenice stared over the gold and ruby rim of her goblet, waiting.

'The king should return the gold to Yusaf in the morning,' Hypatia said. 'Moreover, he should do nothing to stop the Syrians building on the land around the synagogue. Let them set a brewery, a pork butcher and a shrine for laying out the dead at every wall if they want to – but let the king first move the synagogue itself, stone by stone, to a new location within the city.'

Berenice's hand tightened on her goblet. The gold bowed, but did not dent. 'Where to?'

'I don't know, but for the worth of eight talents, a place could surely be bought. Only let it be paid for openly by the king. If the Hebrews wish to give him gold later that's their affair, but to begin with, if the land is seen as the king's gift, none will dare insult it as they have done the synagogue.'

'She's right.' Drusilla nodded, smiling. 'The question is whether our brother will allow it.'

'No, the question is quite different.' With her eyes still on the queen, Hypatia asked, 'How close is Saulos to your brother?'

'Ah.' A reclining couch stood behind, upholstered in a blue just a shade deeper than the queen's gown. Abruptly, Berenice sat on it.

A breeze hissed in through the windows. Hypatia moved to close the shutters, and paused, holding them half open. The moon was there, shining disc of Isis, past its height, sliding down towards the west, cast in replica on the ice-black water. She kept her back to the two royal sisters, hiding her face.

The whole world knew that Berenice, queen in Caesarea, had left her last surviving husband to return to the city of her birth. Some said that she, who lived for the joy of the hunt, had pined for the quality of the ibex and gazelles that ranged on the low hills to its south, being in want of equal quarry in the lands of her husband. Others said she loved her brother and had returned for the love of his touch. A very few said that she might have loved him, but that her brother, the king, could not bring himself to mate with any woman, even the few times necessary to beget a child.

The Empress Poppaea, who had best reason to know, had it differently. *Agrippa didn't call his sister, I sent her, and she went for love of me. Agrippa is not fit to rule; he's weak and too easily swayed by his latest . . . attraction. Berenice has the heart of a monarch and she knows that her people's interests are Rome's interests. She will rule better than him or any of the idiot governors we send.*

Hypatia closed the shutters. Berenice was still on the couch, watching her. Drusilla mustered a small smile.

Hypatia turned to face them. 'Has he . . . Have they . . . ?'

'They are as brothers,' Berenice said, crisply, which did not entirely answer the question Hypatia had not entirely asked; in this family, brothers might still be lovers.

'Then there is no point in our discussing what may or may not be done with Yusaf's gold. If Saulos has the king's trust so completely, you will go to Jerusalem. Whatever they have been in the past, today, here, now, the riots outside are a tool and their purpose is to move you, to bring you more completely into Saulos' power. Your question, then, is whether you are willing so to be moved.'

Dark stains grew in the armpits of Berenice's gown. A greenish tinge marked the corners of her mouth and eyes, a sure sign that sickness was coming. She kept her head high. 'What is your advice? Personally, not as the Chosen of Isis.'

171

'The two are the same, lady. Unless you are ready to face Saulos down, you should appear meek in his company.'

'How will I know if I am ready to face him?'

'You will know. If you are not sure, then you are not ready. For now—' Hypatia gave Drusilla her goblet, and rubbed her hands briskly. 'There may be little time. Choose what you need and then what you most want. Pack them, or have them packed. Be ready, for the order to leave will come when you least expect it, and—'

The door crashed back with a force that broke the mosaics on the wall behind it.

Kleopatra, fully dressed, quite awake, stood framed in the entrance, twisting away from Polyphemos even as he tried to restrain her. Her black hair was wild about her shoulders. Her eyes were pale as ice, and burning.

'Mother! Aunt Berenice . . . that is, your majesty! We have to go *now*!' The emphasis robbed the sentence of everything except its urgency, but that was enough to bring the queen, her sister and her new counsellor to the doorway.

Berenice said, 'Kleopatra, comport yourself. Polyphemos, what is she saying?'

The steward, too, was imperfectly dressed, and the unctuous hand-wringing had been swept away by a terror that left him grey. 'Rioters have broken through the outer gates, majesty. To the east, the Hebrew synagogue is on fire. Men are fighting in the streets: Hebrews against Syrians, fighting to the death.'

'Then the governor must—'

'No, lady. Governor Florus took horse for Jerusalem when the king stood to speak in the theatre and now the Syrians are calling for the blood of the Herods to slake the foundations of their new buildings, and the Hebrews are calling on it for heresy, and for taking their gold without fulfilling the promise. For safety, you must go. We all must.'

'No! The Syrians are our people, not our enemies. Polyphemos, find the king, tell him—'

'He's here, lady.' Hypatia caught the queen's elbow, turning her.

Agrippa stood in the corridor with a broken vase at his feet, scarlet tulips strewn across the black-on-white tiles. Water stained the gold tissue robes.

'We must stay,' Berenice said.

'We can't.' Agrippa did not sound like a child, but not like a king, either. His voice cracked as he spoke. 'Berenice, the riots are happening again, as they did when Father died. They're setting us in effigy on the inn roofs, naming us whores, calling for our blood. We can't hide in a cupboard now – they'll tear the palace down to get to us. We have to leave. I've ordered the horses made ready. Jucundus of the Watch is here with a century of his men. We'll go in two troops: Saulos and Iksahra will ride with us, Kleopatra and Hyrcanus with you.'

'And Hypatia,' Berenice said, and in that conceded defeat, even as she claimed a small triumph of her own. 'The Chosen of Isis comes with us.'

Chapter Seventeen

News of the governor's departure reached the crowd around the theatre at almost the same time as did news that the king had taken eight talents of Hebrew gold to use against the Syrians.

It didn't matter that Agrippa hadn't taken it, and wouldn't have used it against the Syrians if he had: facts had reached that malleable state where they fitted the prejudice of any individual and, when enough people held the same prejudice, the result was incendiary.

News that the royal family were also planning to leave the city was the spark that lit the combustible mass, that pushed the simmering crowd into screaming hysteria, into rolling chants that called for Hebrew blood, for Syrian blood, for Herodian blood, for Roman blood . . . and soon, inevitably, just for blood.

Pantera thrust through the mass, seeking Mergus. If anyone thought him a Nabatean archer trying to flee the violence they were welcome. If they thought him an agent of the emperor, trying to undo the damage, they were equally welcome. As long as nobody thought him either Hebrew or Syrian and tried to slide a knife between his ribs, he was happy.

He shouted, 'Make way, make way,' alternately in Latin and in the desert tongue of the Saba brothers and cared not if nobody understood either; at least he wasn't speaking Greek or Aramaic.

He came to a small square with a nine-pillared fountain whose pipes had been wrenched out of line, spilling water darkly, like free-flowing blood, across the pavings and none at all into the fountain. Beyond it stood a temple to Jupiter Dolichenos that had not yet been sacked and then a long blind wall. Beyond that, men fought to put out a fire. Others stood and watched, as they had in Rome, as if fire were an entertainment, not a danger.

There was no obvious route through and yet every time Pantera turned west towards the palace, where Saulos must be, the prickle in his spine drew him east again, towards the synagogue, like iron to a lodestone. He turned left, therefore, and pushed his way through the thinning crowd. At its margin, a tall, dark figure was forging a straight line through its thinnest edge.

'Menachem!' Pantera shouted, and was not heard. He turned at a sharp angle and wove, ducking, past a Syrian fishwife and her three grown sons, who were shouting useless advice at the unheeding fire-fighters. He came up to the zealot from behind and shouted again, and saw a stocky figure beside him turn, and had time to call again 'Menachem—' before he must twist sideways and round and thrust his arm up and block the blade that came for his throat.

'Moshe, no!' Menachem, too, had gripped the same arm. The man they held between them was more wiry than stocky closer up, with hair wild as a bush and a beard to match. He set his lips in a hard line and shook himself free.

Menachem said, 'Tonight, he is a friend,' and his tone suggested he was speaking of both, to each. He carried a charge with him of simmering excitement, not unlike that of the rioters. Even as he dropped Moshe's arm he was pushing through the crowds again, so that Pantera must follow, or be left behind.

Pantera said, 'I'm looking for Mergus.'

'I know. We have found him.' Half turning, Menachem said, 'On my orders, Moshe followed Mergus away from the theatre while we were inside. Mergus, in turn, followed the man Kleitos who has just sacrificed a dove on an upturned urn in the porch of the synagogue. If the rest of Caesarea finds out, the city will be ash and rubble by morning.'

'Kleitos wouldn't do that alone,' Pantera said. 'He hasn't the courage.' And then, 'How many with him?'

Moshe turned, scowling darkly. 'Five to begin with, but others were coming as I came away. At least a dozen.'

'And we are three,' Pantera said. 'If we can go past the Temple of Mithras, my bow is there. It will even the odds.'

'You can shoot in the dark?' Menachem asked, with interest.

'I can try.'

*   *   *

In the dark and flying shadows around the synagogue's porch, the war-bow sang three times. Three men died

176

with arrows in their throats before the rest realized they were under fire and dropped out of sight.

In the clot of heaving bodies at the back, only Estaph was clearly visible, a mountain of muscle, flanked on either side by shimmering iron as his axes spun and spun and now and then impacted with a skull, breaking it open with a noise that was audible far down the street in a fight that was otherwise marked by its lack of noise.

Even close to, Pantera heard little beyond the contained grunts of the battling men, none of whom wanted to attract the wrong attention and the majority of whom wanted to escape as soon as they realized whose side the bow was on. Hunting men as they fled was a sordid task at the best of times, made harder now by the necessity to be sure that each shape seen in the dark was not Mergus.

Pantera shot three more times, and then dropped the bow and drew his Saba blade and sliced it forward and outward, fast and fast and fast, and a man was dead and another had lost half the skin of his scalp and was blinded by his own blood so that Menachem, fighting with a ruthless efficiency at Pantera's left side, was able to kill him without fuss and then the one that came after. Somewhere on Menachem's other side, Moshe acquitted himself well, which is to say, he killed and did not die.

And then came the moment when no man was left standing except the three of them and Estaph, facing each other over a slippery mass of man-flesh with a smashed urn between them that might once have held the corpse of a sacrificed dove.

Seeing it, Pantera came to realize he had light enough to see by, that the flames from the burning theatre had wrought night to day, dispelling shadows. He turned on his heel, counting, in growing dread. Kleitos was not among the dead. Mergus was not among the living.

He came full circle, facing Estaph. 'Where is he?'

'Kleitos has him.' Estaph stepped over the bodies, sheathing his axe handles in his belt. The battle-light was dying from his eyes, replaced by concern. 'He was fighting Kleitos and three others away from me, and then . . . not. I couldn't get to him. I'm sorry.'

'We must find them swiftly.' Pantera looked across the road. 'Is your family still here, when there are flames fit to roast the city?'

'No.' Estaph smeared another man's blood from his face. 'I sent them to Damascus, to my wife's father.'

'Then why,' asked Pantera, and he was already running, 'is there torchlight coming from the back room of the house you were renting?'

Pantera ran with Estaph a bull-shadow at one shoulder and Menachem a black-eyed ghost at the other and, because they were all three hunters and ran in the dark, quietly, Kleitos neither heard nor saw them as he stepped out of the small, neat house at the end of the row, the one newly empty, that had been Estaph's.

He bore a lamp with a small flame; they could not miss him. Pantera swerved across the street and felt Estaph move in behind him.

'*Alive!*' he called, as they met, bone to bone, forearm to jugular, with Kleitos crushed between. 'We need him alive.'

And they had him alive, but not the two men who were with him, who died as they rushed forward. A third died to Menachem, who used his long, lean, narrow-pointed

178

knife after the manner of the Sicari zealots, sliding it into the man's chest and out again, leaving a small half-moon opening and no blood. It killed just as quickly as had Pantera's.

'And so answers,' Pantera said, stepping back.

Estaph had Kleitos by the shoulders and was pulling outwards and backwards, as a man might to break a board of wood. Kleitos was a child in his hands, a puppet, jerking wildly with his feet not touching the ground. He shook his head wildly.

Pantera stood in front of him, face to face. He was shaking, not only with the aftermath of battle. 'Where is he?'

'You will die! You and all who fight with you: the centurion, the Alexandrian witch, the dove-boy and his father, these men here; all will die the slow, Roman death.' Blue-faced and flecked with spittle, Kleitos spat. Estaph sighed and did something small with his hands that made the other man scream.

'I said you would remain alive,' Estaph said in his ear, 'I did not say you would remain whole.' He twisted again. Kleitos' scream was hoarse this time and too high to hear clearly.

'Where is Mergus?' Pantera laid his knife on Kleitos' face, pressing the tip close to his eye. 'Tell me. Or I will tell Estaph to give you to me.'

'There . . .' Kleitos' head gave a spasmodic jerk, back towards the house that had been Estaph's.

'In the back room?'

A nod.

'Alone?'

'Yes.'

'Hold him.'

Menachem had gone away and come back. The channel of his blade was dark with blood. 'Another two were in the house next door.' By his tone, they were flowers, cut from a field, to be forgotten even before they fell. 'Where's your centurion?'

'Through here.'

Wordless, Pantera pushed through a goatskin curtain to the windowless, airless, lightless place beyond. The stench of human faeces hit him as a physical blow, wrenching bile up his throat, to his nose, so that he had to bend over and thumb it out, choking.

'Light!' he called, back to where there was at least the glimmer of torchlight. 'Get me light!'

Menachem brought a filthy, smoking torch, that called skeletal shadows leaping from the margins of a room so small that four paces in any direction might reach a wall. Most of it was filled with dried camel fodder, spiky with thistles. Broken beams of timber, hastily ripped from other places, had been cast on top with little care for how they settled, only that the resulting heap would burn. And among the florid odours of human ordure and sweet hay was the swell of lamp oil, poured liberally everywhere, over the hay, the timbers, and the pile of rags in the corner . . .

That was not a pile of rags, but a man, bound and gagged and . . . Pantera knelt, turned him over, felt at his throat for a long, desperate moment, and there, *there!* was a pulse, thready, fine, erratic, but leaping live under his fingers. He sat back on his heels and swept his hands over his face.

'He's alive?' Menachem said, softly, from behind him.

At Pantera's nod, he shouted back to Estaph, 'He's alive. We need water.'

Pantera called, over him, 'Estaph, kill Kleitos now, before I am tempted to roast him here. And keep the torches safe; a stray flame will burn us all.'

Moshe brought water and wool and Estaph came in, cleaning the head of his axe on a rag. The giant Parthian lifted Mergus like a child, carried him out past Kleitos' pallid corpse and laid him on the pallet in the front room, away from the risk of fire.

There, Pantera pulled the gag from his mouth and cut the cords at his wrists and ankles. With Estaph's help, he stripped him, and washed away the filth about his body, and the matted blood from the wound on his head, and dressed him again in his own tunic, with the worst of the blood rinsed from the wool.

Then, with fire raging in the city outside, and the sounds of riot building, they began the unpleasant work of bringing him back to consciousness, with water poured on his face, and into his throat, so that he must choke or drown and then, after choking, swallow.

Mergus moaned and turned his head away. Pantera tilted the beaker over his face, and let another half-cup dribble on to his nose. He choked and cursed and struggled, and Pantera held him steady until he opened his eyes, and peered, and blinked and made himself focus, and stared.

Pantera smiled down at him. 'Does your head hurt?'

Mergus shook his head and then stopped. In a moment, whiter, he said, 'Not as much as my hands.'

'The ropes bit tight. Your hands will hurt until the blood comes back to them. The first hour is the worst.'

Mergus closed his eyes. A while later, he opened them again. 'Kleitos?'

'Dead.'

'He said I was the first; that Saulos planned to kill your friends one by one by one: Hypatia, Estaph, the dove-boy, the priest of Tyche – even Menachem and Yusaf whom you barely know, with you at the last, knowing them all gone.'

Mergus' cold fingers struggled for grip. With care, Pantera held them, and chafed them between his palms. Quietly, he said, 'I will not let it happen.' And then, because it didn't seem enough, 'We have thwarted him twice tonight. He will become more desperate after this, and make mistakes. All we need is patience, and we have enough of that, between us.'

Outside was a small flurry of men arriving and leaving and Menachem, who had gone to the door, came back again. He stood in the doorway, with the goatskin curtain pushed back on his arm. 'The royal family has just departed for Jerusalem,' he said. 'Saulos is with them. He has lead place in the king's retinue, behind only Agrippa himself.'

Pantera said, 'Where's Jucundus? He'll need to know about this, to stem anything else that comes of it.'

'Jucundus is leading the king's train, riding at the head of five hundred horse,' Menachem said. 'His second, Acrabenus, has command of the Watch. He will contain the fires as readily as Jucundus might have done, which is to say not readily, but well enough to— No!'

Mergus was trying to rise. Pantera caught him as he toppled and lowered him back to the floor, sitting this time, not lying.

'Don't,' he said, 'not yet. We'll tie you to a horse until you can hold the reins yourself.' He looked up to where Menachem waited. 'We ride for Jerusalem, now, in the king's tracks. Will you come with us?'

'We are four,' Menachem said. 'Myself, Moshe, Aaron, whom you have not yet met – and Yusaf, who was dismissed from the king's side before they departed.'

'The king turned down Yusaf's petition?'

'No, Saulos did that.' Menachem smiled, tightly. Over the guttering light, his deep-set eyes sought Pantera's and held them. 'Thus does your enemy, indeed, become our enemy. And so we will ride together after him to Jerusalem. We have defeated him here when we did not know him as a common enemy. Knowing it, we may more readily defeat him there.'

CHAPTER EIGHTEEN

Caesarea was behind them, a ribbon of tiny lights stitching the dark land to the darker sky. The roar of the riot was too far away to be heard; the desert rang instead to the soft pad of hoof on sand, steady, never stumbling, picking a route by starlight, striving always to keep to the path, which was no path, but was none the less obvious by daylight.

Ahead, torches showed the queen's party had stopped for food, for water, and were mounting again, stringing out along that same not-quite-obvious route. Hypatia was there; Pantera could feel her in much the same way as he could feel Mergus and for much the same reason; these two were his true family. He had not thought of them as such before this, but after the night just gone, it was impossible not to.

Further ahead, if Pantera strained to look, the lights of the king's group stretched across the horizon, heading always south. Saulos was there, and the Berber hunter with her beasts.

He had heard the cheetah was trained to hunt like a

hound, and did not want to find out that it was true, here, in the dark desert, where a hound could take a man from his horse and break his neck before anyone even knew it was there.

And then he heard a change in the rhythmic footfall ahead. Pantera drew his horse to a hard halt and raised his hand. A scream cut the night.

'It's the girl,' Pantera said. 'The royal princess. Her horse has fallen.'

'How do you know?' Menachem pushed up alongside, his eyes dim in the starlight. 'It could be anyone.'

'Who else is reckless enough to throw her horse at a canter away from the lit path and the watchmen?'

'The boy is. Particularly if the Berber woman has rebuffed him.'

'No. Hyrcanus rides with the king's group and they're a mile in front. Watch the torches; the queen's men are veering off the track now to find her. Hypatia's ahead of them, I think. If the girl's neck is broken, then they'll have to . . . but it isn't. See?' Pantera pointed to the gather and squeeze of the moving lights, now together, now apart. 'They're carrying her back to the track now.'

He looked back, at his own party. Of the five horses gathered by, Yusaf and Moshe held the rear, while the other three kept to a row with Estaph and Aaron staying one on either side of Mergus, to keep him safe; an hour into the journey they had untied him so that he could ride freely, but he wasn't secure enough to be left entirely alone.

Ahead, the torches of the royal train danced back to the trail. Pantera said, 'They'll have to carry her, which means they'll move more slowly. If we want to reach

Jerusalem before daylight, we'll have to swing out round them and get back to the track well in front.'

'And risk running into the back of the king's group? You said they were only a mile ahead.' That was Mergus, speaking from just beyond his horse's left haunch. By a miracle, he kept the pain from his voice and was a centurion picking out a particular problem; nothing unsurmountable.

Pantera laughed softly. 'If you've tracked Eceni warriors through the forests of Britain at night, you can track a group of minor Herodian royalty carrying torches along a desert pathway that's been used by every passing merchant for the last hundred years. And you can do it without having to take the same path.'

He turned his horse off the track and eased it forward on to the shadowed sand beyond. 'Follow me. Don't speak. Keep your horses out of step with mine so we don't set up a rhythm the guards can hear. And' – this last with hollow humour – 'don't scream if you fall.'

They moved uncertainly at first. The thumbnail of an old moon did not so much light the desert as sharpen the shadows, painting the treacherous dips and hillocks in stark relief. The horses baulked at imaginary traps and had to be nursed round lines in the sand that curved like snakes. They moved so slowly that there was a real danger dawn might come and see them still crossing the desert, visible to any who chanced to look.

In the dark, Pantera halted his horse. 'Dismount.'

Yusaf caught his elbow and leaned down, bringing his face close. His nose was heavy, his lips thin, his beard a hedge about his face. His midnight silks swayed, thick with the scent of balsam, and the odour of money. 'Are you suggesting we walk to Jerusalem?' he asked.

'No, I'm suggesting we run until we come back on to the track on the other side of the queen's party. Then we ride.'

He saw them look, one to the other; Moshe to Aaron, who was smaller, wirier, older. Estaph to Menachem, and then to Pantera. 'Run?' Estaph asked. 'Even Mergus?'

'Even Mergus. It'll help to ease his muscles, to stop them stiffening. It's easier than you think. Trust me.'

They didn't trust him at all, but he kicked off his shoes and gathered his reins and began to run, digging his toes into the cooling sand, feeling the grit and the balance and the slope. His horse, after the first reluctant steps, ran with him, increasing in confidence. This close to the ground, the moon became an ally, showing the way; the sand became a living thing that gripped his feet, the hillocks loomed larger and more clearly, and the pits were obvious and easily avoided.

After a while, he heard the others slide down from their horses and begin to run. Of them all, his concern was most for the city-bred Yusaf, the bearded counsellor in his ruinously expensive silks who had never seen war, but he proved fitter than he looked, and not given to complaint. Mergus, as Pantera had promised, became looser in his stride, and did not fall behind.

He led them in a long curving line past Hypatia's part of the royal group and back to the track, where they paused a moment, to drink water, and to rest.

'You've done that before.' Mergus was leaning forward with his hands on his knees, panting, but he was

187

breathing more easily than he had when they started. 'One day, you can tell me the details.'

'There are no details to tell,' Pantera said. 'I used to live here; my father made me do this when I was a child. The desert climbs up to the mountains. On the other side are the trees: pine, cedar, olives in groves. It'll be easier going then.'

'Your father is the man who taught you how to throw a knife?' Mergus' eyes gleamed in the dark. He was in pain still, but less than he had been, and he was a warrior; the challenge of a night run pushed him beyond his own exhaustion. 'How old were you?'

'Twelve.'

Shaking his head, Mergus accepted Estaph's help to mount and rode on down the track. Pantera followed, and considered as he rode the vagaries of luck, or chance, or the push of the gods, that had brought him back to this road. His father had made him ride it a dozen times in his youth, each time pushing him further, testing him harder, making him run or ride faster, later into the night.

On the last occasion, Pantera had been given blunt arrows and a knife with the tip filed away and his father had set men along the route pretending to be brigands. The boy had hit four out of eight. None of them had hit him. His father had been quietly pleased. One of the men he had failed to hit had come to him later and told him how close the arrow had gone. All eight had taken him out and given him beer and sworn, drunkenly, with some weeping, to be as a brother to him evermore.

It had been a good night, seared from Pantera's memory by rage at his father's later treachery. He remembered them both now, the night and the anger, as if they had happened to somebody else, but they had laid the foundation of what he was. And what he was in that moment was . . . alive.

They had walked knowingly into Saulos' grasp in Caesarea and come out alive. He had not died and, more important, nor had Mergus. The realities of Saulos' power were not diminished, but, somewhere in the dark, easing his horse forward over ground he could barely see, spreading his hearing like a net over the flat sand, tasting the air, alerting his skin to the felt-senses that had kept him alive through worse nights than this, Pantera realized he was breathing freely for the first time since the horror of Rome's fire, and that he was glad to be alive.

He sent his thanks through the night and heard again the echo of another voice – Seneca's – speaking to the youth he had been. *You need to be pushed to the edges of your being. Your soul has always craved that kind of challenge. What you lacked was the knowledge of how to survive when you got there. I have taught you everything I can of survival at the edges of being. Now we shall find out if I was good enough.*

Good enough to get him here. And good enough, presently, to know that he was no longer the only hunter in the desert.

'She's here,' Pantera murmured quietly to Mergus.

Estaph, close by, said, 'Who is?'

'The Berber hunter. Iksahra.'

Nobody, this time, asked how he knew. Menachem said, 'What do you want of us?'

'Keep grouped close together so she can't easily tell

who we are, or how many. Mergus, if you can bring your scarf up over your head and keep close to Yusaf, it may be that she can be made to think you're his wife. The longer Saulos thinks you dead, the better.'

'Why let her live?' Estaph asked, with blunt simplicity. 'We are seven; she is only one.'

'Because we're caught between the two royal parties and I want to be in Jerusalem before Hypatia, which means we have to keep moving. If we have to split up, go in by the farmers' gate down at the far edge of the wall and meet up again at the Inn of the Black Grapes – if the inn is still there?'

'It's still there,' Menachem said, and then: 'How did you know?'

Pantera smiled into the dark. 'I lived most of my child-hood in Jerusalem. Saulos has forgotten that. Here, we have a chance to defeat him.'

CHAPTER NINETEEN

The torchlit ride from Caesarea to Herod's palace at Jerusalem was a nightmare from the start. Hypatia hated every stride.

It wasn't anyone's fault. Jucundus of the Watch had been more than thorough in his preparations: the horses were of good, sane stock, well fed and rested, able to keep up the breakneck speed set by the leading riders. To prevent them from stumbling in the dark, the watchmen all held pitch-pine torches in their nearside hands and carried others unlit on slings over their shoulders, enough to last them three times the night's duration.

Jucundus had arranged a stopping place where food and water were unloaded from pack mules and it was possible for the royal riders to relieve themselves, to rest, to talk a little with those around them without the relentless drumming noise of hooves on sand that made it necessary to shout and so easier to remain silent.

At the break, Hypatia found herself caught in the eye of an argument between Drusilla, whose smile was beginning to crack under the strain, and her daughter, who was bright-eyed with a fury that made no sense, until Hypatia found that Kleopatra had wanted to travel with the king's group and had been forbidden to do so.

'Are we so dull to ride with?' Hypatia asked as they remounted.

The girl spun, blazing. 'She has them all with her! The falcons, the cheetah, your hounds. How could you let her take them?'

Iksahra then: the early interest was fast becoming an infatuation. The girl had wrenched her horse away. Hypatia followed, laid a hand on her bridle. They were alone now, on the borders of the party. The watchmen had packed with quiet efficiency. Their leader was already on the path, torch bobbing in time with his steady horse.

Berenice was close by, with eight guards around her. The queen rode fast, with a sober determination that made Hypatia want to be with her, to talk, to consider what they might do in the morning. Instead, she was left with a petulant girl.

Taking a breath, she said, 'The hounds had to come to Jerusalem. I wouldn't leave them in Caesarea where men might stone them to death, or the slaves might fail to feed them. Iksahra had already loosed them when you came to get us. They are safe with her, and they'll enjoy a night's run. What did you want me to do, wrest them from her?'

'If you had to. Don't you dream at all? I thought you were the Chosen of Isis?' At which the Princess Kleopatra kicked her horse to a violent run, leaving Hypatia in the dark, watching her fly over unseen desert, too far from the torches to see the ruts and hillocks, the holes made by small beasts, perfect to trap a horse's foot and trip it.

She was turning back to fetch a watchman with a torch and a fast horse when she heard the girl scream.

Hypatia kicked her own mount forward into the dark. The watchmen came later, slower, spreading their slick light across the sand and rock and desert shrubs. Hypatia watched for snakes by habit – in Alexandria, they made riding at night close to impossible. Here she had seen none, and still saw none as she dismounted by the girl's fallen body.

'Kleopatra? Can you hear me?'

Hypatia could see no blood, nor smell any, and scent was the more reliable here in the uncertain light. The girl was breathing. A pulse beat at her neck in a solid, steady rhythm. Her limbs were intact and – harder to check without causing harm – her spine also.

To one side, her horse moaned and snorted and then, suddenly, shuddered and blew hot foaming blood across the sand and those upon it. A watchman had cut its throat.

'The leg was broken,' he said, standing. His knife was dull in the torchlight. Black blood soaked the sand around, and the air stank. He said, 'It stood in a hole. You shouldn't ride in the dark, that's why we carry lights. The girl, did she break anything?'

He was Syrian, of twenty years' service; they all were sworn to Jucundus first, the governor a distant second and their Hebrew king's niece not at all, except that they were old enough to be fathers, to have had sisters, and so might have some compassion.

A horse padded over the cool grit: Drusilla was nearly

193

upon them, and Berenice, coming more slowly, because her watchmen were more alert and were keeping her from riding hard once she was away from the path. 'Is she hurt?' the queen called.

Hypatia stood, lifting the princess. She was a dead weight, heavier than she looked. 'She's alive,' she called back. 'Nothing's broken.' And then, to the girl herself, 'Kleopatra, can you lift your head?'

She could, evidently, though with effort. She opened one eye, screwing it against the torchlight.

'You can ride with me,' Hypatia said, without knowing why. The closest guard was the one who had cut her horse's throat and had only now realized he might be required to give up his own horse and walk. To him, she said, 'Hold her while I mount, then pass her up to me. Kleopatra, you have as long as it takes me to mount to decide if you're well enough to ride behind me, holding on, or should go in front, where I can hold you.'

Infants and the chronically sick were held in front. Asking the question was a risk and possibly a stupid one, but it worked to the extent that Kleopatra tried to raise her head and declare loudly how very ready she was to ride entirely on her own, neither behind nor in front of anyone, and, in failing to do so, proved neatly enough to her watchman, her mother and her aunt, the queen, that she wasn't fit to ride on her own at all.

Berenice was there by then, leaning over, with her hand on the girl's brow. 'We could send back for a litter.'

'Caesarea is not safe, majesty. If we send anywhere, we would have to send ahead to Jerusalem and that would be too slow. If your majesties will permit, I will happily bring her.'

She spoke to both the queen and Drusilla, but it was Berenice who made the decision, who spoke first. She should have been commanding armies: her mind had the right speed to it, and grasp of broader strategies.

She said, 'You'll need men with you, to see you're not taken by brigands. You—' She singled out the officer, marked by a red badge on his shoulder. 'Take a dozen men and form an escort for the Chosen of Isis and the princess. Their lives are as yours. If you return and they're dead, your ghost will follow theirs to the afterlife. Is that clear?'

Thus it was that Hypatia of Alexandria, Chosen of Isis, rode through the second half of the night with a fourteen-year-old girl clasped in front of her saddle. Her watchmen took exceptional care of her. They rode at a wiser, safer speed which meant that they reached Jerusalem quite some time behind the others, and a long time after the seven who had been riding behind.

Hypatia had become aware that there had been seven men riding behind soon after she first knelt to help Kleopatra. She had sensed them walking their horses nearer, keeping their steps out of rhythm so that the watchmen might not pick up the sound of their approach.

They had passed by, wide to the east, going faster than she was, faster even than Berenice, who had slowed to keep Kleopatra in sight. Knowing they were there, Hypatia had listened hard, sifting through the night-sounds of beasts and stray winds, of ifrit and ghûls and scrabbling scorpions, and heard enough to have some idea, or perhaps hope, of who they were.

The watchmen were good, but they rode with the earpieces of their helmets down as protection against missiles, which made sense when they were the ones carrying the lights and so made the best targets for any arrows that might fly from the dark. It didn't help them to hear a spy and his companions as they ran round in a wide arc that brought them back to the track a long way ahead of Hypatia and her guards, so that by the time dawn spilled its slow light across the land, they were gone.

Hypatia's small group reached Jerusalem an hour after sunrise. As they wound down the side of the Mount of Olives towards the northern gate, Kleopatra raised her head and vomited over the side of Hypatia's horse.

Thereafter, she slid back into unconsciousness, but she continued to grip Hypatia's wrist with both hands as she had throughout the ride, so that her fingers left blue marks dented into the flesh, and, when they reached the palace without mishap, she let herself be lifted down by the watchman and carried up the palace steps to her mother and her aunt.

There, as she was set on her feet with all the care one might hope for, she turned back to where Hypatia waited at the stair foot. 'My head hurts,' she said, with crystal clarity. 'The Chosen of Isis will know how to cure it.'

*   *   *

Iksahra sur Anmer did not enter Jerusalem at dawn on horseback through Herod's vast, ornate gate with its images of the sun and the moon lighting her way and her falcons on the pommel of her saddle and the queen's new hounds behind her.

She came on foot, the cheetah her distant companion, ghost-like in the dark. She came with a swathe of linen over her face, to keep the sand from her lungs and to cover her dark skin against the gaze of whoever might choose to spend time watching the uncelebrated routes by which slaves and servants entered the city.

She came dressed as a slave, an insult forced on her by Saulos at the start of the night's ride, when he had said she must hang back, to see if Pantera followed, and, if he did, who was with him. He had said it smiling, thinking that she was his to instruct, that no station was too low, no insult too great. He had taken the falcons on his own horse, whistled the unwilling hounds to heel, and they, trained always to obey, had gone with him.

Iksahra had thought of killing him then; it would not have been hard in the milling chaos of horses and watchmen, slaves, servants and stewards that had marked the start of their escape from Caesarea. He had turned on his heel and walked away from her, leaving his throat unguarded, and her hands had drawn the silk cord from her waist before her mind had caught up with the thought. She had let him live, not because she was afraid of killing him, but because he was still her greatest – her only – chance of avenging her father. She did not expect to need him for ever, and the different ways he might die were daily occupying more of her thoughts.

This night, though, she chose to do as he asked, and so she had left her three fleet horses in Saulos' care and had run on foot like a slave, save that slaves were not hunters, and a slave would not have known how to slide safely through the desert at night, keeping clear of the snakes, the insects, the undead evil that stalked the dark. A slave would not have kept the cheetah at a distance, always her shadow, always her first line of attack, her last line of defence.

A slave would not have heard Berenice approach from far enough away to find a hiding place in time, so that the queen's train passed close enough for Iksahra to touch her horse's oiled hooves, nor would a slave have lain prone on the cold sand with her lips closed against the grit, until the queen's sister followed later, weeping, nor waited on until the Alexandrian witch came with the black-haired royal girl held in front of her saddle like an infant.

A slave, if one had been there at all, might have let these pass and gone after them, thinking the night empty, but Iksahra sur Anmer, hunter and daughter of hunters, had turned away from the track and pressed her ear to the ground and heard the men whom Saulos had said would follow the royal train.

He hadn't said how he knew Pantera would be coming, nor had Iksahra asked, but she had set herself a new goal: to learn Saulos' sources of information. When she had them, he could die without loss to her or the world.

Meanwhile, she had run out across the sands, following the new sounds, and, because she was the best of the best, she had found them, and cut in ahead of them, and lain still in the night until they passed her, riding now; seven shadows set against the starlit night. Then she had wrapped her robes around her in such a way that nothing flapped and set after them.

To track seven horses in the dark was a skill few possessed, even among her people. To track them when they were led by a man of infinite suspicion, who took care to hide the traces of his passing even in a desert at night, who stopped at random intervals and slid down from his horse to listen to the air and press his ear to the ground and then set his horse forward at a canter on the remount, who turned to face the rising sun, making his god-signs to the aching red blade as it cut open the night, and even then made use of the light to search the land behind . . . to track such a man was an act of genius and Iksahra alone could have achieved it.

She learned a lot about her quarry in the course of the chase; she always did, but she had never been as certain that her prey knew she was there. By the end, when they were among the trees, he made no secret of it, and kept his horse steady, waiting for her, looking east to the sun in such a way that she might come to know the contours of his face, might see the scar above his right eye, the weakness of his shoulder and the lame left ankle, where the foot would not bend as much as it should.

She saw his eyes and the way they scanned the earth, exactly as her father's had. She saw his dry smile and the way he listened to the others who clustered around him before he spoke; always he listened more and spoke less, but always his words carried more weight. The men with him showed no sign that they knew Iksahra was there. If he told them, they had more discretion than anyone she had met.

Pantera, too, did not ride in through Herod's Gate, but pulled his small cavalcade east towards one of the livestock gates where the wall bounded the lower city. Iksahra left them then, and slipped round the wall in the opposite direction, heading south and west and then south towards the slave gates at the junction of the upper and new parts of the city.

Saulos was waiting for her in a shadowed alley not far inside the gate. Breathless with urgency and the need for her news, he did not offer her water, or a melon, or any of the small courtesies that were her due as a returning hunter. He watched the cheetah as it came to press its head on her hand, and tried not to let his eyes grow wide.

Iksahra had her own water skin hidden in her robes with a mouthful of water left against just this eventuality. She took it out and drained it dry, watching Saulos wring his hands and sway from one foot to the other in his anxiety. If he knew the insult she offered by not sharing the drink, he showed no sign of it.

Wiping her mouth with the back of her hand, she took the time to settle the empty skin inside her robes, tight against her belt, then said succinctly, 'Pantera is here. He will ride in through the lambs' gate at the lower city soon. Maybe he has already done so.'

Saulos frowned. 'You are sure of this?'

No man had ever questioned her tracking. Not one. Ever. Her father had killed the only man who had ever questioned his own abilities. His daughter had not needed even to do that.

Iksahra stared in silence and Saulos stared back a moment, expressionless, before a smile cracked his face. 'Of course you're sure. How could you not be? The great Pantera, the Leopard himself, bested by a woman of the Berberai!' He forgot himself and patted her arm. 'I knew you were good. I didn't know you were the best. I apologize.'

Iksahra nodded. Her eyes never left his face.

Saulos looked down, smoothing his palms over the sand-coloured silk of his topcoat. 'Your hunting birds made the journey well,' he said, as if it were his own gift to her. 'I thought perhaps you might like to take them out to hunt?' He moved to one side. Behind him, in the alley's deepest shade, was a small basket of woven grasses with its lid tied down. A dove's yellow eye peered out through the mesh, blinking placidly. An ivory message cylinder was bound to its left leg.

Iksahra said, 'You mean you want me to ride out of the city under pretext of exercising my birds and release a messenger-bird so that it can return here as if it had flown from Rome. In doing so, I am to stop my birds from killing it, and am, instead, to ensure that it reaches its roost in safety.'

Saulos' hands sketched an apology in the air. 'You understand me well. The bird bears the message you took from the air nine days before Pantera arrived. I have cut off the last sentence, but it bears Nero's mark at the head, which is hard to counterfeit. The governor will trust it, and whatever else he sees at the same time.'

He peered at her from under lowered lids, his eyes wide as a girl's and full of flattery. 'It would make our plans more difficult if the bird were to die as it flew to the palace. You have the best eye for a hunting falcon. If anyone can keep it alive, you can.'

'Then I shall do so. Although I assume you wish me to hunt any other doves that are seen to be flying towards the city?'

'That would be most useful. And later, if you are unoccupied on your return, it might be . . . instructive

201

if you were to follow the woman who brought the two hounds from Rome's empress?'

'The Alexandrian witch,' Iksahra said.

'Is she a witch?' Saulos' brows snapped up. 'I didn't know. Certainly, she's Pantera's creature, but the Sisters of Isis never do anything for men without another, better, reason of their own. She's drawing closer to Queen Berenice and the Princess Kleopatra than I had thought she would. Such a thing may be either useful to us or dangerous. We can only turn it to our cause if we know what's happening.'

'Then I will follow the witch if she leaves the palace. I can't promise to follow her within it. I am too obvious.' A single gesture took in her skin, her hair, the great cat that shadowed her heels.

'You could, perhaps, do without . . .' He talked with his hands, this man; they waved now, vaguely, uncertainly, at the cheetah, and then withdrew. He shook his head. 'Of course not. And in any case, you are, as you say, remarkable; someone to draw all eyes. In that case—' His hands swept wide, taking in the whole of Jerusalem. 'I can take care of all that needs to be done in the palace. You will have your own apartments, of course, and permission to make use of whatever help you need. Herod had the baths built to his own design. They are renowned across Judaea. We're not in the desert of your home, but this place has its own attractions. Do what you need to make yourself at home.'

She watched him leave, and wondered that he had never thought to ask her who was with Pantera, whether the mountain-man was with him, or the Hebrews, or why the centurion had dressed as a woman.

Because he had not asked, she had not told him, but kept the information to herself, in case it might be useful later in the plan she was beginning to make, which was significantly different from the one she had nursed on the ship sailing in from her homeland.

JERUSALEM
EARLY SUMMER, AD 66

IN THE REIGN OF THE
EMPEROR NERO

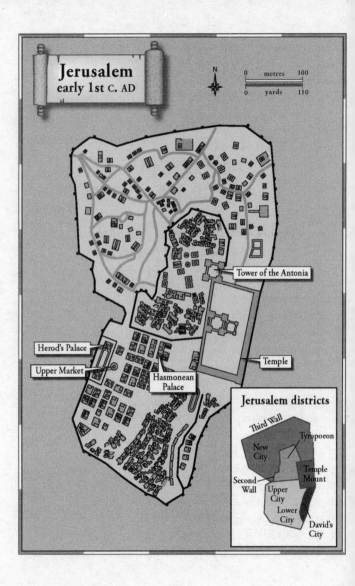

Jerusalem
early 1st C. AD

N

0   metres   100

0   yards   110

Tower of the Antonia

Herod's Palace

Upper Market

Hasmonean
Palace

Temple

Jerusalem districts

Third Wall

New
City

Tyropoeon

Temple
Mount

Second
Wall

Upper
City

Lower
City

David's
City

CHAPTER TWENTY

Jerusalem was old: older than Alexandria, older than Rome, older possibly than Athens or Corinth.

Riding in at dawn with Kleopatra slack as a corpse before her saddle, Hypatia had caught the ripe scent of a dunghill and noted it – Caesarea had no dunghills – but she had not yet been struck by the differences between the city of David, scarred by war, built and rebuilt over and over by the pride and blood of the Hebrew nation, and Caesarea, youthful city of Herod, whose grandson sat on the throne, whose mason marks were still sharp on the buildings, whose carpenters still used the tools their grandfathers had held when they built it.

She saw it now with the morning sun hard on each detail. Where Caesarea was young, bright, shining, with wide streets of white stone, with cleansing sewers the height of a man that carried ordure and storm water equally into the ocean's depths, Jerusalem was . . . wizened, wise, balanced on the shoulders of forested hills, with dry wadis all about and steep valleys cutting through her heart. Her crooked, arthritic streets crabbed along valley sides, up slopes, twisting, knotted; sore, yes, but with her history written in every angled stone, and such a history . . .

Where Herod's city, named for a Roman emperor, claimed to be the Roman capital of Judaea, and boasted a temple to the deified Augustus, Jerusalem, named for peace, was the Hebrew capital, sanctified by Solomon, by David, by the Hasmonean monarchs who had last held her free; here was the Temple sacred to the heart of every God-fearing Semite across the empire.

Here also was Herod's palace, four storeys high, built in the Greek style and set on the westerly wall, where the king might enjoy the fruits of his labours and yet not overlook the Temple and the sacred works performed therein.

Hypatia stood now on its steps, and looked east across the city to the Temple and the fortress of the Antonia. She breathed in the scents of the Upper Market just below her; of saffron and garlic, of olives and oil and wine and fresh meat and dried fish, and began the slow process of knowing in the way she might, in other times and other places, have come to know a lover; slowly, over time, and fully.

In that coming-to-know, she had another task: the finding of herbs for Kleopatra's head. She was not a healer of headaches in fourteen-year-old girls and had said so several times in the sleepless morning that followed their arrival. Nevertheless, she had trained to her vocation in the company of healers whose skills had cheated Anubis of far more certain souls than Kleopatra's and she did have a reasonable grasp of what herbs and poultices might prove effective.

Sadly, Herod's magnificent, many-storeyed palace, while being larger, more stately and possessed of far more intriguing layers and corridors than its counterpart at Caesarea, had proved to be shockingly poorly provisioned. Hypatia had lost half the morning searching through cold stone kitchens, cluttered, dust-rimed storerooms and an unused infirmary on the fourth floor of the western side before one of the permanent understewards who staffed the lower levels thought to tell her that the High Priest preferred prayer to the use of herbs and she was unlikely to find what she sought anywhere in the palace.

Thus it was that in the worst heat of the day, when every other member of the royal household from servants to king had retired to bed to sleep off the effects of the ride, Hypatia petitioned a drowsily amiable Polyphemos for a new, anonymous tunic to replace the green silk of the night's ride and, minimally refreshed, left the palace for the undying heat of a Jerusalem afternoon.

She looked out across the Upper Market, which grew as a riotous, many-coloured fungus below the steps, almost to the palace walls. It sold silk, evidently: colours exploded from every stall; cerise, midnight blue, turquoise, searing yellow, spring-leaf greens. She thought she saw a herb-seller somewhere behind the flagrant colours and set off to find her.

'Wait!'

Kleopatra stood, flushed, on the wide marbled porch. She, too, had abandoned her theatre silks for an undistinguished tunic, belted with rope. She was barefoot and her hair was caught up under a boy's cap. From a distance – even close up – it was impossible to be sure of her gender. She ran down the steps, clumsily.

'Kleopatra, go back. You're not fit—'

'I am your princess. It's not for you to say whether I'm fit or not.'

'Really?' Hypatia turned fully round and arched one brow. 'Tell me, when did you gain rule over Isis? I must have missed it in the night.'

Grown men – governors, princes, kings – had withered before that look and that tone. Kleopatra of Caesarea halted, balanced between one step and the next. She looked mildly discomfited; hot.

'You're barely conscious and the sun's at its height. Even if you don't still have a headache, it would give you a new one,' Hypatia said reasonably. 'I'm going to look for valerian and monkwort or whatever I can find in the market that will take away the pain in your head. I'll bring it back as soon as I can. You'll be far more comfortable if you stay here.'

Kleopatra shook her head. 'You'll need a guide to find what you need.'

'I doubt it. I have travelled in other cities; I can find my way to—'

'Jerusalem is different. The streets wind and bend up and down like a maze. You could be lost here and not even know it.'

'Then I'll find a guide I can trust. Thank you for your advice.'

'I'll be your guide. You can't trust anyone else.' Kleopatra came closer, a step at a time, punctuating each short, sure phrase. 'I was born here. I've spent half my life exploring the Jerusalem markets. And I know where the herbs are sold. There isn't anything you want in the Upper Market, you need to go into the lower city. I can show you the way.'

It was still possible to send her back. The Chosen of Isis had had command of armies in the past, and of their commanders in the nearer times, but . . . but . . . There are days in life where each moment passes and is remarkable in its own right, but not particular. Then, occasionally, there comes a day when a particular moment holds the key to different futures, and the gods hold their breath upon its turning.

Hypatia studied the girl who stood before her, whose dark hair mirrored her own, whose high, smooth brow was exactly that of the queen, whose stormy eyes belonged to nobody but herself. The black dots at their centres were small now, and of equal diameter, which they had not been in the night.

And so a choice was made. 'Come then,' said Hypatia, and the gods breathed again. 'Keep close to me. Your family's not well liked and news of Caesarea's riots will have spread with the dawn. If the merchants come to know who you are . . .'

'They won't.'

'To be certain, we will say that I am a Greek woman seeking herbs for her husband and you are my niece. Speak Greek unless I say otherwise. Lead me to the herb-sellers, but not directly. Saulos will have set someone to follow us.'

CHAPTER TWENTY-ONE

Thus it was that Hypatia discovered the hills, the valleys, the sacred pools, the riotously loud markets, the quiet places of worship, the narrow lanes and dark, hidden alleyways of Jerusalem not in pleasurable solitude but in the company of a fourteen-year-old girl. The early surprise was that she found herself not at all unhappy with the exchange.

Passing swiftly through the Upper Market, Kleopatra showed an easy familiarity with the city's angular back streets and blossomed in the role of leader and guide. She led at a fast pace, taking random turns to left and right, up slopes, down hills, a sharp back-turn here, a long, lazy arc there, keeping always in the shade, so that whoever was behind them – there was someone, Hypatia could feel a presence and thought she knew who it was – could not readily follow.

They passed down steep alleys and along streets where the mud-brick houses reached four storeys or more and leaned over almost to touch one another above the street. They passed through small, open squares where the sun flooded in, and lit the bricks to gold. In Rome or Corinth or Caesarea, they would have housed a fountain in the shape of a dolphin or a satyr. Here they played host to a stall where a woman or a girl or a youth sold melons, or dates, or peaches.

Elsewhere, they skirted round courtyards in which middle-aged men in dark robes sat in a semicircle and debated points of law and religion, and in between all of these, in the markets that clogged every free area, they threaded through throngs of men, women and children, who eyed them with a degree of loathing Hypatia had rarely encountered.

Kleopatra ignored them all; her clear Greek etched out the architecture and the politics, but not the immediate press of people.

'This street leads to the Temple. Only priests live here, but you can tell who's out of favour, for those close with the High Priest have the north side, sheltered from the sun, and those he hates are moved to the south side, and bake through the day.

'Over there is the street of the knife-grinders. The priests buy most of them; they kill a million lambs for the Passover so they need dozens of knives and replace them monthly.

'That's the Hasmonean palace. Would you not want to live there, with all those beautiful round towers, rather than the square edges of my great-grandfather's?

'This is the lower city. The best markets are here. To your left are the silk merchants. Did you ever see colours like that?'

'In Alexandria, possibly.' Hypatia turned slowly, looking about. No one was behind, and had not been for the past three blocks. 'But not so many in one place. Alexandria has one great market spread over acres of land, not dozens of small, close stalls cramped into a hundred different markets as you have here.'

'I've never been anywhere except here and Caesarea.' Kleopatra had lost the imperious stance of the palace steps. Here, her face was wide with a child's curiosity. 'Tell me about Alexandria. No – just tell me about Isis. Tell me where you trained as the Chosen, what you did, all of it.'

'I can't tell you all of it. About some parts, I am sworn to secrecy.'

'Tell me what you can.'

It wasn't possible to give a lifetime's teaching in an afternoon, but it was still a day for god-held moments, not to be ignored. Hypatia let the god guide her voice and Kleopatra, listening, asked intelligent questions that led the conversation along unexpected avenues, so that by the time they reached the far edge of the lower city Hypatia had agreed to take her to the Oracle of the Sibyls in the Temple of Truth when her business in Berenice's court was over.

'That won't be soon, though,' she said. 'I may have to stay for the rest of the year.' And then, 'Someone's behind us again.'

'Let's go.' Kleopatra caught hold of her elbow. 'This way.' They passed left and right and right again down a dark and steeply sloping passage and came out into the heady scents of a small fruit market. A beggar spat at them as they passed. Kleopatra rolled her eyes. 'Ignore him.'

'If I took notice of everyone who spat at us,' Hypatia

said, 'we'd still be in the upper city. These people hate us, and they don't even know who we are.'

'If they knew you were the Chosen of Isis, they'd stone you to death in the street.'

Ducking under a saffron-yellow awning, Kleopatra bought a net full of peaches, and handed the fruit to Hypatia. In her lightly accented Greek, she said, 'For my aunt, a gift from her niece.' And more quietly, 'Are we safe yet?'

'I'm not sure. Keep moving. And keep talking so I can look around. Tell me why so many people wear blue here, when further back, near the valley, it was yellow?'

Kleopatra set off at a brisk pace. 'It's to do with factions and their hatred of each other. Yellow is for the War Party, led by Menachem, grandson of the Galilean who led the zealots out of Galilee and died fighting to rid the land of Romans. His people think they can do all their grandfathers did, but better. They rule the land around the valleys and they're pledged to destroy the king and his family.' She said this as if they were distant people, seen perhaps twice in a lifetime.

She went on. 'Blue is for the Peace Party. Those who wear it are pledged to rid Israel of Rome by peaceful means, by prayer and diplomacy. They're led by Gideon, known as the Peacemaker. The War Party want his death almost as much as they want the king's. Menachem is the only one holding them in check. He says they're not ready to fight yet, that they risk annihilation if they act too soon.'

They passed under an arch. A crowd of blue-clad women stepped aside, hard-eyed. The blue was not all one colour; some were paler than dawn sky, washed almost to white, some were the deep blue of woad traded from the far side of the empire, some were stained with berry juice and almost black. A prick at the back of Hypatia's neck said someone was following still, but she, who could see through the heart of men's souls, could see nothing.

Kleopatra was deep in one-sided conversation, following her own inner line of thought.

'It's all the fault of Ananias, the High Priest. The Hebrew god is jealous of the other gods which means his people have no choice of worship. They pray to be rid of Rome and Rome stays, therefore the Hebrews believe that the invaders have been sent as a punishment for their poor behaviour. If they hate us, it's only because they hate themselves more.'

'Did someone tell you that?' Hypatia asked. They turned right into a narrow alleyway and had to pass a throng this time of men and youths marked by patches of hidden yellow, a fleck on a neckerchief here, a thread through an armband there. They parted to let the women go by.

'Who would tell me?' Kleopatra gave a short laugh. 'Men have been stoned for saying such things.'

'What makes you think you're safe?'

'Nobody listens to a girl. I can say what I like as long as I'm careful who I say it to. Hyrcanus knows what I think, but he won't tell anyone.'

'He might tell Iksahra,' Hypatia said, absently. She scanned the market, trying to see what did not fit.

Kleopatra shrugged. 'Maybe. But she hates everyone also. Was she the one behind us earlier?'

'Possibly. One of them.' Hypatia was turning circles

now, trying to see through the blue-clad crowd that followed as they passed out of the narrow alley and into yet another teeming market square. 'I think there are two, maybe three. The question is whether they are together or apart.'

'Really?' Caught by the new urgency in her tone, Kleopatra said, 'If we run, we could lose them. We could go left here and across the square and—'

'No, wait.' Hypatia caught the girl's arm. 'Not everyone who follows is an enemy.' She turned the girl round so that she could hold her shoulders and look down into her eyes. 'Do you trust me?'

'Yes.'

Hypatia read no hesitation in her face. Truly the afternoon had wrought miracles. 'In that case, will you stay here for a moment? I won't be long.'

The girl's eyes flew wide, but she nodded, and stepped back under an awning and crouched down. Fast as a mouse, and as delicate, she swept up a dozen small stones and balanced them on the back of one hand. Transformed, she was a street child playing knuckle-bones.

Hypatia plunged back through the blue-clad throng towards the alley on the square's western edge, following a flutter of linen that might not have been there, and a half-sensed feeling that was old and yet new.

The alley ran from east to west and was dark along its length. Halfway along, on the north side, was a house of only a single storey nested between two others far taller. A set of stairs sloped down from its flat roof. A bundle of rags twitched in the tight angle of the stairs' foot. As she reached it, the rags unfolded in a single fluid movement. A knife gleamed once in the shadows and was still.

She said, 'Pantera?'

Pantera grew from the dark. There was barely light enough to show the lines of exhaustion on his face, but Hypatia was trained to see beyond the outer skin, and what she saw was the man she had met in Alexandria, a man whose will shone like polished iron, and was as hard. He had lost that polish on the day after Rome's fire. It was back now, just as bright and sharp and hard as when she had first met him.

He was studying her with a disconcerting frankness, one brow raised. 'Are you all right?' he asked.

'I am. You, on the other hand, look exhausted. Have you slept at all since you left Caesarea?'

'No.' His gaze still fed on her face. 'Am I alone in that?'

She gave a wry smile. 'Not at all. But I'm on my way back to the palace where I have a safe bed, while you will need to find somewhere—'

'We have somewhere. Yusaf has a house here. He is giving us refuge.'

'Yusaf ben Matthias? The counsellor who petitioned the king?' A memory flashed between them of absurdly weighty silk, of a weightier beard and eyes sunk so deep they were hard to read. 'The petitioner whose failure tipped Caesarea into riots last night?'

'He's safe company for now.' Pantera looked both ways down the alley's length. 'We don't have much time,' he said. 'Iksahra is following you. We can't be seen together.'

'I thought we'd lost her in the markets round the Hasmonean palace,' Hypatia said.

218

'You did. But she'll find you again soon enough: she knows you're looking for herbs for the princess. There aren't many places to look.'

'So tell me what I need to know.'

He gave his report with military precision, listing points on his fingers. 'Saulos knows that you and I are linked. He tried to burn Mergus last night and his man named you in the list of those whom he intended to destroy. I will do what I can to prevent it, but his resources are many. We think he has blocked the message-birds so we can't send or receive messages from Rome. I sent one to Jerusalem from Caesarea, but it hasn't arrived. The dovecote is at Yusaf's house; he knows all that comes and goes.'

'Iksahra will have caught the message-bird,' Hypatia said. 'She hunts them with her falcons. At Caesarea, the birds fly along the water's edge, where the air lifts over the waves. They are barely sport.'

'Does she take the ones coming in or just the ones leaving?'

'Both, I think.'

'Which means they will have read the messages we sent. Everything that went to the Poet in Rome, and all the orders she sent back.' Pantera took in a long breath and let it out slowly through his teeth.

He had about him the sense of a drawn bow, tense, but alive, waiting for the loose; of a falcon at the moment before the stoop; of a man, hunting, and near his quarry.

She said. 'Is Mergus . . . ?'

'Sore, but whole. He knows he's a target now. As are you.'

'You warned us of that before we left Rome,' Hypatia said.

'I said I would not let it happen.'

'But if he knows you at all, Saulos will know the depth of your care for us and he will use that as his weapon against you. There may come a time when you have to choose between saving a people or your friends. If it comes to that, remember that death is a release; the dead do not grieve their loss of life, only the living.'

Pantera closed his eyes. Across his face, briefly, passed the stain of an old grief; of a woman slain, and a daughter dead in his arms.

Hypatia said, 'We should part now, before Iksahra finds us.'

'We should.' Stooping, Pantera pressed a dry, unexpected kiss to her cheek. 'Stay safe,' he said. 'Whatever happens.'

And he was gone, leaving her in empty silence.

At the alley's opposite end, Pantera stopped and drew a strip of torn blue linen from his tunic, and wound it round his arm. Blue for the Peace Party which today, by some alchemy he wished never to learn, had control of this side of the lower city. Jerusalem wasn't like Caesarea, there were no riots yet, but the pressure of inaction was worse; here, gangs roamed the streets with no greater purpose than that they must keep the other faction away.

Mergus came up softly behind him. He, too, had a blue flash wrapped about his wrist. He gave a brief nod, barely there, and they moved out into the street together, to merge with a pack of Peace Party youths.

'How many?' Pantera asked.

'Three,' Mergus said. 'The Berber woman followed Hypatia and two Iberians followed her.'

'Good. We go this way . . .' Pantera turned sharply left down a smaller alley, leaving the youths behind. 'When did Iksahra catch sight of Hypatia?'

'Not until she went into the herb market. She'll follow her back to the palace and the Iberians will follow her. Menachem's trackers are following the Iberians and Estaph is following them; he won't lose them, even if the trackers do.'

Menachem's 'trackers' were beardless youths – boys, really, who refused to wear the Peace Party's blue markers, even here, in the wrong quarter of the city where to be caught was to die.

'Menachem's followers are well disciplined, at least,' Pantera said. 'His grandfather would be proud of him.'

Mergus said, 'His grandfather, from what I've heard, came near to driving Rome out of Judaea. Menachem isn't close to completing the job. Do you trust him yet?'

'No, but I still have no reason to distrust him. If anyone is going to sell us to Saulos, it won't be Menachem; he is a man driven by ideals, not by money.'

'Yusaf is driven by money.'

'Yes, but Yusaf has been loyal to Seneca for decades and seems as loyal to his memory as he was to him in life. We have to trust him, too, as far as we may without being overtly stupid about it.' They came to a junction where the narrow alley divided into two smaller ones that parted at right angles. Pantera closed his eyes and drew for himself the streets he remembered from his childhood; nothing here had changed in all that time, except that paint was older, and the colours of the parties were new. Sure now of his bearings, he turned right, away from the palace, deeper into the lower city.

'Where are we going?' Mergus asked.

'To see if we can persuade Gideon ben Hiliel, leader of the Peace Party, to meet Menachem. Don't look at me like that; nothing is impossible. Yusaf may look like a merchant, but he trained with their priests in all aspects of their law and he's one of the few men respected by both of Jerusalem's factions. He thinks there's a chance of bringing Menachem and Gideon together under one roof. He's offered his house as the meeting place.'

'And if they both come,' Mergus asked, 'what then?'

'Then we'll see if we can persuade them to stop trying to kill each other and instead, for the sake of Jerusalem, join together in common cause against Saulos. Or at the very least not let him provoke them into a civil war designed to destroy their nation.'

CHAPTER TWENTY-TWO

'Do you love him?' Kleopatra asked, from the pool's far side.

The palace was, to all intents and purposes, asleep. In the bathing pools on the lowest floor, slaves pattered on soft feet, bringing towels and bowls, pouring flavoured salts into the water. Hypatia lay in a vault of rose-scented steam, turning slowly pink under the lupine eyes of a mosaic left by Herod the Great, who counted Romulus and Remus amongst his ancestors. The wolf-mother had milk enough for a nation. Her twin boys hung back, afraid of her teeth.

Hypatia lowered her gaze and stared across the pool. 'Do I love whom?'

Kleopatra lay with her elbows on blue-veined marble on the pool's far side. Her black hair was plastered around her face. Her eyes reflected the colour of the water; green, tinged in places with blue. She said, 'The man you met in the alley this afternoon. The one with the scar over his right eye. Do you love him?'

The man Kleopatra was not supposed to have seen.

Hypatia opened her mouth to answer, considered, and changed what she had been about to say. 'I love him as if he were a brother,' she said. 'Not in any other way.'

'Does he love you?'

'I hardly think so.' Hypatia ducked her face under the surface and came up, streaming water. Her ears popped. She shook her head and felt her hair make wet ropes about her shoulders. 'He loves an Alexandrian healer called Hannah. She conceived his child on the night Rome burned. He put her on a ship the next day, bound for Mona, the dreamers' island that lies to the west of Britain. He grieves for her still. We all do.'

'You knew her, too?'

'I've known her since I was your age.'

'I'm sorry.'

'So am I.'

A brittle silence fell, in which Hypatia stared fixedly at the shimmering ripples on the water where sunlight from the high windows met its own reflection and cast the surface gold.

It was a technique designed to keep her mind from straying. She had learned it when she was fourteen years old, sitting in front of a branching candlestick in the Temple of Isis, counting the wavering lights. It worked after a fashion; in nine breaths or ten, she was able to give most of her attention to the changing textures of the water, and no more than usual to the memory of the woman who had gone to safety on Mona.

Across the pool, Kleopatra let go an unsteady breath.

Hypatia said, 'What?' It came out more sharply than she had intended.

'This is my dream.'

'Lying in a pool of hot water with a woman who still grieves for her past is your dream?' That, too, was more cutting than Hypatia had meant it. She sluiced water on her face; found it too hot, suddenly, cloying.

Looking through the steam, she found that Kleopatra was biting her lip, staring down at the water. She may have been weeping.

Small-voiced, the girl said, 'No. The dream is being with you . . . like this.'

'Like what?'

'Angry. You're angry with me and I haven't done anything. I just asked a question. And that man is here; the one you think doesn't love you. The shadow who draws danger to him. He's what starts it all.'

The shadow who draws danger to him. Hypatia's throat closed and it had nothing to do with the steam or the flavour of roses. A bubble of silence settled on her, so that the only sound was the rush of her own pulse in her ears and the drift of her own voice, decades before, sitting in the half-dark of a temple before a woman who terrified her, saying, *It all starts with the shadow that sings to danger. He's the beginning.*

She had forgotten the terror of that; the first dream, first speaking of it, the sandalwood and frankincense, the sticks of dried thyme, smouldering. Lying amidst other scents, a lifetime's dreams came into sharp, devastating focus.

Hypatia forged her way across the sluggish water. She pushed past the floating sponge-bowls, the lilies on leaves, the pumice stones, carved to fit a hand. She came to stand in front of Kleopatra, close enough to smell the

225

salt of her tears over the rosewater and rosemary, to see the red rims of her eyes through the steam.

Hypatia pushed aside her own terrors. Carefully now, she said, 'Is this the dream you told me about? The one that frightens you?'

'Yes.'

'In the dream, are you afraid because I'm angry?'

'Yes . . . No. Not only that. People are angry with me all the time, it's not that. It's that I don't want you to die. You, or Pantera, or me, or my aunt, or the other men whose faces I haven't seen yet.'

Kleopatra was hugging her knees to her flat chest, breathing in short, sharp jerks. Hypatia took her hand and rubbed the palm with her thumb, absently. 'Do I die in the dream?' she asked. 'Does Pantera?'

'I don't know. It changes. Each time it changes . . .' Kleopatra stared at the water as if it might part and reveal the past, or the future. 'I'm so frightened when I wake up that I never remember exactly what's happened; the order of it, or who died, or where, or how. I just lie in bed trying not to scream. But Pantera – is that his name? The Leopard – it suits him. He's always there, and then Saulos comes and Iksahra and you and there's gold and blood and pain and death . . . so much death; sometimes you die, sometimes he does, sometimes me and Aunt Berenice, and other men I don't know yet, and the worst thing is, I don't know any of it for certain; it's hazy and confused and I don't want it to be real.

'But this, here, now . . . this is real and it's always the start. The smell's the same and you're . . .' Kleopatra's eyes were wide, full of tangled passions. 'You're different from anyone else here. When everyone else is hazy, I

226

always know who you are, where you are. I saw you when you first came into the palace, to Aunt Berenice. I knew then that it was you.' She was looking down into the water, at the place where her fingers were knotted together. She ran out of words, or did not want to remember more of that first meeting at the palace.

In the silence, Hypatia had time to speak. 'Gold and blood?' She fought to keep her voice level. 'You said, "gold and blood". Are both in your dream?'

'Yes. The blood comes from a hanged man. Pantera, I think, but the gold comes first; lots of it, like the eight talents Yusaf ben Matthias gave to the king last night, only more of it. And then later there are crowds, screaming, and then cold and black, the opposite of the gold, but still full of death.' Kleopatra's eyes grew slowly wide. 'Can you see my dream?'

'I have . . . had one like it.' Hypatia let go of the girl's hand and edged away to where the beating of her heart might not cause waves in the water. 'If any more of the dream comes back to you, will you tell me?'

Kleopatra nodded. 'I will.'

Hypatia stepped up out of the pool, and sat on the side, rubbing herself dry. Presently, Kleopatra leaned across to Hypatia and touched her arm. 'If Saulos is in both of our dreams, shouldn't we try to find out what he's doing?'

'Saulos is too dangerous for the likes of you and me to spy on.'

'Even if I know of a way we can do it without being seen?'

'Kleopatra . . .' Hypatia turned to her. 'Is spying on Saulos part of your dream?'

'No, but he's just ordered Governor Florus to admit him to his suite. The slaves were saying so to each other, but they were speaking Syrian and it's taken me till now to work it out. Florus is asleep. They've sent a man to wake him and help him dress. Saulos won't be there yet so we have time to get ready.'

Hypatia lifted the girl's hands in her own. Her fingers were in the half stage, midway between childhood chubbiness and the lean strength of a woman. Their ends were wrinkled with water and steam. She turned one over. Two lines crossed on the palm, below the fourth finger.

She studied it a moment, closed the fingers over on themselves, hiding the futures. 'Listen to me now, because this matters. If Saulos caught you spying on him, he would kill you. Not openly, but you would have the kind of accident you nearly had in the desert last night, only that it would be you who died, not only your horse.'

'I know.' Kleopatra's hair hung down in thick, damp ropes. Her face was scarlet with heat, and quite serious. 'I've watched Saulos since he came here, two months before you; I know the risks. But I've also lived half my life in this palace. My great-grandfather built it, and he had tunnels put in the spaces between the walls and listening passages made so that his agents could listen to the conversations in every room. I know them all. He won't know we're there, I swear it.'

'Show me the tunnel. I'll go alone.'

'No.' Kleopatra reached for another towel from the pile the slaves had left. 'I'll show you where the listening place is,' she said. 'It's safe. You'll see when we get there.'

CHAPTER TWENTY-THREE

Gessius Florus, governor of the entire Roman province of Judaea, had dressed hurriedly and badly. His breath, he knew, smelled of sleep and the silvered mirror in his suite showed that his hair had been combed by a madman with a horse brush.

On top of these things, or because of them, he was in a foul temper, but too afraid to show it openly, which left him irritable and sweating and added a twitch under his left eye that had only afflicted him twice before. His father had beaten him the first time it appeared. The second time, Nero had given him governorship of his most eastern province, which post ought to have ensured his wealth for life. It ought not to have necessitated a desperate night ride across a haunted desert in the company of a king too weak to control his own counsellors.

Florus thought of saying these things aloud. The words crowded on the brink of his tongue, jamming up against his teeth, so that when the king's latest favourite flung open the door to the governor's private chambers

– unannounced, no slave or steward in attendance – no words came out; he simply stood there, gaping, as this man, this nobody, this silk-clad, sleek, smooth, invisible, too-visible intruder stood on the threshold.

He was a spy; Florus was not an especially clever man, he knew that, but he was also not as stupid as his reputation claimed. So he had realized early that this man who could melt into a crowd and disappear faster than ice on a hot day was not all that he seemed.

Soon, it had become apparent that he was a favourite not only of the king, but of the Emperor Nero. In Florus' experience, Nero had always favoured unusual men and Saulos was certainly that.

Florus had studied him harder after that; had found him fluent, voluble; he used his hands a lot when he spoke. He was excessively neat, always dabbed his lips with a clean patch of linen after eating, but physically he was still a nobody, of indeterminate height with indeterminately brown eyes that sometimes might seem to lighten to grey, with mid-brown hair cut to mid-length which curled, but not too tightly. He was terrifyingly indistinct. And he was here, in Florus' room. And he was dangerous.

'My dear Florus!' Saulos offered a deep bow. Florus was compelled to return it, at least in abbreviated form, and when he rose again he found that Saulos had dismissed the half-dozen slaves that had been attending to Florus.

Even as he turned, the last remaining pair were backing out of the room, covering their faces with their hands to hide relief. Saulos held his smile fixed until they had gone, and then turned and thrust a fragment of something pale into Florus' hands. He thought it might be a cloth to wipe his lips, then realized there was writing on it, and the emperor's personal mark, and that Saulos was speaking.

'This is the original message. It's in code, as you can see. This' – another fragment was pressed into his hands, this one neater, less fragile – 'is the translation. I can show you how the one becomes the other if you wish?'

'No, just let me read it.'

Since childhood, Florus had read with difficulty, moving his lips as if speaking the words aloud. Today, he moved them less than he had ever done before. His tutors would have turned cartwheels of delight. The thought calmed him.

From the Emperor Nero Claudius Caesar Augustus Germanicus to the Leopard, greetings and our good will on your endeavour. We learn that you are in Caesarea safely, and that you will shortly be in a position to uproot the enemy of our peace. Your reward is our blessing and our lifelong care. Daily, we await further news.

Florus lowered the paper. 'Nero wasted a message-bird for this? It says nothing.'

Saulos smiled as if Florus were his student, and had successfully parsed some difficult point of grammar, or understood the finer points of geometry. He said, 'My lord proves yet again why his appointment here was so well deserved. This was a test to see that the birds were reaching me untampered. We arranged the text before I left. Anyone trying to counterfeit a message would not say so little.'

'They surely would not. When did you get this?'

'It was waiting for me here in Jerusalem. Along with this . . .'

Saulos opened his hand to show another translated message. With dread pooling in his gut, Florus smoothed it open and read again.

From the Emperor Nero Claudius Caesar Augustus Germanicus to Gessius Florus, governor of all Judaea, greetings. You are ordered to aid us in our repair of Rome after the devastations of fire. Our treasury is sorely pressed. We require, therefore, that you relieve the Temple in Jerusalem of its funds, of which our need is the greater. Do this with all speed, by our order.

The paper fell from Florus' fingers, a fluttering moth, ignored by them both.

'We are to take the gold from the Hebrew temple?' Florus asked. 'All of it? This can't be true.'

'Not all of it. Not the sacred treasure, the many-branching candlestick, the table, the trumpets, the altar. Those can be left. If we take only the coins now, that should be enough. I am told there could be as much as fifteen talents in gold.'

'*Fifteen talents*? Why do they keep so much?'

Saulos' vocal hands described a small, pious movement in the air. 'Their god requires gold for his works, I imagine. But if Nero needs it to rebuild Rome . . . We would have to say his need *is* the greater.'

The sinking sensation in Florus' lower abdomen became fluid and turbulent until he thought he might disgrace himself there, in front of this fastidious, smiling demon. He folded his arms over the small mound of his belly. Somewhere high in the walls, a rat twitched;

even the vermin, it seemed, were appalled at what he had said.

He began to pace to keep his bowels closed, and, pacing, he spoke as he thought. 'Nero wishes peace in Judaea. He told me so at every meeting before we set sail and he has sent message-birds to me three times already this year, saying exactly the same. *After the bloodbath of Britannia, and after the fire, we cannot afford another war.* Those were his words exactly; I have the messages yet if you wish to peruse them. And he is right; however poor the treasury, however stripped of funds, if the emperor orders us now to rob the Hebrew temple of its gold, the War Party will have their holy war and not a man in Jerusalem will stand against them. You must understand this. If we try to do as this asks, there will be war – and we may fail. If the High Priest stands against us, if he sets his holy men at the temple gates to block them . . .' Florus closed his eyes against the image of Roman legionaries hacking their way through a wall of unarmed priests to gain access to the Temple's wealth. 'We can't do it,' he said, with finality.

'Ananias won't stand against you,' Saulos said, as if that were consolation. 'You forget that Rome has the power to command him, not the Hebrews or their god. He takes his orders from you and you take them from Nero. That's why he's High Priest. If he disobeys, then we find another to take his place who understands where true power lies.'

Florus found that his fingernails were digging into his palms. He forced open his hands. 'Everyone knows that true power lies with the man who commands the largest army. Do you know how big the Jerusalem garrison is –

or should I say how small? We have half a legion, all of them infantry.'

'We have half a legion of solid Roman soldiers, not the Syrian trash who kept the peace in Caesarea. They are famed throughout the empire.'

'Fame does not give strength of numbers. We have three thousand men, of whom five hundred are at Masada. In Jerusalem there are, at any given time, one hundred thousand Hebrews. If Menachem can rouse them all, if he can arm them against us—'

'He can't arm them all, he can't arm even a hundred of them; it's why he hasn't attacked you yet. He has men whose only arms are a food knife and a big stick and he knows it's not enough.'

'Do you say so?' Florus swept a hand through his hair. Discretion abandoned him. 'You are a spy, your sources are impeccable of course, I bow to your wisdom, but if Menachem decides that a knife and a cudgel are sufficient, have you thought what will ensue? We will be outnumbered by fifty to one. I don't care how famed your garrison is, they will lose, and we will die – and Rome will have lost all of Judaea.'

He turned on his heel. The room was placid, painted in pastel yellows, with flag irises in an urn faintly scenting the air. He wished he were back in Rome. Or Corinth. He had liked Corinth. Nobody had tried to kill him there.

At the turn's completion, he came to a decision. 'Get me a scribe. We will send a message to Rome. It may be that this was written wrongly, that a fault was introduced when the code was transcribed. We will ascertain—'

'You will do as you are ordered, and you will do it now.' Saulos was standing some distance away, fingering a fruit knife that looked longer than anything required to cut pomegranates. His voice was distantly cold. 'I carry Nero's seal. I am his representative in the east. You have no authority except what I lease to you and that lease is running out. I could appoint Agrippa as governor in your stead.'

'Agrippa? Ha!' Florus' laugh was pitched higher than he intended. The skin under his left eye jumped. 'Are you completely mad? He wouldn't stand against—' He stopped, like a man who has taken a wound, and only now knows himself dying. 'He is yours, heart and soul and body. He will do as you say.'

Saulos smiled.

Florus looked away. 'Have you planned a way to do this that will not kill us all? Or will it kill everyone except you?'

'It will kill no one who matters. It will achieve the aims of the emperor, and there will be peace. The High Priest will play his part, you will play yours and the Hebrews will mutter and throw stones, but they will not dare revolt. They may be a hundred thousand, but they are an unarmed, disorganized rabble gathering in derelict houses and we will make sure that they remain that way.'

Florus said, 'Someone, somewhere, will throw a stone at a legionary. Blood will be spilled.'

'Of course. And so someone, somewhere, will be crucified. You will see to it, I'm sure. It won't be the first or the last, and it will cool their ardour for long enough. Now, we must discuss—' Distantly, a bell rang, silver-pure. Saulos snapped his fingers in irritation. 'We have exceeded our time. It would have been good had you been able to rise earlier from your slumbers. As it is, I must leave.'

Florus let his gaze be caught and held. He sustained the contact longer than he thought humanly possible and in that time he decided that Saulos was, indeed, a ghûl, one of the undead, sent to walk amongst the living. What else had eyes so utterly devoid of feeling?

Saulos recovered first, laughing softly. 'I will leave now,' he said. 'We shall take a day to prepare. Tomorrow, we shall mount the steps to the Temple. Be ready then. And be more . . . clean.'

'Gold! Gold and blood! I don't believe it. I don't want to believe it.'

Kleopatra knelt on the floor of a small, disused attic room and stared down at fingers black with dust and grime. She wanted to sneeze and did not dare for fear they would be heard; two walls and a ceiling grille separated them from Florus, who stood in his chamber where Saulos had left him. She wanted to weep, but the world had become too difficult for that.

She raised her head and peered at Hypatia. The Chosen of Isis was staring at the wall, at the closed door that hid the long, hot listening tunnel that led to the governor's room. Kleopatra said, 'I moved when the governor read out his orders. I'm so sorry. If they find us, it's all my fault.'

'Nothing's your fault.' Hypatia roused herself. 'They thought it was rats. They're too busy planning how to take the temple gold.'

'Why, though? Why would Nero want to rob the Temple? Does he not understand that the gold is given to the god?'

Hypatia shook her head. 'Nero didn't send that order. The emperor is strange and wild and uncontrolled, but he isn't mad.'

'So the message is a forgery?'

'It has to be. If Saulos wants to destroy Jerusalem – which he does – he will need to enlist the power of the legions to do it. To get them to invade, he needs a revolt, and there's no better way to rouse a revolution than to rob the Hebrew god of its gold.'

Hypatia stood with her fingers pressed to her temples. She was filthy. Dust smeared across her face where she had pushed her fine black hair out of her eyes. The nails on her left hand were broken where she had levered open the tiny trapdoor set in the tiles high in the wall. Her tunic was black where she had crawled along the tunnel and lain in the baking heat, high up, right under the roof, had lain listening to the planning of an abomination that was more than simply theft.

Kleopatra said, 'If Saulos takes the temple gold, then the dream is happening, isn't it? The dream of blood and gold and death.' Her voice was too high, too querulous. She did not know how to change it.

'It is happening. Our question now is which of the several possible outcomes will take place.' Hypatia looked older, wiser, more distant; almost returned to the coldness of that first meeting when Kleopatra had stuck out her tongue, just to see if she could break the woman's brittle shell. She regretted that, now.

She said, 'Not all of the endings were bad ones. Can we make one happen and others not?'

'We can try. Why else are we sent the dream, if not to know what is possible?' Hypatia looked down at her hands, at the broken fingernails. 'I need to tell Pantera what we've heard. But first . . .' She turned, surveying the room. 'We need to sweep the dust so that nobody knows we've been here. Help me.'

In a cupboard at the room's far side they found brooms and cloths and used them. Where the track to the hidden door was too obvious, they moved a crate to cover it.

When they were done, Kleopatra dusted her hands, looking down at her ruined tunic.

'You look as if you've been breaking horses in a dust yard,' Hypatia said. 'You should bathe again and then change your clothes.'

Kleopatra raised a brow. 'Not just me.'

'But you can go to the baths and say that you were in the market, whereas I must to go out into the city.'

'To tell Pantera that the dream has started?'

'Yes.'

'Can he stop this?'

'If anyone can. But only if he lives long enough to escape the gold and blood in the dream. If I were to leave the palace by the slaves' door, can you lie for me and say you don't know where I am, that you haven't seen me since we returned from the market?'

Kleopatra grinned. 'You have no idea how well I can lie.'

CHAPTER TWENTY-FOUR

Yusaf ben Matthias' house in Jerusalem's lower city was mirror to the man; richly, even sumptuously decorated, but never brash, it screamed restraint, and whispered of immense wealth, and wisdom.

Pantera, Mergus and Estaph dined under many-branching candlesticks, lying in the Greek style on couches of plain oak and carob wood; no jewelled inlays here, but a quality of workmanship that left Pantera stroking the wood, feeling underneath for the joints, just to know what they were like and how they were done.

Woven mats on the walls kept out the heat and on them were designs that would have put the temples of the empire to shame; intricate sworls and leaf-like spears in arrays of subtle hues: dusky lavender, pale sky-blue, a hint here of yellow, there of a red deeper than wine.

Mannerly servants brought fish and then fowl: a wild goose, stuffed with apricots. After it was lamb, roasted in garlic with a sauce of capons and vinegar. Dates followed and fresh figs, and pomegranates, with ivory picks to lift the seeds. Three wines were served, and when Pantera demurred, well-water came, cold as winter, so that beads of condensation furred the outside of the perfectly plain, perfectly proportioned silver beaker.

And through all of it, they talked; of trade, of travel routes, of cargoes, of camels – a lot about camels, the memories of a month spent travelling overland were still ripe – and of taxes.

They spoke of history: of the Persian kings Cyrus, Darius, Artaxerxes; of Alexander, who followed them; of Mithridates and Tigranus and the satraps who followed the King of Kings in Parthia and together made an empire to rival Rome's. They spoke of trouble in Alexandria, where the Hebrews were forbidden to take up public service, and of that which might soon follow in Corinth. They spoke of the Hebrew prophecies, of her king who would come and rule the earth in peace; and they spoke of faith and the exigencies of faithful service. They spoke not at all of the riot in Caesarea, or of the opposing factions in Jerusalem, ripe with mutual loathing.

Presently, a steward brought wide, soapstone lamps swimming with good oil that filled the wall niches and the host moved his guests from the dining benches through to a courtyard open to the sky, planted on all sides. The scent of lilies sweetened the night sky. Fish moved lazily in a central pond.

'This is very Greek in its style,' Pantera said.

Yusaf gave a wide, open smile that made the most of his long face. He wore a cap to cover his baldness and, because it was of velvet that matched his coat, it did not seem untoward, or pretentious or unworldly.

He said, 'I find it sets my foreign visitors at ease. And there is, perhaps, less chance of our being overheard as we speak. In Jerusalem, you understand, one is never certain . . .'

'Not only Jerusalem,' Pantera said.

They stood around the pool, three men looking in at the silvery fish, and soon there came a knock at the door in a particular rhythm. The steward opened it to a round-faced man whom Pantera did not recognize.

Menachem arrived before the door shut, but from the other direction, so that he and the other man met on the threshold. There was a moment's silent conflict before Menachem took a half-pace back and let the stranger enter ahead of him.

He walked with purpose, this newcomer, but not arrogance. He was older than either Menachem or Yusaf and stockier than both. His mild gaze hid an unmild mind. Pantera caught his eye and was held a moment and let go. He thought he had been recognized.

At a nod from Yusaf, the steward vanished into the interior, from where the scent of cooking fires still permeated. Yusaf himself served the wine and stood on the threshold of the courtyard garden.

'Gideon ben Hiliel, allow me to introduce Sebastos Pantera, Appius Mergus and Estaph of Parthia, all three in the service of their emperor.' Not *our* emperor. 'Gentlemen, for the avoidance of doubt, Gideon leads the Peace Party in Jerusalem; Menachem ben Yehuda ben Yehuda, grandson to the Galilean, who so discomfited Rome, leads its opposite, the War Party.' Yusaf gave to each leader a small, formal nod of his head. 'You are both welcome under my roof. Here no man has

241

ascendancy; here, our god is paramount. You have both come knowing that, and prepared to talk. Menachem, your cousin Eleazir is not with you. Did he not receive my message?'

'He received it. He did not agree with its contents.' Menachem had found the second of two places in the courtyard where the lamplight did not reach. Pantera was already standing in the first.

To Pantera, as if he were the one who had asked, Menachem said, 'My cousin Eleazir is a grandson of the Galilean just as I am. He believes war with Rome is inevitable, and that it should begin sooner rather than later. He will not attend any meeting with those who argue for peace.'

Pantera said, 'If you die, will he become leader of the War Party?'

'He will. I do not, of course, intend to die, but if I do there will be war with Rome within days, whether the men are armed and ready or not.'

'Then they will all die,' Gideon said, flatly. 'And bring catastrophe on our heads.'

'Of course. Which is why we shall be brief. I would not leave Eleazir long alone.' Menachem lifted his deep-set eyes to his left. 'If ben Hiliel would speak, I will hear him.'

Gideon ben Hiliel spoke with the gravelled voice of the learned, so that the others fell naturally still, the better to listen.

'We are here at the behest of Pantera, the emperor's man.' He gave a measure to the name that sounded at once honourable and faintly distasteful. 'He asserts, I believe, new reasons why conflict with Rome is un-

242

thinkable at the present moment. Before we go further, I would hear him speak.'

They waited. At Yusaf's nod, Pantera stepped out of his shadow into the half-moon of lamplight that held the south edge of the garden pool. Water lilies kissed the edge by his feet.

'You have no weapons,' he said. 'You have men, but they have sticks and stones and knives and nothing more. Menachem's grandfather, the Galilean, began his campaign by assaulting the armoury at Sepphoris, and was able to arm his zealots for a generation, while—'

'While', said Gideon, 'the women and children of Sepphoris were sold into slavery and the men and boys were crucified. Ten thousand died so that the Galilean could wage his war. We forget that at our peril.' His gaze was on Menachem. The words had the worn feel of an argument chewed over so long that neither side truly hears it.

Menachem gave a small shrug. 'We know the capacity of Rome for vengeance,' he said. 'We do not forget. You know our state.' He tipped his head towards Pantera. 'So now we know your spies are good, and you have the wisdom to understand what they tell you. What can you tell us that is new?'

'A man has come. His name is Saulos and he holds in his hands both the soul of King Agrippa and the courage of Governor Florus. He, too, is a spy. He, too, knows your state: everyone does from the imperial palace to the far borders of Damascus. The difference is that Saulos wishes the destruction of Jerusalem. He will do whatever he can to achieve it and the best way by far would be to foment a revolt in which untrained men armed only with sticks and stones hurl themselves on trained and armoured legionaries. You might win a battle. You probably would. You could not win a war.'

'This is true,' said Gideon. 'Every Sabbath, I preach this. I teach what the scriptures say, that—'

'We know it without hearing you preach.' To Pantera, Menachem said, 'This spy, is he sent by Nero?'

'No, although he will pretend that he is.'

'What will he do to provoke us?'

'That I don't know, only that it is his stated intent and that he has already—' A knock came at the door, a new rhythm; they had thought themselves secret. Menachem spun, his knife out. Pantera leapt the pond; they reached the door together.

Pantera flung it open, stepping back, wide, his knife ready . . . and then not ready.

On the far side stood Hypatia, simple in a slave's garb. 'You said you would be at Yusaf's house.' Her startling gaze shifted to Menachem. She held up her hands, palms out. 'I bring words, not weapons and certainly not guards. May I come in?'

At Menachem's half-nod, they stepped back, together. Pantera sketched a bow. 'Gentlemen, allow me to introduce you to Hypatia of Alexandria, Chosen of Isis. She is a guest under his majesty's roof. She comes, I think, with news of our enemy, Saulos.'

'I do.' She was tired, she was dirty, she smelled of rosewater and dust and the smoke of the evening cooking fires, but she was still Hypatia; beautiful, brittle, bright-spun, terrifying in her self-assurance, in the unhidden shine of her intellect. As she stepped fully into the room, it was impossible for any man to look elsewhere.

Wordless, Yusaf brought her a beaker and poured for her. She came to stand under the largest of the lamps and tilted the beaker a little, until the flickering lights of the candlestick met and merged on the wine's velvet surface.

Pantera joined her in the light. 'What is it that Saulos plans?'

'He has a message he claims came from Nero that orders Florus to seize the temple gold: fifteen talents of wealth which is kept in gold bullion in the temple precinct. They are to ship it to Rome to pay for the rebuilding works after the fire.'

Silence met that, broken, at length, by Mergus, who had remained on guard by the door. 'No one will believe that Nero would command such a thing.'

'Of course they will.' Menachem was caustic. 'We are two months' journey from Rome. All anyone here knows of Nero is that he kicked his wife to death and has taken a gelded boy to bed in her place. They'll believe anything they're told unless someone with credibility can name it a lie.'

'In which case,' said Gideon, 'there will be riots the like of which Jerusalem has never seen. I can preach calm and restraint against some things, but against a defilement of the Temple . . .' He ran out of words. His eyes closed against the horror of it.

Hypatia said, 'Florus has been told to deal with any insurrection using all necessary force. According to Saulos, the Hebrews are used to crucifixion.'

'Saulos actually said that?' Gideon was solid now,

a thick-set trunk in the midst of the courtyard. It was easier than it had been to imagine him preaching restraint to the fiery people of Jerusalem. 'When does he plan this defilement?'

'Tomorrow.'

They fell silent, each man staring at the others, waiting.

'It would seem,' said Yusaf, at last, 'that the only escape from calamity is for someone to denounce Saulos as the traitor he is. Someone with credible proof that he is lying. Someone, perhaps, who bears the emperor's ring.' He was looking at Pantera.

'Does he?' asked Menachem. 'Do you?'

'Yes,' said Pantera.

'No!' Mergus exploded forward. 'Saulos knows him. Sebastos, you can't do this. He'll have you crucified before you open your mouth.'

'He can't do that if I've gone to him as the emperor's emissary,' Pantera said. 'It's not legal to crucify a Roman citizen.' He turned to Hypatia. 'Is Yusaf right?'

Hypatia had been watching the pond; now she lifted her head. The dark light in her eyes was deep as the Nile, wide as the night sky. The last time Pantera had seen her like that, she was the Oracle in the Temple of Truth, and barely human.

'He might be,' she said. 'But you risk death if you do as he says.'

Pantera shivered. Everyone saw it. 'Have you seen this?'

'I have dreamed it. As has Kleopatra. This is the start of an unknown time. Our dreams have many different endings, but in very few of them are you entirely safe.'

'Is anyone safe?'

'Not if you fail, no.'

She was holding something back, he could feel it sliding through the air between them. He caught her arm. 'Tell me what you know.'

'There's nothing else I can say. Nothing is clear, except that there are times when the world turns on a single act and this is one of them. If you succeed, if you expose Saulos as a traitor, and have him arrested, it is possible we might live. If you fail, then those of us with you will die. Everyone in this room and most of those in the city outside will die with us. There are no half-measures.'

'And Jerusalem?' Gideon asked, soft-voiced. 'If we are all dead, where stands Jerusalem?'

Hypatia made a short, hard gesture. 'Jerusalem will be lost, no two stones left one atop the other. It will cease to exist and Saulos will rebuild it in his own image.' She turned her gaze on Pantera. 'When you were in Alexandria, what did the Oracle tell you to do?'

'You don't know?'

'Truly, I don't. It speaks through me, not to me. But what was said then matters now.'

Pantera closed his eyes, remembering. 'I was told to find the truth, always.'

'Then do so. Think. Is it right to do this? If it is, how may it be done safely? On your answer hang all of our lives.'

He did not close his eyes this time; he did not have to. The glassy water of the pond became his window and through it he saw Mergus, bound, surrounded by living fire, and in his ears rang his own voice: *I will not let it happen.*

Out of nowhere, he remembered his father as he had last seen him, pacing the length of a garden, guarding the tomb therein, and the corpse that lay in it. Except there had been no corpse, and he had not guarded against those who came to take away the living man, brought down early from his cross.

His father had lived for honour and dignity and obedience to his superiors and yet he had thrown all of those away that night to help a zealot and a pregnant woman steal the Galilean to safety. The Galilean, who was known in Jerusalem as Yehuda, and was loved for all he had done. Yehuda, who was grandfather to Menachem, and father to Hannah. Yehuda, whom, against all reason, Saulos had named the Messiah.

Nothing simple. Nothing ever as it seemed. From deep in the fish-stirred pool, his father said, *Some things matter more than the smallness of our lives.*

'What must I do?' Pantera asked.

What can you do? his father said, and was not his father alone, but a young god, beautiful in his youth and vigour, with a Phrygian cap and a great bull's blood on his hands, who demanded truth from those who chose to follow him.

Pantera opened his eyes. Hypatia stood between him and the pool with her hands on top of his and her gaze level.

She said, 'What?'

He took a steadying breath. 'At dawn, I will meet the High Priest on the temple steps in front of all the people of Jerusalem. I will dress as befits my station and I will show him the royal ring that I bear. With him as my witness, I will tell the city of Jerusalem what Saulos

248

plans to do, how he plans war with Rome, which will destroy them. Governor Florus will come; he will have to if the multitudes are there. When he hears the truth, he will side with us and Saulos will fall. This is not certain, but it is possible. I have to try.'

CHAPTER TWENTY-FIVE

Saulos' visitor came so deep in the night that the stars barely gave him light to find his way.

Iksahra was asleep in the stables when she heard a shoulder brush along the oak fence that separated the beast garden from the city. She was there to care for a sick horse, or so she had told Polyphemos. In truth, she was tired of the old air in Herod's palace and of the scurry of nervous slaves that filled it night and day. Sleep came more easily among the beasts, who welcomed her presence and didn't make signs behind their backs to ward off evil every time she passed them by.

And so she slept in the straw, lightly, as a hunter sleeps, with the cheetah at her side, and when she heard footsteps outside the big cat rose with her and together they tracked the maybe-intruder by sound as he scuffed along the dust on the far side of the fence towards the palace.

She couldn't unlock the gate without being seen and the fence was too high to climb, but the gods smiled and the interloper stopped at the end of the fence where flamelight from the palace torches spilled bright across the ground, sending a solitary shadow sliding under the fence.

The stranger had picked his time well; by Iksahra's estimate, he had a quarter-hour to do what he needed before the guards who made their circuits of the palace were likely to return. She watched his shadow shift and shift and then stop beneath Saulos' chamber.

It took a cool mind and a careful arm to throw a pebble up four storeys and hit the shutters that covered Saulos' window. Iksahra was impressed by the stranger's accuracy. Time after time after time – five in all – he threw his pebbles and hit the centre of his target.

On the fifth stone, the shutters opened and Saulos' round, white face showed moon-like in the dark window. He looked out and down, waved a white kerchief three times and withdrew. His visitor gave a grunt of satisfaction and began to make his way back along the fence.

Iksahra followed until she reached the cheetah's empty cage and slid in behind it, keeping her head low.

Saulos passed the hound kennels; they caught his scent and stirred restlessly. The horses shifted in their stalls and a mongoose chattered alone in its pit. Unheeding, Saulos walked on through the garden, towards the dungheap at the back.

With half a hundred different animals emptying their bowels through the day and all of it dumped in that pit, the stench was ripe, and the rats sleek. Saulos did not go all the way up to the barriers that bounded the pit, but stepped to one side at the last moment and pressed his head sideways to the oak fence.

A knot hole pierced the wood there, wide as a man's

bent thumb. When she first came, Iksahra had seen the faint shimmer of grease around it from faces pressed to the oak and had thought it a trysting place for lovers. Perhaps it was; certainly Saulos and his visitor had used it before.

Saulos knocked on the wood three times in simple rhythm. A knock came back, and a hoarse whisper. 'Who is the third son of David?'

'Absolom is third son of David. Are you he? Or his emissary?'

'It's me. No one else is to be trusted this close to the end. I bring news that the Egyptian witch is in Pantera's pay.'

'Is she? And young Kleopatra so smitten with her. How immensely unfortunate. Thank you.'

It was not a secret: Saulos had told Iksahra the same before they left her people. Which meant that he kept his spies in the dark and let them tell him what he already knew; it fitted with the kind of man she had seen him to be.

On the other side of the fence, the voice said, 'There's more. Tonight, the War Party and the Peace Party met together under one roof for the first time. Pantera was there. He plans your death.'

'Of course he does.' Saulos sounded amused, in so far as a whisper could impart feeling. 'He is, after all, a worthy adversary. Remember that, my friend; if you are going to fight a mortal battle, fight it with someone you respect, however much you hate them. Victory is sweeter that way. What does he plan?'

'He personally will denounce you tomorrow in front of all Jerusalem as an enemy of Judaea.'

'And you think he'll succeed?'

'I am afraid of it. More than that, I am afraid he is right. Are you an enemy of Judaea?'

'I am an enemy of those who would destroy her with their petty squabbles. I will restore her to glory.'

'Under Rome?'

'Of course under Rome. But as an equal partner in the Kingdom of God. You know this. My friend . . .' Saulos placed his flat palm against the fence and leaned his cheek on it. His voice was warm with care and reason. 'We have talked of this so many times, over so many years. How can you doubt me now, when we are so close?'

'How can I not? They say you will destroy Jerusalem.'

'And so you come here in person to find the truth, as is fitting. I taught you to doubt even the hand in front of your face, did God not show it you first.' Saulos pressed his cheek to the fence. 'Jerusalem will fall, but she will rise again by God's hand. The Kingdom cannot be built but out of the rubble of what has been. When the time comes, tell that to those you command.'

'And what do I tell them of the women? They speak already of the witch, and the beastwoman who is more demon than witch, and they know that you consort openly with both of these.'

'But not for long. You know – who better? – that in pursuit of our goals we must pretend to be that which we are not. Trust me in this, neither the witch nor Iksahra has turned the course of my heart. They serve their purpose, which is my purpose, but when their use is done they will join Pantera in Hades. We can do this, except only if you doubt me; faith is everything and without yours I am nothing.'

A silence came from the far side of the fence, a waiting, and then, 'My faith is as it has always been. And my trust in you.'

'And mine in you. Go back whence you came, my friend. Sleep and know your warning fell on fruitful ground. Tomorrow, Jerusalem will begin to die, that you and I may raise it living from its own ashes.'

The visitor left then, his footsteps fading into the black night. Iksahra laid a hand on the cheetah's broad brow and another under its chin and held its mouth still until Saulos had walked past and let himself out of the garden, back into the palace.

Then she breathed in the scent of the cat, of the horses, of the hounds, of the night, and considered her hatred of Judaea and her contempt for Rome and how, exactly, these were outweighed by her utter loathing of Saulos the Herodian, snake in the night, who must pretend to be what he was not, yet was blind to those around him who did the same.

CHAPTER TWENTY-SIX

O n the morning of the sixth day of the month of Ab, high summer in Jerusalem, a bird sang to greet the dawn. A hot, dry wind blew from the east. High over the hills, a hawk soared in hunting spirals, scanning the early land.

On that morning, a night and a day and a night after the riots had begun at Caesarea, a single night after Hypatia had come to tell him that Saulos was planning to rob the Temple of its gold . . . at dawn on that day, under the high, shimmering call of the hawk, Pantera stood alone on the second to top step leading up to the Temple of Jerusalem and watched the High Priest of Israel step out through his breathtaking, jewel-studded gates and look down on the gathered people of his city.

Ananias ben Ananias was a man of average build and average features. His head was a fleshless skull, with eyes set too far up to his brow and a wattle neck like an ageing hen's.

Beyond that, he would not have stood out in a market, or a hippodrome or a battlefield, but that he was robed in silk of porphyry that shimmered in the sun, and tiny gold bells sang on the lower fringes of his coat, so that he was a songbird in motion. Black onyx stood out from his shoulders with the names of the twelve tribes of Israel engraved thereon, and other gems in emerald, in aquamarine, in ruby, studded his cuirass, each bearing the name of a different tribe. A polished gold plate fixed to the turban of his headpiece proclaimed him holy in the eyes of his god.

Chiming in gold, splendid in purple, he paced forward to the edge of the heights on which his temple was built and looked down on the gathered people.

A sea of blue-marked men and youths and girls too young to marry, too old to be left at home, looked back up at him. Silence settled on them as a moth settles in the evening, softly, without their noticing.

These were the Peace Party, come out in their multitudes at the request of Gideon, the Peacemaker. At their back, around their edges, stood the War Party, brought by Menachem and his cousin Eleazir, distinguished by their flashes of sun-yellow. All around, in their unmarked but remarkable long-coats, stood the merchants summoned by Yusaf ben Matthias, who bore no affiliation to either party, but whose future turned on the morning as much as anyone else's.

It is possible we might live.

Hypatia's promise rang in Pantera's ears as the last echoes of a thunderstorm. He felt as if his skin had been shed and grown back again, thinner. The world was sharper around him, with danger so clear he could taste it as iron on his tongue and feel it in the sweat on his back.

He watched the High Priest come forward and counted his own heartbeats by the soaring in his ears.

'Your excellency—' He clasped Nero's ring in his hand; gold and turquoise, with a lyre engraved on it, and the chariot that was this emperor's sign. He raised it up so that Ananias might see it, and the crowd might know that he carried gold.

'Your excellency, I am Sebastos Abdes Pantera, known as the Leopard. I come in the name of the Emperor Nero, bearing this, his ring. I bring news of one who would rob your temple, taking the emperor's name in vain.'

Pantera had fought on battlefields; he knew how to pitch his voice to carry. A sigh came from the crowd. They loathed Nero as the author of their woes, as the man who had thrust Governor Florus upon them, and held the legions in the palm of his hand, ready to crush them if they rose against the excesses of his greed. Even so, the sound of the imperial name carried the patina of royalty and the gold flashing in Pantera's hand took on new meaning beyond simply wealth.

They drew a long inward breath and Pantera let it lift him that last step up to the platform on which the Temple stood. The walls faced him, white and brilliant in the sun, their glorious gem-studded gates hanging open only by a foot's length, enough to let the colours catch the morning sun, but not so far that it was possible for Pantera to see inside to where the Hebrews worshipped their god.

The crowd's sigh became a low hum, not yet angry, but not cheerful either.

Ananias, High Priest by appointment of the emperor, turned his head. His fat eyes rested on the etched lyre on the ring. When he raised them, they were hard as flint.

'You do not come from the emperor,' he said, and his voice, too, carried out and down to the sea of ears below. 'You are a liar and a traitor to your emperor and to your god.'

The crowd drew another breath, harsher than before.

Pantera made himself smile. He scanned the horizon for signs of Mithras: a raven, a bull, a hound. He saw none of these, only the soaring hawk. 'Your excellency, I am loyal to my emperor and to my god, who is not your god.'

The crowd was muttering now, so that it was harder to be heard. Beneath their rumblings, Ananias said, 'And if I choose not to believe that?'

'Then the emperor who commands both of us will wish to know why.'

'I see.'

They might have said more, but a gong sounded from inside the walls and on that sound, drowning it in a crash of hooves on stone, Jucundus rounded the corner at the head of two hundred and forty cavalry, breasting the crowd like an ocean ship in a high swell.

In the chaos of their arrival, the fury of horses and mail, the screams of men, women, boys who had never faced cavalry, Pantera's sense of danger sharpened. It came not from the armed men below, but from the flurry of quiet movement behind the temple walls, from the command given in a voice he knew too well, so that when, finally, the oak gates opened wide, flashing their jewels to the morning, and a figure walked out, sleek in sand-coloured silk, to stand beside the High Priest, Pantera was beyond surprise.

Two years evading capture had drawn a few new lines about Saulos' eyes, but he was still the smooth-faced, smooth-voiced enemy Pantera had known, invisible unless he chose to show himself, but when he did, the power of his ambition could draw a thousand eyes. It was doing so now.

'You are not the emperor's man.' He spoke crisply, but not loudly, so that the crowd must quiet themselves to hear. 'I doubt even if you are the Leopard, for he is known to be loyal. We will find your true name in due course. The questioners are even now preparing the tools of their trade. The people of Jerusalem are diligent in their love for the emperor and will honour him by allowing the High Priest to donate fifteen talents of gold to Rome for the repairs after the fire. Your blood will seal the gift.'

Fifteen talents? Nobody in the crowd believed that. They made no sound.

'I bear the emperor's ring,' Pantera said.

'A forgery.'

'Perhaps we should await the Governor Florus and ask for his opinion. He alone has seen it on the emperor's hand.' Pantera spoke to Ananias alone. 'I bring also a letter from the emperor to the governor, commending me to his service in the search for the man who would destroy both Rome and Jerusalem in pursuit of a broken prophecy. His name is Saulos. He stands at your side.'

The message was rolled in his belt pouch. It was written on imperial paper and sealed with the imperial seal which was identical in all ways to the imperial ring. Pantera had written it himself, sitting alone in the night at the table in Yusaf's room when sleep would not come, but Saulos had no sure way of proving that, short of asking Nero himself.

'Truly? Let me see.' Saulos stepped out of the High Priest's shadow, and, by that single movement, made it clear who had command of whom.

Below, the crowd sucked in another, greater, breath: a hundred thousand breasts, affronted. A murmur became a rumble, became a torrent. With a single shouted signal, Jucundus deployed his men in a row along the bottom of the temple steps, forcing the people back.

In front of them all, Saulos took the message Pantera had written and tore it across and across. 'This is not real.'

Pantera turned to Ananias and spread his hands wide. 'Your excellency, we each speak and you cannot be expected to discern the truth. But the emperor knows. If you wish to send a message-bird now, I will compose for you a message which will confirm the truth of what I say.'

Ananias pursed his lips. A flicker of doubt burned in his eyes. He said, 'It will take a handful of days to send a bird and get one back.'

'Then we can wait. You cannot empty your treasury in less time than that. And in the meantime, I beg leave to commend to your lordship the words of our emperor when he sent me here: *Say to Ananias the High Priest that we approve the quality of his leadership and wish that he may continue in his place until his nephew is fit to wear his robes.'*

Pantera kept his gaze level. Very few men in Rome or Jerusalem knew that neither Ananias' sons nor his grandsons featured in his plans for the future of the priesthood. The Emperor Nero was one of those who did.

Ananias' eyes flickered back and forth, too fast to follow. He closed them, and when he opened them again, a small shake of his head was the only sign that he had come to a decision.

This time, when he raised his arm and the gong sounded, a troop of armed legionaries marched from the temple compound. These were not Jucundus' Syrian auxiliaries, but legionaries of the Jerusalem garrison Guard; Roman citizens all, raised in perfect certainty of their superiority to every race on earth.

Two hundred men such as this in columns of fifty, four abreast, marched from the Hebrew temple, their very presence a defilement. Each man bore across his flat palms a single bar of solid gold, his muscles corded and sweat-rolled with the strain.

They came and they came and they filled the temple platform, their gold glittering in the sun like so many scattered grains of new corn on the threshing room floor.

Below, the crowd believed at last that which they had previously denied, and were struck to silent sorrow. The want of noise was as deafening as the night before battle when the ears ache for the song of the stars and there is nothing to hear but the sound of a thousand souls preparing themselves for death.

Into that silence, Ananias, High Priest of Israel, said, distinctly, 'He is a traitor. Take him.'

He was pointing to Pantera.

Chapter Twenty-Seven

'What's happening? Is it war? It sounds like war.'
Caught too far from the tall, narrow window,
Kleopatra tugged at Hypatia's elbow, trying to see past
her to the shouting men, the clashing weapons, the
screaming, stamping horses that were causing such
mayhem around the Temple below.

She was used to people who stepped out of her way.
She was used to a lot of things that Hypatia, Chosen of
Isis, did not do, and just now, Kleopatra wanted to see
what Hypatia was seeing, and could not.

'It sounds like war,' she said again, in frustration.

'It's not,' Hypatia said, pressing her brow to the
window's edge. 'It's the prelude to an execution.
The High Priest has arrested Pantera and the men of
Menachem's party are trying to free him.'

She stepped out of the way at last, and Kleopatra
pushed past in time to see two men of the War Party
hurl themselves at the line of the garrison Guard. The
legionaries, by a miracle of self-control, held up their
shields but did not respond.

'Why are the Guard not fighting back?'

'Someone's ordered them not to,' Hypatia said. 'They're trying not to provoke a war.' She turned at last away from the window. Her face was white, frightening in its intensity. 'Where are prisoners kept in this palace?'

Kleopatra closed her eyes, the easier to think. 'There are two places: the beast garden and the cellars. For questioning, they take them to a man-cage in the back of the beast garden, behind the stables. Sometimes, if the prisoners won't answer, they set the wild beasts on them: hounds or boar. The Hebrews can't bear it. Before an execution, they keep them in the cellars.' She opened her eyes. 'But in the dream of blood and gold, Pantera is always in sunlight. It's how we can see the blood. The cold and the dark come later.'

'And Saulos will want to "question" him, even if he already knows the answers.' Hypatia gave a tight, hard smile. 'Go now, find your aunt and tell her to petition the king for his release. Use whatever power she can. I'll go to the beast—'

Hypatia was already leaving. Kleopatra grabbed her arm. 'You can't leave me behind. You can't! It's my dream too. I'm always in it.'

Hypatia stopped. 'In the dream, are you watching, or are you acting?'

'Both. Sometimes one, sometimes the other. It's always different, you know that.'

'But some things are always the same. What happens now, in the next hours, will change everything.'

Desperate, Kleopatra said, 'I can show you the swiftest way to get there, through the slaves' entrance. At least let me take you there. I won't ask to go further.'

Hypatia took a moment longer to reach her decision. 'Lead then,' she said. 'As fast as you can. But only to the door of the slaves' entrance, no further.'

The fastest route to the beast garden ran through the slaves' corridors on the first floor. Kleopatra led the way at a run, down the stairs and down again, then left along a corridor and right.

They passed three slaves, two carrying silver baskets of grapes, peaches, apricots. The last carried wine and goblets of gold, chased with emeralds. They smiled dutifully at Hypatia, in friendship at Kleopatra.

When they were safely gone, Kleopatra pointed along the corridor towards the vast oak door at the far end. 'We need to go through that door.' Black iron banded it and the lock was a hand's length high. 'The feeding room's on the other side. The beasts are all fed at dawn; nobody will be there at this time of day. The door will be locked, but the key's in a box on the right. People might break in, but they never think anyone's going to break out.'

'Thank you,' Hypatia said. 'Now go to your aunt. Tell her— What?'

Kleopatra set her jaw, mulishly. 'You said I could come to the door. All the way to the door. We're not there yet and there's someone on the other side. You might need help. You promised.'

She spoke to Hypatia's back; the woman was already walking forward, silently now, as if her feet made bare contact with the floor. The door to the feed room hung a hair's breadth ajar. Even with so small a crack, the air in the corridor was heavy with scents of fresh meat

265

and old fruit, of grain and milk and water. By the time Kleopatra reached her – walking silently was difficult and slow – Hypatia had laid her head against the heavy oak, pressing her ear into the grain.

At her gesture, Kleopatra came forward and did the same. With her ear hard on the wood, she closed her eyes and sent her mind through the door, a thing she had been doing since childhood.

She thought she might hear slaves preparing feed for the animals brought in late. What she heard instead were the soft movements of someone moving amongst the crates and jars and buckets and bales, picking things up, moving them. A slave would not have been so confident. Kleopatra inhaled, and smelled cat, and so . . .

She signalled towards the door. Hypatia shook her head, held up one finger, pointed it to herself and made a walking motion with her fingers; then, with emphasis, she held up the flat of her hand in the same signal she used to order the hounds to stay still.

Kleopatra took a breath to argue, saw the look on Hypatia's face – and stepped smartly back to the corner, from where she watched Hypatia push open the door.

A blur of white skin and black; a taken breath; a woman moving – two women – and between them knives, as silver birds, flying.

The knives hit wood, solidly, to stand juddering, vibrating tuneful as arrows, but on a lower note.

One hit Iksahra, the Berber woman, on the shoulder. Or didn't. Looking again, Kleopatra saw that the knife's point had caught the loose flow of her draped clothes just above her shoulder, pinning her to the wooden panel behind.

Iksahra's own knife stood out of the oak doorpost where Hypatia's heart had been. But Hypatia was there no longer. She was in the room, to the right, by the tall barrels that held grain for the horses.

'Will you drop the other knife now? Kleopatra, stay out. She has another, hidden.'

She has a cheetah, Kleopatra thought, *what need has she of another knife?* But the cheetah wasn't there; she could smell it, she could hear its breathing, but not see it. Outside the door, possibly? Or elsewhere, ready to leap out when they least expected it.

If Hypatia was concerned she hid it well, and Iksahra was . . . Iksahra; ice wrapped round fire, hating the world and everyone in it.

For icy calm, they matched each other; both dark-haired, both tall, both much too full just now of unspoken rage. When it seemed their fury might crest, might spill over and cause untold damage, a blade clattered to the worn wooden floor, and then another, to lie among the feed bins.

Iksahra had held two knives in secret, then, not just one. But now none. Having thus disarmed herself, she crooked her finger and the cheetah was there, creeping belly-low from its hiding place behind the feed bins, ears flat to its head, white teeth flashing, tail a-twitch. It was commanded to stillness.

'Why are you here?' Hypatia stooped to pick up the dropped knives by feel; her eyes never left the other woman's face.

Iksahra stood where she had been when the door

267

opened, a figure of black and white, wreathed in loathing. 'My business does not concern you.'

'Everything you do concerns me,' Hypatia said. She laid the blades on a workbench at the side, beyond reach. 'Why do you hate the Hebrews?'

Iksahra blinked. No other muscle moved, but it was as great an expression of surprise as if she'd thrown her hands in front of her face as the Gaulish slaves did when they saw a snake.

When no answer came, Hypatia said, 'We are here to free Pantera, prisoner of Saulos. You are Saulos' servant, and yet you, too, are here, bearing knives and in the company of your cat which can kill a man as easily as it might an antelope. Whom do you seek to kill?'

'Him.' Iksahra jerked her head back, towards the beast garden. 'The prisoner. Saulos has asked that I set the cat on him.'

'To kill him?'

'What do you think?'

'I think it will take a remarkable degree of control to set a cat on a man and then call it off before it kills, while it has yet done enough damage to satisfy Saulos.'

'You think I have not the skill?'

Hypatia smiled, not kindly. 'I would not question your skill. I would question that you let Saulos command you so. Has he honour? Is he the kind of man your father was? Is he worth your service?'

Kleopatra wanted to cover her eyes, to stop her ears. No one had ever told her exactly what the Berber did to those who impugned their honour, but she had an imagination, and it fed her visions of bloody, raw-red vengeance.

She watched Iksahra take a step forward, and then stop. 'What do you know of my father?'

Hypatia raised a brow. With a rare diffidence, she said, 'I know that his name was Anmer ber Ikshel and he served as beastmaster to Herod the Great and then to his son, Herod Agrippa, grandfather to Kleopatra who is standing so quietly by the door. He was renowned for his skill in training beasts; it was said that he had a great cat that followed him everywhere as a hound follows an ordinary huntsman. But it was his horse-breeding that was his undoing. Anmer ber Ikshel bred the best, the fastest, the most beautiful horses the world had seen. The best of them were the colour of almond milk with black manes and tails and they could outrun the wind for days at a time. Shall I go on? Shall I list for you the ways that your father met his end?' There was compassion there, if you listened hard for it. Kleopatra was listening very hard indeed.

So too, in her way, was Iksahra. Her eyes were wide, showing white at the rims as a horse does when wary. Her long, lean fingers shaped the signs that dispelled ghûls and kept ifrit at bay. 'How do you know this?' Her voice was steady, but the effort required to keep it so was clear.

'There are ways to find out things that do not take a message-bird,' Hypatia said, gently.

'What ways? Have you dreamed him? Have the witches of Alexandria sent you his ghost?'

'Your father was famous, Iksahra. Everyone knew of him and even those now dead told their children details they will remember beyond their last breath. All I had to do was ask the slaves, ask Polyphemos, ask the men of the Watch who were detailed to escort me. They all knew his name, they all knew how he came to die. Shall I tell you what they said to me?'

With cold courage, Iksahra said, 'Tell me. I would hear it from you, who have no love for me.'

'King Herod Agrippa was in debt. That was not surprising, he was a profligate man and always so, but unfortunately on this occasion he owed significant sums to Gaius Caesar, known as Caligula, emperor of Rome, who had the power to break him. But Caligula was known for his love of horses and so Herod Agrippa conceived a plan to give Anmer's horses to the emperor in repayment of his debt. He couldn't pay for them, of course, he had no money, and he could not be seen to steal them from a man held in such high esteem. So he manufactured a crime, some fictitious treason, and had Anmer ber Ikshel killed, and claimed all his goods.' Hypatia's features had softened, and her voice was almost kind. 'Anmer was warned by those who loved him of what was coming. He could not escape it, and did not try, but I heard that he sent away his nine-year-old daughter, that she might not see his ending, or know how it happened.'

'I was told about it when I came to adulthood,' Iksahra said, and her voice was thick with grief and loss. 'They said he was torn apart between four of his own stud colts. My mother hanged herself. I knew nothing. Three days before, I was sent away to live with my father's people. I didn't know why and hated both of my parents, calling them names because they were sending me away from a place and a life that I loved, to live in a tent with people who slept with their horses.'

Iksahra raised her head. Her voice was dry as the desert wind, and as implacable. 'Then I learned to sleep with my horses. And I learned what had happened to my father and mother. My people are taught how to nurse hate, to hone it, to keep it sharp and ready. When Saulos sought me out, I knew before he had finished his first word that he was the vehicle the storm gods had promised, that I might savour my vengeance. I came with him as he asked, but you are right, he has no honour; less than that, he has its opposite. When the time arises, he, too, will die.'

'After he has destroyed Jerusalem?'

'Perhaps; if I can wait that long. But certainly before he has rebuilt it.' Iksahra tilted her head. 'You did know, did you not, that he wishes first to destroy this city, but then to rebuild it in the image of his god, to make it great, as Rome is great, with himself as king.'

'I knew. It has always been Saulos' dream, but it is not widely known. Did he tell you of it himself?'

'Not directly. I overheard him tell another, here, at the beast gardens. He spoke last night in secrecy with one who came with news that you were sworn to the service of one Pantera, called the Leopard. That Saulos knew already, but he did not say so to the one who came.' Iksahra glanced up under lowered lids. Hypatia had fallen still. Iksahra said, 'That one told Saulos also that this Pantera planned to denounce him before the High Priest this morning. Your Leopard was betrayed. His death was certain before ever he mounted the temple steps. Did he know this?'

'He knew it was possible, yes.'

'But still he went.'

271

'He seeks to prevent war.'

'This is not his land. Why should he risk his life for its people?'

'He has honour. He is the opposite of Saulos. He is, I think, very like your father, but I am not the one to say that; you would have to know him yourself.'

The air came to rest that had swayed back and forth between them; the ferocity of feeling, of grief, of ice-hot fury. And as it rested, it was different, so that Kleopatra could taste on her tongue an opening, a possibility of change.

'It seems to me,' Hypatia said, slowly, 'that Anmer ber Ikshel might best be avenged by your aiding us, not Saulos. And that, avenged or not, he might walk more peacefully through the afterlife knowing his daughter has not sold her honour for the cheap coin of a traitor.'

There followed a long, painful silence. Nobody moved. Nobody spoke further. To Kleopatra, it seemed as if the whole world had been caught somewhere on an inbreath and could do nothing but hold it.

And then Iksahra looked down at her hands, at her knives that lay out of reach on the workbench, at the one that lay in Hypatia's open palm.

'Will you kill me, if I choose to differ?' she asked, and it was the tone with which she asked that said a corner had been turned, more than the words, or the half-smile behind them.

Kleopatra let out her breath in a rush. Hypatia closed her eyes. Relief washed through her. She put her hands together and when they came apart again her own knife had gone. She moved forward to the window that gave out on to the beast garden, leaving Iksahra free either to take up her own three knives, or to join her.

Iksahra did both, and they stood, shoulder to shoulder, black skin to olive, looking out at what had become a place of busy men, of marching guards and shouted orders.

Presently, with no word spoken, and no glance back to Kleopatra, the two women walked together out of the feed room with the great cat at their heels.

Chapter Twenty-Eight

The place to which they took Pantera was a vast, open-fronted cage in the back of the beast gardens, caught in full sun, dazzling, hot and disturbingly open.

Always before, he had been questioned in the dark, in low, cold places where a man's agony could not reach the sunlight, where the intimacy of pain and humiliation was shared only with his inquisitors. Here was big enough to host a banquet and open to the watching beasts, to the flies that gathered waiting for an open wound, to the slaves who dallied, staring, as six vast men of the Jerusalem garrison Guard stripped Pantera of his tunic and tied him to the central stake, with his hands above his head, hauled up, so that his feet held barely half of his weight.

Around his feet was beaten earth, polished black with old blood. There was, however, no fire lit yet, no brazier with which to heat the irons that might burn out his eyes, or draw lines of pain on his body. Pantera fastened on that fact and held it close.

They settled him in his new position and tied off

the ropes. Already, his hands began to burn. He drew a surreptitious breath through his mouth and held it and tried to measure how hard it was to lift his ribs and make the air slide into his lungs, how much extra weight it put on his arms. He thought he could speak, at least in short bursts.

The giants who had tied him stepped back to study their handiwork. None of the six was fully dressed; a loin cloth and belt, both easily replaced, was their only covering, but on his belt each wore the corn sheaf of the Jerusalem garrison Guard which labelled them as Roman citizens.

By their size, by the red-gold hair, he put them as the sons of the sons of Caesar's famous Batavian guard, the men of myth and legend, great Germanic tribesmen, twice the bulk of any other man, and loyal to the point of idiocy. None of them was an officer; they were bred and trained to the taking of orders.

With his nurtured breath, Pantera said, 'Like you, I am a Roman citizen. It is not lawful to do this.' He spoke Latin, in the accent of the Senate, which gave orders to men such as these.

They hesitated. He met each troubled gaze in turn, said, 'If you were to fetch Governor Florus and explain to him the circumstances, the emperor will look kindly on it when this is brought to his notice. It does not, I believe, contradict your orders.'

None of them hit him, to keep him from speaking; it was a start. Pantera glanced down at the neat pile of folded linen that was his tunic. The turquoise ring lay within the folds, for these were honest men, who did not steal from prisoners.

He tried again. 'You see that I bear the emperor's ring. You must know that it is real. What harm in bringing the governor to hear my case?'

One was smaller than the others, although still vast by Roman standards. He nodded, checked with a sideways glance that none of his fellows was going to stop him, and stepped backwards out of the door.

He was gone – perhaps he was gone – before Saulos came, for Saulos came very quickly on the heels of his leaving. The remaining five men stepped away, and stood in a line; a human barrier that made a wall in front of the cage, and gave a degree of intimacy to those inside.

Saulos had changed his clothing. Fastidious to a fault, he had stopped somewhere to exchange his sand-coloured silks for a slave's tunic of plain linen with the old stains washed out, so that only a man who had seen inquisitors' work from beginning to end might recognize the uniform of his trade. He wore a belt with two knives in it, and a small lead weight, rounded to fit a man's palm. Pantera's stomach rolled over, remembering.

Smiling, Saulos lifted the weight and tossed it from hand to hand. 'Are you comfortable?'

'No.'

'But you will remember, I'm sure, how comfortable this is, compared to later. You can look forward to your death. It will happen long after you want it, but it will still happen.'

Saulos moved as he spoke, lazily, swinging round in an arc, like a dancer pretending to practise. At the move's end his fist, made heavy by the lead, hammered into Pantera's solar plexus.

There had been warning of a sort in that inelegant swoop, and Pantera did not let his feet come off the ground. In the puking, retching, black-blue star-spattered agony, as he fought to breathe, and heard the raucous noises of his own pain soak into the dirt beneath his feet, that was his victory.

The pain in his diaphragm became less. He caught a breath and treasured it, nurtured it into his lungs, even when sanity said he should have abandoned breathing and let himself go into the blackness.

He lifted his head. Saulos was smiling, white-toothed in the dazzling sun.

'Very good. You were questioned in Britain, I understand, so none of this is new. Such a pleasure to work with someone who understands what's happening. In the old days, sometimes, when we released men to be informers and they refused to inform and we had to arrest them again, then they were like you. But there were few of them, and we stopped it soon enough when it was obvious they were lying. After that, men only came once, and left as food for the big cats.'

'You worked here? In this place?'

'I was here in the time of Caligula and then Claudius. Seneca sent me to suppress the Hebrew insurrections led by the Galilean's lieutenants. They made me the lead inquisitor under High Priest Ananias; the elder, not the current craven idiot. We thought that pain and executions would do it.'

'And when you found they didn't, you took the Galilean's death and made it the cornerstone of your new religion, speaking of a god that needed only faith, not deeds?'

It was not necessary to say that, or even useful; nobody knew Saulos' history better than the man himself, but there had been a change in the padding noises of the beasts in the sun beyond the cage and it mattered that Saulos not hear it.

Pantera let his voice run on: 'You freed the Hebrews from the twin burdens of circumcision and the table laws so that they might love Rome and the Romans. Yet when you last came to Jerusalem, the zealots bound themselves with oaths not to eat or drink before they had killed you. How much did you hate them for that?'

'No more than I hated them already, with their petty, pusillanimous carping.' Saulos smiled. 'The governor is coming,' he said. 'Did you think I had not heard?'

He began his graceless, looping dance again, slower this time, so that when Florus appeared in the gap between the standing guards, the only sound was Pantera's flailing breath.

CHAPTER TWENTY-NINE

'We are not yet ready. Pass it on. Tell everyone, of any party; Menachem says we are not ready for war.'

Menachem was a man transformed. His eyes were alight with a blackening fire that scorched the men on whom it fell. His voice rang with authority, his smile was bright and sharp and his men lived for the touch of his words, so that when he had said for the tenth, the thirtieth time, *Not yet. We are not ready for war*, they let go their stones and their staves, and paused in their screaming of insults long enough for his message to pass unchanged down the lines of command, dimming the mob's hysteria, bringing order in the chaos, not only among his own men, but among the Peace Party, too.

Nobody spoke for peace now, not even Gideon, just that they were not yet ready for war. Even the men of Eleazir's faction of the War Party, those who lived for war yesterday, or war today, or war tomorrow at the latest, accepted Menachem's edict and were subdued.

Trapped in the midst of the chaos, Mergus saw the

men around him pause for breath, but not shout again. He caught Estaph's arm.

'They've taken Pantera to the beast garden at the back. There's a wooden palisade around it. There must be a way in.'

'If not, we will make one.' Estaph's axes hung at his belt. He was not smiling now, had not smiled since the night when Pantera had said what he planned. His big, broad face was pinched below the cheekbones, thumbed in below the eyes. 'What once we're in?'

Mergus said, 'We create a distraction: start a fire, kill some men, do whatever we need to get the attention of the Guard and then we hope that Hyp—'

'Mergus, you can't.'

Menachem's voice came from behind him, still ripe with the power of leadership. Mergus turned. 'I didn't ask your permission. We will do what it takes to get him out. You have no right to hinder us.'

'I know. And I know what he is to you, and what he has done for us. But do you not think we have lost men we loved as deeply to that cage? From the time of my grandfather's father, men have died in there whom we loved, and I swear to you, we have done everything we could think of to free them, and when they could not be freed, we have done everything we could think of to end their agony. We have failed. If you try to do the same now for Pantera, you will die with him. As you said, I cannot stop you, but I can ask if your deaths will help him. I don't believe they will.'

'But we have an advantage,' Mergus said. 'Hypatia is in the palace and she does not want him dead. Is there a way she might get them both out?'

Menachem took his time to consider. At length, he said, 'There's a gate in the beast garden palisade that leads out into the Upper Market. The slaves use it for the beast dung. It is the least guarded of the gates, though closest to the man-cage. If Hypatia reaches it, and if there were men waiting on the outside able to hamper those who followed her, she could perhaps reach freedom.' He gave a tight, smile. 'We never had anybody inside who might help.'

'Will you take us to the gate?' Estaph asked.

'I will take you, and I will leave Aaron with you, who grew to boyhood in the market. If Hypatia reaches you, with or without Pantera, he will take you all to safety. In this, there is hope.'

Pantera had no hope, but at least a degree of respite while Gessius Florus, the peevish, frustrated, uncertain governor of all Judaea, held on to Saulos' arm, and insisted on being heard.

'I have not my lord Saulos' extensive experience, but in the past, when I have had cause to question a man, we have on occasion allowed him breath to speak.'

The governor was doing his best to exert his authority, but Saulos wasn't listening any more than was Pantera. They were dancing together, or at least he, Pantera, was responding to every move that Saulos made and Saulos was moving in a continuous slow rhythm, lazy and graceless as ever, but entirely effective: he didn't have to work hard to ensure that Pantera couldn't speak in Florus' presence.

And yet, the next blow was late. Florus spoke and Saulos did not swing the lead and Pantera had time to study the governor's toga, with its thin purple band at the hem, to smell the governor's sour sweat and to register surprise that he could smell anything beyond the vomit – and lately the urine – that puddled beneath him.

His feet had long since left the floor, but nothing had broken yet; not the bones of his arms, not the strings of his shoulders, not his ribs, not anywhere that might lead to bloodshed and an early death. Even so, his body was a single, searing point of pain. Had he breath, his screams would have reached the palace, but he had no breath. He heard Saulos answer Florus from a thick, unreachable place, beyond the wall of his misery.

'There is no need to let him speak yet. He won't say anything of benefit.'

'You know him?'

'I know his kind. They break slowly, over hours and days, not early, at the first hints of discomfort.'

'But the men say he's a Roman citizen. If it is true, both you and I will suffer for this.'

'It is not true.'

Pantera dared not open his eyes. Saulos was facing him, talking to Florus as if he were an inconvenience, which he was. But he had not lifted his hand again, had not begun his dance afresh. Pantera knew the changes in the air when it happened; already his body cringed away from them as a trained animal from the lash. Now there had been a dozen heartbeats without. He took the first part of a clear breath and was pathetically grateful.

An arm's reach away, Florus was still speaking. 'I am told he carries the emperor's ring. The turquoise with the lyre and the chariot engraved thereon.'

'A forgery,' Saulos said. He raised his right hand . . . and dropped it again into the palm of the left. Pantera sucked in another part of a breath.

'Let me see it. My wife has the ring's companion, made at the same time by the same jewelsmith in Athens. There are making-marks that cannot be counterfeited. I will know them.'

'The ring has gone. It was lost in the crowd.'

'It is in the folds of my tunic which lies on the floor. It is real.' Pantera squandered his precious breath sending his voice as far as he could, which was not far.

It earned him another blow from Saulos' leaded fist, but Florus had heard him. Knowing that was enough to keep Pantera's feet on the floor and a part of him was amazed afresh at how so small a measure of hope could change the tenor of things.

'I will see the ring,' Florus said. 'I will not be undone in this. If this man is talking truth, he may not be used to set a precedent. When once a citizen is hung thus, any one of us might follow. I will see the ring.'

A sweating hand reached past Pantera for the tunic that lay near his feet. He retched afresh at the imagined pain and then the hand was gone, and the ring with it; a kingfisher flash before his eyes. Somewhere, something whimpered like a beaten infant. He realized it was himself, and that if he had air to make noise, then . . .

'Send a message-bird to the emperor. Ask him who speaks the tru—' Saulos' fist slammed the words away. He struck twice this time, first in the diaphragm, in the centre of the flowering bruise, second to Pantera's nose, so that blood sluiced like a waterfall, and one more way of breathing was lost.

In the hell that followed, Pantera heard Florus shout a command to the men who stood guard over them.

'The ring is real,' said Florus, when he returned. 'As he says, we should send a message to the emperor. He will know who is speaking the truth.'

Saulos laughed. 'We would lose six days waiting for a dove to reach Rome and a reply to get back.'

'He has the emperor's ring.'

'It was stolen.'

'From the emperor's jewel chests? Just this one among the many hundreds our lord has been given as proof of his people's love for him? Or are you telling me that this man stole as many as he could carry and then gave them away and chose to live in penury in Jerusalem, bearing just this one as a keepsake? A moment ago, it did not exist. Now it exists and it is real. Therefore his story is real.'

'It is not, and he will tell you himself and then you will tell the king and the High Priest and it will be established beyond doubt that we have questioned not a Roman citizen, but a fraud. If we release this man, and allow him to take ship for Rome, what tales do you imagine he will carry to the emperor? You have just ordered fifteen talents of gold to be taken from the Temple. It was done in your name. If you wish the emperor to know of it, you have only to say and I will, indeed, send a dove . . .'

Florus' mouth flapped, uselessly. Saulos snapped his fingers. Two of the guards came forward slowly, burdened by weight. Over the baked noon air, Pantera smelled fire and hot iron. He would have vomited afresh, had he breath left to do it.

The men deposited their load and stepped back into their line. Saulos pumped the small hand bellows and the heat became a fire's heat, and close, so that Pantera's skin blistered.

Saulos lifted the first of the irons. 'You asked that this man be given breath to speak. He has that breath. He has spoken his lies. Let him now speak the truth for you to hear it. He will tell you that he stole the ring, and that he is the bastard son of a Syrian archer, that he plans insurrection against Rome, that he is in league with the War Party and has met often with Menachem who leads them. And then he will lose his tongue, for we shall have no further use for it.'

CHAPTER THIRTY

Over the reek of vomit, through the buzz and tease of horseflies, Saulos' voice floated out across the beast garden, fine in all its arrogance, its petty ruthlessness.

Hearing it, Iksahra sur Anmer began to run. The cheetah was her shadow, stilt-limbed, fluid, head high, the mask of its pelt dazzling gold under the sun. Hypatia matched her on her other side. As they passed the hound kennels, Hypatia opened the gates, so that by the time they reached the stables they were two women and their beasts, walking again, but swiftly.

Eight guards stood across their way; big-muscled, part-naked men with red-gold hair and iron eyes, standing in a line in the open ground behind the stables, where a man-cage was the only thing against the back wall.

Hypatia smiled at them, meeting their eyes. She made her hounds halt, one either side, and laid her hand on their heads. 'You know us both from the palace,' she said. 'It shames us that we must ask for permission to pass, when there is a battle outside and you are prevented from taking part. But Saulos has called for the hounds and the cat, to threaten the prisoner. Please call him if you wish to confirm our right to be here, or if not let us through.'

Dangerous, dangerous woman. Iksahra stared ahead, that the men might not see her eyes grow wild.

Flattered, they chose to be gracious. The biggest wore his red-gold hair tied at the side in a warrior's queue, with bear fat streaked through it. He smiled, showing teeth fit to rip a raw bull apart.

'The shame is all ours. As you say, we should not be here. Tell the lordling, if you dare, that a riot is building outside the walls and our place is with our brothers, holding fast against the rabble.'

The lordling. Iksahra smiled then, and saw the guards step away with the same looks on their faces as the slaves had, making the same signs against evil, but they waved them through and they passed on; two women and their beasts, welded together by the heat.

The air on the other side was hotter, and even as they approached the cage the stench of vomit was overlaid by the particular searing odour of white-hot iron, and then, unexpectedly, of burning flesh.

A man's scream split the air.

'Pantera!' Hypatia said it, but Iksahra knew already. She had never heard him speak, this Leopard she had tracked across the desert, but she had come to know him through the turns and twists of the night, so that she knew the tone of his scream, the early holding, as he fought not to give way, the suddenness of release, the hoarse ending, as if his throat had broken, as well as his will. The cheetah pressed against her, hissing.

Ahead stood the cage, big enough to house a grown lion; smoke issued thinly from it.

The cage had no door, but an open front which pointed towards the stables. Six guards stood before it in a line. Seeing the women, they stepped forward, arms crossed. Iksahra stopped, waiting for Hypatia to spin her magic again and get them through.

From inside, she heard Saulos say, wearily, 'And now you will tell the governor your birth, that you are not a Roman citizen, that this ring—'

Gold flashed in the air, raised on a bloodied arm.

From somewhere close behind, Kleopatra screamed, 'Hypatia! Stop them! *That's the dream!*'

Hypatia was already moving. Her hounds leapt forward, fast and high, carrying the cheetah with them.

Kleopatra stood in the shadow of the stables and felt the boundaries of her world fold around her in a crashing kaleidoscope of gold and blood.

In the first moments after she had screamed, there was only movement, too much, too fast. Gold: the ring, the cheetah's pelt, more gold than black in the noon-day sun, the hounds, one gold, one dark, with flashes of silver on their collars; Iksahra, black limbs and flying black robes and a silvered knife that sang forward, that sank into the flesh of a guard whose red-gold hair flew back, whose blood was a fountain rising and rising, beat upon beat, and then falling away.

Exactly as she had done in her dreams, Kleopatra stared about her, too stunned to move, deafened by the high keening voices of the dead.

And so, exactly as she had in the dreams, she missed

the moment when the first hound died. For half of her life she had lain awake in the night, trying to take herself back, to watch the line of the guardsman's sword as it sang through the air, the particular thrust, the angle that caught the hound on the side of the neck and sliced on downward, to cleave its foreleg from its dying carcass.

But, as in the dream, she heard only the scream of a hound, dying, and knew before she turned her head that Night was dead and that Day was hysterical now, in a killing rage, and that Hypatia was standing over the still-warm body, icily calm, too calm, more frightening than if she had fallen into a like rage, using her own knife, flashing fast, but not fast enough. These guards were the best in the empire; they moved faster than a hunting hound, so that Hypatia's knife flew to where her assailant used to be, but not where he was, and she was left standing alone with her hound dying at her feet and behind, eight more guards, alerted.

'Stop! I command you to stop!' The queen's voice came from Kleopatra's right, surprisingly close. Kleopatra had sent word calling them, and had been assured that they were on their way. Running on ahead, she had not been there to see the moment when Berenice and Agrippa had arrived at last at the beast garden. Better than anyone in the palace, they knew the use of this cage, and what happened here, and the queen, at least, knew what she must do.

But, as in the dreams, she was a long way too late.

And so Kleopatra did what she had done on a hundred different nights; turning, she dragged the jewelled display dagger from her uncle's belt and, running forward, threw herself bodily on the back of the nearest guard and sawed at his throat with her eyes shut, feeling the thick cords of his neck beneath the blade, feeling his fingers reach for her, wrapping themselves in her hair, round her neck, yanking forward, to smash her downward on to the ground. In some of the dreams he succeeded, and she died there, by the fallen hound, her neck broken, her head askew.

But in some . . . she stabbed deeper, felt the rush of scalding hot blood, heard his curses bubble and fade and began the strange, silent conversation in her head that she held with the dead in her dreams, and heard her aunt's voice again, full of royal power. 'Back! I command you, *back*!'

The guards hesitated, unsure of whose authority was paramount. In that time, the one under Kleopatra died. She felt his body crumple, heard the high whispered voice of a soul released and launched herself forward, to roll on the earth in the way her riding master had taught her to roll after a fall from a horse.

She came up disoriented, with the world back to front, and too many voices all around.

Everyone was moving. Iksahra was behind her now, killing a guard with a clean thrust to his bared chest. The cheetah hung on the back of another, its great jaws clamped on his skull as the claws of all four feet ripped open his flesh. He fell as its hind feet stripped out his kidneys. Its victory-scream covered any sound he might have made in dying; a yarling, yowling demon-song, the noise of Hades brought to the living, and even the giant men of the garrison Guard covered their ears not to hear it.

Kleopatra's own blood sang in her ears, in harmony with the cat. She balanced on the balls of her feet. In the dream, Agamemnon was there, the Germanic slave who had taught her to ride and then, secretly, to fight. In life, now, she heard only his voice through the rush of her ears: *To kill, you must have surprise, small one, or you will die; this is the law of the battle. Get your man before he expects you to do it, or he will get you.*

A guard had his back to her. She still held her uncle's over-jewelled knife. Rubies shone dully now, outdone by the blood, but a garnet sang proud on the hilt, and an emerald strove to bring another colour to the day. By its light, she stabbed the guard in the back, to the left of his spine. *Go between the ribs, small one. You have only one chance. Make it count.* Her blade skidded on bone, slid forward and in to the hot vitals beneath. She twisted as she had been shown, but had never done, pulled out, ducked as he turned.

His own blade was a cavalry sword, as long as she was tall; no jewels there. It hissed over her head. She slashed at his thigh, aiming for the big vessel in his groin, scratched the skin and had to back away. Then her stab caught up with him and he toppled sideways, surprised. She watched him, astonished; saw the colour drain from him and leak blackly on to the packed earth. She heard his voice in her ear, *Am I dead?*, but could not stay to answer, and did not know how.

Keep moving. Never still. In battle, the still men die.

She turned away, saw Iksahra throw a knife that seemed to bend in the air, and come straight again, on its path to a man's heart. She saw the cheetah fly past on golden wings, blinked, and saw it again, without the wings, saw it leap up and cling to the chest of a guard, its face at his face, yarling its song from Hades, raking his manhood with its killing feet. He died of terror, no blood spilled, or none that Kleopatra could see.

'*Saulos!*'

She heard Hypatia's high song-voice and heard a hound's curdling yell and turned again, with dream-stilled slowness, and saw Hypatia . . . Hypatia running through the last of the guards to stand over the body of her second dead hound and face Florus, the governor, who had lifted a blade that he clearly did not know how to use.

He stood waving it as if the breeze of its passing might cool him, might cool the battle, might stop the woman with the ice-cold eyes from walking straight up to him and slicing her knife, back-handed, across his throat.

He died, folding up, hissing like a punctured bladder.

And then there was stillness. Stillness and blood and gold; the emperor's ring lay on the floor by the brazier, which was cool now, unbellowed, a deep cherry-red, darkening by the moment.

Kleopatra turned a full circle. Hypatia: safe. Her hounds, Night and Day: both dead. Kleopatra could feel the pain of that, like an icicle sawing at her heart, but Iksahra was safe, and her cheetah too. It stood, head high, scanning, just as she was doing, looking among the dead, to the living, to the four remaining guards, who stood aside, kept still at last by Berenice's command, with sullen faces and murder in their eyes, to the king, whose eyes held loss of a different kind, to the dead who cluttered the earth, to the cage, where a man hung . . .

Hypatia reached him first, but Iksahra was there with

a knife to cut the cords high above his head, so that he fell forward into Hypatia's arms, and that was so exactly like the dream that Kleopatra dared not look into his mouth, dared not ask, dared not listen for the first bubbling, tongueless mumble.

Instead, she stepped behind him, away from the red-white marks burned across his chest, and struggled with the cords that bit into his wrists. Her fingers, which had been so nimble with the knife, were wooden sticks; uselessly haphazard.

'Let me.'

With care, as if she were fragile, Iksahra took Kleopatra's hands and folded them away and slid her own knife under and cut the cord with only a small split of skin, and even then no blood welled up, because no blood was in his hands; they were green-grey and cold.

'If you can rub them?' Iksahra was gentle, her black eyes questing, not hating. Kleopatra found she might weep. 'Have you killed before?' Iksahra asked, holding Kleopatra's two hands in her own.

'Not men. Not anything, actually.' She had thought about it, but never done it. 'I think . . . I think I can hear them. After they're dead.'

Iksahra's black gaze pinned her still, banished the whispering. She nodded, said, 'Later, you can ask Hypatia. For now, be still. Wait for us. We will attend him and then there will be peace and time to attend you.'

'Has he . . . ?' Kleopatra craned her neck, trying to see, still not wanting to.

'He is whole, see?' Iksahra slid aside so that Kleopatra could see all of him, naked, bruised, lying flat on the bloody earth with his head cradled in Hypatia's hands and Hypatia's tears hot on his face. She saw him shift his head a hair's breadth and look at her, meet her eyes, and then he looked at Iksahra, and then the cheetah – a small smile at that – and then last to Hypatia. She saw him take in a breath, saw how much it hurt, saw him focus his will, the effort of it, saw his mouth form the single name before it came out.

She heard Hypatia say, 'Saulos is gone. I'm sorry. We couldn't get through the wall of guards in time. Florus was his scapegoat. He is dead.'

She did not say, *I sent the last of my beloved hounds after him, or he would have plunged into your heart a white hot poker, and you would be beyond anyone's reach.*

Neither did she say, *The hound took your death for you.* She didn't say it, because there was no need; Day's body lay still beside them, warm, with a poker, dulled to black now, standing proud of his chest.

Pantera drew in another breath, and asked his second question.

'War?' A whisper.

'Yes. We will prepare for that. But first we have to make you safe. There's a gate where the beast ordure is taken away. It leads into the Upper Market. Iksahra says Mergus and Estaph are waiting there. If we go quickly, before Saulos gathers his men, we can lose ourselves in the city and then, later, find Menachem. If anyone can keep you alive in what Jerusalem will become, he can.'

CHAPTER THIRTY-ONE

There was a point when Pantera's pain ceased to be red, sooted with black, or black speared by a thousand dazzling points of crimson, and became simply white.

It was not less, only that the texture of it changed so that he was put in mind of silk bandages tied to trees and let fly in the wind; of gulls swooping over fishing boats in a harbour – any harbour; of hawthorn blossom in Britain in spring; of Hannah, so that his heart clenched tight and his soul wept.

Somewhere, a door opened and closed again and a new texture of white wove round his head. This was mist of the kind that hung over marshes, and caused men to see things that weren't there. Within it, he smelled wild flowers, faintly, and they took him back to Alexandria, to a woman he had met there, who had once frightened him.

Drifting, he traced her thread through his life since then, to Rome, to Caesarea, to an image of her dressed in green silk, with silver at her ears and neck, sitting alongside Queen Berenice in the theatre, and then more recently, fighting with her hounds, fast as any warrior. He thought he could see her soul then, and that it shone. He struggled for her name, drew it slowly to his breast as a man draws a fish: *Hypatia*.

The effort exhausted him. He fell away from the mist, and when he came back, the bed was surrounded. He could feel the press of half a dozen hearts; their concern, their impatience and grief.

'We need to move him.' Yusaf's voice rained down from an impossible height, worried and trying to hide it. 'Saulos has the garrison Guard on house-to-house searches. He can't stay here.' A man's breath touched his cheek; he felt the heat of a face. 'Is he awake yet?'

'Not yet.' Hypatia dribbled cool liquid into his mouth, slowly. Her finger stroked his throat for the swallow.

'How much longer?'

'As long as it takes.'

He was struggling to reach through the layers of mist when an idle, malicious voice said, 'If you don't want war, you should give him to the Guard. They'll pick up someone else, otherwise, to make an example. If they crucify an innocent man now, we'll have war whether you like it or not.'

Yusaf drew himself up in a murmur of silks. From high over the bed, he said, 'We will not give him to anyone. If the men of both parties remain indoors, the Guard will have no reason to pick anyone for reprisals. There will be no war. You are not ready.'

The slick, sliding voice said, 'We are as ready as we are ever going to be. All we need is weaponry enough for those who would wield a sword or a spear. Our grandfather assaulted the armoury at Sepphoris and took arms for himself and his followers. I say we do the same now.'

'No!' Yusaf slammed his hand on the bed's side, remembered himself, and drew it back with an oath. In the slightly startled silence, he said, 'When the Galilean stole the swords of Sepphoris, the legions crucified every boy and man in the city in retaliation. They sold the women and children to slavery. Even now, the city has not recovered. I will not allow you to do that again.'

'You think you can you stop it?' said the stranger. 'You are not the Peacemaker. You can never be.'

Someone new moved to the bed. Caught in the grey half-land between waking and sleep, Pantera felt a new quality to the silence and knew who had come and was grateful.

'I will stop the war,' Menachem said. His voice was quietly reasonable, as it had always been, but resonant now with a new authority. 'Yusaf is right, we are not ready. I will give you to the guards myself before I will allow you to drag us to our destruction.'

'Then what do you suggest, cousin? We will have war; even you cannot stop it. As Yusaf has rightly said, my death would bring it on faster, not delay it.'

'*Masada*,' said a whisper of dry linen dragged on stone. Pantera's throat hurt, hearing it, as if someone had just scrubbed his windpipe with a fistful of sand.

'He's awake!'

Three voices said it together. A single hand clutched his, then withdrew, swiftly, but it was enough to wrest his eyes open, to let him see that he was, indeed, the centre of a circle of heads bent over, looking down on him.

Hypatia was nearest, still with the feel of silk bandages about her although her hair was a black flag, caught behind her ears. He sought her hand, which lay still on the counterpane. 'The hounds . . .' he whispered. 'Sorry.'

She pressed his hand again, shook her head. 'They died in battle, a credit to their ancestors.' He wanted to believe her.

His eyes roamed on. Mergus was next to her, grey-white and sleepless, his face pinched as a gull's, and next to him stood Estaph, a ghost of a bear, watching with great, hurt eyes that smiled a little when Pantera's gaze settled on them. Iksahra was there; he smelled her cat first, and his eyes found her second. He sent her thanks with his gaze.

Yusaf was next, then Menachem, who might yet become his friend, and then . . . he did not know who was next, except that it might have been Menachem's paler brother, his hair one shade lighter than black, his eyes a shade towards grey, his soul . . . his soul very different from Menachem's.

His identity was couched in his tone as much as his words. *What do you suggest, cousin?* Enlightenment came with the memory, and Pantera let his gaze rest on Eleazir ben Simeon, younger cousin to Menachem, who wished to lead the War Party, and was not fit.

Menachem lifted Pantera's hand, brought his wandering attention back. 'Did we hear you aright? Did you say Masada? That we might get our weapons from there?'

Eleazir hawked and spat, fluidly. 'Masada's a death trap. No one can get near it.'

298

Pantera closed his eyes. Darkness gave him solitude and allowed him strength to push the necessary words past the fire in his throat.

'My father said . . . your grandfather, the Galilean . . . should have raided Masada. The armoury is bigger than the one at Sepphoris. It lies on a bare rock, guarded only by Romans. No Hebrews there to be slain in reprisal.' He felt better, speaking, than he had when silent. He opened his eyes again.

Menachem was staring down at him thoughtfully. 'Even so, my cousin is right,' he said. 'Since Herod built his first palace there, no one has assaulted the rock of Masada. There is one path in, and that is so narrow that two guards could hold off an army. There are five hundred legionaries on the rock. If there is a safe way in, or out, nobody knows of it.'

'I do.'

They dared not believe him, except Hypatia, who closed her eyes and raised one brow, as if questioning a voice within, and at the end of it said, 'Tell them.'

And so to her, to Mergus and Estaph, to Yusaf and to Menachem, he said, 'My father took me to Masada. I have walked inside its walls. I know a way it can be assaulted so that no innocent life will be lost.'

'Why would you do this?' asked Menachem. 'It does not prosper your battle against Saulos. He has taken control of the fortress of the Antonia, next to the Temple. He commands the garrison Guard and the cavalry from Caesarea. Only the auxiliary from Caesarea under Jucundus is still loyal to the royal family. If we take you, and wait until you heal . . . it will be nearly a month before we return. Saulos' power will have risen by then like leavened bread under a morning sun.'

This close, Menachem's eyes were not black, but a deep, deep brown, shaded in places with amber. They were the eyes of a man who has taken the harsh decisions of leadership, who bears the weight, and has not fallen under it, who can think clearly, and weigh risk against gain and keep his ardour for when it was needed.

To Menachem alone, therefore, Pantera gave his dwindling breath. 'Saulos plans a war that will destroy Jerusalem. If we cannot stop him, then we will make war on our terms. A war we will win.'

He lay back, spent, and heard them argue as to his fitness and how he might be healed, and what must be done and could be done and might be done, here, or in the desert, where men lived as healers.

In the end, sleep claimed him, and so he was spared the pain of movement, as they loaded him on to a litter and carried him along narrow alleys to a gate used chiefly by the night soil collectors.

He woke at night in the desert, to the sounds of emptiness and the songs of the stars and a morning sun that spilled bright, prophetic blood across the sand.

MASADA AND JERUSALEM
MID SUMMER, AD 66

IN THE REIGN OF THE
EMPEROR NERO

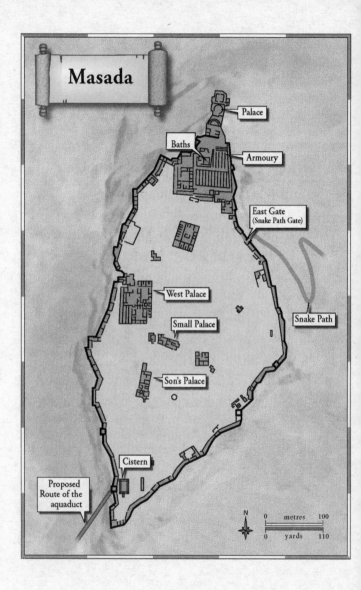

Masada

Palace

Baths

Armoury

East Gate
(Snake Path Gate)

West Palace

Small Palace

Snake Path

Son's Palace

Cistern

Proposed
Route of the
aquaduct

N

metres 100

yards 110

CHAPTER THIRTY-TWO

In the red desert mountains south of Jerusalem, a bloody sunset scorched the western sky, blurred to lilac at its margins. In the lengthening shadows, a lioness stalked a long-horned oryx as it drank from a drying wadi.

Pantera lay belly-down on a ledge a spear's throw above, with his chin propped on both fists, barely breathing. His bladder ached with the need to empty; he ignored it, as he ignored the sharp stones digging into his elbows and the dull ache from his diaphragm that accompanied every careful breath, each one timed with the lion's footfall, that the sounds of her own movement might keep her from hearing him.

She was ten yards away . . . eight . . . five . . . effortlessly balanced on three broad feet, one forelimb lifted, frozen while the oryx raised its white head and twitched its tall ears a full circle and snuffed the light evening breeze. The lion was downwind of her prey, as Pantera was downwind of her, so that their scent came to him mingled, sweet-sour fermenting grasses overlaid with the hunting cat's mellow meatiness. Water dripped from the antelope's muzzle, splashing fat drops on to the dust; a profligate waste in this land, where water was scarce as gold, and infinitely more valuable. The beast stared at the sunset a while, and then turned, ears a-twitch, to contemplate the distant inland sea whose waters were poison to drink.

A slow cloud crossed the sky. Its reflection crossed the sea's surface, perfectly mirrored. Pantera and the antelope watched it together, while the she-lion stood, carved out of time, waiting.

Presently the oryx dropped its head again. Pantera breathed. The lion made the last step and drew in her long back, shrinking into herself until her hind legs were coiled beneath. Her tail flagged left to right and was still.

Pantera held motionless by an effort of will, the pain in his torso, his elbows, his bladder lost in the lilac night. The lion was the best he had seen in eighteen days of looking out for lions from his desert ledge, where the vultures had watched early for his death.

He would not have minded dying here in the austere beauty of the desert, away from the palms and the olive groves, far from the timid sheep and the stench of humanity and its politics.

Here was only sky and rock and wheeling hawks and the small locusts that fed on dust, and mountain ibex that could spit a man on their scimitar horns, and wild asses that could never be tamed, and white oryx, whose beauty made poets weep. And the lioness who must make a kill here, now, that she and her young might not starve.

There passed a stillness long enough for Pantera to breathe and breathe again, and then she was flying through the air, swift as a thrown spear, perfect in the certainty of her intent.

The crack of the beast's neck breaking rebounded threefold off the rocks. It crashed to the ground, its galloping legs sweeping the dust long after it died, carrying its soul to an afterlife set aside for white antelopes, where they might graze on lush grass on gentler inclines, where wadis ran with clear water, where the lions fed on other beasts.

The lion held herself aloof until the flailing hooves had stilled. Then, she gave a coughing grunt that summoned her three cubs from a fissure in the rock.

Too young to hunt, too starved to live much longer without food, with knife-sharp ribs staring through their mottled sand-coloured hair, they crept forward on their bellies until the smell of meat drenched their fear and, in a delirium of bloody joy, they hurled themselves to the feast. Goaded by their mewls, their dam ripped open the belly and let the guts spill out, and set her jaws to the steaming liver.

Pantera slid back then, dry-bellied and soundless, back along the ledge to a place he could wriggle into, and stand up and turn round and slide across the top of the bluff to the other side. Here was a fissure with steps cut in the side so that he could climb down, and find a place – at last – to urinate, and then climb back up to yet another hard, harsh rocky plateau on which was a camp that was both hidden and yet had a view across the whole of Judaea in any direction.

Menachem waited for him, sitting on a rock with his

saddle bags tied, and his knife across his knee, and his eyes trained on the darkening sun: no lilacs now, only deep, bloody red and purple, like a bruise. His black hair shone in the reddening light. His brows were solid lines, carved by the hand of a god. A scroll lay rolled and fastened at his side. 'Did she come?'

He held up a water skin. Pantera took it and drank. 'She came, she killed, she has fed her young.'

He had seen the lion first on his third day here, and had watched her daily since. The desert healers had thought him sun-struck, but they had also thought he was going to die and had been content to let him occupy his mind with something other than the pain of breathing.

That he could observe her now with little pain was down to the healers' ministry; to the bindings of linen and poultices of black mud from the poison-sea that were said to suck the illness from any wound, of body or soul. Their care had been exemplary and effective, but the day he had shown himself well enough to get to the ledge by himself they had washed their hands in the ritual vessels set beside him and turned away, not wishing to soil themselves further with one not given to their god.

Menachem had paid them with his own gold as they left, and, with the ever-present Mergus, had taken over the application of the stinking black mud to Pantera's abdomen, to his shoulder, to his left ankle, which had never fully healed after the interrogations in Britain. It was improving now, or they had told him so, and he had not the strength to disbelieve them.

The days had passed in a stupor of hot, stinking mud,

but they did pass, and with each one he had been less prone to sleep without warning and more inclined to discourse and always, when he woke, Menachem, not Mergus, had been the one at his side, awake and willing to talk.

Over the course of a dozen nights, they had discussed the mountains, the desert and the beasts that lived therein. They had talked of the sky, the stars, the naming of the constellations, which was different in every tongue and creed, and the ubiquitous presence – or otherwise – of the sand-spirits that the Syrians believed in, the ghûls, the ifrit, the djinn.

If it was late, and they were tired, they discussed the differences between their gods: Mithras, god of truth who required of his followers that they face their own fears, that no man might have mastery over them, but had no written creed, and desired none, lest men come to worship the written word over the truth; and the Hebrew god, whose name could not be spoken, whose laws were so plentiful and written so completely that men did, indeed, fight and die to uphold one or other truth of them.

'There is a simpler truth beneath all the written laws,' Menachem had said, 'and the people are ready to hear it. But first we must take Jerusalem, or they will not have peace to listen.'

And so they had discussed the possibility of taking Jerusalem, which was under Saulos' control now; ruled from the tower-fortress of the Antonia that was built so close to the Temple as to be part of it. They talked of how the tower could be taken with the least loss of life; how the garrison Guard might be lured out into

307

full battle and outflanked; how, if that failed, they might drive tunnels under the walls of the Antonia to collapse them, and how the emperor might be brought to denounce Saulos in ways so unambiguous as to be fatal.

What they had not ever discussed was Masada and the possibility that they might assault it.

The whole idea might have been a dream born of a fever, except that each day of the last five Pantera had walked to the top of the nearest mountain and stared south towards the high, flat bluff on which Herod had built his stronghold, with its impregnable wall all around and its astonishing hanging palace, and its storerooms to provide for any who lived there: enough food and water – and weapons – to last a thousand men for ten thousand days, or so it was said, or ten thousand men for a thousand days, nobody was ever clear which, but enough, certainly, to take Jerusalem.

Pantera came to sit now beside Menachem. 'We have waited long enough,' he said. 'We should go.'

'The lion's kill was an omen?' Menachem stretched a rare smile. 'I did not think you a man of superstition.'

'The omen, if we need one, was that I could climb up unaided on to the rock, and lie for an afternoon still enough for a lion and an antelope not to see me, and climb down again afterwards. I am fit enough, therefore, to lead you into Masada.'

Menachem's smile faded. He turned his face to the east, where the first silver blade of the moon sliced open the night, letting the stars leak in, one at a time, dimly. He looked down at his hands. 'I did not betray you.'

'I know.'

'I thought perhaps—'

'That we had not spoken of Masada since we came here because I feared you would betray me further? That was true at first.'

'And now?'

'Now?' Pantera rose, walked a few paces and scooped up a small stone and juggled it from hand to hand. 'You are a patient man, but Saulos is not. If you were going to betray me, I would be dead.'

He threw the stone hard and fast, slanting across the desert. It bounced five times before it fell. 'The traitor, therefore, is someone else. Perhaps someone in Jerusalem.'

'Which means that Hypatia is in danger,' Menachem said. 'Iksahra, Kleopatra and Estaph also.' They had stayed when the rest left: Hypatia, for a dream; Iksahra and Kleopatra, because they would not leave her; Estaph because . . . Mergus had not been clear why Estaph had stayed behind. It seemed most likely he had been asked to cleave to Hypatia and thereby make Jerusalem safe for Pantera's return.

'We are all in danger,' Pantera said. 'Which is why we must assault Masada.' He nodded south, whence came the fickle, blustery wind that made knives out of dust and scraped them across his eyes.

Menachem came to stand beside him. Together, they gazed at the distant mass of rock that hogged the horizon, the only truly flat-topped mountain in the whole Judaean desert.

'If a man were to stand on the edge of the casement wall and fly a banner of white silk enough to clothe a tall man,' Pantera said, 'I think it would be seen by a sharp-eyed observer who sat here, waiting. Who among your men could see it best?'

'My cousin Eleazir has especially long sight,' said Menachem. He glanced sideways at Pantera, so that he did not have to say, *Eleazir might be the traitor who sold you to Saulos.* Both knew it might be true, but had no proof, and so could not yet act.

Pantera said, 'Would you trust your cousin to convey news of a victory to the rest of your men?'

'I would. He wants the weapons as much as we do. Afterwards . . . we will worry what happens afterwards if we are alive.' Menachem stretched his arms above his head until his shoulders cracked. 'When you say "the rest of my men" – which will they be?'

'The nine hundred we will leave behind when we ride for Masada. We can take no more than one hundred with us. You need to pick those among your warriors with the best head for heights, but also the most experience of combat. If you have any with experience of combat?'

'I have men who have fought each other in practice. They have killed when they had to, but in small numbers and always with the advantage of surprise. They have never faced trained legionaries in full battle.'

'If I play my part right, we will have the advantage of surprise. As to trained legionaries . . . my father was never clear who was sent to Masada. As a child, I thought it was a place of punishment, where men were sent to march away their time stranded on a rock in the noonday heat with the wind that can flay a man's skin in an hour and the rains that come twice a year if you're lucky.'

'And now? What do you think now?'

'I have begun these last days to wonder if it was not perhaps a place of reward. Herod's three-tiered hanging palace is there. It is said to surpass anything in Jerusalem for luxury. There are baths, and a gymnasium, and food to keep a thousand men for ten thousand nights. For men who dream of Rome—'

'It would be a posting given by their gods; safe, secure from attack and free from the daily harassments of the city.' Menachem began his long-limbed pacing. 'If you are right, then are these men old, about to retire? Or the best of the garrison, sent to rest and recover?'

'I don't know.' Pantera found his nerves strung newly tight. He folded his arms across his abdomen, and looked south towards Masada. A young moon was rising, made yet pale by the old sun's gold.

He said, 'Do you know the story of how Alexander of Macedon took the Sogdian Rock?'

'Tell me.'

'The Sogdians were vicious mountain people, who had a mountain fortress that was said to be impregnable: easy to defend, impossible to assault. When Alexander's troops first approached it, the defenders laughed at him, and said he would need to teach his men to fly if he were to reach them.'

'Let me finish.' Menachem gave his rare smile, which lit his face. 'Every boy learns this story, even here. Alexander ordered that three hundred of his best climbers go up in the dark, past the Sogdians to the summit. They lost thirty men on the way but the others succeeded. When they reached the top, they unfurled the silk banners that had been wrapped round their waists and let them fly in the wind. Alexander called up to the defenders that he had, indeed, found men who could fly. The Sogdians surrendered without a fight, thinking him god-blessed.' Menachem looked away from the moon. 'Are we, too, going to fly to the summit of Masada?'

'No, we will climb, and if necessary we will stuff our mouths with silk as Alexander's men did, so that if we fall, we will not cry out and alert the sentries. But then, if we are lucky, they'll think we have flown. You should tell your men this story before we leave. Surprise is the greatest asset in any assault, but in this it is doubly so, for if we succeed, we will have done what everyone believes to be impossible: we will have taken Masada without a thousand-day siege.'

'Shock can weaken even the hardest of veterans,' Menachem agreed. 'I will tell the tale to the men who are coming with us. But what about those left behind? What do I tell them?'

'Tell them to be patient until tomorrow's noon. If they see the white banner, they can ride in and collect their weapons. If they don't – if we fail – they can do whatever you think best. If you were to ask my advice, I would suggest they send runners into Jerusalem saying that you have succeeded and that you'll fall on the city like a flight of locusts. Half of a battle is won in the hours before it starts. If they're lucky, panic will spread among those who have most to lose and the garrison commanders will pack up the royal family and carry them to safety at Antioch, leaving the city open for your men to enter, with or without you at their head.'

Menachem turned to the rising moon. 'If we fail in Masada, I will leave instructions for my men to do as you say.' He bowed from the waist. 'But we are makers of luck, you and I. We will not fail.'

CHAPTER THIRTY-THREE

In her dream, Hypatia was a lion, stalking her prey. By scent she knew him, by the subtle changes of his fear; he was Saulos, and he knew that she was coming.

Pad on slow pad, with the taste of blood sifting past her teeth to her tongue, she advanced down a darkened alley. Or perhaps it was a fissure in some distant mountain; the part that knew she was Hypatia, and so knew that she was dreaming, could not tell where she was, except that the air smelled of new rainwater and man-urine together, and someone, or something, whispered in a tongue she did not know.

The air was tactile, teasing, feeding her facts. She knew Saulos was round a corner to her left, that he bore blood-wet iron in one hand, that he was afraid, and desperate, and yet . . . she snuffed the line of wind that carried news of him to her and found that he was not alone. She sat back on her haunches in surprise, and cocked her head and heard him laugh and speak a name: hers.

Hypatia.

In the dream's mirage, she saw a glint of sunlight on

metal, and smelled the stink of Saulos' exultation. She hated that. Her tail lashed. Biting down on her tongue, she made herself wake up.

'Hypatia?'

A hand touched her shoulder. Her eyes sprang open and met other eyes, cat eyes, gold and black in the soft light of morning. Hot, meaty breath warmed her face. Whiskers pricked the fine skin of her neck. Behind them stood Iksahra.

She pushed herself up. Iksahra's hand remained on her shoulder for a moment, and then withdrew. 'You called out,' she said. 'I came.'

She did not say how she had been close enough to hear, or why she had come; they had fought together in battle, had each saved the other's life more than once. The exertion of that, the physicality, the stretching of one's soul to the ends of existence – all of it was as intimate in its own way as the bedchamber and it moved them beyond the need to ask obvious questions.

Iksahra had been near, she had heard Hypatia call out.

And now she was here. In Hypatia's bedchamber, which held, after all, its own intimacy, different from the battlefield.

'What did I call?' Hypatia asked.

'Saulos. You called Saulos by name. Is he close?'

Hypatia shut her eyes. The dream hovered over her, fine as morning mist and as hard to hold on to. She pressed her fingertips to her eyelids, and caught at the wisping memories. 'Not close to here, to this palace, but close to success. He's sending a message-dove that he believes will help him.'

'He's sending for reinforcements.' Iksahra gave a soft laugh. 'He has the entire garrison Guard with him in the Antonia. We have Jucundus' detachment from Caesarea. Does he still not feel safe?'

'He may have news by now of Pantera and Menachem. If he thinks there's a chance Menachem can arm his men and march them into the city, he won't feel safe.'

Hypatia rose as she spoke, and only thought afterwards that she was unclothed. Iksahra did not step back, or look away, but sent the cheetah off to the room's edge with a crook of her finger.

They stood face to face in the dawn's peach light, close enough to touch, to breathe in the other's out-breath, to smell the layered wildness of horses, of hay, of hunting cat, of healing scars. It occurred to Hypatia that this was the first time another woman had been in her bedchamber since . . . Since Alexandria, which was not a safe memory. Since Hannah.

She took a step back. 'Can you hunt Saulos' message-doves as you once hunted ours?'

'With pleasure.' Iksahra's smile caught Hypatia somewhere under her ribcage, leaving a sharp pain. She reached for a robe to cover herself. 'Take Kleopatra,' she said. 'See if you can keep her away from the palace long enough for the council to meet this morning. It's not safe for her here.'

'She won't want to come.'

'It will do her no harm to find that she cannot always have what she wants.' On impulse, too fast to let herself think, Hypatia reached for Iksahra's hand. 'Stay safe.'

'I am always safe,' Iksahra said, and squeezed and let go and was gone to the beast gardens to find her falcons and her horse and the princess who did not want to be with her. Her cat paused in the doorway and gazed back with baleful yellow eyes.

Hypatia stood until it had gone, then dressed with care for the day ahead.

The sun was twice its own height over the horizon when Hypatia, the royal family and their closest attendants met in the audience room of the palace, which had become, perforce, their war room and council chamber.

They were grouped on dining couches; Berenice and Hyrcanus on one, Drusilla on a second with a gap where Kleopatra might have been. Agrippa, on the third, was at the head, with Polyphemos directly behind him. Hypatia took the fourth.

Estaph stood behind her, a solid presence, carved from mute flesh. He alone wore no silks, and kept his war axes at his either side. His parting from Mergus had been painful to watch, and Hypatia had said more than once that he should go with Pantera, to guard him, but the Parthian had his own path and had sworn himself to her protection for Pantera's sake; he would not leave.

Hypatia had doubts as to what one man could do in the nightmare that Jerusalem had fast become, but she felt safer in his company than without it, which was a thing rare enough to be cherished.

They breakfasted on dates, olives and flat bread, and drank watered wine. Slippered slaves came and went, silently, with only the occasional anxious glance to show how far it was from being any ordinary day.

Then Jucundus brought eight armed guards, four more than had been at any of their previous daily meetings, and destroyed the illusion. He stationed them at the doorway, half on each side, with the door, a hand's breadth of solid cedar, closed and barred between.

Before he had walked the breadth of the room, Berenice said, 'Have you word that we are under assault?'

The officer came to a halt within the half-circle of their dining couches. He saluted, crisply, as he had each of the past eight mornings since the king's retinue had found themselves confined to the palace, unwilling to stay, unable to leave. He met Berenice's eye and then Hypatia's, and last the king's.

'Not specifically, lady, but Saulos has had the Guard search the entire city for Pantera and not found him. This palace is the only place to which he cannot gain access. He knows Pantera is not here, because people saw him being carried from the city, but still he will want to look, and in looking he will want to fix his hold on power.'

Agrippa still held the throne in title, if not in fact; they deferred to him, let him speak first. He stood, thinking it made him more royal. His silks were of sun-yellow, with red at the margins; they made him smaller than did the gold of his public appearances, or the plainer white he favoured in private.

Presently, he turned to Jucundus. 'Are you suggesting we invite him into the palace?' he asked. 'The usurper who would take a city and destroy it?'

'Avowedly not, sire. But he has two and a half thousand men of the garrison Guard and we have five hundred Syrian cavalry not accustomed to siege warfare. They are all sworn to give their lives in your majesties' service, but they will not live long if we are assaulted directly.'

'Then we should assault them. Gain the advantage of surprise.' For a moment, with the kind morning light behind him, with gold on his head, with iron in his voice, Agrippa sounded like a commander, and a king; only his words undid him for their lack of strategy.

The silence lasted a heartbeat too long. Hypatia held the queen's gaze, until Berenice, too, stood.

'My dear lord,' she said, 'I have no doubt our soldiers and yourself would fight with great courage in any assault, whether of our choosing or our enemy's. But it remains the case that the numbers are overwhelmingly against us. You would die bravely, but you would still die, and all your men with you. And then, if we were lucky, we, too, would die – your women.' She swept an arm that took in herself, Drusilla, Hypatia, the gap for Kleopatra. 'If we were not lucky, we would be sold as the spoils of war, sent to the highest bidder, or to Rome, at Nero's pleasure.'

'There is also', Jucundus said, with a note of apology, 'the possibility that our assault may start the war we have striven so hard to prevent. Your subjects will not take well to seeing their king slaughtered in the streets with less care than a Passover lamb. They will fight, and once they start they will not be stopped, even if we are all dead.'

'Which is precisely what Saulos intends,' said Hypatia.

Agrippa closed his eyes against the sun's soft touch. 'We are a small nation; Rome is vast, with greater resources than any we can ever garner. Set against

319

them, we cannot prevail.' His eyes sprang open. 'What then is your counsel? Should we leave this place? Flee to Antioch in Syria? To a Roman governor who will glory over our discomfort?'

'Your majesty is ever wise.' Jucundus bowed his relief. 'The governor of Syria is not foolish. He will see the advantage in granting succour when it is most needed; he will know that this situation cannot last, that Saulos must be made to give up his hold on the city, and that when that happens he will be rewarded both by yourself and by the emperor for his grace.'

'When should we go?'

'Tonight, if it please your majesty, under cover of darkness. The gates to the east of this palace are held by our men, and even now I have auxiliaries scouting the countryside under pretence of a hunt. We shall have a safe route by nightfall.'

Agrippa paced the breadth of the room. Polyphemos tried to follow, but soon fell still, and stood winding his hands round each other until Hypatia wanted to choke him.

Mid-stride, Agrippa paused. 'What if Saulos has already petitioned Syria for help? The Twelfth legion is there. It may yet be that he could call them here on a pretext, to help him secure his hold on our city.'

'I believe he may have endeavoured to do so, majesty,' Hypatia said. 'But the message-birds fly only in daytime, and in daytime Iksahra's falcons can hunt. She and Kleopatra are out now with them. He may send a courier by horseback: that we cannot stop. But I believe he will not succeed in calling aid by any faster route.'

'Good!' Agrippa smiled for the first time that

morning. 'We are well served!' He clapped her on the back as if she were one of his captains, until Estaph stepped forward, alarmed at the assault on her person, and the king moved back.

Jucundus bowed as he left the room. 'Tonight,' he said. 'At the dark of the moon. Be ready to leave when I call for you.'

CHAPTER THIRTY-FOUR

With Mergus riding at his shield side, Pantera led a hundred men on a moonlit ride far more exacting than the one from Caesarea to Jerusalem. Near midnight, he brought them to the foothills south and east of Masada, leading them to a place where they could find shelter from the ruinous wind.

They tethered their horses in care of one boy to every twenty mounts and, wrapping their faces against the grit, came as close as one hundred men reasonably could to the base of the vast, flat-topped bluff that was Masada. Menachem, Mergus and eleven hand-picked climbers moved forward to gather round Pantera.

'Masada is a diamond shape . . .' Pantera took up a stone and drew a rhomboid in outline on the flat piece of rock at his feet. He felt clear-headed again, as he had on first entering Jerusalem. This time, newly, he felt the presence of the god, close as a lion's breath behind his right shoulder. Mergus held the left, quiet as a ghost, viewing every Hebrew as a potential threat.

Pantera closed his eyes and took his mind back to his childhood and, with the shapes fresh in his mind, drew his stone in a line along the map.

'The rock's long axis runs north to south. Herod's three-tiered hanging palace lies here – at the north end, sheltered from sun and wind: we will not attack that, nor near the water gate on the west side. To the east, the snake path runs up to a narrow guarded gate: the Romans believe this is the only way men can enter. Moshe—' Moshe stepped forward, the only man of the eleven in armour. 'You will lead your men up this path as soon as night falls. You will need to walk with care, one foot in front of the other, feeling out the route. A misplaced step will spell your deaths.'

'Such a death would not be quiet,' Moshe said, frowning. 'If we scream, the legionaries will hear us.'

'When Alexander had his men climb the fortress of the Sogdian Rock, they stuffed their mouths with silk scarves so that they might not scream and alert the defenders. I took the liberty of bringing some.' Eighteen silk scarves spilled from Pantera's saddle bag. Black, fine, perfect.

Moshe stared at him. He was a small man with arms furred like a goat, perfect for climbing. Stony-faced, he said, 'Alexander paid the first man to the summit an entire talent of gold.'

'You will have weapons enough to take Jerusalem.' Mergus' voice came out of the dark. 'Would you rather have gold?'

In silence, Moshe took the scarves, noosed them on his arms and returned to his team. Pantera watched the other men, who did not have to climb the snake pass in the dark, and did not know yet that it was the easy route.

He said, 'The gate at the top of the pass is guarded by two men at any one time. They will not sleep on duty, you can depend on that. Therefore, keep out of sight until you hear us. Menachem has already told you the signal.'

'If Moshe's men wait on the only route up, how are the rest of us to gain access to the top?' asked Aaron, who was older than most, balding all the way to a line that crossed behind his ears, so that it looked as if he shaved the front half of his head. Nevertheless, he sat at the head of the ten decade-leaders who sat in the moon-shadows beneath the bluff; by their silence, he had their respect.

'We will gain entry in the south, here.' Pantera marked a circle on his map. 'The palaces and guardhouses – and their storerooms – are all north of the east-west line. The south is minimally guarded, if at all.'

'There is no access from the south,' Menachem observed quietly; the first time he had spoken since their arrival. 'Which is why it is not guarded.'

'The garrison believes there is no access from the south,' Pantera said. 'But my father was part of the garrison here and he brought me to Masada when I was twelve years old, not long after my mother died. We were here for three months and he set me the task of imagining how I might assault it. I chose the south. And I tested it.'

'Did your father tell anyone of your success?'

'Not that I know of, but I left Jerusalem soon after-wards. Which is why I will go first. If I'm wrong and he

324

shared what we found, or if someone else has discovered the same route, then I will die, but the rest of you will have time to withdraw and to call back Moshe's men from the snake path.'

'I have studied this place all day,' Menachem said, and indeed he had wrapped himself in cloth the colour of grit and wormed closer to the rock in the afternoon's heat. 'I see no way to ascend the south of the rock unless you would have us climb a sheer wall in the dark?'

'Did you see the aqueducts?'

'I saw a channel cut in the southern mountains, leading away from the wadi. And yes, an aqueduct crossed from there to the rock of Masada. It emptied straight into a cistern cut in the heart of the rock at the southern end. It casts a shadow now, even in moonlight, like a thread of a spider's web.'

'It is stronger than spider thread,' Pantera said. 'And it empties into the side of the cistern, as a pipe might empty into a jug, so . . .' He drew a square box, and then at one side drew a lipped opening. 'The engineers cut it so that there's a lip that juts into the interior, so that none of the water is lost. If we lower ourselves down from the aqueduct, we will land in the waiting water.'

'Unless the cistern is empty,' Menachem said. 'In which case we'll fall a great distance on to solid rock. What are the chances of that? A garrison of legionaries must use more water than this holds many times over and there hasn't been rain for months.'

Pantera rubbed his hand over his sketch. 'Herod intended that this place keep a thousand men for ten thousand days,' he said. 'There's another aqueduct to the north that fills cisterns to supply the fountains and baths as well as drinking water, and two others nearer to the barracks. The one we will enter is the furthest distant from the garrison and is drawn from only in extremity. There will be enough water to cushion our fall.'

Ten uncertain men huddled round him. Each led nine others. To reach the hundred, then, he must reach these ten. Pantera turned a slow circle and squarely met the gaze of each one.

'Nobody will force you to come. If your ten wish to stay here to greet us as we come down, no one will think less of you for it. Speak to your lieutenants and let them know what we plan. Those who wish to come with me should wind their tunics tight about their loins and have no scarf hanging free. You must be as if you were naked, while still clothed. It will be best to leave your sandals behind.'

He did not look at them as he took the hem of his own tunic and pulled it up between his legs to fasten in his belt. He did not listen to the murmurings in fast, accented Aramaic as he took the scarf that had protected his eyes against the withering wind and wound it so tight about his head that it became a second skin. But when he was done, and looked round, ten men stood likewise ready, and the ninety behind them were finishing what must be done.

Not a man of the hundred remained unprepared, and when he and Mergus led them, not towards the giant bluff of Masada, but up the rock face that rose from the desert behind them, they followed without protest.

*

Pantera had been twelve years old when he climbed to the aqueduct. Then, the places chiselled into the rock where feet and hands might find purchase had seemed impossibly far apart. Now, if anything, they were too close together so that he must hinge his body about his waist, or risk pushing his weight too far back.

But they were there, precious handholds, even more precious toeholds, that made of the sheer rock if not a ladder, then at least something that could be climbed in the dark, nursed on by the spare light of the rising moon, while the vagrant wind, that blew from the north as easily as the south, flung grit in his eyes, up his nose and through his teeth to his throat.

He spat away a mouthful, and reached up into a shadowed cleft. He stroked the rock; he had come to love it, to care for it as he cared for a good horse, or a well-balanced blade. Sliding his fingertips over rough-ness and projections and cracks . . . there, he found the ledge, a finger's length long, where he could brush away the accumulated dust and rubble of three decades and fasten his hand on the flat ledge beneath, and hold himself steady while he crooked his leg up a foot's length and his bare toes sought a counterpart ledge below; and found it, and it took his weight and let him ease on up and up again, with the rising moon at his back and a hundred men below, testing the selfsame handholds and finding them, silently.

The climb did not go on for ever, only seemed to. The moon was not at its full height when Pantera's searching hand felt over the next small ledge and did not stub his fingertips at the back, but slid on a full arm's length to find a small fissure angled down and back, so that he could fix his fingers in it and haul himself bodily on to a wide platform with a water channel cut through the centre, and a half-pipe aqueduct stretching away on a small incline towards Masada.

There was no time to look at that: already an arm came up over the ledge, fingers stretching, seeking. Pantera lay flat on his belly and leaned over. Menachem's scarf-huddled eyes came level with his.

'We're here.' Pantera guided his hand to the hold. 'Stay by me when you're up. The others can move to the back, out of the wind. Tell them to drink and eat, but sparingly.'

Mergus came next and then, after him, the Hebrews. A hundred times, Pantera guided a hand. At the hundredth, there was room on the ledge for perhaps three more men. It was Pantera's father who had made the estimate of how many it could hold. He sent thanks to his memory.

To Mergus and to Menachem, he said, 'That was the easy part.'

Mergus grimaced. 'I thought it might be.'

Masada stood below them, an elongated platter, stretched under the moonlight: they had climbed its height and half as much again. The aqueduct stretched down into the night, a single strand of spider's web that swayed in the wind.

'The aqueduct is bigger than it looks,' Pantera said, 'and it takes a weight of water when it's full that is far more than the weight of unarmoured men. We crawl down it with two body lengths between each man, lying flat, and don't bring our heads above the edges.'

'Is it big enough to hide us?' Menachem asked.

'It was when I was twelve years old.' From somewhere beyond the reach of memory, Pantera found a smile, and saw it repeated, nervously, through the massed men behind him. In the desert, they had not believed him; he had been a stranger, spinning fables. Now, they sucked in his words, and used them to bolster their courage.

'You are all lean. Nobody will get stuck,' he said to them now. 'And at the bottom, we drop off the end into the lip of the cistern.

Menachem drew his scarf tighter around his head. 'Which is the worst part, I assume?'

'It is,' Pantera said. 'If you can do that, you can do anything at all. After that, all we have to do is swim across the cistern. If we're lucky, the stars will shine in to guide us.'

'And if we're not lucky?'

'Then it will seem like the edge of Hades, and we will have to hope that I can find the ladder that leads up out of it. If we don't we'll be climbing back along the aqueduct. And going back, it's all uphill.'

CHAPTER THIRTY-FIVE

Kleopatra had not wanted to go hunting with Iksahra. She had made it clear, in fact, that she considered Iksahra's offer to be a bribe that dishonoured them both. But she pulled herself together enough to hold her tongue while the slaves presented the horses, and Iksahra lifted the tiercel that had been her cousin's bird and set it on Kleopatra's gloved fist; her temper had not spilled over into making a scene in front of the slaves.

In crisp, uncomfortable silence, they rode from the women's gate below the palace, trotting north over sloping pastures where goats grazed in the perpetual shade of Jerusalem's wall, and out past olive and lemon groves and pomegranate trees, along the ridge above the wadi, to the higher ground, where Iksahra released the falcon, sending her high on the morning's warm air.

The bird climbed in slow, lazy spirals until she was a speck against the lightening blue of the sky. Iksahra had no sight of prey, but there was something in the bird's attention that made her look where it looked, so that she saw the moment when it slewed round in its turn and gave the sharp, high cry that was the signal for oncoming prey.

Iksahra directed her gaze west, where the old night still held the sky. There, a blur sped along the hazed horizon, flying hard and straight in the way of a message-bird, bred for speed. The falcon reached the top of the sky and cried a second time. The tiercel heard its mate and bated from Kleopatra's fist, hurling itself against the jesses, screaming.

'Hold him,' Iksahra said, without turning. 'Talk to him. Tell him how proud he is, and how well he will hunt when his time comes. Keep him still or he'll throw her off her kill.'

She spoke as she might have done to a skittish horse, not looking, not scolding, yet certain of the outcome, and was rewarded presently by the beginnings of a murmur and the sounds of the male bird rattling its wings, and the small chirruping whine that said his pride had been dented, but he was prepared to be mollified.

Iksahra felt a depth of satisfaction that surprised her. It seemed to her then, under the morning sun, with the dew still wet on the grass and the yellow-eyed goats stepping sideways from the cheetah, that the day shone, and her heart ached and she was not sure, yet, that she wanted to name the reason.

The falcon cried, high in the air. Iksahra raised her hand to shield her eyes.

'See now?' For Kleopatra's benefit, she jutted her elbow out towards the soaring falcon. 'She's at the top of her rise, where the air thins and won't hold her any more; she can't go higher, but she can hang there, resting, as you rest in calm water when you swim in a

331

river.' She wasn't sure that Kleopatra had ever swum in a river, but the point was made. 'And if you look along the tree line, you'll see the message-dove coming in, there – where the land meets the sky.'

'Just above the lemon grove? Where the trees are taller than the olives?' Kleopatra was engaged, in spite of herself.

'Exactly there. The falcon will wait until it comes out across the lighter pasture, where the goats are grazing. We can move the horses down there and be close to the kill. Carefully now; there are stones among the grasses, it's not safe to go fast.'

They went slowly, moving with the sway of the horses, stepping around the boulders that had been left, perhaps, for this reason: to stop men riding hard in a straight line towards the city.

From behind, without warning, Kleopatra said, 'Is Saulos going to kill Hypatia? Is that why she's sent us both away, so we'll be free from harm?'

The warm and mellow morning became suddenly chill. Sweat grew in cold drops along the flat blades of Iksahra's shoulders as she spun her horse. Flatly, she said, 'Saulos is not going to kill Hypatia.'

'Are you sure? She's set herself against him and he's the governor now in all but name. He could.'

'He won't.'

'Saying it won't make it true.' Kleopatra brought her horse alongside. She was still white, but not now with rage. Her gaze flicked past Iksahra's shoulder. 'Look, your bird is coming down for the kill.'

The falcon was dropping from the sky, wings closed in the impeccable moon-curve beloved of the Berber people. It was as perfect a stoop as Iksahra had ever seen and it should have roused her to a fierce and savage passion where the glory of the kill was hers as much as the bird's.

Today, now, she watched through fear so dense that it took an effort of will to reach through it, to lift the bird from its kill, and unwind the message cylinder from the leg of the stricken dove, to open the tiny capsule and lift out the paper therein and—

'What does it say?' Kleopatra asked.

Shaking her head, Iksahra passed it over. Saulos had never imagined she could read. She did not know if Kleopatra's easy assumption was a compliment, or its opposite.

'It's in code.' Kleopatra was frowning at it, biting her lip. She looked younger than she had done moments before. Her mouth moved as she read, framing the words, then stopped. 'Latin writing, but not Latin words.' She looked up, her features brightening. 'Pantera will be able to read it. He knows the emperor's codes. If someone can get it to him in the desert, he'll know what it means.'

'It might not be one of the emperor's codes.'

'Even so, Pantera will be able to read it.' Kleopatra levelled her gaze at Iksahra. Her eyes were the blue of a late-night sky. Her grandmother's, it was said, had been the same. She was fourteen years old and could have been forty, or four hundred. 'We should go back.'

'Not yet,' said Iksahra. 'It's too soon.'

'By whose accounting?'

'My own.'

'No, it's not!' The girl wrenched her horse round,

sawing at its mouth. 'Hypatia made you do this! She wants me kept away from the palace, so I can't sway the king, or my aunt or mother or any of the others and make them stay. They're going to flee again and leave Jerusalem in the hands of that filth, to . . .' Kleopatra straggled to a halt, and put her hand to her throat, and then her face. 'To those men who are coming for us,' she said, flatly.

Ahead, a company of men trotted four abreast along the path that led from the city. Iron glinted in the sun, and polished brass on their helmets.

'We must run.'

Iksahra caught her reins. 'No. It's too late.'

'Those are Saulos' men. Our horses are better than theirs. We could—'

'They have archers. I will not risk your life.' Iksahra took her hand from the girl's bridle. The day was young, and bright, and she wanted to hunt, and to kill, and, for the sake of a child, could not. 'We will be civil to them, and expect they will extend the same courtesy to us. I will command the cat not to hurt them, and you will hold the tiercel.'

'But the message cylinder . . . the one you took from the bird – they'll find it!'

'What cylinder?' Iksahra spread her arms and both the naked hand and the gloved one that had borne the falcon on its wrist were empty. She fixed Kleopatra with a stare of the kind that calmed horses. 'Don't speak of it. We will not be harmed.'

Iksahra spoke to the cat, and when the men came, it did not fight, but settled behind her horse. Iksahra addressed them civilly, and Kleopatra archly, in the tones of royalty, so that both were allowed to direct their horses into the midst of the company as it turned back to the city.

They were even left with their hunting birds, and thus did Iksahra return with the falcon feeding on her fist, each twist of its head throwing out evidence of what they had caught.

It fed to fullness before they reached the city and she had time to drop the dove beneath the feet of the trotting horses, and hood the falcon, so that when Saulos met them at the city gates, all that remained was a spot of blood on her hunting glove.

'Your majesty!' He was dressed in his sand-coloured silks, fulsome in his greeting of Kleopatra, smiling his victory. 'If you would be so kind, the full council of the Sanhedrin has convened in the heart of the city to address certain matters pertaining to the recent . . . disturbances. We will honour them with our attendance.'

He nodded to Iksahra, as if seeing her for the first time. 'Your beasts will be treated with utmost respect, I guarantee it.'

Polyphemos brought the message, written on papyrus, rolled and sealed. It came to Berenice, in her private apartments, not to the king. Hypatia alone was present.

Hypatia watched the queen break the seal, and read, and sit suddenly, pale to the point of death. She saw her wave Polyphemos from the door; he did not want to go, so it took a swifter motion than it used to.

'What?' Hypatia asked, when he was gone. Dread lay on her like a morning fog, draining her as surely as any ghûl.

Berenice spoke in a voice devoid of inflection. 'They have Kleopatra. And Iksahra.'

'Where?'

'They stand before the Sanhedrin. They will be charged with killing Governor Florus. The penalty is death by stoning.'

Hypatia said, 'I killed the governor.'

'I know that. Saulos knows it; he saw you. This is a trap. You will not walk into it.'

'I must,' Hypatia said, and heard her own voice as if from a distance, with a tunnel's echo between. 'Kleopatra is the next Chosen of Isis.'

Berenice turned her head. Her eyes were blank channels that led straight to her soul. In their depths, Hypatia saw a name form, and saw it taken away again, out of tact, or kindness, and was grateful. If Iksahra had been named aloud, she might well have lost what remained of her composure.

Berenice, queen in Caesarea, rose. 'Then I will come too,' she said. 'No – do not argue. You are my gift, given by the empress. Saulos cannot touch you while I am present.'

She rang a bell for her personal maid. 'We must change our clothing. The men of the Sanhedrin have . . . certain ways of viewing women. I am a widow before I am a queen and must be seen as both. You are my handmaid, and must be appropriate. We will do this alone, you and I. We have too much to lose to leave it to anyone else.'

CHAPTER THIRTY-SIX

The aqueduct was a black thread in the night's weaving, but it was behind him, and Pantera had not vomited, nor lost control of his bladder, nor screamed aloud his terror as he crawled down the long concrete trough held up on stalks of stone that looked barely strong enough to withstand the scrub of a mangy goat should it choose to scratch its back along them.

In that regard, he was a man, not a child. In all other ways of measuring, he had returned to his childhood, so great was the hold of the past in this place, where he had come to manhood, with his father pushing him on.

A slight lip rose under his fingers, which was how he knew he had reached the end of the line. The only light was from the stars which rendered everything a faint grey; his fingers, the concrete, the rock wall ahead of him that stretched, it seemed, for eternity in all directions – and the gap that was left between the aqueduct's end and the lip of the cistern. When he was twelve years old, that gap had been big enough to fall through. For years after he had been here, his dreams had seemed all to lead to this place, where he looked over a lip of fragile stone and found himself staring down on to the backs of the circling vultures, and then down, and down, and down to the antelopes that ran, small as ants, across the desert below.

The gap was still big enough, but the vultures had gone, and with them had gone some of the certainty that the earth must suck him from this place and drag him down to become another ant lying dead on the valley floor.

His heart tripped at the memory, his stomach lurched. He made himself remember that the gaping mouth in the side of the rock was more than big enough to take a grown man, as long as he got the angle right when he jumped.

He rolled over on to his stomach, turned in his own length, and wriggled backwards, holding on to the concrete edges of the aqueduct, gradually taking more weight on his hands until his whole body hung straight. Menachem was above him, his eyes wide as the moon. 'We do this backwards? On our bellies?'

'It's the only way. Tell each man to tell the one behind him as he comes to it, but no sooner: there's no point in letting them worry all the way up the line. Wait for me to call. In case there's no water . . .'

'You said there would be water.'

Pantera had already let go. Falling, the ghost of his youth came with him, sucking in the damp, cold air in a great breath just before he hit the water – the deep, cold, marrow-chilling water.

He bobbed to the surface, choking. Menachem's voice echoed down, drily amused. 'I hear that you were right.'

'Come quickly. I'll move out of the way.' Pantera paddled backwards, watching the spout cut in the rock. There was more light above than he had thought, but only in contrast to the utter darkness that was the cistern. Here, it was impossible to tell the water from the walls.

Menachem arrived in a ghostly splash, vanished, and came to the surface. '*Cold!*' he said.

Pantera's teeth were already chattering. 'We need to be fast. When we have ten men, we'll make a chain and I'll find the steps up.'

'It seems to me that a ladder would rot or rust in the time since Herod,' Menachem said.

'It's made of rock. There are holes cut in the wall that let a man climb up to the surface. I used them once; we have to hope they're still intact. We don't want to have to climb back along the aqueduct. Uphill, the swaying is worse.'

'You've done that?' Menachem's voice skipped over the water, sharp with surprise. 'You've been up and out, then back along the way we came?'

'My father thought it would be a useful learning. I was sick with fright halfway along, and thought the sway set up by my puking would make me fall, which made me wet myself. My father said the only thing I did not stink of at the end was dung. He was right.'

Mergus dropped from the aqueduct, and then Aaron, who always followed him. They bobbed up near them, swearing.

Menachem said, softly, 'Did he hate you?'

'No, I think he loved me.' Unexpectedly, Pantera found his throat too tight to say more.

'I am not a father to offer love, but I will be in your debt for life if you can find the ladder that will take us out of this place as swiftly as you said.' Menachem's teeth, too, were chattering. He fought to sound even.

Pantera smiled. 'I brought you in here. There is no debt if I lead you out again. Follow me, and make sure the men follow you in a chain, so nobody gets lost.'

He closed his eyes and called on his childhood, and then, neither twelve years old nor fully a man, struck out for the opposite side of the cistern. Men had been dropping in at regular intervals, cursing the cold. They made a line behind him, trusting.

At a certain point, he stopped. 'Here.' And then to Menachem. 'Look up.'

They looked together, past the lightless stone of the cistern, and on, up through a black tunnel to . . .

'I can see a star!' Menachem made himself whisper. Even a hand's breadth of sky seemed too close to the Roman garrison. 'Why is there only one? The sky should be full of them.'

'There's a well house above us, roofed over to keep the wind-blown grit from contaminating the water. Years ago, when I was here, I cut a small hole in the roof to see through, as you are seeing now.'

'At your father's behest.'

'Not entirely. I became lost down here the first time because I couldn't see the way out. Before the second try, I cut the hole. The ladder is here.' Pantera took Menachem's hand and raised it high. 'Can you feel steps cut in the rock? As long as they haven't worn away, we can climb out.'

He reached up to the first of the projecting spurs. He

had to jump to reach it when he was twelve; now it was not even a particularly long stretch.

Menachem caught his elbow. 'How many men will be able to stand in the well house?'

'My father thought fifty. We will bring up the first five decades, and then move them out to shelter. That'll be the time of most danger. I'll go first: if there's a guard, it will be best he believes I have come alone. If I live, I'll whistle to call you up.'

The ladder took Pantera to the surface faster than it had done when he was young; he was stronger, and he hated the water more. No guard waited in the well house. He knelt, with his face next to the well opening, and whistled softly. Menachem joined him, and then Mergus and Aaron and then the others of the first five decades. They fitted closely in the well house, wetly cold. Pantera knelt by the door, feeling for the hinges, and the bolts that held the latch.

'Is it locked?' Menachem asked.

'It never has been. A wooden latch lifts on the outside. There's a knot hole that a man might reach through to tip it up . . .' His fingers were a child's, searching across the grain until he found the knot and hooked his knife's tip around it and drew it inwards, slowly.

The knot came free of the wood. Wind hollered through the tiny gap, small foretaste of its fury. Pantera put his eye to it and, for the first time this day, saw the grey-pink dawn.

He cursed, softly. 'We've lost the night. We will have to call Moshe and his men soon, or they'll be seen.'

'Where do we go?' asked Mergus, who had worked his way to Pantera's shoulder.

'The women's palace is ahead and to our left. We can hide behind it, and call the rest up. This is the best time to attack, just as the night Watch changes with the day Watch. Those who have stood all night will be tired, those who are waking now will still be lagged with sleep. We will have all the advantage.'

Pantera's knife slipped in the sweat of his hand. He wiped it dry on his tunic and gripped it again, drew back and back and – *there!* – let fly . . .

A man grunted, softly. Iron chimed on stone. From somewhere close by, Menachem said, 'I would not have thought it possible with the wind as fierce as it is, with the man turning against the light, to put a blade between his cheek plates and the neck of his mail like that.'

Pantera forced his eyes open, not knowing they had closed: that was a thing his child-self had done that his man-self had abandoned long ago. 'You have to do it like that,' he said, suddenly shy. 'If you don't hit the larynx, they cry out and alert the others.'

Menachem was looking at him queerly. He shook himself and forced a smile. 'He was alone. We should go on to the sons' palace. It's smaller than this one.'

'Herod's sons?' Aaron asked, and spat.

'Yes. They lived here before he had them slain. There's room there for all of us. We'll join and then go forward together.' Pantera raised his arm in signal. Three groups of ten men slid out from behind the women's palace in whose shade they had been hiding. The remaining seven groups made a long, narrow line, sliding along the shelter of the casement wall.

He retrieved his knife and ran with them. At a certain

point, he left the safety of the wall and dodged inwards, across the open bluff, to hide in the shelter of another tall stone wall. A malevolent wind backed with the sun, catching sand and grit to hurl at the running men.

'Make your scarves into masks again. Leave only your eyes free. It'll help you breathe.' Pantera did it faster than he had done on the valley floor. The child in him was small now, watching the man do things it had barely dreamed about in his youth. He took up his knife and drew on the back wall of the palace.

'The main palace is here, at the western edge of the casement. There are storerooms there which will still hold weapons, but the garrison has its quarters in the north, around the upper tier of Herod's hanging villa. There are baths and stores there; it's easiest for the men. Their weapons will be there. We will attack while the Watch are looking eastward at Moshe and his men.'

He turned to Menachem. His smile came easily, bright and sharp. 'Now is the time to whistle. And be ready to run.'

CHAPTER THIRTY-SEVEN

Hypatia and the queen left the palace together in secrecy, and, in secrecy, they arrived at the small, unremarkable hall set behind the Temple, in which the city's councillors gathered to give their opinions on matters of law and faith, these two being inseparable within the walls of Jerusalem.

Berenice was dressed in simple blues of a hue so deep it could have been taken from the night sky. Her dress and the long-coat over it were cut in the style of the Hebrew women: modest and unfussy, with not a thread of silver or gold. She wore no jewels at neck or ears or fingers. No hint of balsam sweetened the air where she had been.

Her slippers were of satin, and she walked on clouds of righteousness. Her hair was bound back in a black sheaf of perfect modesty – the first time Hypatia had seen it so – and covered with a veil of the night-blue silk. No Hebrew councillor could have deemed her anything other than what she was: a widow and a queen.

The men of the Sanhedrin had not seen her yet; the

three windows of their council chamber and the tiers of candles cast their light into the centre of the hall, where Iksahra and Kleopatra stood together, black skin welded to white in their closeness. By not a flicker, not a trembling of a hair, did Iksahra show that she knew Hypatia had arrived.

Hypatia stood in the doorway, holding herself to stillness against the turmoil of her heart. She did not let her eyes rest anywhere for long, but glanced instead at the small, low-ceilinged hall, and the sixty or seventy men packed into it, dressed in their long-coated finery, crushed on to benches in a rough semicircle.

Yusaf was there, near the front, and Gideon not far behind him, but no others of the city laity that she recognized.

The High Priest, Ananias, sat in state before them, a gold-encrusted crab trapped in the curve of a net. He rose now to speak although his voice had lost its power since he had addressed the multitudes from the temple heights.

'It is unquestionably the governor's duty to deal swiftly with—'

A figure rose in a flurry of linen. 'Have the accused answered the seven enquiries? Have the witnesses who speak against them answered likewise?' The voice was the opposite of Ananias'; it rang with righteousness, bounced off the walls with its own power.

'Yusaf.' Hypatia mouthed the name to Berenice, who stood with her. 'Although he is now a merchant in Caesarea, he was trained in the law in his youth.'

'I know.' Berenice made a finite motion of her head. 'Ananias didn't expect difficulty. Listen. He flounders . . .'

345

'I don't think there is reason—' Ananias' voice drew out, threadily.

Yusaf cut it off at its thinnest. 'It is the law of this court, which is God's law; there must be witnesses who will testify against these women, and they must be questioned separately to see that they concur. They must answer in what week of years the crime took place, in what year, in what month, in what day, in what hour. If they agree on that, they must answer the nature of the crime in detail. I have not heard the accused speak in their own defence. I have not heard the witnesses speak for the accusation. I have not, in fact, heard any enquiries, nor their answers. We do ourselves a grave disservice if we let the rule of Rome remove from us the due process of law. One of these women is a princess of Caesarea, one is a native of the Berber lands. We may not—'

'They reside in Jerusalem, and therefore they are bound by our laws. We may—'

'Gentlemen, forgive my intrusion, but time is brief and our city lies in perpetual danger. Will you hear the address of your queen?' Beautiful, royal, exemplary in her modesty, Berenice stepped out of the dark porch and into the light of twenty-seven candlesticks.

The men fell silent; what else could they do? She was a vision of all they held dear, and if they remembered that they loathed her grandfather, and despised one of her husbands, it was with a small part of their minds that did not stop them from drawing a breath, and murmuring to each other.

Except for Ananias, who rose late, bowing a little, before the force of her majesty. 'My lady, this is not a place—'

'For women. I am aware of this and I crave the council's forgiveness for intruding upon the affairs of men. But there are times when a queen must set aside her fears and act as majesty requires. One of these women is my niece. The other, as is well known, has come here to render unto us the same service as did her father, whom we all know was ill-treated by our ancestor. I would be in dereliction of my duty did I not come here before the highest court of the land to speak on their behalf.'

She flattered them, and they accepted it as their right. Along the benches, greying heads inclined with a new gravity and murmured to their neighbours, adding weight to the different components of her argument. The volume rose, and rose, until they could have been in a market place, except that nobody, yet, was bargaining openly. The scents of rosewater and jasmine folded before the waves of man-sweat.

To Ananias alone, Berenice murmured, 'My lord High Priest, if these women are spared now, it may be that my brother the king can take news of your compassion directly to Rome when he journeys westward this summer. The emperor is known to look fondly on the men who stand against the forces of corruption in the heart of his empire.'

The emperor was known to have men skinned alive who failed to take a stand against open corruption, and the fact that they were priests of a minor local deity had never yet inclined him to mercy.

Ananias knew that as well as anyone. He pressed his lips to a white line. His eyes flicked from Berenice to the shadows in the far side of the room.

Aloud, she said, 'But before you can speak, we must

hear the charges against them. What is said of these two that warrants a convention of the full Sanhedrin?'

All eyes turned to the room's darker side, where Saulos held the shadows close about him, as a cloak.

Slowly, with careful majesty, Berenice, too, turned her gaze there. Alone among them, she had the courage to speak.

'Saulos of Idumaea. You came to Caesarea claiming friendship to my brother, and then you betrayed us. You came claiming that you held the friendship of Caesar, and in that you lied. Now you would bear false witness against my niece? Is there no end to your calumny?'

The chamber held its breath, so that air became a scarce thing, to treasure. Hypatia took a breath, and held it and let it out, and in all that time, Saulos did not step forward into the patch of sunlight that spread before him.

When he did deign to move, it was with his arms folded across his chest, so that his hands were almost hidden in the sand-silk; his face he arranged in thoughtful pose, of a man considering a fine point of law. His honeyed words reached them all equally.

'My lady.' He inclined his head; a dutiful subject. 'I regret that I have fallen from your favour and will do whatever I may to right that. I regret also that you have been deceived by men and women sent for that purpose. I do not lie. I have never done so. I speak always the truth as God gives it to me.'

He sounded humble and frank, but Hypatia heard an echo to his words, exactly as she had done through a lifetime's dreams, so that she knew each sentence before it was spoken: his and Berenice's. She knew, too, the actions each must take and the responses each must give. If nothing else, it gave her time to prepare herself.

'What is your truth now?' Berenice asked. 'I have heard that you accuse my niece of murdering the governor. You were present, as was I, when Gessius Florus lost his life. You know that my sister's daughter did nothing during the unfortunate violence in the beast garden besides protect herself from assault. I know of no man among the Sanhedrin who would not wish of his daughter that she defend herself from infamy.'

Until that moment, Berenice had not looked directly at the council. As a woman should, she had kept her eyes cast down, her hands looped in front, long fingers linked.

Now, she let her hot, hard gaze rake across them, one brow arched, and Hypatia saw them nod before her, as grain before a storm wind. But they rose again after and their eyes were all on Saulos, while his, at last, were on Hypatia.

'You were in the beast garden? I confess, lady, that in my haste to leave the carnage after the governor's untimely death, I had not seen that. I do now realize, though, that I was mistaken in my belief that your niece had held the knife that killed him. As you say, she defended herself with great courage against men she believed were set to ravage her, as any maiden should.'

He was walking now, and not a man in the room could look away as he came before Kleopatra, and knelt, and took her hand and pressed it to his brow. 'My lady, you have been sadly wronged. You will, of course, be released upon the instant.'

'And Iksahra?' Kleopatra's voice was the mirror of

349

her aunt's in its hauteur. 'If I am innocent, then no less is she.'

Saulos rose, the perfect image of magnanimity and grace. 'Of course. In my haste, I was mistaken. The guilty woman had dark hair, but not dark skin.' He bowed to Iksahra. 'My lady, please accept my apologies. You will be recompensed for your discomfort. Your beasts, too, will be returned to your care. Let me offer you an escort back to the palace. I understand the king will be leaving tonight for Antioch. I will take the palace as he leaves. It is right that I do so.'

Two guards came on his word, glittering efficiency. Even as they led Kleopatra and Iksahra from the chamber's minor exit, Saulos let his gaze drift past them to the entrance, as if searching for other guards, to give more majesty to the occasion. None were there; none had been stationed there. Instead, by that single act, he drew all eyes to Hypatia.

She had not left when the chance came, even with the echo in her ears that brought a warning. In too many dreams she had walked away, fearing what might come – what was now certain – and then she had seen Saulos twist the men around him, until stones rained down on innocent heads.

In the dreams, she had not known the two women accused, she had not known their names, or the contours of their skin, but she had known that their deaths would snap the thin thread of hope that she nurtured, that might yet lead a nation, and the world beyond it, to a kind of peace – and that therefore they must live.

'My lady!' Saulos bowed to Berenice so deeply that his brow brushed the floor. 'I am overwhelmed by your consideration. I see that you have delivered the guilty party into our hands. Your gifts to us are boundless. We—'

'You are not yet king, my lord. It behoves you not to speak as one. The king may yet remain in Jerusalem and you have no right of blood or law to occupy the royal chambers. You have already wrongly identified my niece as a murderer. Would you now also indict my handmaid, who was granted to me as a gift by my beloved sister, the late empress?'

'Most assuredly not. But, as Yusaf ben Matthias has asked, I would allow her accusers to be questioned according to the law, each separately, so that they may not confer. Four men of the garrison Guard will stand as witnesses to the governor's murder. I ask only that this woman be held in safety while they give their testament.'

The guards were already moving; eight men, not any of those who had been in the garden. They came prepared, with chains and locks. Nobody thought to ask why the witnesses had not been brought forward to testify when Kleopatra was named the killer, or what had prevented them from conferring in the nine days since the governor's death; under Saulos' sway, men did not question the facts laid before them.

Berenice, who did, moved to bar the guards' path.

'Stop! Your duplicity is obvious to those of us who know you. Hypatia will leave here with me, now. If you wish to press charges, you may do so when the witnesses have given their testament.'

'No, lady. Forgive me, but we will do so now.'

He lifted his hand. The guards moved with the speed of men long ago in receipt of their orders. They encircled

Berenice, and then, fluidly, Hypatia, drawing the two women into a ring of iron and sweat and Latin diction, where royalty carried no weight.

Saulos' mellifluous voice poured over them, calming the men of the Sanhedrin. 'Your majesty will accompany my men to the palace, where we may consider at greater length your role in the events surrounding the governor's death. We may—'

A muffled shout filtering through the closed door interrupted him. Outside, iron clashed on iron. A man swore in Latin, viciously. Another bellowed in Parthian. Briefly, the doors appeared to buckle, as if fine old oak could bend like metal; the edge of an axe appeared at the centre, embedded in the ancient wood.

Saulos took a step back. 'The Parthian,' he said, crisply. 'I want him alive. Tell the men that the one who kills him will suffer the death that would have been his. They would do better to die here than that.'

Even as he spoke, the door splintered open. Sunlight spewed over the black and white floor tiles, spattered now with crimson blood as a dozen armed garrison guards were hurled bodily into the chamber.

Hypatia was swept aside, caught by the eight guards who surrounded her, who lifted her bodily and carried her sideways and set her down again, with a surprising degree of courtesy, away from the scrum of heaving, bleeding flesh and armour that occupied the central part of the floor.

It ended faster than she might have thought, with only one man dead and that one not Estaph; he was unconscious, bleeding from a wound to his head. It took four men to carry him from the chamber.

In the shiver of disarray that followed, Hypatia felt a touch on her arm and turned to see Berenice, tight-lipped and tall. 'Would it have been better had he died?' asked the queen.

'I trust not.'

'And us? Would we also be better dead?'

'Not yet,' Hypatia said. 'Not all the paths from here lead the way Saulos would want,' and then there was no time to speak because Saulos was there, in a space made for him by the guards.

His gaze ripped over them all, but it came to rest on Hypatia last. He smiled then, with the freedom of a man who has reached the limits of his own control and finds he can do what he has always wanted, and no one has the power to stop him. Nero had found that, and Caligula. And now Saulos, who hated Hypatia and the Herods equally.

Then he looked away, to the gaggle of frightened old men, and waited until they took their seats, one by one. This time, when he spoke, he raised his voice, and his words were fashioned from frost and stone, not mellow honey.

'These women came here to continue their pursuit of sedition, treason and murder. They brought with them a Parthian mercenary as proof of their guilt. The recorders of the Sanhedrin will note it as such. As the emperor's representative, we thank you for your legal expertise and we will proceed to execution. Not—' He held out his flattened palm against the first thoughts of a murmur. 'Not today, because the Sabbath begins at sunset and we must not leave a dead man hanging, nor bring down one yet living, which he will surely be. Nor

353

tomorrow, which is the Sabbath day. They will die at dawn on tomorrow's tomorrow.

'By that time, your king will have departed for Antioch in Syria. I have given orders that one company of the garrison Guard might accompany him on his journey to safety. His sister, meanwhile, who is not a queen of Judaea, will suffer for her acts here. She will walk now back to the palace that was once hers to command. It will be instructive for the people of Jerusalem to see what has become of a woman they once held in respect.'

He turned and nodded beyond the door. 'Do it.'

Three more men entered, led by Vilnius, chief of the garrison Guard. They were all Romans: Saulos would not trust anyone else with this.

Vilnius stood before the queen, and saluted. 'Madam, you must disrobe.'

'Here?'

Vilnius flushed. He may have been Roman, but he had been posted in Judaea for three decades. He must have known Berenice since she was a child; certainly he was old enough to be her father.

He said, 'Only to your undershift. The emperor's envoy requires that you walk barefoot in your shift to the palace. As a penance.'

The emperor's envoy. Not a man of the Sanhedrin dared to murmur against the new, ungiven title.

Berenice turned her back on them and untied her robe. Her eyes were flat, unseeing, her fingers moved neatly. Her robe slipped free. Her undershift was of linen so fine it might have been silk and it hid nothing of her body. Men behind her shifted in silence; still they did not dare speak.

'Penance?' Berenice's gaze was on Saulos and there was life in it; a challenge, and a question that Hypatia could not read.

He said, 'A full penance. You will go with your hair shorn.'

'Tell my people I do this for them, to prevent war,' Berenice said, and bent her head, and Vilnius, with shaking hands, lifted the first of her tresses across the upturned blade of his knife. Black sheaves of hair fell like blighted corn across the floor.

Hypatia removed her shoes. Nobody asked for her clothing. Nobody touched her hair. There were limits to what even Saulos dared to do.

CHAPTER THIRTY-EIGHT

The road was hot and gritty and painful underfoot. Hypatia walked alongside Berenice, shoulder to shoulder, matching her pace for unflinching pace, providing solace and support and dignity.

Saulos did not come with them. They walked the first few dozen yards alone, with only stiff-backed Vilnius ahead and the retinue of his garrison guards about, but soon the city came alive as word spread of what was happening and men and women, young and old, War Party and Peace Party, gathered in their handfuls, in their hundreds, in their thousands, to line the route from the council hall past the old Hasmonean palace that was Saulos' new headquarters to Herod's new palace with its prison cells underground in the cellars.

They gathered by the same alchemy that drew iron to lodestones and caused moths to die, dancing in the flames of a night-time fire. They came without care for their own safety, without understanding fully what it was they were watching, unsure even if they were there to support their queen, or harry her.

It was a Jerusalem crowd: inevitably, a stone was thrown, and then a few more. The guards moved closer and Hypatia welcomed them.

They reached the foot of the hill and turned a little south, down a long, broad road. The crowd filled the street now, leaving only a narrow channel along which they could walk. Chanting started, as it had in Caesarea, rising to a low, rolling boil, and within it the usual slanders of Herod and his lineage, cut with the War Party's hatred of Rome.

Vilnius' back was hard as stone. His guards loosened their swords in their sheaths. Hypatia began to wonder if they could run down some side street. Her feet might be cut to shreds but worse had happened in the past.

And then she felt a tug at her soul and the crowd parted a little and Kleopatra was there, and beside her, veiled and cowled that her black skin and ram's-head hair might not stand out amongst the Hebrews, stood Iksahra, tight-lipped and tall. Her eyes promised murder and vengeance, all of it heaped on Saulos. Hypatia wanted to smile and could not. She nudged Berenice, and saw that she, too, had seen them.

Aloud, so that those nearest could hear, Hypatia said, 'If your people knew that you chose this penance, to ask their god to keep the city safe from war, they would applaud you, not throw stones as they do.'

She did not have to shout; Iksahra had the best hearing of anyone she had met. She did not turn to look as they passed, but lifted her hand as if to smooth the hair from her face. On the edge of her vision, she saw the girl turn away. Iksahra had already gone.

The crowds did not part immediately, but within a hundred paces a sigh swept through them, carrying the rumour that the queen had taken a vow to walk barefoot in her shift, with her hair cropped close as a shorn sheep, to keep the city from war.

The stones stopped first, and then the shouting. There was silence then, because this was new to them: that the queen might be an object of veneration, not of loathing. Then, from nowhere, a young woman threw on to the road ahead a bunch of small, white, four-petalled flowers, of the kind that grew along the coast near Caesarea, and in the cultivated gardens about the city.

The bouquet fell in the dust in front of Vilnius. Without breaking stride, he stepped long across it, and so did not crush the flowers. His men, too, veered away from them and so they were whole when Hypatia picked them up. She gave them to Berenice, who held them to her nose – there was little scent, but it was the gesture that mattered – and smiled her thanks into the crowd.

It all happened in a moment, but it tipped the mood of the crowd to a place they had never been. A hundred paces later, the road was littered with white flowers so thickly that Vilnius could no longer step over them. Hypatia found herself walking on crushed petals, balm to her feet.

Soon after, palm leaves came, thrown with care across their path. They smoothed the road and made their walking effortless.

Berenice was a woman transformed. Made light by

the day's dry heat, her face glowed with a life of its own, claiming the sun. Her pace lengthened and quickened, so that she was floating forward, ever faster.

Hypatia touched her arm. 'Slow,' she said. 'They love you, and Saulos is not so confident in his power that he can stop them. Smile now for your people as they call your name.'

Slowing, Berenice smiled for her people, who screamed her name as if she alone had the power to save them. Hypatia looked at the sun's searing orb and the sky around it, and became aware of the mass of people, the scents of garlic, pepper, lemon.

She smelled something else, more raw, like the breath of a hound, or a hunting cat, and turned her head a fraction, and saw Iksahra again, close by. Hypatia caught her eye, nodded thanks, and made a single gesture, and saw it acknowledged.

'Vilnius. May you tell me where we are to be taken?' She spoke loudly enough for him to hear, which meant that those closest in the close-pressing crowd might hear also.

'I regret you must go to the prisons, my lady. The ones beneath King Herod's palace where no man can gain entry except he tunnel through solid stone.' His response was from the parade ground; it rang across the furthest reaches of the crowd.

'And no sun can gain entry either?'

'I regret, no light at all, lady, except by candles.'

'Then we must make our own light, and hope that the queen's family may be allowed to visit her.'

Vilnius said nothing, only stiffened his shoulders

further. When Hypatia dared look again towards the crowd, Iksahra and Kleopatra had both disappeared once again.

She walked on beside Berenice, over palm leaves, and her feet felt them as silk.

CHAPTER THIRTY-NINE

'Menachem!'

Pantera screamed the name above the havoc of combat while all around him other men screamed to their gods, to their brothers, to themselves, in agony, in victory, in the sheer exertion of striving to live, which meant striving to kill first, before a sword swung from nowhere, and one more name was lost in the maelstrom.

For an eternity after Pantera called out, Menachem did not move. Then he tilted his head as if his god had tapped him on the arm, and nodded and, turning, dropped his right shoulder, and the blade that would have split his skull instead sheared away the side of his tunic, taking a collop of flesh with it.

He bled. Therefore he was alive. Mergus was with him, shouting, holding a shield. Pantera saw that much before a body, perhaps living, perhaps foe, slammed into his back.

He took the power of the blow and let it catapult him forward, flying free of the carnage, suspended in the air, out of reach of the enemy behind, not yet within reach of the one in front.

The ground came at him fast; the hard, red rock of Masada, bounded by Herod's double-skinned casement wall that had stopped him from falling over the edge at every other point along the perimeter, except here, at the gateway to the snake path where it wound up from the ground: here was the opening, and no wall – and falling was not just possible, but probable. It was a very long way down.

He tucked his head in, curved his shoulder, arced the sweep of his arm as the ground rushed to smash him, so that he rolled forwards and came up on his feet, facing back the way he had come. It was a tumbler's move, learned as a boy, and it was his only weapon, now that he had thrown both of his knives.

A sheet of shining mail blinded him as he rose, so dazzling was its polish, so bright the morning sun beating against it. The legionary whose shirt it was shouted an oath to Jupiter and ran at Pantera with his sword held straight forward, like a spear.

Pantera dropped sideways, and rolled in at the coming feet, tripping them. Thrusting up on one elbow, he pushed out with his hands and let momentum hammer the other man hard against the edge of the wall even as he ripped the sword from his hand.

Bones cracked under the impact. A scream was cut off halfway as Pantera sliced the man's own blade across his windpipe and the great vessels that hemmed it on either side.

Blood made a splashing fountain behind him. He ran from it, fast; he had seen men die because they had lost their footing in the gore of the man they had just killed. In the barracks afterwards, those who lived named it dead man's revenge.

Pantera had a blade now, but no shield. He came at a man from behind and speared his new weapon upwards, under the edge of his enemy's mail. It was a coward's move, but he had no shame; it gained him a shield and he used it as a weapon, smashing the boss into the face of the next man who came at him, as he bent and cut low, to slice his enemy's tendons. That one fell, and died, and Pantera walked over him, stamping, as the legions were taught to do.

The new blade was sharp and well balanced and it was the last proof, had Pantera needed it, that these men were the best veterans of the Jerusalem garrison, sent to Masada as a reward, not the lazy, the lame and the disobedient sent for punishment. They were, in fact, men exactly like his father, who had brought him here to show him its magnificence.

Pantera killed twice more, each time more difficult, each with increasing respect. The men that were left on both sides were tired, but they were alive because they were faster and better, and luckier, than the men who lay dead on the rock. Nobody was left who was slow or weak or deaf or part blind.

For a moment, nobody tried to kill him. He took a chance to look down the snake path, and saw no one sheltering there. He believed there might be bodies on the ground at the rock's foot, but it was too far to see and he had no intention of stepping closer to look.

He pushed his shield against the casement wall and thrust himself back into the battle. The worst of the fighting was no longer here, near the gateway where Moshe had brought his men up to the plateau, but further north, near the Herodian storehouses.

Menachem, Mergus and Aaron were in the heart of it, fighting as a trio, back to back to back. Only Mergus had a shield and he was using it to cover Menachem. Five legionaries stood before them in an arc, pushing forward with their shields locked in classic tight formation. They had their backs to Pantera. Nobody stood between him and them.

He grabbed another sword from a dead man's hand, and sprinted forward, wiping the hilt free of blood as he went. He jumped a body, and a shield, and chose not to take it up. Aaron faced towards him, Mergus and Menachem away. He shouted, 'Aaron!' and threw the sword as if it were a knife, sending it to turn, blade over hilt in the air.

Graceful, flashing in spinning rhythm, it curved over the heads of the five Romans. Aaron reached up and snatched it from the air and it must have seemed that the sky had opened and the gods sent a blade into their enemy's hand, for the inexorable forward advance halted, and five legionaries stopped to gape up at the unbroken blue above.

Pantera hit them from behind with the shield held sideways across his body, so that it smashed into the kidneys of two men at once and caught a third under the ribs with one sharp edge hard enough to knock him off balance. That one stumbled under the fall of Aaron's new blade, and died for his ill luck.

Four left, two of them down. Mergus and Menachem turned to fight the two still standing at either end as

Pantera ruined his new blade by stabbing it down through the angle between the helmet and the mail of one of the two who had fallen before he could recover and rise. That one died nastily, but swiftly enough.

The second was not as winded. He rolled away, hunching himself against Pantera's seeking blade, and writhed round, swinging his own sword out in a circle that hissed past Pantera, as close as any blade had ever come. He jerked back, cursing. The tip sliced on past and caught Aaron on the thigh, but it was at the end of its swing, when the power was gone, and Pantera did not have time to look.

He did not have time to do anything now but wrench himself sideways as yet another blade cut down past his head. His reflexes saved him, but sluggishly, slowed by exhaustion. He spun and parried and hacked and knew that each stroke was slower and later than it should have been and that he was only alive because the man he fought was as tired as he was.

This latest punched his shield into Pantera's face. Pantera grabbed the top edge of it and thrust it down at his attacker's foot, reeling sideways, to keep away from the stabbing, searching blade.

For a few frenzied moments, he fought for his life without thought of anyone else. He punched, he kicked, and, when a flash of flesh passed him by, he bared his teeth and bit.

He thought he was about to die and there, then, when it was not the slow death of Saulos' pleasure, he discovered how much he wanted to live.

And he did so. By luck as much as speed or force, he ducked under a backhanded swing at his face and was there, with a short, savage gladius tucked tight to his side, so that he could spear it upwards at the wide, red mouth that roared death in his face.

The blade grated up through his enemy's hard palate and lodged in the plates of his skull. Pantera let it go as the Roman fell and wrested the other's blade from his dying fingers.

He wanted to rest, to sit with his back to solid rock and tip a skin of water over his head and down his throat. He desperately wanted water; just the thought of it made him dizzy. He spun on his heel to look behind, because this, too, was a time when good men died: when they had just killed, and were too shocked at their own survival, too wretchedly tired, to see the fresh death that came from one side or another, or behind.

There was no one nearby. Mergus was fighting a dozen yards away, but safe; even as Pantera looked, he made the death blow and stepped in to finish.

Closer, in the wreckage of the last melee, Aaron was down. Menachem knelt beside him, his tunic drenched with wet blood down the side where his arm had been hit. Of their five attackers, none was left alive.

Pantera turned a full circle, counting. He had led a hundred Hebrews along the aqueduct in attack against a garrison of five times that number. Now, at the battle's end, of the ninety or so men left standing, very few were Roman and even where they were knotted in small groups, none of them was fighting.

The fight had reached that point where men on both sides were so numb with exhaustion that it was all they could do to stand up. They wanted to sit, to celebrate the fact that they were alive, that they could see the sun, feel the wind, taste the water they craved. Nothing tasted as good as water after a battle, nothing felt so perfect as the wind's caress.

'Pantera?'

Menachem's right arm hung limp by his side. Across his face were written new lines of grief.

Pantera forgot about water, and winning. 'Aaron?' he asked.

'Dead.'

He nodded. He could think of nothing to say. A blade's point had nicked the man's thigh; he remembered that, vaguely. He had not thought it deep, or fatal, but even if it had been, he could not have done anything.

Menachem began to speak a prayer, slowly, as one who searches for the words. Pantera stood with him, and tried to remember the last time he had prayed with any meaning for someone dead, and found it far back and too painful to remember.

He stepped away then, and surveyed the scene and presently said, 'The legionaries have ceased to fight. You have won, my lord.'

Menachem turned to look where Pantera was looking, north, to the storerooms, where a huddle of legionaries stood still, facing thirty or forty of their own men. The clash of weapons had stopped, and all were still.

He said, 'Why are they not fighting?'

'They're spent,' said Pantera. 'So are we, but there are more of us than them. There's a moment in a battle when everything stops. I've never known why it happens, but it does. Come—' He began to walk, picking his way over the dead, past the still-living. 'You will need to take their surrender.'

They came close, and the men parted to let them through. The legionaries were led by an optio; all their centurions were dead. He was lean and wiry, Roman to the ends of his toes. He took his sword and held it across the flats of his palms and knelt, and put it at Menachem's feet. He was bleeding from a wound on his shoulder, not badly. He said, 'We are dead men. We commend ourselves to your care.'

Menachem looked down at the sword, at the notches on its blade made in the battle just gone.

'A prisoner,' he said, in the clear Greek they all spoke, 'is the man who in the last breath was trying to kill me, and in the next wishes me to feed him and give him water.' He turned to Pantera. 'What do we do?'

'If you were Roman,' Pantera said, 'you would crucify them in sight of their brethren in Jerusalem so they would know what awaited those who stood against you.'

'I am not, and I will not.' Menachem spat. A ripple ran through his men, of pride, perhaps.

'You could let them fall on their swords,' Pantera offered. 'Or walk off the edge of the plateau. Either death is swift, honourable and takes considerable courage. They would go cleanly to their gods. You would be doing them a kindness.'

A long moment passed, with no words to fill it, nor none needed. At the end, Menachem turned to Moshe and nodded, and with that as the only order, his men opened out and made a column, lined on both sides, between the stores and the edge of the plateau, to the one place where there was no wall to keep men from falling. They did it with pride, and with a sense of honour that shone from them.

The legionaries watched it and they too did not need to speak. With a glance at Menachem for permission, the optio bent to retrieve his sword, buckled it on and turned to face eternity.

His men fell into line behind him, two on two; thirteen of them in all. A standard-bearer took the hindmost place, for all that their only standard was a small military pennant; the eagle of their legion was miles away.

In the heavy silence, the optio spoke aloud his own name, and that of his god. His men spoke after him, all at once, so that for a moment the sound was once again the discord of battle. And through that sound came Mergus, breathing hard, sweeping blood from the hilt of his sword.

He said, 'My lord, there is another way. If you will allow me?'

Menachem's eyes flashed. 'Does this way avoid bloodshed? And yet leave my men safe?'

'I believe it may.' With a bow, Mergus laid his sword on the ground in place of the one just lifted. Beside it, he laid his helmet, so that he stood bareheaded, his hair slick to his scalp with sweat. In short order after these, he shed his mail shirt, his undercladding and his shirt, until he stood before them half naked.

The Hebrews turned away, but Romans took in the marks of his past and his present; the scars of old floggings, ubiquitous in the legions, the tattoos of his rank: centurion of the Twentieth; the brand of Mithras on his sternum and the later marks that took him from the lowest rank of Raven to the higher one of Lion, a priest of that cult.

In Latin, in the cadences of the parade ground, Mergus spoke.

'I am Appius Mergus, centurion of the Twentieth legion, in Judaea in the service of my emperor. With me is Sebastos Pantera, known as the Leopard, citizen of Rome, made so by the hand of the emperor himself in consideration of his services to the city and the empire. The one who has taken control of Jerusalem is a traitor and a spy. He it is who burned Rome two years ago; we fought him then, and we fight him now. I swear to you now in the name of my god, by the bull-slayer, first Father, god of the nights and of the days, that this is true. If you join with us, if you take a new oath to Menachem, rightful king of Judaea, you will be rewarded for it by the emperor when this conflict is over.'

The silence when he finished was more dense than it had been before. Mistrust flooded from both sides, from men who had killed and had no desire to take the enemy as a brother.

Only from Menachem was there a measure of equanimity. In good, clear Latin, he said, 'If you will swear an unbreakable oath to serve in my interests, I will accept it.'

For a dozen slow heartbeats, Pantera dared to hope. Then the optio shook his head and turned back to face the edge of the plateau. He looked over his shoulder at Mergus.

'If it offend you, I apologize; I would not go to my death carrying one more man's hurt. But I prefer to die now, than to serve against my brothers.'

He marched as he would to war, fast and straight, two dozen strides to the edge, kicking up dust to his knees so that he seemed by the end to float on a cloud of heavy air.

He might have gone on walking on that cloud, out into oblivion, but the weight of his armour caught up with him, and he was gone, suddenly, shockingly, fast as a stone.

Not a scream came from him or from the four ranks of men who followed, dropping in pairs, so that there was silence, for a while, and only the faintest crashing impact as they met the valley's floor.

Menachem had closed his eyes and was speaking a prayer to his god, and so he did not see, as Pantera did, when the standard-bearer changed his mind.

'Strabo, Silanus, Ralla, Bassus, on me! About *face*!' The order snapped and the four named men snapped with it in a perfect turn. The rearmost, who had been foremost, teetered a hand's breadth from the edge; the merest gust of a breeze would have pushed them over.

It did not come. They stood square and straight. The standard-bearer planted the end of his pennant on the rock. 'I am Gnaeus Galerius, called Naso, optio of the fourth century, second cohort of the Fourteenth. I served in Britain under Paullinus. Did you march to Mona with him?'

His question was directed at Mergus. 'I did. We marched there to fight the dreamers and back to the battle with the rebel forces and on down to the south to relieve the Second. Did you march with us?'

'No.' Naso sounded sad that he had not. 'We left before that war. Gallus sent us to Claudius with a message after some small skirmish and Claudius kept us in Rome. When he died, the new emperor, Nero, kept

371

us on. He sent us to Judaea less than a year ago.' Naso smiled, thinly. 'I believe it was a gift for good behaviour.'

'You are not seconded to the Tenth?' Mergus asked. The nine men who had gone were all of the Tenth legion, the marks on their belts had proclaimed it.

'Not seconded to, not friends with, not particularly impressed by . . . no.' Naso picked his nose, thoughtfully. 'And unlike the Tenth, who have been in the east so long they have begun to believe every rumour they hear, I have seen Nero, watched him as a boy and saw him come to a man. He is . . .' Naso might have been close to death, but he was not stupid. He swallowed his opinion of Nero. 'He is a man I would trust with the truth. And Mithras is a god I would trust with my life.' He eased his blade from its sheath. To Menachem, he said, 'Would you take our oath, to defend you at all times, from all harm, until death?'

'We march next on Jerusalem,' Menachem said. 'The men of the garrison Guard are legionaries of the Tenth under Saulos' command. Unless we can persuade them to abandon him – and I do not hold out much hope for that – we will attack them. Will you fight against your brothers?'

'It would hardly be the first time,' Naso said. 'And I doubt if it will be the last. Caesar fought Pompeius with his legions and then Marcus Antonius fought Octavian who became Augustus. The legions fight for who pays them and whom they trust. I will trust you if you will trust me. And my men go where I go, all of them.'

'Then I take your oath,' Menachem said. 'And, in turn, give you mine, not to send you into danger that is ill-thought or ill-judged, not to ask of you more than a man may reasonably give, and never to hand you to the authority of another, should your emperor decide that he does not wish, after all, to support these two, who carry out his orders.'

The five Romans knelt. As one, they spoke their oaths, in the name of Mithras and of Jupiter Optimus Maximus.

Menachem spoke his own oath in Latin, Greek, Aramaic and Hebrew. The men behind him shifted at this last, but none of them spoke against it and at the end they parted to let the five men, newly of their ranks, step away from the cliff's edge and oblivion.

Mergus kept close to them, as a father with children. He took them a little way apart, and brought them water. Slowly, the rest began to disperse, to find water, to gather weapons from the dead, to eat, to sit, to rest.

Watching, Menachem wiped the heel of his hands under his eyes, leaving paler streaks in the battle-dust. It made him look more savage than even the blood on his pale tunic. 'That was well done,' he said. 'This is not a time for needless deaths.'

He was not alone in thinking so. From their place by the store houses, one of the Romans made a joke in sketchy Aramaic. Nearby, a Hebrew man laughed. Death fled from the air.

Pantera said, 'Mergus will set the banner for Eleazir to see so that the rest of your men know we have victory. If you have doves that will home to the city, have the men send them now so the word is spread as widely as it can be. This is not a time for secrecy; let them know that we are going to drive the legions out of Jerusalem.'

'And you and I?' Menachem asked. 'What are we

going to do while the others act for us? Stand and watch?'

The blood on his arm was clotting now, the flesh already beginning to shrink around the wound. He was shaking all over with exertion and the shock of living when others had died.

Pantera, when he took time to look at himself, was exactly the same. It occurred to him that they had not slept in over a day, that they had just fought to the death, and that Menachem did not yet know what the lives and valour of his men had bought for him.

'Come,' he said, and held out his hand. 'Let me show you what Aaron died for.'

The sun was a sheet of spun gold, angling through a window set high in the vaulted roof so that the plane of its incidence fell square across the intricate patterns of red and blue, gold and green, black and white picked out in fine marble chips across the floor.

Menachem stopped at the edge; the brilliance held him back. 'Herod was Greek, wasn't he? Not by birth, obviously, but in his soul he worshipped the sun as the Greeks do.'

'I think he worshipped wealth and power and what they could do for him.' Pantera had seen the mosaic before. The impact was no less a second time. He said, 'In this place, he has captured the sun. One does not imprison one's god.'

'No.' Menachem looked down. 'My feet are soiled.'

'It's blood, which is a sacred gift, and in any case, the floor will wash. We must go across. The greatest of Herod's storerooms is on the far side.'

'It'll be locked.'

'I know where the key is kept.'

Stepping inside, they left smears of old and new blood across the patterned floor, marring its beauty. At the far side, marble steps led down through a high-arched doorway. Beyond, water shimmered under sunlight.

'Are these baths?' Menachem asked, in wonder.

'Have you never seen them?'

'No. But that was not my surprise; rather that Herod should use water for bathing in a place where every drop is more precious than balsam.'

'You swam through one of his cisterns and it was neither the largest, nor the nearest. The rock is riddled with others. When it rains here, water drowns everything. All Herod's engineers had to do was find a way to catch and store it.'

'They were remarkable men.'

'They were Hebrews, as you are.' Pantera stepped into the bathing room and, kneeling at the edge of the baths, ran his fingers along the under-ledge until he came to a recess and in that recess a ball of wax.

Bringing it out, he cracked it open between his hands, as he might crack the egg of a large bird. A four-tongued key glimmered in the centre.

Menachem was standing at the water's edge, looking down at the mosaics in the pool. Here were gods and nymphs and fantastic beasts with wings and hooves and horns.

'A golden key?' he asked.

'Polished brass.' Pantera buffed it absently against his tunic. 'The storeroom is here, by the door to the caldarium.'

The key held the surface shimmer of the wax. It turned the lock with a satisfying solidity. Pantera swung the door back and looked inside.

And looked.

'Menachem?' he said.

Menachem came slowly, still mesmerized by the water and the shapes beneath it. 'I see why our teachers forbid images of men, of women, of beasts. They are too alluring. What have you got in here that could compare to— *Oh!*'

Momentarily, he was a child, seeing gold for the first time. Or a starving man offered a banquet. Or the reality, which was a leader of two thousand men who lacked the armour and weapons with which to fight a war that was no longer avoidable.

Softly Pantera said, 'Herod imprisoned the sun here, too, that it might burnish the arms and armour of his guard.'

Light blazed in from a dozen different windows. It tumbled down on to rack upon rack of mail shirts, of helmets, of greaves, of shield bosses, of sword hilts. It danced, dazzling from shoulder to crown to shin of a thousand imaginary guards.

'There's enough here to arm a thousand men, and rearm them when their blades break or they lose their shields over the edge. Elsewhere, there are provisions enough to feed them for ten thousand days.' Pantera heard pride in his own voice and, this once, did nothing to smother it. 'These are only Herod's supplies. The garrison will have had their own: enough for five hundred, plus repairs. With these, we can fit out the foremost among your men as if each one was a legionary.'

Menachem was at his side, shoulder to shoulder, heartbeat to thudding heartbeat. They stood together, welded by sunlight and purpose. 'And then all we have to do,' Pantera said, lightly, 'is teach each man how to fight as if he was Roman.'

CHAPTER FORTY

In haste, but with Jucundus' impeccable planning, the royal family of Judaea had abandoned Caesarea. In greater haste, with less planning, they packed to flee Jerusalem.

Kleopatra left Iksahra tending her great cat and the falcons in the beast gardens and pushed her way into the palace where slaves, servants, guards, attendants, secretaries, grooms, cooks, vintners, chambermaids and collectors of firewood for the royal family seemed bent on creating for themselves a unique kind of hell in which no one person could speak coherently to any other, or hear what was being said, but where each vied to increase his or her own volume, the better to be heard, and thus, manifestly, reduced the chances of anybody's hearing him. Or her.

'Where's Jucundus? I said Jucundus. Have you seen Juc—' Kleopatra let go the slave she had caught and ploughed down the corridor to a half-open door beyond which danced a helmet plume in black and white.

'Jucundus?' She caught him by the elbow. 'They say you're not going to Syria? Why not?'

His eyes were brown and sad, like an aged hound left behind in the kennels when the hunt bays on a fresh trail. 'I am sent back to Caesarea, lady.'

There was a shadow in his voice that was worse than the pain in his eyes. She knew him, as he knew her: after Agamemnon, he had taken the rough skills of a wild rider and given them a stately polish. He had taught her to fire a bow and to use a sword in the way of the legions, which was more disciplined than Agamemnon's wild warrior swings.

He had taught her history and Latin and the ways of men in the world. If she had a father, it was not the distant king in a foreign land, who had died too soon and sent her mother back to the court of her childhood, it was this man, who stared at her now, shaking his head, with his lips pressed in a string of silence that warned her – begged her – to ask no more.

He said, 'I heard what befell you. I am sorry. I . . .'

'It doesn't matter. I'm well. But my aunt and Hypatia . . .' She was more afraid than she had let herself know. She dashed away new tears with the back of her hand and scowled at Jucundus.

He said, 'Your lady aunt, the queen, is held below, in the cellars. It might be wise to take her food and water.'

'She has none?'

Jucundus took her shoulder and turned her in the direction of the kitchens. 'The guards are from the garrison, but some are men who know you. You would be permitted entry, I think, when we are not. You could take what she needs.'

'Where's Saulos?'

'On the fourth floor with Vilnius, discussing plans for Estaph's crucifixion. They want it to be public, but not to cause a riot.'

Kleopatra gaped. 'Anything will cause a riot. They could crucify a dead sheep just now and it would cause chaos, you know that.' She caught at Jucundus again, suddenly young. 'Don't go. Please.'

'I would stay if I could, but my orders are unambiguous. I am to return to Caesarea and take control of my men. They have . . . not acted as I would have wished. Go now.' He pushed her again, more firmly. 'Think of your aunt, not me or yourself. She needs you.'

The slaves' corridors were blocked with a panic of near-naked men and women, rancid with the stench of fear, unbearably hot. Kleopatra barged and bullied her way through until she came to the door to the cellars. The guard who stood before it was one she knew by sight, although she could not remember his name.

As an alternative, she produced her most blinding smile. The guard flushed, which was a good sign. She made her eyes wide. 'Have you seen my cousin?'

'Lady, he was in his chambers, making ready for the off.'

'It's true, then, we are leaving? Where to?'

He eyed her with genuine concern. 'Were you not told? You're leaving for Antioch in Syria at tomorrow's dawn at the latest. Lord Saulos had his men searching for you all morning.'

'They found us. I had gone hunting, with the beast-woman. We caught a quail. See? I cooked it for my aunt.'

He had already looked at the basket she had brought from the kitchens and had smelled the stolen meat beneath the warming cloth. She grinned at him, as if that simple act made him a co-conspirator.

The guard became flustered and picked at his mail. She saw him dead with a knife through his throat, and closed her eyes that he might not see it too.

She said, 'Are you going to Damascus with us?'

He was older than she'd thought; lines etched his eyes, his mouth, the prickles of beard beginning on his chin, where white mixed with black, to the detriment of both. He said, 'Lord Saulos has ordered that one company is to go, the rest to stay. The centurions will draw lots to choose those who will leave. If they have done so, I haven't heard the result yet.'

'Which do you want? To go, or to stay?'

He drew himself tall. 'A courageous man does not fly in the face of battle.'

'Of course.' Kleopatra looked up at him. 'I am told I must go with my uncle, but I would take food and wine to my aunt first.'

Her basket was full: a flagon of wine, dates, almond cakes, a roast quail stuffed with garlic from the previous night, a bundle of the hard, unleavened bread that the hunters took on long days and swore kept them happy from dawn until dusk. She held it up a second time. 'With your permission?'

His orders were to let no one through; they both knew that. Behind them, chaos held the corridors, but within it were only slaves. He winked. 'Be quick.'

She stood on her toes and kissed his cheek. He was smiling as the door shut behind her.

Three more guards blocked her way. The first was at the top of the stairs and the second stood by the lit torch in its wall bracket, at the place where the corridor branched, right to the wine cellars, left to the dungeons. Both of these let her past on the grounds that if she had got through the door at the top, it must be with permission.

The last was less easy, but he was at least a man she knew by name as well as by sight. Surinus of the second century of the garrison Guard stood round the corner from the cells themselves, out of the line of view of the prisoners, lest he be bewitched by the two women within. He kept his sword permanently drawn and had on enough armour to face down a squadron of Parthian heavy cavalry.

This deep underground, this close to the prisoners, he was a lot more unsettled than his brethren, less willing to allow a relative of the queen's to pass. His blade blocked her path, unyielding.

She held up her basket, as she had three times before, so that he could see the innocence of its contents. His blade did not move. 'Lady, I can't let you pass. I'll be flogged and you'll be taken to Damascus in chains. Go back. I'll let them know you tried.'

'They know already,' Kleopatra said. 'They can hear every word. It's like a grave in here, there's so little sound.'

He shivered, and tried to hide it. She raised her basket. 'They need food,' she said, 'or they'll die and then how will Saulos treat you?'

His blade wavered.

'You'll hear what we say and I can't possibly enter

382

the cages. What harm can it do?' Surinus had been her friend, one of those who had turned a blind eye when she left the palace by the slaves' door. She laid her hand on his blade, pushing, pushing, said, 'Nobody will know. You'll be on the road to Syria by tomorrow.'

'Only one company leaves. My centurion might not win the ballot.'

'So leaving would be winning?' She tilted her head. 'When did I ever lose at dice?'

A smile grew round his eyes. 'I didn't know you had a hand in the drawing of lots.'

She grinned. 'Nor does Vilnius, but can you see him denying me the chance if I ask him right?'

Surinus laughed then, roughly. At last, his blade swung away from her resisting hand. He jerked his head to the cells. To her retreating back, he called, 'Don't let her bewitch you. Not your lady aunt; the other one.'

Swiftly, Kleopatra turned the corner, away from the torchlight and hazy warmth into a place so cold, so dank, it made her gasp, and clutch her tunic closer.

Light leaking from the corridor lit three pale faces turned to her. One of them was a man; the giant Parthian. She had time to take that in, to understand the enormity of it – a man and two women in the same small room, without privacy, without decency – before one of the women stood, and took a tentative step to bars set in the immovable stone of floor and ceiling.

'Hypatia!' Kleopatra ran the last strides, thrust her hands forward. They met, palm to palm, through the bars. 'You're so cold.'

She said it loudly, to give the Chosen of Isis time to gather herself, to look at and read the scrap of paper

383

that had passed between them, that had come from the message-dove and was, if she were truthful, her reason for being there.

She looked past the exhaustion on Hypatia's features to Berenice, who stood just behind.

'Your majesty . . .'

Her aunt was filthy, exhausted, cold beyond imagining. Her eyes were twin pits burrowing in below her high patrician brow. Kleopatra read despair in their darkness, and chose not to believe it.

She said, 'Let me get a torch. I can't see you properly.'

Surinus flushed full of shame when she stormed back, and did not stand in her way, but gave her his spare torch, and let her light it from the one propped in the wall bracket. Pitch and tight-bound wool fizzed and spat. Bright light hurt her eyes, already widened by the dark.

'Majesty, Hypatia, Estaph . . .' She tipped the light to flow over each one as she spoke. Estaph was more bruised than the others, but whole. He had taken the opposite side of the cell, eschewing the warmth of proximity for the probity of distance, as if anybody cared how they sat, here in the dark and the cold.

'I brought food. Not very much, but . . .' She emptied her basket a piece at a time and pushed it through the bars. Estaph turned to her at last, showing bloody bruises on every angle of his face. Someone had wiped him clean in the dark, with no water, smearing the blood so that he stared at her through a mask of red and blue and black. He was so still, she thought he might be undead, a ghûl with lost eyes to steal her soul, until he took a breath and levered himself upright.

He smiled, showing broken teeth, and bowed, stiffly. 'My lady, I thought you a vision, conjured from thirst and hunger and cold,' he said. 'And you have brought food and water and warmth. Thank you.'

She thought, *You won't thank me if you're stronger for it when they crucify you*, but she had not the will to say it. He knew it anyway; it was in his eyes. After a comfortless pause, she said, 'I could bring herbs if it would help. They might let me back in again.'

'They won't.' Hypatia was still at the bars. Her eyes said, *I have read the note. I cannot speak of it aloud.* 'We heard sounds upstairs, as if the whole garrison were there. Have they taken control of the palace?'

'Saulos is in the king's chamber now. My uncle is making ready to leave.'

'You'll go with them,' Hypatia said. Her voice was cold, distinct, set to carry to the corridor's end, where waited a man afraid of witchcraft.

'Yes,' said Kleopatra and shook her head.

Hypatia signalled to Berenice, who bent and dragged the pile of food across the floor. The sound echoed off the ceiling.

'You and Estaph need to eat first,' Hypatia said. 'I ate this morning, before I came to you.'

They did, with alacrity, and, beneath the sounds of their feeding, Hypatia murmured, 'This message must get to Pantera and Menachem. Yusaf can arrange that – he has contacts among the War Party and some of them must still be left in the city. You must leave here as soon as you may. Tell Iksahra that if she were to take you to Alexandria, I would consider it a personal favour. She should find a woman named Athanasia who tends the shrine of Isis in the road of the Golden Scorpion, near the Temple of Serapis. Iksahra is to tell Athanasia that the Chosen of Isis has named her successor. She will be able to choose her reward. Tell her that. And tell her . . . tell her she knows the shape of my heart. She will know what that means.'

'Iksahra is the new Chosen?' Kleopatra asked. It did not seem likely, but then a great many unlikely things had happened in the past days.

Hypatia said, 'No,' and waited.

Kleopatra gaped. Her blood surfed in her ears. 'I am not . . . I can't be . . . I don't . . .' She gathered herself. 'I don't see the dead. The Chosen always does. I heard so.'

'I didn't at your age,' Hypatia said. 'There are twelve years of training in the temples of Egypt before you step out and take the name for yourself. And I must be dead, of course, for that to happen.'

'I don't want you to be dead.'

'Hypatia . . .' Berenice came to the bars, bearing the almond cakes. She said the name aloud, for the guard, and then, more quietly, 'Are you sure? You said it earlier, but I thought—'

'That it was an excuse to join you in the council chamber?' Hypatia pulled a wry smile. 'It was, but it was also true. Unless you forbid it?'

Berenice shook her head. 'Kleopatra will be safer there than here and Damascus would not suit her; without my word against it, my brother and sister would try to find her a husband. Isis will treat her better.'

Kleopatra had to stuff her fist in her mouth not to speak, not to let spill the noises crowding her throat.

Those given to Isis did not squeal; she was sure of that, and she was too close to squealing.

When she could find the right breath, she said, 'But you will be freed. We won't leave until you are.'

'No. You have to leave.' Hypatia reached through the bars to catch her hand and held it.

'Iksahra won't leave you,' Kleopatra said. She did not know how she knew that, but she was certain it was true and Hypatia showed every sign of believing it. She had closed her eyes and turned her face to the floor.

'Tell her it's my wish,' she said, presently, and looked up. 'Tell her that if she thinks we can't get out of here without her, she does no honour to my reputation.'

'But this is the dream.' Kleopatra's eyes held Hypatia's, not letting her go. 'This is the cold, black part of it. Where the pain starts. I have seen it. So have you.'

'I know.' Hypatia broke the lock of their gaze and twisted free of Kleopatra's grip. Stepping back, she placed a kiss on the heel of her hand, and stretched through the bars to touch it on Kleopatra's wrist. 'But the dream has many endings, and not all of them are bad. Trust me. I do not intend to let your aunt die, or Estaph. We have work yet to do before the gods weigh our hearts against Ma'at's feather. Go now. Take the message to Yusaf. Tell him to find whoever he trusts most to take it safely across the desert to Pantera. Then go to Alexandria with Iksahra. We will find you there when we can.'

Chapter Forty-One

Iksahra rode south under the high sun.

Her mare was the pride of her father's breeding. Her hide was the colour of almond blossom, her mane and tail unblemished charcoal, her feet black as onyx, and as hard. She was fleet as the hot south wind and could go all day at a canter without need for rest or water. Her one colt foal was a yearling now, the hope and pride of Iksahra's own breeding herd, left behind in her homelands under the care of a woman who had seemed competent and interested and useful; at least that had been the case in last year's summer, before a man had dangled the sweet meat of vengeance within Iksahra's grasp, before she had discovered that vengeance did not feed her heart's hunger.

The ghost of her father joined her as she passed the palms, the olives, the green pastures south of Jerusalem. He complimented her on the mare, on the cheetah that ran ever at her heels, a living ghost, a shadow in gold and black.

He sat cross-legged on the horizon at the level of her

shoulder and tilted his head and asked, *Why do you do this? Why are you riding from one man to another with a message you cannot read, the contents of which they will not share with you?*

'Because Hypatia asked it of me.' It was not entirely true; Hypatia had asked that Yusaf send the one deemed most reliable and Iksahra had named herself that, leaving Kleopatra in Yusaf's care. It had seemed the same thing at the time, but sounded different now, when she spoke it aloud in the echoes of her own head.

The ghost that might not have been her father gazed at her askance. *And you always do her bidding, this woman?*

'She may die.' *She may die, and my heart will die with her.* She did not say so, even in the echoes of her head, but the ghost heard her anyway, and his laugh was a long stuttering titter, which disrupted the smooth rhythm of her horse. That was how she knew it was not really her father; he had never laughed at the things she cared about.

Under the hot sun, Iksahra spoke the words Anmer ber Ikshel had taught her for the dissipation of ghûls and kicked her mount faster along the route Yusaf had drawn for her in the dust on his floor.

Noon came and went. The sun devoured them, spat them out, ate them again. The olive groves and date palms became scrubbier and less frequent and gave way finally to rocks and sand and waterless desert wadis.

Soon, rocks grew on either side, as scorching ovens. Heat became pain, and burned away the memories of a night when nothing had really happened, but which, even so, had left her feeling torn from her past without sight of a clear future.

Near the end now, Iksahra urged the mare on. The cheetah ran nearby, never tiring. They raced faster. The world was blinding light and hot earth and ropes of saliva frothing back from the bridle and the cat's hot breath at her heel.

Sometime later, the mare pricked her ears and the cat grunted a warning. Ahead, a spark of light flickered where an ignorant man let his sword blade catch the sun, not knowing that the ifrit used such things to discover where men camped, that they might trap them in the night.

With a curse at his idiocy, Iksahra lay low on her mare's neck and urged her into a full, flat-bellied gallop across the last miles of rugged plain to the foothills north of Masada.

She came fast from the north, from Jerusalem, a black woman dressed all in white riding a mare the colour of starlight with black points and black feet, and with a cat running in her shadow.

It was the black-and-whiteness that spooked the lookouts who stood at the northern edges of the heights, more than the fact that she knew where they were. They may have been God-fearing Hebrews, but they had grown to adulthood hearing daily the tales of what lived in the desert at night; in the darker corners of their mind, the things that might hurt them most looked just like this.

Eleazir of the long sight saw her first, and called Mergus who had the authority to stop the lookouts from using her for target practice with their slings.

Pantera waited on the heights until she had reached the mouth of the cleft through which any rider must pass to reach the hidden camp.

'Iksahra!'

He ran down, leaping from rock to rock. Behind him, men who had been afraid to look earlier came to the edge of the heights now, jostling for a better view. Closer, she was no less exotic: a black woman on a milk-white mare with a cat at her heels that was more like a hound.

Pantera reached the last rock and stood above her, looking down. Her mouth was set in a straight line. Tightness held her, where before had been only supple fluidity.

He said, 'Who's dead?'

'I don't know. I can't read the message. Estaph is alive, but taken prisoner. So too are the Chosen of Isis and the Queen Berenice. They are imprisoned. Read this. I will tell you of them after.'

Her palm was held flat and, on it, a message cylinder for him to take. Dried blood on one end flaked off as he uncapped it and tipped out the contents. The fragile paper was in an old code; one of the first, and so the easiest, that Seneca had taught his spies. He read aloud as if it were plain Latin, but quietly, privately, not for the men above.

From Ishmael, keeper of doves, to Gideon, greetings. Blood flows in the streets of Caesarea. Orders came from Jerusalem: let all the Hebrew men and women die. The men of the city Watch came last night in the darkness and by morning all were dead. All. Six thousand men,

their wives, mothers, sons and daughters, even the
newborn, hurled naked on the streets. Twenty thousand
souls in all. My father died trying to save a friend. I
write to warn you, lest death comes also to Jerusalem.

He thought of a boy with eyes like a gazelle's and
a father he had never met. His vision blurred. Iksahra
was staring at him with something close to pity, which
was so unlikely as to startle him to steadiness. She was
speaking. He cuffed away the tears and made himself
listen.

'Yusaf read the message. He knew what it said,
although he didn't tell me, but he did give me this second
scroll for Menachem. He said . . . he said you would
understand it, if he did not.'

Between thumb and finger, she held a scroll tied with
linen thread sealed by a blob of beeswax that bore the
imprint of a man's thumb as its only seal.

Pantera said, 'Menachem is—'

'Behind you. I heard what you read. Caesarea is a
graveyard.' The words came from a sword's length
behind, to his left, deeper into the cleft that led to
the hidden valley in which they camped. Menachem
extended his hand to Iksahra. 'Horses cannot come into
the valley. Will you let Moshe care for your mare?'

It was a decision made without forethought, but it
was good, evidently, for as soon as Iksahra nodded,
Menachem's chief captain skipped down the cluttered
rock as if they were steps and came to hold the mare's
bridle. Even before he reached her, the look on his face
was that of a man besotted.

Menachem's patience was a finite thing these days,
measured in grains of sand that grew fewer with each

passing day. The pressure of his waiting was tangible by the time Pantera, Iksahra and the cheetah reached the neck of the gully, where it gave way to the hidden valley.

Ahead, all about the valley's floor, two thousand men, less a few dozen lookouts, sat cleaning their new weapons, or trying on new mail. At one end, a tailor with three fingers missing on his right hand sat in the shade of the high walls and assessed men by sight as they approached him, and allocated them a mail shirt from the numbered piles about him.

At the valley's other end, Mergus and his handful of Romans held classes to teach men to use Roman weapons in ways that would kill more of the enemy than their brethren. Between classes, men flaunted their new armour, vain as girls in coloured silks.

All this halted when Menachem began to walk to the centre of the valley. A hundred men, more, laid down their weapons and clustered around, keeping a respectful distance, but still close enough to hear and be heard.

Pantera's look sent them back. Catching up with Menachem, he walked with him towards the uninhabited centre, although even at this distance, he spoke softly. 'You heard Ishmael's message? The city Watch in Caesarea has slaughtered the Hebrew community. Twenty thousand dead.'

'I heard,' Menachem said. 'Jerusalem will be next if we don't act soon.'

'Saulos has less than three thousand men,' Pantera said. 'One hundred thousand Hebrews live in the city, even when it is not crowded for a feast day.'

'He has sent for help,' Iksahra said. 'I went out this morning to hunt his doves. I caught one with a message coming in, not going out. If he hadn't sent one already, he will have done so today.'

Menachem walked ahead of them awhile. When he turned, his face was tight, his lips made a fine, hard line. 'They'll send the Twelfth to assault us,' he said. 'It's a ten-day march, maybe more if they bring the local infantry with them.'

'If we march now, and set camp overnight, we can be at Jerusalem by tomorrow's dawn.' Pantera turned to Iksahra. 'How is the Guard arranged?'

'They are in the fortress of the Antonia, next to the Temple, all but one century that will have left by now, escorting the king and his family to Damascus. Except Berenice. She and Hypatia are imprisoned. Estaph's death will begin on tomorrow's dawn if Saulos has his way. The women will follow him.'

'What of Kleopatra?'

'She is safe with Yusaf. Hypatia wants me to take her to Alexandria.'

'Will you?'

'Not while the Chosen of Isis remains alive and imprisoned.'

Iksahra had turned away from him so it was impossible to see her face, to read more beyond the changing textures of her voice.

They came to the valley's end and climbed steps cut in the rock to a high, hidden place from where it was possible to see Masada to the south and, almost, if one stared hard at the horizon, Jerusalem to the north. The sun stood overhead, shrinking their shadows.

Pantera said, 'You said Yusaf had sent you with a second message?'

394

'Here.' Iksahra withdrew the scroll of papyrus from her belt pouch a second time. It was blotted with ink, creased, torn at the corners as if many men had held it. Menachem cracked the seal between his thumbs and unrolled it with reverence, as if it were sacred scripture; which it was, almost.

Over Menachem's shoulder, Pantera read a litany of names written in Hebrew, beginning with Menachem's own and rising back through his father and his grandfather and his great-grandfathers and others and others strung up the page in ever widening lines. At one side, a column of signatures had been added, a little apart from the rest. Yusaf's name was first, then Gideon's, then all of the Sanhedrin, one after the other.

At the end, Menachem let it spring closed. He raised his eyes, found Iksahra, and then Pantera. 'Tell me what you have just read.'

'Nothing that you don't already know. You are of the line of David. You fulfil the promise of the psalm that the fruit of his body shall sit upon the throne of Israel. What is new in this, what changes everything, is that every man of consequence in Jerusalem has signed the proof of your lineage. The whole Sanhedrin is here. They are saying that they will acknowledge you as the rightful king of Judaea. You only have to take the throne.'

'If Saulos saw this . . .'

'He would crucify every man who had signed it. They take a risk, in order to support your risk.'

Pantera gazed out across the open plain. Here, this close to Masada, it was empty desert, home to the antelopes and hyenas, but the haze in the distance was many shades of green, where cedars grew thick as fleece across the hills, and date palms and olive groves wrought patchwork patterns on the fertile slopes around Jerusalem.

Thoughtfully, he said, 'We must anoint you king in a river, as it says in the scriptures. Gideon can do that, with witnesses who will swear to it. Everything must be done as it was written.'

'And if I am not that king? How does your god punish hubris?'

'My god punishes no one. Men do that to each other, or to themselves when they think they have reached too high. You are not reaching too high.'

When he heard no reply, Pantera turned back, away from the plain. 'Your city needs a ruler. The whole of your nation waits for someone who can bear the weight of sovereignty with wisdom and fortitude. Did you think the chance to rule was a gift? You could have asked Nero, or Claudius, or the poor mad fool Caligula. They could tell you that ruling is a curse. It takes a strong man to withstand its pressures. You are that man.'

Menachem's gaze seared his face. 'What would you have me do?'

'Enter Jerusalem as Israel's anointed king. Fight anyone who stands against you. Do whatever it takes to secure your nation's future as a strong and stable state. You can do this.'

'You can do this,' Iksahra said in echo, from his other side. 'You must. It is why I was sent.'

CHAPTER FORTY-TWO

The mule was not only lame, but massively over-burdened, or such was the assessment of Laelius, the harassed garrison guard on duty that Sabbath dusk at the small southernmost gate leading into Jerusalem. He and his gate partner, Bibulus, had watched for half an hour now as the unfortunate beast grew from an ant on the horizon to a full-grown gelding, plodding forward, ears flopping down to its muzzle.

A skinny Syrian trotted along behind, cursing and thrashing the beast with unnerving monotony: thump, thump, thump, once every third stride, just out of rhythm with the lameness. He didn't even have the sense to beat the mule, but struck the left-hand pannier, giving forth with each stroke a pungency of garlic so thick and so strong he could have carved up the very air and sold it at market.

The Syrian did not consider that; he was as foolish as his mule, while the veiled and hooded woman who slumped astride it humming discordant Syrian lullabies was . . . vast. Overwhelming. Too huge to contemplate and certainly too big for the unfortunate beast that was forced to support her.

With awe in his voice, or disgust, Bibulus said, 'She's pregnant.'

Laelius felt his gorge rise as his mind supplied unwanted images of a skinny gap-toothed Syrian and his vast wife locked in the throes of coitus. They passed uncomfortably close. The Syrian smiled at him; his wife crooned her ditties. Among the garlic, Laelius caught an eye-watering stink of civet. The mule was definitely lame.

Neither guard made an effort to stop the pair; there had been no specific edict against men walking into the city at night, only about their leaving it.

Laelius held his breath until they had gone, then leaned in relief against the wall and took a long drink from the wine jug that was better company than Bibulus. He ached for the sound of Roman voices speaking Roman thoughts. He offered a prayer to Jupiter Dolichenos that the rumours were true and his legion might evacuate this godforsaken city before the full moon.

In Yusaf's elegant house in the city, Kleopatra woke from dreams of death and cold and the awe of being Chosen when she had no idea what that meant or what to do. She lay muzzily on a pallet nursing the panic that had begun when Hypatia had named her, and only when her heart had stilled did she hear voices in the air around her, and her name, spoken twice in fast succession, once by a woman.

She opened her eyes and found that there was a mule in Yusaf's beautiful dining room, which had become, perforce, her bedchamber, and a figure with black teeth who stank of garlic leaning back against the wall with his eyes shut, plainly too exhausted to stand much longer, and certainly beyond the care it might take to wash.

From the gloom of too few candles someone handed him a beaker and he drank as if it were the first water he had seen in months. Someone else tugged on the mule's bridle and pulled it sideways. Something shimmered in the erratic light and there echoed about the small room a slither of metal on metal.

Kleopatra rubbed the back of her neck and rolled sideways, hunting for the few remnants of clothing that she doffed for sleep. She found her sandals first, functional as legionary caligae, then a leather belt with the shape of a horse at each of the tie-ends, and a comb for her hair.

She was sitting when the gap-toothed man noticed her, and he only did that because he had lifted a rag of wool with which to clean his face, and in dipping it in his water – or perhaps his wine – he happened to turn.

'Kleopatra,' he said, and bared his lips, the better to rub the candle-soot from his front teeth. 'We were trying not to wake you.'

'Pantera? *Pantera!*' She threw herself to her feet and might have hugged him, had he not been so filthy.

Instead, she stood close in the hazy light, taking in his presence, noting the weariness on his left side that was worse than it had been, the new lines about his eyes, carved by wind and sun, and the newly sharpened angles of his cheeks that spoke of long days without food and a pain that might haunt him still.

But all these were small things when he was manifestly alive, whole, healed, all the things Kleopatra had believed impossible when she had last seen him.

She dragged her eyes from him and looked around at piles of iron links that stole light from the candle to make a thousand flaming points, and lean, long swords, bare-bladed on the floor, and helmets, enough for a tent-party of eight . . . And Iksahra, sitting on the floor, with the cheetah draped about her ankles.

She was no longer dreaming, but reality was stranger than she had imagined. Stooping, Kleopatra ran a hand over the armour on the floor; shining, serpentine links, enough to equip half a dozen men.

'You took Masada?' Hypatia had told her they planned it, in the days when Hypatia was still free to speak to her.

From behind, Pantera said, 'Two days ago. We will take Jerusalem in the morning.'

Kleopatra spun back to face him. 'What was the message? The one that Iksahra's falcon caught. Could you read it?'

'I could.'

'What then? What did it say?'

'Gideon will tell you.' Pantera caught her eye and directed her attention towards the uncandled shadows on the room's far side where a shape detached itself from the dark and Gideon the Peacemaker stood before her, looking older than he had in the council chamber, as if the night had stolen years from him.

He answered her question in a voice in which grief and rage measured every word. 'The message was from Ishmael, the dove-keeper in Caesarea. It came with news that his city is a bloodbath. Twenty thousand are dead; every Hebrew in the city, down to the last child, has been killed by the city Watch. Saulos ordered it.'

Kleopatra covered her mouth with her hands. 'Jucundus,' she said, faintly. 'He wouldn't . . .'

Pantera said, 'He wasn't there.'

'He tried to tell me what had happened. I didn't listen.' Kleopatra closed her eyes and then opened them again; against all probability, the bloody gallery of her mind was worse than the horror etched across Gideon's face, the pain, as if he had seen the acts himself.

Quietly, Pantera said, 'We will not sue for peace now. We must fight and win, else Jerusalem will wade thigh-deep in the blood of innocence. And we must do it soon, before the legions march from Syria.'

Kleopatra could not look at either man. Instead, she looked down again at Iksahra, and at the piles of chain mail shirts that surrounded her. 'How did you get these in?' she asked. 'All the gates are watched.'

'On the mule.' Pantera shrugged, as if it was an easy thing. 'The blades and helms were in one of the panniers. Iksahra wore the shirts bunched about her body. The guard thought . . .'

With a wry grin, he glanced at Iksahra, who ghosted a shadow of Pantera's smile and said, 'We choose not to imagine what he thought. But he did not search us.'

'And the cat?'

'The cat was in the other pannier, on the right-hand side. It will forgive me eventually, particularly if we fight in the night.'

The cat had come to tolerate Kleopatra, if not to like

her; she could come near it now and it did not harden its eyes.

She reached past its head and lifted a mail shirt from the nearest pile. She had seen them often worn by the guards in Caesarea and Jerusalem, but never held one. It rippled across her hands like sharkskin.

'How many did you bring?' she asked.

Iksahra said, 'Nine. Mergus is coming later with some men, but he won't need all of them. We think that one will fit you.'

'Me?' She spread it out, looking at the width between the shoulders, at the length. 'It could—'

Pantera was ahead of her. 'Iksahra, no! We spoke of this.' He caught Kleopatra's arm, drawing her towards him. 'You should come with me to the encampment, or at the very worst stay here until the fighting is over. Nothing else is safe.'

'So you say, and yet Kleopatra of Caesarea has killed once already in my sight. She has, I think, practised with the sword more than any other member of her family.' Iksahra stooped, scooping a blade from the floor, and passed it, hilt first, to Kleopatra. 'Is he right? Must you be kept safe with men about you for protection while we open the city's gates from the inside to let in Menachem's army?'

In a clear invitation, Iksahra lifted a blade of similar length and held it out, as men will who offer a fight to another.

Kleopatra took a step away from Pantera. The blade she had been given was fine, well balanced, a little shorter than the cavalry blades Jucundus had given her to practise with, but she swung it once, twice, and found that point of harmony where the end of her elbow became the true end of the blade, so that its killing edges were a part of her arm, and she could defend without thinking. Or attack.

She swept a strike at Iksahra's head. The other woman swung her sword up in a block that hurt all the way down Kleopatra's arm to her feet, but she let the power of it throw her own blade out and round and down, cutting for Iksahra's ankles. The second block was faster, but she was ready for it, and already moving, twisting, angling sideways and up and through and . . . so close, but not close enough; Iksahra was faster, sharper, harder and continued to be so for a spray of strikes, again and again, and again, until the world was a whirl of iron and Kleopatra's sword arm was numb from the impact.

She sprang back, breathing hard, and held her blade high above her head in surrender. 'How are we going to open the gates?' she asked.

'By stealth, for the most part.' Iksahra lowered her own sword. 'We have to remove the guards in such a way that they don't alert their brethren to the possibility of attack.'

'Are we alone? We two?'

'No. Mergus will bring five men into the city as soon as Pantera has left, in case we need to attack. Gideon goes with Pantera.'

'Gideon is invited to go with me,' Pantera said. As his gaze sought the Peacemaker, there was a challenge in it that Kleopatra did not understand. 'Does he wish to accept?'

'I do.' Gideon laid both hands on his chest. 'Before

God, I will do whatever may be done to aid Menachem. I have not done so in the past, but the bloodshed at Caesarea changes everything.'

'In that case, we'll need to make you as large as Iksahra was with her mail shirts. If necessary, we'll cut up some of Yusaf's bedding rolls.' Pantera shifted his gaze to Iksahra. To her he said, 'It's not too late to change your mind. I could still take you and Kleopatra to safety outside the walls.'

The Berber woman laughed, softly. 'No guard is so stupid as to let you in with one pregnant wife and then let you out that same night with two wives and a fourteen-year-old daughter.'

'Guards can die.'

'Guards will die, but if they do so before dawn their brethren will know that you are on your way and your surprise is lost. Without it, you will lose the battle that is to come with the sunrise. I will not allow that.'

Pantera ran his tongue round his teeth, nodding, as if she had said something quite different. 'Hypatia is not dead yet,' he said, slowly. 'We don't know the time set for her execution. We may still—'

'Don't! Don't speak of what we may or may not do, when the first parts are not yet even set in train!' Iksahra spat at him, not a throaty human spit, but the hissing, teeth-baring spit of the cheetah. It rose, stiff-legged, like a hound, and pushed its broad muzzle into her hand.

Iksahra shook her head at its touch, and spoke to it in her own tongue. It settled again, crouching at her heel. In a short, violent movement, she jerked her head towards the open door.

'Leave now. Kleopatra and I will do what needs to be done so that Menachem's men may enter with the dawn. That is our task. Yours is to make sure Menachem is ready to lead them.'

CHAPTER FORTY-THREE

Scarcely an hour after the crazy Syrian and his wife had entered the city, they returned to the gate.

That was against the law, but a sliver of silver was slid into Laelius' palm, and another to Bibulus, and each looked at the other and shrugged. These two were not so crazy, Laelius thought; leaving now was a sure sign of sanity. He waved them on through.

A short while later, a centurion approached from the hills south of the city, cloaked against the dark, with five men at his back.

Mindful of his duties, Laelius stood in his way. 'State your business.'

'Mentos of the Twentieth.' The man let his sleeve rise up, showing the marks on his arm, of valour in the worst of circumstances. 'Our business is the emperor's. We are seeking a man dressed as a Syrian, who takes with him another man, dressed as if he were his wife. They may have an ass or a mule.'

Laelius felt his bowels churn. Fervently, and silently, he cursed the crazy Syrian and his fat wife. He considered the lies he might tell, and abandoned them. Nearly twenty years in the legions had taught him that honesty was generally less trouble. He said, 'Centurion, I know the man you mean. He and his accomplice entered the city at the night's dark and left again less than a quarter-hour ago.'

'Excellent! Then we may yet be in time to find the men they came to meet.' The centurion produced a salute of a crispness that the garrison Guard had long ago abandoned, and a silver denarius, still sharp from the mint. 'Spend this in my memory when you are next off duty. Your name?'

'Gaius Laelius.' Out of charity, Laelius said, 'And this is Publius Vera. We call him Bibulus.'

'I will remember those names.' The centurion gave a small and solemn bow. 'But best for you both not to say anything to anyone. If we succeed, your names will be mentioned. If we fail . . .'

If they failed, it was safer to know nothing.

He resisted the temptation to bite the coin to see if there was copper beneath the bright silver and dropped it instead into his belt pouch. 'Not a word,' he said, 'unless I hear from you.'

'Magnificent. May the rest of your watch pass in peace.'

The centurion marched his men through the gate and turned left, where the crazy not-Syrian had gone.

Laelius watched him go and set about forgetting the meeting. Soon after, he and Bibulus were relieved; he said nothing to his replacement. There was no need to talk, really, only to listen as the relief men spilled out the not-quite news that the royal family of Jerusalem was to be escorted to Antioch in Syria. The queen, obviously, was not included in the family. There was some doubt as to whether she remained alive.

The bad news was that only one century of the garrison Guard was required to attend the king as escort; the rest had orders to remain in Jerusalem and defend it against the potential attack from the south. Laelius' century was the third of the Guard, a detachment of the Tenth legion that had grown, over time, until it was as big as the legion itself. This third century was not going to Damascus.

Laelius walked back up the inner line of the wall and reached his barracks within the half-hour. By the call of the next watch, he had drunk enough wine to believe himself back in Rome, where all salutes were crisp and legionaries were not spat on in the street.

Some time in the night it came to him that he had seen both the centurion and the crazy Syrian before, but the wine had softened the edges of his memory and he slept before he could think where that might have been. Asleep, he dreamed of Rome, and a girl he had known before he had been posted east.

In the dream, she was as beautiful as when he had met her, twenty-three years previously, unaged and perfect. Laelius brought her red wine, and Judaean olives and a lame mule, and she kissed him for it and offered her body. He was poised over her, about to enter, when a lame Syrian rose from beneath the bed and drove his sword between Laelius' naked ribs.

Laelius knew that face, had seen it on the temple steps, and again, walking to the prison in the beast garden under armed guard; an uneven, asymmetrical face, impossible to forget. Except that he had done. And the man who was his accomplice was said to have been a centurion of the Twentieth; his name was Mergus, not Mentos.

Wide awake, struggling to breathe, Laelius stared at the dark and prayed for help from both his gods. From both, it seemed, came an answer that had always been a possibility; something he had planned without ever consciously admitting to it.

Silently, he rose and, eschewing his mail shirt and sword, donned a plain tunic. He took the seventeen silver coins he had saved from their hiding place beneath his bed and added to them the few he had earned in the night. Then, armed only with a knife, he left the barracks. Nobody stopped him; men went into the city and returned all the time.

Laelius went into the city now, but he did not plan to return. Instead, he delved deep into the lower quarter where lived a woman and her bastard son; his son. On his instruction they packed their bedding rolls, some food and some fodder on to their mule and drove it north, out of the opposite gate to the one Laelius had been guarding.

By noon of the following day they were far enough away to ensure that, had he been caught, the commander would have crucified him for desertion. They were not caught, and presently they came to Antioch and then to a small village in the northern mountains where lived his lover's parents. Swiftly – overnight, in fact – they became his parents-in-law.

Laelius apprenticed to his wife's father in his dotage, and when the old man died he became the village smith, in which role he lived a far longer, more prosperous and more fulfilling life than he would have done as a member of the Jerusalem garrison.

The visitor came to the cellar beneath the prison just after the changing of the guard.

Hypatia heard the second set of footsteps and nudged Berenice to warn her. They were sitting back to back for the warmth, with Estaph an arm's reach away. She stretched out her foot and tapped his.

He whispered, 'Saulos?'

'I think so.' Their voices sank into the stone and were lost.

Standing was hard, for the cold had seized their joints, but she wanted to meet him upright, face to face, near the bars, as far away as possible from the corner they had chosen to be their latrine. The stench was every-where, but they could at least distance themselves from it this much.

She heard him give good evening to the parting guard, and exchange commiserations with the one who took his place, and then he was walking down the corridor slowly, unwilling, when she had expected brisk triumphalism.

He turned the corner. Surprised, she said, 'Yusaf?'

He brought a small oil lamp, with a handle that spooned over his hand. The flame lit the lower half of his face, sending blurred beard-shadow sprawling up-wards to cover his eyes.

'Why you?'

'I am a member of the Sanhedrin.' His face tightened. 'Better me than anyone else. I am to tell you that Saulos has ordered us to attend your deaths tomorrow.'

'Our deaths?' Hypatia felt her hands tighten on the bars and made them loose again. 'All of us?'

Estaph said, 'In the morning?'

'Beginning in the morning,' Yusaf said. 'Estaph is to be crucified. Hypatia and the queen are to be ligatured about the neck, to hang on the cross, below his feet, one on either side. It will be faster.' He did not say, *Even so, they can make it last hours*; they all knew that.

He would not meet her eyes. He said, 'We tried to speak against it, but Saulos has taken the governor's place and no one can stand against him.'

'He will bring war to Jerusalem,' Hypatia said.

'I know. They say he wishes to raze it to the ground and rebuild it in the image of his god.'

'He said exactly that of Rome before he burned it.' Hypatia stepped back from the bars. 'You should leave. Thank you for coming. Can you tell us what hour it is, and how long until . . . how far until morning?'

'The guard will change twice more before they come for you,' said Yusaf. 'You have six hours left of peace. It is possible . . .' He shook his head. 'No. It's not. I'm sorry.'

'Say it.'

He opened his mouth and closed it again twice more, like a fish. 'It is possible Menachem and Pantera may return by then. They have stormed Masada and emptied its armoury. They will be here within the day, and their army with them, but I fear not by dawn.'

'Too late for us then, but perhaps not too late for Estaph if he is strong. Crucified men have been cut down before and lived.' Hypatia reached through the bars, and laid her hand on top of his. 'Don't fear for us, Yusaf. We will not hold this against you.'

'You may not, but I shall.' He left them, as disconsolate as he had come, taking his meagre light with him.

CHAPTER FORTY-FOUR

In the night's dark, a shadow stumbled where no shadow should have been. Pantera caught Gideon by the arm and dragged him off the path, one hand gripping his shoulder, the other covering his mouth.

'Don't speak.'

Gideon nodded, in so far as he could. Pantera let him go and eased down to a crouch.

The swiftest route back to Menachem saw them on a goatherd's track running south-west from Jerusalem, through olive groves and sloping pastures. All around, forested hills made the land uneven. Stars scattered enough light to make out the rocks, the hills, the distant herd, tight-gathered in a fold – and the figure of a man walking up the path, fast, and frighteningly unquiet.

He passed them by, unseeing in his haste. Smooth as any hunting beast, Pantera rose from the shadows behind him. As he had with Gideon, he clamped his hand over the newcomer's mouth, pulling him off balance.

As he had not with Gideon, he laid the flat of his knife across the expanse of bearded throat. 'Yusaf,' he said, flatly. 'You have news for us?'

Tight-voiced, Yusaf answered, 'Estaph will be crucified when the sun first touches the hill behind the palace, that is at the third hour after dawn. Hypatia and Berenice will hang from ligatures beneath him.'

It wasn't news, only confirmation of what they had feared. Pantera felt his heart clamp closed, and ignored it.

Stepping back, he slid his knife away. 'Did Saulos send you to tell me this?' he asked.

'Not specifically.' Yusaf gathered his dignity, smoothing his long-coat, his hair, his beard. In the grey starlight, his face was heavy with sorrow. 'I was sent into the cellar dungeons to tell the prisoners. Afterwards . . . I didn't consider it at the time, but Saulos let me go too easily. I think he knew I would try to find you.'

'Which means in turn that he believed you knew where to look. Were you followed?'

'No. That is, I don't think so; you would know, would you not? But I should go back to the city. If Saulos doesn't know that I have come . . .'

'He'll know. If you go back, you will join Hypatia and the others in the cellars if you're lucky. If not, his questioners will spend the night learning all that you know before you hang. Either way, you can be sure Saulos plans your death, only the time and the manner are uncertain.'

Yusaf chewed on his bottom lip. His nervous hands worked the silk of his sleeve-ends over and over through his fingers, gathering his courage. Just when it seemed he might never have enough, he raised his head. 'May I join you and Menachem?'

'It would seem you will have to.'

'What will you do about Estaph and Hypatia?'

Pantera stared at the hard sky, at the unmoving stars, at the fast cloud sailing across. 'It may be that we can be in the palace by dawn. If not, they will have to rescue themselves. If such a thing can be done.'

Two hours after Pantera had left it, Mergus arrived at Yusaf's costly town house in Jerusalem, bringing five Romans who had sworn fealty to Menachem. They drank wine and ate Yusaf's olives and bread and checked their weapons and stole away as softly as they had come.

When they left, Iksahra and Kleopatra went with them. Kleopatra wore a cloak over her mail shirt which, by happy chance, also covered the short stabbing sword at her belt. Mergus' men took her in their midst and did not question her ability to keep up with them as they marched swiftly through the dark.

Iksahra led them and she was not like the others: she wore no armour, her knives were shorter than even the short gladii of Rome and her cat kept to her heels in a way that made the legionaries step away so that Iksahra had a bubble of ten feet about her into which only Kleopatra and Mergus dared step. She despised the others for that, and they knew it, and hated her the more. It was not a good start to the night.

Silently, Iksahra led her small group out to the city's margins, towards the gate through which they and Pantera had entered. A new guard held it now, not the one who had seen them.

Within sight of the gate, but not within earshot, Iksahra moved sideways into an alley and had the group gather as close as they dared.

'We need to remove the guards from the gates in such a way that they believe they have left of their own accord, so that they return to their barracks in fear, but not alert to danger. Such a thing requires stealth: Kleopatra and I will do this one. If it goes wrong, Mergus knows what to do.'

'These are men of the Tenth,' said one of the men. 'They are small-minded and parochial, but they aren't stupid. They won't be frightened by two women. We will have to fight.' His hair was white with age, his skin browned by sun and wind until he was as dark as Iksahra, nearly.

Iksahra gazed at him with liquid eyes. 'Your name?' she asked, mildly.

'Gnaeus Galerius. My men call me Naso.' His nose, Kleopatra thought, was big enough to warrant the name. His knuckles were pale as he held both hands tight, but he stood his ground. 'The guards on the gates will fight; they won't retreat. It is what they are trained for.'

Iksahra's smile set them flinching. 'They fight when they think they can win. I am here to prove to them that they cannot. Kleopatra will help me with the first one. Watch, and you will learn what must be done.'

'Who's there?'

'It's me. Kleopatra, princess of Caesarea.' Kleopatra walked openly down the road. The guards at the gate were not ones she knew, which made it easier to do what she had to do. She said, 'Have you a flame? A

416

torch, perhaps, so you can see that it's truly me?'

They had a small soapstone lamp with a dirty wick. The taller of the two retrieved it from a niche in the wall and spilled light across the nearest part of the roadway, meanly, as if it was his own gold, and he might at any moment go on hands and knees to gather it back.

Kleopatra said, 'I am supposed to go to Antioch with my family.'

The Romans hated her: their eyes were flat with loathing. The taller said, 'You're at the wrong side of the city. Go to the palace. They'll leave from the west gate, behind the beast gardens at the palace, if they haven't already left. You don't have to— What in the name of all the gods is . . . *that*?'

'What?' Kleopatra spun. Iksahra was moving up the road, arms outstretched, white robes billowing behind. Even had the guards' eyes not been dulled by the lighting of the lamp, it would have been impossible to see her arms and legs and head. Her robes, it seemed, came on of their own volition, rippling softly. The cheetah stalked at her side, taller than it seemed in daytime, its eyes aflame in the meagre lamplight.

As she moved, a line of Romans marched across the road, blindly, steadfastly forward, as if on a long, long route. She flowed through them, or they through her, or each through the other, as ghosts are wont to do.

'What?' Kleopatra peered down the road in evident confusion. 'What is it? I can't see—'

The smaller guard was already running. The taller dropped the lamp. The light guttered bravely on, leaving a glow in the air as he turned, feet scrabbling, and ran, high-kneed, up the road towards the palace.

Kleopatra picked up the lamp, shaking her head. Iksahra came to join her, bubbling with silent laughter. Mergus and his men gathered a short distance away, grinning in spite of themselves.

'You could have killed them easily,' Kleopatra said. 'Why did you not?'

'Because a terrified man spreading fear among his brethren is more useful tonight than that same man safely dead. We did what we needed to do. There are seven more gates to clear before dawn. Shall we go?'

The guard to the cellar dungeon changed in a clatter of lock and key and footsteps, with a new torch lit and the old one left to smoulder, to help fight back the dark. Nobody came to visit the prisoners, although the new guard paused a moment in the entrance to the tunnel and stared towards them, to be sure they were still alive.

Hypatia stood by the bars after he had gone. Her cheek felt cold metal, her feet cold stone. Her mind was a tumble of memories, of dreams, of a lifetime's nightmares, all different in small, definable ways, all leading to this place, this time, this cold, this dark.

All her life she had thought that if she did things differently, if she turned a different way at each of the crossroads to which fate had brought her, she might be able to escape this. And she had failed. She took a bitter breath and looked ahead, down the pathways of the dream.

Only two paths stretched before her now, and one of them so rare, she had dreamed it just three times. The first, the common one, had haunted her life. She knew by heart each moment of this long, cold night and the messy death that followed.

But the path of the rare dream was not yet unravelled; she still walked its route, the point at which the two diverged yet to appear. Closing her eyes, she pressed her forehead harder against the bars and began to clear the fears that cluttered her mind, to leave space into which the god might choose to come.

She let out a breath and another and on the third she did not breathe in again, but stepped forward in the dark space of her mind, into the void that was deeper than water, wider than the oceans, emptier than the dungeons at night. And in that space, she asked of the listening silence the only question that had ever mattered: *What would you have me do?*

Nothing came, and less than nothing; no word, no sign. Resting on the cusp of a breath, as near to death as she might come and still live, she thought she was forsaken, lost, alone.

Then she felt the hot press of a living pelt against her calf, and smelled the meat-mellow breath of a hunting cat. She heard its breath rasp by her ear, recoiled at the sharp prick of whiskers against her cheek, and when she looked deep in the dark, there was the smudge of black against paler black in a patterning she almost recognized and two green-amber eyes, that grew stronger as she gave them her attention.

She thought it was a leopard, sign of Pantera, and said so. Somewhere, the god laughed. The beast drew back its lips and padded closer until its outline was clear, taller than a leopard, longer-legged, with a muzzle more square, and a head held higher.

From all of these, she knew it as Iksahra's cheetah, a beast that had viewed her with nothing short of disdain since the day she had first seen it. Nevertheless, it was here, in the space of Hypatia's unbreath. She touched her forehead, as she might have done to Isis, or Ma'at or Apis, bull-god of Memphis, and waited. And waited. The beast blinked at her; the only movement in the void.

Again she asked, *What would you have of me?* Again the beast blinked, and in that movement she saw through the patterned pelt to the black skin of a woman behind, saw through its eyes to gold-brown eyes, saw black hair, tight as a shearling ram, and the flash of white teeth.

Pain flooded her then, the twisting knife that leaves a heart in fragments; the pain she had thought set aside, safely, that it might not undo her this close to the end.

She closed her eyes, and when she opened them again both woman and beast were gone and in their place was the whistle of wings and the far, high keening cry of a falcon, bird of Isis, hunting.

Somewhere far beyond it, the god said, *I would have you taste the true cost of life. There is no escape from this.*

Hypatia breathed in, a great gulping swallow of air, of life, of cold and the present moment. Her head ached, as if the god had struck it in passing.

She took another breath, and stilled it, and came back to herself, to all that she had lost and gained and might lose again. Aloud she said, 'Thank you.'

From behind, she heard Estaph take breath to speak. Without turning, she said, 'No.'

'You don't know what I was going to say.' They both spoke quietly and directed the sound at the floor: already they had learned what would carry to the guards and what would not.

'You were going to suggest that you could kill us both now, and leave only yourself alive for the morning.'

'It's the only way.'

'It's one way,' Hypatia said. 'But if we take it, you will spend two full days dying and Saulos will have won. I have dreamed this every night of my adult life. I will not let you do it.' She stepped to the centre of their small circle, standing between them. 'If anyone should stay alive, it should be me. There may be a limit to what even Saulos will dare do to the Chosen of Isis.'

'There isn't,' Berenice said. 'He does this for his god, and his god feeds on the blood of others. There is no limit at all to what he will do. If you have dreamed this, you know it is true.'

Whatever else she had dreamed, Hypatia had certainly dreamed this moment, these words; now. Perhaps a dozen times in her life, the many branching pathways of possibility had brought her to this, the last of the turning points. Two pathways lay ahead, each one distinct from the other: the first, the easiest, led to certain death. The other . . . she wasn't sure where the other led, she had been along it only twice in her life, and each time was different. Still, she was the Chosen of Isis, and she was not given to procrastination. She made her decision swiftly, took a breath, and let it out again.

Berenice saw a moment's indecision and gave a small, tight smile of triumph. 'Shall we draw lots for it?' she asked. 'The loser is the last one to remain alive.'

Chapter Forty-Five

Among the hills north of Jerusalem, a thousand small cooking fires showed the size of Menachem's army.

Of those thousand, a hundred clustered close around the shoulder of a low hill and beneath their light a spring bubbled and sang, gold and silver as it passed from fire-light to starlight.

In this place of drought and desert, a stone channel poured water down into a plunge pool deep enough to take one man standing upright and cover him to the crown of his head.

Stone steps led down into the water. Menachem stood naked on the topmost tread with his head bowed, watching the torch-made dapples shiver across the water. About him, about the spring, his army waited in such silence as was possible for two thousand men dressed in new mail, with new weapons and tired horses and a battle ahead.

Pantera stood apart, on the spring's southern side, holding by the bridle the almond-milk mare that had been Iksahra's parting gift to Menachem, that he might have a mount fit for a king. The mare was anxious. She stood, watching the fires, the men, the silver stream. A single foreleg struck the ground, calling thunder from the earth.

Menachem looked up at last. His gaze met Pantera's and his mind returned from the distant place where it had been. He clasped his hands together. Black hairs grew in strong lines down his arms and thick swards on his chest. They stood upright now, testament to the morning's chill.

'How much longer?' he asked.

Gideon stood with his back to them, staring at the faint strand of silver strung along the horizon. 'Soon,' he said.

And soon, soon, with goats grazing in the distance, and morning cookfires of Jerusalem threading the morning sky, with cockerels crying a greeting and small birds taking up the call, then did the shy sun blush over the edge of the mountains behind, and burn the dew off the thin grasses, so that the mare dropped her head at last to graze.

Pantera said, 'In two hours, Hypatia, Berenice and Estaph will die.'

'They will *begin* to die,' Menachem said. 'But we will be in Jerusalem by then. The city will be ours.'

'It may not. If Iksahra has not ripped the hearts out of the garrison Guard, this will be a battle of a different mettle than the one on Masada.'

'Even so, this is our home. You may be surprised—'

'Look,' Gideon said. He pointed at the rock at the pool's lip, and they fell to silence, and watched as the sun lifted the shadow from Menachem's feet to his thighs, to his torso, to his brow.

Between one breath and the next, he was bathed entirely in light and the stream flowed liquid gold. Then Gideon said, 'Now,' quietly, so that only Pantera, who was closest, might hear, and Yusaf, who stood a little behind.

Thus, in the first opening of dawn, before the gathered multitudes of his army, Menachem, grandson of the Galilean, stepped down into the liquid light, and under it, completely, so that only the very top of his black hair showed.

When he stepped out again, Gideon came forward with a jar of perfumed oil and drizzled it on to his streaming hair and raised his voice, so that it rang from hillside to hillside, to the two thousand men and their horses, to the goats and the rising hawks and the distant, discordant city.

'I give you Menachem, of the line of David, of the tribe of Judah, grandson of the Galilean, greatest of Rome's enemies. As spoken by the prophets, he shall ride into Jerusalem on an ass, symbol of peace. He shall cleanse the Temple of its iniquity. He shall free us from oppression. For in his righteousness is the path to peace, and he shall set the sons of Zion upon the sons of Greece, and shall dispel them, that our city, and our Israel, shall live without war, in a time of harmony, under the eyes of the living god!'

They heard their priest in silence, the army of the king of Israel, and for a heartbeat more they held that silence, and then they lifted their new blades, and beat their hilts on the hard bull's hide of their new shields, and the sound rocked the earth and the roots of the hills and the pillars of the sky, and surely it must also have rocked the city, wherein waited men and women in their hundreds of thousands for the king who had been promised.

Menachem opened his mouth to speak.

'Not here. Go to the head of the spring where they can see you,' Pantera said, and like a blind man Menachem turned, and stepped up and up to the spring's head.

The sun cast him in gold. The spring sang out of the earth at his feet and when he bent and cupped it in his hands, and sprayed it over the men nearest, they were drenched, lightly, in liquid silver.

He raised his hands high, as the priests did on the Sabbath. The rolling thunder of hilts on shields rose and fell away. His voice rang out over the heads of his men, straight to Jerusalem.

'I am of David's line. I am son of my father's father, Yehuda, the Galilean, who should have been king of all Israel, and would have been, did he only have you at his side to make it happen. Today, we shall complete what he began those many years ago when he assaulted the armoury at Sepphoris. Today, we shall drive Rome from the sacred places of our people. By tonight, all Jerusalem will be ours under one god. You have waited for this, you have worked for this, you who have been true from the start . . .'

He spoke to men by name, drawing them forward, naming their courage in particular battles at particular times, or brothers lost, or children dead in their absence. They came and knelt and went away again, shining with love for him and pride in themselves and their army.

Pantera backed away and stood with Gideon and Yusaf on the lower ground by the spring. 'He looks good there, with the newborn sun at his back and the water before him. We must remember this, if he is to speak often: it is what the men will recall, later, when the terror of combat has burned away their other memories.'

'But not our other memories,' said Yusaf, drily. 'Or at least, not yours. Do you ever feel true fear like mortal men?'

'Of course. You would not believe how often.'

'We do not believe you now,' Gideon said, in a tone that matched Yusaf's exactly. 'One day you must show me how you hide it so efficiently. Meanwhile, we must find ourselves a donkey colt. Zechariah was a rambling idiot who contradicted himself with each second word, but every child knows that the king comes in righteousness and salvation riding on an ass. We can't let it pass.'

'We can,' Pantera said. 'We must. This is battle, not a coronation. He will ride Iksahra's mare. Nothing less will keep him alive.'

'The ass is to signify peace.'

'And righteousness, I heard. But to get to peace, he must live through war, and this mare is battle trained. Lay your hand here, on her hide, and feel the shiver of her sinews. She knows there's a fight coming and she's desperate to take part. You won't find a donkey that'll fight for you.'

'But—'

'But nothing. He'll look better mounted on that mare

426

than on anything else, trust me, and there are prophecies enough to go round: one of them probably mentions a white horse with black feet if you look hard enough. Put your effort into seeking that out if you find yourself with time on your hands through the morning.'

Chapter Forty-Six

Six of Jerusalem's seven gates cleared smoothly through the remaining hours of darkness. Six more pairs of legionaries fled to their barracks, carrying stories of a ghûl abroad in the night, of ghostly legionaries marching to nowhere, of monsters greater than any they had seen.

Iksahra gained in stature with Naso and his legionaries with each gate, so that by the time they approached the last, set in the western wall behind the beast gardens, they were no longer drawing wards against evil when she passed them by, but were sketching instead the sign for good luck.

The process was not fast, though; the city's cockerels were clearing their throats and the small coloured birds of the gardens and groves were already courting by the time they reached that last gate, tucked away behind the palace. The morning was lighter than it should have been; the perimeter of the beast garden was etched clearly across a grey sky.

Kleopatra caught Iksahra's arm. 'It's too late; dawn's nearly on us. They'll see you're not a ghûl.'

'I know. This time we have to fight. They are ten and we are seven, but we have the cheetah, and Mergus' men have the advantage of surprise: the Guard will not expect to be attacked by men they know. Still, we need to get closer. Will you go forward now and ask them if your family has already left? Keep them talking until we get near.'

It was easier, this time, for Kleopatra to walk up the road, and, this close to the palace, the guards were civil.

'The king left before dusk, lady, and all his family with him. You've missed them, but you can't leave now. The zealot army is already outside the walls. They've armed themselves and moved north of the city in the night. There'll be a battle before noon. You should be indoors.'

It was the captain who spoke, first of ten men, stationed five on each side of the locked and barred gate. Each of them held his sword out, his shield off his shoulder, ready against ghûls and zealots equally.

'I have to join them.' Kleopatra bit her lip and stared at her feet and found that the morning had progressed so far that she could easily see the detail of her toes. She looked back up at the guard. 'Would it be possible to—'

His raised hand stopped her. To his men, not to her, he said, 'Here she comes. See? It's the king's Berber beastwoman. I told Antonius it wasn't a ghûl. Make a line on me and advance on my word. My lady, if you could step behind us, you'll be safer there.'

They made a line of iron and bull's hide; men who had fought and killed all their adult lives. They guarded the gate nearest the palace, likely first focus of any assault from the north and west.

Kleopatra was pushed behind, so that she saw Iksahra through the gaps between their shields. She was walking down the road with the cheetah at her heels, making no effort at all to stretch her arms, or to appear as an apparition. She came to a halt ten feet away from the line of guards.

There followed a moment's hush in which ten men braced themselves, waiting for an order. In her bones, Kleopatra felt the thrill of preparation run through them. She saw the captain take a breath to shout and slid her own hand into her sleeve where her knife was hidden: better to die trying to cut his throat than to see them crucify Iksahra alongside Estaph.

Iksahra lifted her arm. The captain said, 'Steady, steady . . .'

Iksahra dropped her arm. The cheetah sprang forward as commanded and its fluid gold-black flight merged with Iksahra's battle shout, for as her arm came down her thrown knife caught the first edge of the dawn and carried it forward, lancing the throat of the captain as he, in his turn, launched himself at Iksahra.

The captain tumbled forward, retching, his own blade spinning and clattering to the ground. Iksahra stooped to gather it and so ducked under the swing from the rush of incoming guards: five against one. Their blades hacked out and down – and missed.

Iksahra was as fluid as her own hunting cat, dodging, sliding, skipping back, and laughing in their faces, so that at first they did not see Mergus and his five legionaries who came out of the shadows on either side of the road, advancing fast and silent.

'Look out!' Kleopatra shouted, when she was sure

they'd been seen. 'Enemies to both sides!'

The men of the garrison thought her a friend and shouted thanks even as they turned, five on four, back to back in a single snatched step. Their captain would have been proud of them. He was not yet fully dead; his blood still pulsed in a dark sheet across the road, but the waves were less with each ripple and his eyes had already turned up to show the whites.

Men and iron blurred in the paltry light. One fell from each side, but no more; they were too evenly matched, trained in the same vein by the same men in the same tactics.

Iksahra was there, ahead of anyone else, still singing, with her knife blood-wet in her hand, flashing – it was light enough now for more than a glimmer – as she slashed right and left at the guards on either side. They fell back from her as they had not from their fellow Romans, but not far; the men behind them acted as a wall that held their backs and kept them firm and, with the instinct of men who have trained and fought together for decades, they stepped away together, giving each man more space to move, and then attacked in perfect synchrony, their blades swinging in, hard, at the height of Iksahra's heart.

'Iksahra!'

Kleopatra had stood still for less than three breaths and she was not breathing slowly. Now, with terrible clarity, she saw the blades coming in, set to cut Iksahra in half, and, in the passing of a single heartbeat, she saw the place where she could act, considered it, found it good and, stooping, picked up a blade from the clutter that lay on the ground at her feet.

Lifting became a swing, became a slice up, under the legionary's half-mailed skirt. The blow was the same she had used to kill the guard in the beast garden not ten days before, but this time she held on, and drove it deeper and on until blood spilled from between his lips. Only then did she twist as Jucundus had taught her, and pull out again.

Her enemy choked on his own blood, and sank to the road. Kleopatra stood back, struck to sudden stillness.

It was said that the Chosen of Isis could see the shades of the dead and speak to them. In the beast garden, she had not known she was Chosen, had not looked for the signs of death or tried to see anything. Here, harried by new knowledge and new doubts, with bile stripping the lining of her throat, Kleopatra stared at the dense air about the dead man's head for some sign of life. Or death.

Nothing was there, but in the echo of her mind she heard him say, with some surprise, and no hurry, *Am I free?*

Always before, she had conducted her conversations with the dead in her head, and had thought them hers alone. Now, she answered aloud, 'You are. Go to your god soon, before the gods and spirits of the desert find you.'

She felt, but did not see, him bow to her and turn and march east, to the rising sun.

'Kleopatra?'

Her own name came at her oddly, as if through other ears. She looked up and saw the cheetah first, and wondered how it could speak; then she looked again and saw Iksahra, not ten feet away. The beastwoman had killed another guard and had caught his falling body. She stood, cradling it across her chest like a lover. That one's voice was more distant, softer, but he, too, was glad to be free. Iksahra let him down to lie on the ground. Her eyes were fixed on Kleopatra's face. 'Are you ill?' she asked.

'No.' Kleopatra held herself tight, arms wrapped across her chest, hugging ever tighter. Time was returning to its own speed, leaving her feeling seasick. She said, 'It was too easy. That was my third kill. Each time was the same.'

'It wasn't the same and I don't believe it was easy. You are a credit to your teachers. Look now, we are done: Mergus' men have taken heart from your action and finished the enemy.'

They had, indeed. Eleven lay dead; ten Romans of the garrison Guard to one of theirs, a junior officer whose name Kleopatra did not know. His soul spoke Aramaic, while all around him the Roman dead hailed one another in cheerful Latin.

From somewhere closer, Iksahra said, 'Kleopatra, what is it?'

'When you see how death frees them, it is no hardship to kill.'

Iksahra stood, staring. In the growing dawn, the whites of her eyes grew narrow and then broad again. Kleopatra said, 'You can't hear them, can you?'

'Nor see them, no. Hypatia can, though, I am sure.'

Iksahra drew closer, laid a hand on Kleopatra's arm. Her fingers were stiff with dried blood, and cool. 'My mother told me death was a release. I thought she meant only when the life was lived in pain, or the threat of it, as Estaph is threatened with the cross.'

'These men were not like that. And yet I swear to you, they were not unhappy to be dead.' She shook herself free. 'We have to find Hypatia.'

'Not now,' Mergus said urgently, from her side. 'Now you will turn round and put your back to the wall. Quickly! We are not alone.'

Kleopatra turned and slapped her shoulders against the wall by the guard post. Mergus came in at her left side, and Iksahra at her right with the bloodied cheetah beside her. The other men joined them in ones and twos. And so they stood, seven alone in the still morning, listening to the cockerels take command of the dunghills.

'Hush!' Kleopatra held up her hand. 'I can hear men, marching. And horses. Is it Menachem's army?'

'The horses are Menachem's,' agreed Mergus bluntly, 'and his men are behind them, heading for the gate. But if you listen to the noise from the other side, you'll hear the garrison Guard, and they are faster and closer. We will face them alone.'

Even as he spoke, the peace of the morning was torn apart by the sudden roar of armed men singing, and the ear-breaking clash of a thousand sword hilts beaten on shields, in perfect unison, as the garrison Guard marched up from the Temple.

Chapter Forty-Seven

The king of Israel's army marched towards the sleeping city with the new sun sending long, raking shadows streaming behind them.

Small groups peeled off through the minor gates: a hundred men under Moshe; a hundred and fifty led by Eleazir, whose men believed he should have been king, although he had not said it aloud himself – Pantera thought them safer away from the main fighting and Eleazir had not argued – and two hundred of the Peace Party under Gideon, who was given, now, heart and soul to the coming battle.

The rest advanced on the west gate, the biggest, that was set behind the palace and still in the shade.

Helmetless, his black hair aflame to his shoulders, Menachem rode Iksahra's almond-milk mare at the van. The sound of her feet was the clash of cymbals on the hard road.

Pantera rode at his left hand, to be his living shield. He rode with his eyes on the road, but his attention was fixed on the sun, his mind a sand-timer that drained grain by too-fast grain towards the moment when the light might strike the hill of execution behind the wall.

Aloud in the hollows of his mind he said, *We're coming, we're coming, we're coming. Don't lose hope.* He had no idea if Hypatia could hear him.

And then the dawn peace was broken, smashed against the wall of a legionary marching song drummed to the beat of sword hilts clashing on iron shield bosses. They sounded like thunder on an iron roof, marching to bring death; even as their enemy, Pantera felt it stir his blood.

'The garrison Guard!' Pantera shouted, and raised himself up and gave the battle cry of the new king's army. *'Jerusalem!* For the glory of Israel!'

He kept level with Menachem for the first few yards, but the milk-white mare was turned to lightning by the sounds of war, so that Menachem was through the gates, on a mount who screamed her own battle cries over the havoc.

They turned the last corner. Two hundred yards away, the garrison Guard marched towards them four deep across the road, held in tight formation by a captain in a white plumed helmet who shouted orders from the farthest, safest edge.

With the skill of a dance master, he kept them shoulder to shoulder, shield locked to shield, blades of the front lines naked to the fore. They held absolute order, even as Menachem's front rank of horsemen charged them.

And there, caught between the two hordes, was a clutter of figures at the side of the road. Pantera caught a glimpse of white linen and black limbs and, beside them, long black hair and a single sword held high . . .

'*Kleopatra! Iksahra!* Move back! Keep out of the way!'

He saw them skip back into the shadows of the Upper Market, far enough not to be run down, and then he was past, bearing down on the garrison. He wrenched round in the saddle, torn, unable to slow, or break free. From three ranks back, he heard Yusaf shout, 'I'll see to them!' and saw him peel his mount away from the margins of the group just ahead of the first clash.

In so far as there had been time to think at all, Pantera had hoped that sheer mass of numbers and the weight of their momentum might break the guards' shieldwall early and fast. It did not do so.

The initial impact rocked the garrison back on their heels, but the men of Menachem's army were largely untrained and their horses unused to war; they had no knowledge of how to form a wedge, how to split open the shieldwall and force apart the legionaries into ever smaller packs of encircled men.

Pantera had read of such things and knew them possible, but here, now, he found himself in a chaos of spooked horses and unseated men, of blades held cack-handed that failed to bite, of white, shocked faces and the sight of grown men weeping.

Ahead, the men of the garrison Guard set up a new shout and the rear ranks redoubled the thunderous drumming of their sword hilts on their shields. Hit broadside by the noise, horses reared and bucked in terror, unseating riders as unsuited to war as they were.

Pantera swore, viciously. Flinging his own mount round, he shouted above the throng. 'Men of Israel: dismount! *Menachem!* Order the dismount!'

Menachem tried. For honour, for sanity, for the chance of winning his city, the new king of Israel filled his lungs and bawled the order to dismount in four different languages: in Hebrew, in Aramaic, in Greek and in Latin.

The garrison Guard laughed to hear the last two, and raised the volume of their clamour. Menachem's mounted men either couldn't hear or didn't understand, or were simply incapable of leaving the saddle and delivering themselves whole, on their feet, to the safe, solid ground, ready to fight.

Pantera wheeled his horse. Menachem was a dozen feet away, slashing his own sword left and right. The raging milk-white mare did more damage than a man ever could, striking out with teeth and feet at anyone, of either side, who came within reach.

Pantera saw her kill one of the garrison Guard who made the mistake of running at her, as if to mount behind Menachem. She wheeled, lashing out with both hind feet, and his face dissolved in a plash of blood and bone and white teeth. His body arced high into the air. At the apex of its arc, Iksahra passed him, running at a different, riderless horse. She was mounted before he hit the ground.

She spun the new mount without reins. Her face was spattered with dried blood, pale against her dark skin. Her arm was cut above the elbow; a clean wound, with sharp edges that had ceased to bleed.

'Look out!' Pantera killed the man who might have assaulted her. She swung her mount and let it kill another. He had not realized that this, too, was one of her horses. Perhaps it wasn't, and simply all horses became trained to battle when she mounted; today, this morning, with the sun not yet on the hill beyond, anything was possible.

Feeling more confident, he swung back to face the mass of armed men ahead of them with Iksahra a white and black killing machine at one shoulder, Menachem fighting doggedly at the other and Mergus – blessed of Mithras, he heard his voice above the fray – martialling the foot soldiers somewhere beyond his left flank.

Even so, the garrison Guard was disciplined and well led; trumpeters sounded high, harsh notes and men moved to their command, pushing in, step by brutal step, crushing everything.

To his right and his left, Pantera shouted, 'The captain! We need to kill the captain!'

He pointed ahead to where white plumes, tall as a man's arm, waved like a beacon at the battlefield's edge. Together, he, Menachem and Iksahra fought towards him, slashing, hacking, wounding more than killing, but staying alive, which was all that mattered.

The plumes danced ahead, always a little away from the fighting, always shouting out new orders to the trumpeters, who sent them to the men. As they approached, the Guard split into two groups and manoeuvred in perfect synchrony, so that one part stepped out and round, in a long wheeling arc, while the other pushed inwards.

Pantera shouted, 'Kill him now or we're—'

He stopped because everybody else had stopped; each man's shout cut off as if a god's hand had hammered past, sucking away all the air. But it hadn't been a god; a thousand men had drawn breath all at once, in surprise, in shock, in terror, in delight.

In the hair's breadth of hush, Pantera hauled his mount left, to the city, and so saw what the others had already seen.

'God of all gods,' he whispered. 'Gideon has come.' Nobody heard him, for Gideon had not come alone, nor with only the two hundred men he had taken with him; he had come with the whole of Jerusalem and the moment's silence was annihilated under the sound of their cry: *'Jerusalem!'*

Hundreds came, thousands, tens of thousands, too many to count, all the men of Jerusalem, and their wives, their sons, their daughters, their grandmothers, lame on their sticks; everyone and anyone who could run or walk was flooding now from the streets on either side of the Upper Market, here to free their city from the yoke of occupation.

They surged towards the garrison Guard, armed with kitchen knives and pestles, with sickles and smithing irons and rods with sharpened ends for poking at goats, with axes and hammers and lengths of wood ripped from their doorways.

Most of all, as the hordes of Jerusalem always did, they came armed with stones and they threw them now, hard, aiming for their enemies' legs, for the soft skin behind their knees, for their shins, for their Achilles tendons, where, like the hero, they might be weak.

A dozen or more had slings, and used them with startling accuracy on the men who were executing the pincer movement. Within a dozen heartbeats, thirty men of the garrison Guard had fallen, and the rest were no longer concentrating on the enemy in front, but were turning, haphazardly, to face those behind.

And then Pantera saw their captain. A break opened in the lines, a flash of sun on a helmet that drew his eyes past a trumpeter . . . he saw him in profile: soft nose, a little upturned, curls of dark hair escaping the confines of his helmet, and an arrogance that no other man in Judaea had ever truly matched.

'*Saulos!*'

Pantera's roar outdid the trumpeter. The standing plumes flew aslant as Saulos turned his head, not towards him, but back to a tent-party of eight men who stood a dozen yards behind the others, separate from the fighting. At his shout, they turned away and ran for the palace. He sprinted to catch up and they opened to take him, a smooth move that drew him in and held him secure in their heart. He flung the helmet away as he ran; white plumes lay rocking in the dirt behind them.

Pantera spun his horse so hard that it reared. He caught Iksahra's eye. They did not need words; a look was enough, and in it, one name: *Hypatia*.

Together they pushed their horses away from the conflict, following where Saulos had gone.

Hypatia sat alone in the dark and the abominable cold and listened to the stamp and clatter of the last guard change.

Light flared at the corner. The incoming and outgoing guards exchanged murmured Latin: 'There's war outside; we're winning. How is it here? Are they well? Yes, all well. As well as can be on their last night. They'll be lucky if it is their last night. I've seen crucified men live three days.'

She felt a shudder from both guards and then one left, relieved, banging the door shut behind him. The other locked it from within and then, alerted perhaps by the quality of the silence in the cellar, lifted his torch and brought it round the corner.

The light flooded the cell, blinding after the dark. Hypatia laid her hands over her eyes, but otherwise made no move to rise, to acknowledge his presence. She had shown she was alive, which was more than the others had done. They lay along the side wall, in easy repose, with their hands by their sides as if for burial and a cloth across their brows. Beneath, each face was free of all care, liberated from the travails of life.

The new guard ran at the bars, trailing his light, bright as a comet. 'What's happened?' Panic lit his voice. He banged his sword hilt on the bars. 'Wake up!'

Nobody moved. He crashed his whole shoulder on the iron next to her head. 'What have you done?'

'I have given them peace.' Hypatia took her hand from her eyes. 'What would you have done? I, too, have known men live for three days on a cross.'

'Gods alive!' He was grey with terror. Throughout the empire, if a guard let his prisoners die, routinely, he took their place in whatever followed. His fingers grappled numbly for the keys at his belt. 'You can't do that!'

Hypatia regarded him with quiet curiosity. 'I am the Chosen of Isis. I can do whatever I choose. Don't come in. You can't change anything.'

'You can't keep me out!'

Iron jangled. A key met a lock and turned, shakily. The door crashed back. A flutter of flame came in first, as the torch was thrust into Hypatia's face.

Hypatia jerked back as he threw himself across the cell to the two bodies lying on its far side, then, without rising, she propped both hands on the floor and, stretching, swept her feet in a long arc that met his at its apex, tangling his ankles.

He fell, inelegantly, so that his chin made first contact with the far wall, and then his shoulder. He came to rest head down, in the nauseating pile of ordure at the furthest corner from the door. For a mercy, if only temporarily, he was unconscious. Hypatia struggled to turn him over and wrest his blade from the scabbard.

She turned, blade in hand, and found Estaph looking at her. 'It worked,' he said.

He was cold; the tips of his ears were blue-white and his face was haggard enough to be dead. She lifted the guttering torch from the floor and nursed it to life, this once needing its heat more than its light. She brought it to him and to Berenice as she, too, rose from the frigid floor.

'Is he dead?' Estaph, ever practical, asked and then answered his own question. 'No. And now yes.'

In between these two, a swift wrench of a head; exactly the mercy he had offered to Hypatia and she had refused, because the god did not allow death, but demanded life, and this was the only way she could think of to give it.

She said, 'We're not safe yet. There's a palace full of guards outside.'

'The palace isn't as full as it was yesterday,' Estaph

said, and he held open the door to their cell for her to pass through. 'You should lead. You have the best ears of us all. You can warn us if someone comes.'

And then what will we do? We are worn and cold and afraid and we have one sword between three of us, which is not enough. Hypatia did not say it aloud, but met his gaze and found the same thoughts reflected in the same tight smile.

'We have to try,' Estaph said. 'Your god did not want us dead too easily or too soon.'

Chapter Forty-Eight

The beast garden was a stinking mess. The air was heavy with old urine and rotting faeces and alive with flies. Inside was a cacophony of hunger, of thirst, of bestial desperation that outdid the havoc of combat a bare few hundred paces away.

Seeing Iksahra stand in the gateway, the horses, hounds and hawks threw themselves in a frenzy at the bars of their compounds, howling or screaming or belling, as their nature demanded, for food, for water, for the blessing of release.

Iksahra spat on the ground, eyes ablaze. 'The slaves fled to Damascus and left them untended. They should die for such a thing.'

'They are slaves,' Pantera said. 'It is not given them to act without orders. They are often flayed for exactly that. We haven't time—'

'I know. But we are two against nine. But even two such as we will better prevail if we have—'

'Three,' said a clear voice behind. 'With me, we are three. Or seven, if you prefer.'

Pantera turned, slowly. Kleopatra was wildly bruised; a long welt across her left cheek half closed her eye and promised spectacular colours later. Her forearms had cuts along their lengths, one of them ragged, of the sort that responded better to clean air than to a dressing. None of it detracted from the light in her eyes.

Pride shone from her, and a new determination. 'I'm coming with you to get Hypatia. You need me. I know the fastest way through the palace to the cellars where she's held. And Mergus is on his way – is here.' A shuffle of sandals and he was there, with three others. Kleopatra said, 'He can't go back: the Hebrews don't know him well enough to remember he's friend not foe and they're winning now. He'll be cut down simply for looking Roman.'

Mergus was breathing hard, but not greatly hurt, nor the three men with him. He saluted across the heads of the others, a gesture that promised stories later, when time allowed. He moved to the two women and there was a joining between them, as of men who have fought together in battle, who have saved each other's lives and know the most precious of bonds, closer than many lovers. And now Kleopatra and Iksahra were a part of it.

Pantera bowed to them, for the brightness of their greeting. 'Lead then,' he said, and so it was that five men, two women and a cat walked down the slaves' corridor to its end.

'Left here,' said Kleopatra as they poured out through the door, 'and then left again at the junction at the end. There are stairs fifty paces further on. A guard will be at their head.'

Iksahra said, 'Let me do this. Mergus, if you and the others could appear to form an honour guard? Let him see you as we round the corner, but don't come closer unless I fail.'

As if ordered by an officer, the men fell into line behind Iksahra. She flicked her fingers to keep the cheetah close, and then they were at the junction in the corridor and there was no time to ask what she planned, only to watch as she stalked away, black and white, with her beast flowing gold at her side.

The guard saw the men first. His head went up, and he smiled, and was still smiling when his gaze fell on the cheetah and the woman and his confusion then, of why she should have been thus honoured, slowed his blade.

In perfect Latin, Iksahra said, 'I am the ghûl that assaulted the gate guards,' and it seemed to Pantera that the guard had died of fright before the cheetah had ripped the life from his throat.

He died in a flurry of muffled beast noises, and not one single human sound. The smell of blood rinsed the corridor and Pantera found that, this once, he was not immune to such a thing, and that he was not alone; Mergus and Kleopatra were both paler than they had been.

Iksahra stepped round the mess. 'We go down the steps behind this door,' she said. 'I believe there is a corridor to a similar door, and another set of steps and then a long corridor that winds the length of the palace and brings us to the head of the stairs where Hypatia is being kept. Am I right?'

Kleopatra brought herself past the carnage. 'There will be a guard at each of the doors,' she said. 'We should have questioned this one before he died, to find if Saulos has already gone through.'

'He has. And he knew we were coming,' Pantera said. 'The guard had his sword newly out.' The others turned to stare at him. He shrugged. 'The oil of the sheath still shone on the whetted edge. It dulls very quickly. Seneca taught me.'

'And Seneca taught Saulos,' Iksahra said. 'We have to hope he has remembered less than you have or our passage will not be easy.' She led the way at a jog-run.

Pantera followed, and wondered what he would do if he were Saulos, if he knew what he thought Saulos knew, and if he did not know the things he hoped Saulos would not know.

At the head of the next set of steps, with the gore of the next dead guard sticky underfoot, he held up his hand.

'Wait,' he said. 'When Menachem enters this place as its king, where will he go first?'

He saw Kleopatra tilt her head, bright as a dawn bird, thinking. 'He'll go straight to the king's chambers,' she said, in time. 'Three rooms in a suite at the far end of the top floor. The outer room has a fountain in the centre and windows set high in the north-easterly part of the wall. Two rooms lead off it. The bedroom is to the west, with a wide bed for the making of heirs or . . .'

She broke off and did not detail, as perhaps she might once have done, the things her uncle did there that would never lead to heirs. Her colour high, she said, 'There's a third room that was once a bathing room with sunken baths, but these are laid over with boards now, and it has two dining couches and perhaps a low trestle table, although the slaves may have taken it out. This and the bedchamber connect one to the other, so the three rooms make a ring. There are no weapons in any of them, unless you can use the table. The mosaics are considered the best in the kingdom.'

'And no guard?'

'My uncle's guards fled with him to Antioch.' Disdain made her more like her aunt than she had ever been.

Pantera clapped her shoulder. A man's response to a man, or a boy; not a girl. 'If you are ever in need of employment, I will train you as a spy. The work is half done.'

He faced Iksahra, eye to eye, and then Mergus. 'There will be, at most, half a dozen guards at the entrance to the last corridor; you can deal with those easily, particularly if you use the same ruse to take you close. Go now, fast, and free Hypatia and Estaph, and Berenice.'

'You're not coming with us?' Kleopatra asked.

'No. You don't need me. I have . . . other work.'

'Saulos is upstairs.'

He laughed at her, at the speed of her reasoning. 'I think so, yes.'

She chewed her lip, considering, and then nodded. 'It has to be you, I suppose.'

Mergus, who knew him best, caught his eye for a moment, and held it. Whatever he read there was enough. He turned away, and signalled his men with him.

It was Iksahra who caught Pantera's wrist and held him fast. 'You're going after Saulos? Alone?'

'I have to. If he escapes now . . . Iksahra, I have to kill him. I must.'

'You and you alone.' Her gaze searched his face. 'He will be expecting you.'

'Even so, I must go.'

'Of course.' Her smile was something from the desert, sharp and savage and full of the promise of death. 'Go then.' Her fingers sprang open, releasing his arm. 'Kleopatra says that the newly dead go joyful to their gods.'

'Some of them do,' he said. 'I doubt if Saulos will be among them.'

CHAPTER FORTY-NINE

The door to the king's quarters in Herod's palace at Jerusalem was not built to be knocked upon by human hand.

Cedar formed the frame for carob wood inlaid with ebony and ivory, with lapis lazuli and rubies set on its face in the same patterns as on the floor of the jewel house in the palace at Masada. The thinnest part of it was thicker than a man's arm, and its scent, heady, aromatic, full of promises of wealth and power, filled the corridor for twenty feet in either direction.

It was a door that was built to be guarded, with a niche on either side to take a tall man and his helmet: here more than anywhere was visible Herod's fondness for the Gauls. Nobody else was that tall, except of course Iksahra's people, the Berberai, but nobody had ever yet enslaved a Berber.

No guards stood there now, slave or otherwise, but even so it felt improper to hammer on it with his fist.

Pantera took a moment to breathe, to be still, to remember who he was and why he had come, and what

451

he had to do; he remembered fire and a man's death, and a woman lost for ever, and then unthought each of these, because neither rage nor grief was useful to him here.

Filled with the clarity that comes sometimes in the midst of battle, he reversed the gladius he had brought from Masada and rapped its hilt on the hard wood.

The sound rang down the corridors, echoes rolling in the dust. He called out into the hollow emptiness.

'Saulos! You can circle round those three rooms, but there's no way out besides this door. I can sit here and starve you out, or we can end this now, face to face, with what's left of our honour.'

He thought he had made a mistake, that it wasn't Saulos he had heard, that he had sent Iksahra and Kleopatra into a trap, that he had fallen into one himself, that he had failed Hypatia . . .

The door swung open under his hand. Pantera sprang back from the expected blow, or arrow, or spinning knife, but none of these came; Saulos, too, had taken a step back and so they met at last, alone, face to face, blade to longer blade, for Saulos had a cavalry sword, of the kind given to the guards at the chamber doors, with a blade twice as long as Pantera's legionary gladius. It looked fearsome, but was too long to use in a tight space.

The room into which they stepped was not a tight space; Kleopatra had warned him of that, but it was quiet, a place where sounds of battle rumbled softly, as from a city far away, where men and horses fought and died for other reasons than theirs.

Then Saulos smiled, and all Pantera could see was

that same smile flashing in the black dark of Augustus' temple in Rome, with fire all around and the stench of bodies burning, and all he could feel was the touch of Hannah's skin against his own in the morning, knowing she must go.

He said, 'You look weary. Are you as tired of this hunt as I am?'

'A trick of the light.' Saulos stepped back into the first of nine perfect panes of sun cast on the floor by the windows set in the high wall. Mosaic spirals wound round his feet in a living river of colour, a hundred times sharper than those at Masada, and better set. 'I never tire.'

It was possible to believe that. He had taken time to change his clothes from battle garb to his sand-coloured silk, uncreased except around the hem, where it looked as if he had lain down for some time, and only recently risen.

Encased in his subtle finery, he looked joyful, like a hound that hears a hunt, while Pantera . . . Pantera had no idea how he looked. He was striving for calm and supposed that it showed.

He stepped into the room and felt the door swing behind him. He took a wide step to his left and another and they began to circle, slowly, lazily, with a marble fountain playing between them and the reclining couch behind. It was carved of ebony, padded with silk dyed to deepest porphyry. It sang, siren-like, drawing Pantera closer to sit, to lie, to sleep and never wake.

Saulos asked, 'How did you know I was here?'

'I heard you when we were in the slaves' corridors

below, after Iksahra's cheetah killed the second guard. Where else would you be but here, where the king will retire when he has taken his kingdom?'

'He has to win the battle first,' Saulos said. 'Nothing is certain.'

The air smelled of cedar, and old incense, and wine and, near the bedroom, of balsam. They circled on. They were too evenly matched to take risks; each had too many memories of their last fight to be the first to step in.

Pantera said, 'Does your god still require that Jerusalem be destroyed to bring about his eternal kingdom?'

'Of course. The Kingdom of Heaven will rise from the ashes of two cities, Rome and Jerusalem.'

'But you failed to burn Rome. Your prophecy required that first, before the destruction of Jerusalem. If you fail in the first part, what point in pursuing the second?'

'I burned enough of it.'

'And most of your men died as you did so.'

Saulos shrugged. 'I have enough men. And they will glory in the kingdom God brings to them. You will see it from whichever rank of Hades you have entered.'

The room was exactly as Kleopatra had said: an antechamber, where visitors might be kept for long enough to reflect on the king's wealth and their own insignificance. Windows opened along the heights of the wall opposite, nine oblongs of unblemished blue, casting their cool light in patterns on the floor.

Pantera passed them, and felt a draught of cool, fresh air, and yearned to sit and let it wash him. Not yet, though. Two doors lay behind him, one in the south, one in the west, both hanging ajar: the bedroom and the dining room that was once a bath room. He had an idea and set about testing it.

He leaned in and tapped Saulos' sword with his own. The long blade swayed away and came back again, steady, firm, true.

Pantera stepped back. 'You came here to kill Menachem, but you will fail. Everyone knows you are here; if I can't kill you, others will, and then Israel will have peace.'

Saulos slashed at his face. Pantera felt the rasp of iron in the air, smelled the whet of its blade. He spun away out of reach.

Saulos said, 'Not if the governor of Syria gets here in time with his legions. You know I have sent for him?'

'Iksahra's falcons took your dove from the sky. The governor isn't coming.'

'*Liar!*' Saulos raged forward, through the haze of light from the windows. Their blades clashed and clashed again and they parted, each a little wiser. 'I took the beastwoman prisoner before she could do harm. And Hypatia is dead. I had her throat cut before you could reach her.'

'No. I would know.'

'How?'

'I would know.' He was sure of that. Almost sure.

They came to a natural halt, facing each other across the fountain. The door was not locked. It swayed a little, caught by some unfelt current.

The air was thickening, braiding itself in ropes that drew taut between them, but they were further apart than they had been, each so wary now of the other's assault that they kept to the margins of the room.

Pantera had measured the distance; thirteen paces plus a half. He had planned the two moves it would take, one to pull his knife from his sleeve, the other to throw it, and how much closer Saulos could be by the time of the throw.

And then there was the door, which had moved again, slowly, soundlessly, and was lying open by a hand's breadth.

Pantera moved a pace to his right, so that the high windows' light was not blinding him. 'Yusaf ben Matthias came with me out of the city last night. This morning at dawn, he bore witness when Gideon the Peacemaker anointed Menachem as the rightful king of Israel. I thought you should know; Yusaf is the one who sent us the scroll that proved Menachem's right to the throne. He will be the new king's foremost counsellor.'

'I don't believe you.' Saulos stopped and stared at him in frank disbelief.

Pantera did three things then, fast: he threw his sword high up over the fountain, so that it tumbled down in a dazzle of water-light and sunlight; he drew the knife from his left arm, and threw it; and, as it left his fingers, he hurled himself to the left.

The knife missed: he had known that it would. The falling blade sheared close to Saulos' left shoulder, slicing away a collop of flesh in a mirror to the wound Menachem had sustained on Masada. Saulos grunted like a kicked horse, and swayed away from the threat, as any man would, but he ran forward, which was his undoing.

Pantera continued his roll, tumbling like an acrobat straight through the open door of the king's dining room that had once been Herod's private baths.

He saw the vertical shadow of the doorway pass him by and kicked the door shut as he cleared it, then thrust one hand down, pivoting on it until the bones of his elbow popped, and came round almost full circle, in time to drop the bar across, sending prayers to the old king, Herod the Great, and his paranoia that said every private room must be readily barred against intruders.

He ended near the dining couch, panting, and looked round at the only place in the world where Herod had absolute privacy.

The room was a paean to the hunt: mosaics livelier than anything in life showed antelope and lion, goat and cheetah, dove and falcon, all hunters and hunted, with figures of men, and some women, ordering the kills.

On other walls, naked men wrestled, in the Greek style, holding each other by the shoulders for the throw, while unclothed girls leapt over the horns of bellowing bulls. And in the centre of the ceiling, in the place where a king might look who lay back in his private bath, was an image of Helios, sun-god of the Greeks, picked out in all his daring, blazing beauty.

There was no trestle table covering the hole in the floor where the bath had been, only a rug of six sewn ibex skins, sleek and shining, and under those a board, which moved when Pantera pulled it, enough, he thought, to do what he needed. Perhaps enough. He risked his life on that one thing, having nothing else; his weapons were all gone.

He had not barred the door to the bedroom, only pushed it shut. Saulos kicked it open, abandoning his fabled composure.

'*Ha!*' He brandished two swords, Pantera's short one in his left hand, the long cavalry blade in his right; a gladiator's pose. Blood flowed freely down his arm from the wound on his shoulder, staining the sand-coloured silk.

Pantera stood with his back to the dining couch, unarmed. 'Yusaf!' He sent his voice beyond the walls. 'You may as well show yourself. I am neither blind nor deaf nor stupid.' To Saulos, who had stopped a pace inside the doorway, he offered a dry smile. 'Did you think I didn't know?'

'You didn't know when you first came to Jerusalem. You didn't know on the night he sold you to me for a promise.'

'Sold him?' Yusaf's voice came harsh from the outer room. 'I *gave* him to you for the promise of peace under Rome, which is beyond price. I did not do it for the slaughter of innocents in Caesarea.'

Yusaf arrived at the threshold, a figure of ruined silk and conflict. His long face was pale beneath his beard, but he held a Roman short-sword in his hand, its point high, and steady.

Softly, Pantera said, 'Did you not know he planned such bloodshed? Is it not obvious that he plans to do in Jerusalem what he did in Caesarea? That this has always been his plan?'

'He said he would allow no more violence than was necessary.' Yusaf's attention flickered between them, settling on neither.

'Oh, *please*!' Pantera's voice was a whip cast at his face. 'You've known this man thirty years. Don't tell me you still believe what he tells you?'

'Ignore him!' Saulos threw up a hand. 'He's goading you. Stay where you are while I finish this.'

'Exactly, Yusaf, stay where you are. Be his puppet as you have been from the start while we—'

Pantera stepped smartly back, and sideways, using the dining couch as a shield against Yusaf's charge. He threw up his hands—

And let them fall again, to the muffled sweep of an ibex hide and the crack of long bones on marble, and the silence of a blade, sailing high from nerveless fingers.

Pantera caught the hilt before it hit the ground and swept it down to rest against the bare neck that sprouted now from the floor: all but Yusaf's head and one arm were lost in the pit that had once been a bath.

On the room's far side, Saulos had not moved, but was breathing hard, as if he had done.

'He's been your puppet for a long time, hasn't he?' Pantera said. 'He came to Rome, and before that to Alexandria, to Corinth, to Galatia. Did you let Seneca build him up at first and then seduce him, or was he yours from the start?'

'I belong to no man!' Yusaf twisted his head. Blood welled along the side of his throat where the blade lay hard along it. 'Judaea needs peace and only Rome can bring that. I—'

'Shut up.' Saulos was moving; slashing, hacking, all civility gone.

Pantera stumbled back, caught off guard by the thunderous power of the attack. For a dozen strokes he parried and the shock hammered his arm each time, and each time he felt the wind of the strike slice closer as

459

Saulos' longer reach and extra weapon found the weak places in his defence.

He was being forced backwards round the room, ducking, swaying, spinning, using every trick Seneca's tutors had taught him, and all those he had learned since, in the alleyways of the empire, in the forests of Britain, in Gaul, in Parthia, in the gutters of Rome.

He tried a counter-attack, and had it smashed down so hard he thought his stolen sword would break. It was clear then that Saulos had lost all control, and was more dangerous for it, not less.

He saw a second blow coming straight down to split his brains apart, and flung up his blade, and caught the worst of it on the guard, but not all, so that the tip tilted, and Saulos' cavalry blade sheared down, catching a flat blow on the side of his shoulder.

He felt no pain, but a rush of light to his eyes, as if someone had hit him with a mallet, and it was only his reflexes that saved him as the back cut came slicing in straight across his neck with a strength that would have lifted his head from his shoulders and spun it full across the room.

Dropping his blade, Pantera threw himself down, pivoting on one flat palm, with his arm rigid, and swung his legs across, straight out and together.

His feet hit Saulos across the knees and pitched him forward, off balance, but not enough. Using the momentum of the stumble to take him over across the top of Pantera, Saulos spun round, and threw himself back with both hands on the hilt of his sword, stabbing down in the same killing stroke the master hunter made on the mosaic body of a tiger on the eastern wall.

Pantera rolled along his own length, and came to rest by Yusaf – who was no longer wedged in the sunken bath, but had wrested his trapped arm free and was halfway out.

'Here,' he said, and placed a throwing knife in Pantera's palm. 'Get up and finish it.'

By a trick of the air, he sounded like Seneca; a ghost made real. Pantera's head snapped up. He rolled back and up and round and rose to his feet in time to meet Saulos coming in with a sword in each hand again, and for a pure, clear moment there was a gap between the tips, through which a man might not pass, but a thrown blade could.

He held his ground and drew back and threw, and in the slowing of time that came in death's shadow he saw the knife fly true and sweet, past the two swords that came in for him, missing them by the thickness of a prayer, of a held breath, of a life.

He dropped to the ground, flat . . . and Saulos dropped to meet him, face to face, gaze to gaze, mouth wide, startled, with a hand's length of iron lodged in the hard bone between his brows.

Pantera lay still and watched the life leak from his enemy's eyes, and said, almost too quietly to hear, 'If Kleopatra is right, you go willing to a god that demands blood-price for his kingdom.'

He waited for a response. He wanted one, suddenly, wanted there to be an answer – something, anything to fill the aching, empty space . . .

'Pantera?'

The world was blurred, the air too dense to breathe. Careful fingers gripped his shoulder and rolled him backwards. He looked up, and blinked, and Yusaf's long face grew into focus.

Yusaf's voice was a buzz in the background that moved gradually to the front of his awareness. 'It's over. He's dead. You killed him . . . Pantera, it *is* over.'

His mind was mist, and less than mist; it was an empty field, drenched by winter rain, with a scattering of last season's straw. He sat up, helped by Yusaf, and wondered at the ache in his chest that was so much greater than the one in his head, where the sword had glanced by.

He pushed himself to standing, using Yusaf's arm as a lever, and looked around the room, until the scenes of carnage all about resolved themselves to simple pictures of men at the hunt, and one image in particular, of a king, mounted on a horse the colour of starlight, with black feet.

Pantera looked at that a long time and, when he turned at last, Yusaf was waiting for him, white, and completely still, as a man at his own execution.

'You and I have a reckoning,' he said. 'I betrayed you. For that, Saulos would—'

'*No!*' Pantera caught his arm. With barely held violence, he said, 'I am not Saulos. I kill where I must, not for vengeance.'

'But—'

'I knew who you were and what you had done before I came back to Jerusalem last night. If I were going to kill you, I would have done it in the desert with Gideon as my witness.'

Yusaf's eyes were too wide, still awaiting death. Pantera made himself look away, set his mind to something

462

else. Without warning he thought of Hannah, and then Hypatia. In quite a different voice, he said, 'Saulos is dead; let that be an end to it. Today, we have a king to crown and he will need good counsel in the months to come, if you would be willing to offer it?'

Yusaf clipped a laugh. 'I would give my hope of heaven to be asked for counsel by that man. Menachem is the promised of God, who can unite us all. My only wish is that I had seen it sooner. I might not have made the mistakes that I did.' He swept both hands across his face, and was older when he looked up. 'I am grateful, truly, more than I can say, and will repay you somehow, if a way can be found. But before we set this behind us, I have to ask – how did you know it was me who betrayed you?'

'You are Absolom. Iksahra heard you speak to Saulos. But I knew before she told me. On the temple steps, the High Priest gave way too easily. He wouldn't have done it had he not the backing of someone trusted by all twelve tribes of Israel. Who else knew what was planned, and yet had the authority to sway Ananias?'

As he spoke, Pantera knelt and tugged the knife from Saulos' brow. It took two hands, and some force, to wrest it free and bright blood welled where it had been. It was becoming easier, now, to think of Saulos as gone, to see a future that was not blighted by his presence; easier, too, to be generous in his mercy.

He wiped the blade on the dead man's sleeve and rose again, holding it across the flat of both hands. 'This is yours.'

When, wordless, Yusaf took it, Pantera said, 'We

are different, he and I, whatever he may have told you.'

'I knew that when you came back. Saulos would not have had that courage.'

'And you sent the scroll to Menachem, with the signatures of the entire Sanhedrin beneath your own. That also took great courage.'

'I had just heard of the massacre at Caesarea. I could have done no less.'

Yusaf lowered his gaze; they both did. Saulos' eyes had shut, his face fallen slack, a dribble of saliva slid down to the swirling mosaic floor. The sun had moved on; they were in perpetual shadow now. A few cautious flies began to dine.

'I thought he was the one man who understood the ways of Rome,' Yusaf said. 'That he loved Israel above all else, and would usher in a peace to last a thousand generations.'

'He loved only himself, and the god he had made in his own image.'

Yusaf raised his head, sought Pantera's gaze and held it. 'You could have killed him without my help, you do know that?'

'But you gave me the knife when I needed it.'

'Would I be alive had I not?'

'I hope so.' Pantera stepped back, setting a clear distance between them, him and Saulos, breaking the last tie, so that he could step again, back, out of the door that led from Herod's private sanctum, away from the reek of blood and betrayal, from the still, closed face of a man who had been neither of those things.

He turned away and set his mind to the living . . . he hoped to the living.

He said, 'Hypatia should be safe by now, but we must make sure of it. And after, we will find Israel's new king and crown him before the multitudes, and maybe then you will have your peace to last a thousand generations.'

CHAPTER FIFTY

One last corridor led to the cellars. Behind, eight men lay dead, of beast wounds, and sword cuts, and one of a throat crushed by the hammer-hilt of a blade. It had not been an easy battle, but it had not been notably hard; the incomers had lost no one, nor sustained any serious injuries, and, most important, they had achieved their victory in near silence; not one man had time to shout to the last guard left holding the cellar.

There was no obvious reason, therefore, why Iksahra sur Anmer should be walking down the corridor lost in a memory from her childhood that left her numb with fear.

In her mind, she was a child of no more than nine summers and her father had set her a task that was beyond her abilities. These many years later, she couldn't remember exactly what was so frightening except that it had involved the stud horse of his best line, that all were born entirely black and then grew lighter with age to the colour of almond milk, with slate grey manes and tails.

They were the best horses that ever lived – she believed that as a child and believed it still – but the herd stallion was a fearsome beast and she had been sent to fetch him in from pasture, or to take him out to pasture, or perhaps to take him to one of the mares that was in season, ready for covering.

Whichever it was, for the first time in her life, the child Iksahra had been truly terrified. A strange clammy sweat sprang like dew all over her body and her heart tripped an unhappy rhythm that made her feel giddy, so that for ever after, she associated the smell of her own sweat with the iron-ripe odour of a hot and angry horse, and both with the sensation that her own heart and the stud horse were conspiring to defeat her.

And they had succeeded. When she reached for the beast, her sweaty hand had slipped on the rawhide thong that hung from its halter and it had jerked its head free of her grasp and run away.

She remembered little of the aftermath. Her father had hidden his disappointment, if he had any, and, in exactly the same way he did with his beasts, had set to teaching her the ways to handle the horse without fear, so that the event itself would have been lost, if it had not been for the horror of her own failure that had kept her awake through the night afterwards.

She remembered lying awake under the stars, counting each speck of light as a part of her fear. She had vowed then, before the gods that lived behind the black night sky, that she would never in her life let fear discommode her as it had done that day. It had come, she thought, because she had cared too much about succeeding, and therefore about the possibility of failure. And so, in the small hours of the morning, when the stars were fading and the sun was taking their place, she had made a second, more binding vow: never to care so deeply about anything that it might bring her down.

In keeping the second vow, she had kept the first: in having no great care, she had never known the incapacitating terror of her childhood.

Until now.

With Mergus' men and her great cat left at the corridor's head, keeping it safe, with the newly emboldened Kleopatra walking in the place of the honour guard close behind her left shoulder, Iksahra sur Anmer slid, ghost-footed, along the slaves' corridors of the Herodian palace carrying a blade unsheathed in either hand – and those hands were wet with sweat.

She smelled that sweat and, because memory is made of scent, she smelled also the iron-ripeness of an angry stud horse, so that her terror multiplied until she had to stop and lean against a wall, and scold herself to calmness.

She did not fear death – she never had – but she feared failure now exactly as she had feared it in her childhood, and for the same reason: she cared too much.

Cursing aloud, she pushed away from the wall. A corner lay ahead. 'Stay here.' She felt Kleopatra take a breath to argue, and let it out, unspoken.

Alone, Iksahra turned the corner. A door lay ahead, blocking the corridor. The last of the garrison Guard stood outside, awake, if not alert. Iksahra slid her hands and the knives they held up her sleeves and flashed him a smile of pure relief.

'You're alive,' she said weakly. 'Thank the gods. They haven't got here yet, then?'

'Who hasn't? What's happening outside?' Frantic, the guard's gaze flew from the scratch wound on her arm, to the torn fabric of her clothes, to the many shades of drying blood.

'The Hebrews have attacked. The men of the garrison Guard are . . .' Iksahra looked away.

'What are they? Tell me!' He reached for her, to shake out more news. 'In here, we hear nothing but the distant clash of arms.'

'It's as well you don't. Outside is a massacre – not only outside.'

With something close to regret, she took her hands from her sleeves. One blade slid up under his diaphragm into his heart. She held it tight, against the sudden bucking twist of muscle on iron, then slid her other blade up into the tight gap between his neck bones and his skull, into the living vessel of his thoughts.

He died without a sound. She lowered him to the ground and wiped her blades clean on his tunic. The oak door was closed, as Kleopatra had said it would be. Iksahra pressed her ear against it and listened.

Back round the corner, she heard Kleopatra speak in her soft, certain Latin. 'Go to where is lightest, to the sun. Your friends are waiting. Death is freedom, not loss.'

Shuddering, Iksahra turned, and listened again to the rustling beyond the oak.

Estaph said, 'There'll be a guard outside the door. There has to be.'

469

'Not necessarily,' Berenice said. 'There's a battle beyond the walls, you can hear it if you press your ear to the stone; the guards might all be out there, fighting.'

'Hush.' Hypatia waved them both quiet with a flap of her hand. She pressed her head to the wood. The door was oak, thick as her outstretched hand, designed to withstand any attack.

In the beginning, she heard only the echo of a king's welcome that rang through the walls. With more attention, she found a presence that seemed most likely a guard; a man left edgy by the noises outside who stepped away from the wood with a challenge in his voice and—

And someone died on the door's far side. Hypatia felt the soul slip free of its moorings, but it slipped past too fast for her to tell if it was male or female, guard or slave, friend or foe.

She swallowed on a dry throat. She hadn't eaten since Kleopatra's gift and the taste of garlic still furred her mouth. She was light-headed and weak and her stolen gladius hung leaden as a lump hammer from her fist, too heavy to use. In the still part of her mind, she sought the help of the god and found instead . . . the iron-sharp stench of an angry horse, and beneath it the scent of a woman's fear.

She grabbed at the handle and hurled the door open, already rolling, down and sideways, away from whatever blades might come, that did come; that missed her wildly and clattered down the wall to the floor.

Still rolling, she heard only silence. She rose to her knees, with the stolen sword in both hands. She heard the lift of a breath taken and held.

'Iksahra?'

The Berber woman was standing in the doorway, black on white, framed against the new light from behind. The only sunlight was a single shaft poured in through a high, lost window, but it was the first Hypatia had seen since yesterday's morning and it encased Iksahra in its light, so that her white silks became as gossamer, folded about the fine – the exquisite – lines of her body.

With her heart unstable in her chest, Hypatia pushed herself upright. 'I knew it was you,' she said. 'You must have known it was me, or I'd be dead.'

The Berber woman did not respond. Carved marble had more animation. She was shaking, fine as a leaf, all over.

Hypatia bent and retrieved the two thrown knives and laid them aside on the cool stone floor and walked on through the door to a place where the stench of blood was overwhelmed by the scent of woman-sweat, sweet-ened with new hay and old corn and the raw breath of the hunt. It was a smell of horses and a hunting cat, of wildness, of beauty.

Hypatia herself stank of confinement and privation. Sharply aware, she tried to step back to a place where she might offend less.

She failed because Iksahra moved at last. Her lean black fingers caught Hypatia's right hand and held her still; she could not have moved if she had wanted to. She did not try.

'Estaph is there,' she said. 'And Berenice. In the corridor.' Words fell haphazardly from the turmoil of her mind, none of them useful. 'You're wounded.'

'Not badly. It will heal. I can still throw a blade.' Iksahra took a long, uneven breath. 'We are not safe here. We should leave.'

'Yes.'

Iksahra's hand was hot, damp, unsteady; all the things Hypatia had least imagined. She squeezed and felt the movement returned. Her own hand was not any steadier.

Silence held them both, broadening, stretching, becoming harder to fill. The air grew thin with hope and thick with things unspoken.

'Kleopatra is waiting,' Iksahra said, finally. 'Pantera brought Menachem, newly anointed. His army is fighting the garrison. By the sound outside, I think he has won.'

'And Saulos?'

'Pantera has gone for him. Kleopatra says he's dead, that she heard him take his leave of her. And Ananias the High Priest, also. They found him hiding in a sewer and killed him.'

Iksahra's skin shone like polished horse hide, evenly damp with the sweat of a moment's exertion. She said, 'Kleopatra can hear the dead. She converses with them. She says death is a freedom, as if it were something we all should seek. You have to speak to her.'

'I will,' said Hypatia. 'It's good to see you care. It changes you.' And then, because nothing was coming out as she meant it, 'The god came while we were in the cells to show me the mistake I made in holding my heart closed. What I might lose.' Her fingers were still, her skin too much alive. 'I don't want to lose you.' At last, the right words.

Iksahra's face was still one moment longer, and then bloomed in such a smile as might light the whole day.

'It was my fear this whole day that I had lost you,' she said. 'I will not live with that fear again, nor let you live with it. I would take you to the desert, and the high places, and watch with you as the sun sets and rises and sets again, and we shall do that soon. But for now, we have a king to crown and a city to heal and a queen to make fit to greet her people.'

EPILOGUE

The pool of Siloam on the edge of David's city was fed by an underground stream, so that when all about lay under dust, its surface shimmered under the sun.

On the morning of the king's coronation, the early light tinted it green. A faint scum gathered on the limpid surface, studded with petals of small white flowers, shining as shreds of moonlight under the not-quite-present sun.

The air above it hung heavy with the smell of still water and frankincense and the gathered thousands; all gone now. Where they had been, palm branches lay thick on the ground, frond upon frond, woven by their falling into a mat thick as a man's wrist.

Pantera stooped to lift one smaller than the others; a child's frond, cut for a small fist to wave for the new king and cast before his humble donkey. It served now to distract the flies that fell frenzied on Pantera and his four companions, having no one else left to feast on.

Hypatia was with him, and Mergus, and Estaph,

who had shown no sign of hastening to Syria and his family, and Kleopatra, who sometime since the night in Yusaf's house had ceased to be a girl and become instead a young woman; and that young woman bonded to Hypatia. Iksahra was not there; she had gone hunting with her birds and her cat, loping off before dawn, to escape the gathering thousands.

Without her, Pantera stood now at the pool, famous in prophecy, in portent, which was the oldest part of David's city, itself the oldest part of Jerusalem, and watched the ragged end of the crowds as they surged up past Herod's hippodrome to the Temple.

Somewhere at their head, beneath the banners, surrounded by his armoured men, Menachem rode his donkey in fulfilment of every prophecy in the sacred texts.

His people had seen him anointed in the pool most sacred to their god, they had seen him bend his head before Gideon, newly named High Priest of Israel, had seen him declared as the true king, second only to God, who would lead his people to their peace, where no one was put before their god, neither Caesar nor an empire.

They had seen him mount the donkey that Iksahra and Hypatia had found: a colt, newly broken, as tall as any Pantera had ever seen, and piebald, with one black ear and one white, with its broad brow black as jet and its muzzle white as chalk and its flanks patterned in smooth asymmetry, like a map etched in black ink on perfect papyrus, so that Pantera's eyes had been drawn to it through the ceremony.

His mind was still lost there, now, wandering in new

lands, seeking out new coves among the headlands, new islands lost in the star-white ocean.

To Hypatia, thoughtfully, he said, 'If he has time, Menachem will make of Jerusalem a city fit to match Alexandria.'

'If he has time.' Hypatia's gaze was fixed on the hills outwith the city walls, on the grazed grasslands and the citrus groves, on the herds, and their herding boys; few of those today when most were in the city, greeting Menachem.

She said, 'Iksahra is coming,' and it sounded like a portent of doom.

He looked and saw nothing, but did not disbelieve. 'We could go to meet her?' he asked.

Hypatia's face was closed. 'I think we should.'

They walked together to the small gate through which Iksahra had left the city. Outside, the air was brighter, less clogged with breath and waiting, and the birds sang, when they had been too shocked to do so in the city, silenced by the voices of the crowd.

Presently, Iksahra was there, a shimmer in the morning's haze, black limbs stark against her flowing white shift, with the cheetah lithe at her heels and the hunting birds flying freely above her, not tethered to her fist.

Even as they watched, the falcon swung up, gaining height until she was a fading scrawl against the harsh sky, and turned in her own length came down again, tight as an arrow, and flung out her wings to land lightly, and bent her head to feed on some small, dead thing on Iksahra's glove. Plucked feathers danced around them, caught on the hillside wind.

'It's a dove,' Mergus said; his distant vision was always better than anyone's. 'She's caught a message-dove.'

They ran then, and met her at the place where the land flattened out towards the city.

Hypatia reached her first, and they stood apart, but close.

Pantera said, 'Bad news?' She couldn't read; he had forgotten and remembered too late to take it back. He held out his hand.

She dropped the message cylinder into his palm. 'The dove is red roan, with amber eyes. Seneca bred them; the Poet uses them still.'

A blob of wax sealed the cap shut, bright as blood. He cracked it open and took out the onion skin of paper, so thin they could see his fingers through it. The writing was fine and neat and familiar.

'You're right,' he said. 'This is from the Poet; a new code, never used in Seneca's network . . . Wait a moment, this is not easy.' Latin letters lay in lines across the page, but not in words. Pantera took the first three, and made them numbers, and used those numbers to transpose the letters to make sense of them.

The others waited. Iksahra moved closer to Hypatia. She smelled of horse-sweat and wild wind and wonder. Their hands brushed, back to back, sending lightning across Hypatia's eyes.

Pantera completed his translation. 'My dove has reached the Poet, who in turn sends this to me and to Menachem. Listen, I will read it.' His voice was strained. It echoed in his own ears.

From the Poet to the Leopard and to Israel's new king, greetings. You must know that the Twelfth legion

marched yesterday from Antioch under command
of Cestius Gallus, governor of Syria, with orders to
retake the city of Jerusalem, and the nation of Israel.
Those who have the emperor's ear have tried and failed
to divert them: Nero will not call them back. Defend
yourselves immediately, lest your peace and prosperity
wither on the vine.

He felt the press of their waiting. The light was gone
from Hypatia's eyes. She was gathering herself, becoming sober again, taking on a weight that was not yet
hers.

She said, 'Menachem must be told.'

'I'll do it.' As his gift, Pantera took the weight from
her. It settled about his shoulders like chain mail, and
was not unbearable. 'He will have reached the heights by
now and have formally named Gideon as his High Priest
and Yusaf as his counsellor. When he comes down, I
will tell him and we will plan the defence of Jerusalem.
We have arms and men who listen. All is not lost and we
may yet negotiate with Nero. You . . .' His gaze held first
Hypatia, then Iksahra, and after them the others. 'You
have a day and a night to do whatever you choose. Use
it, and then come back to me in the palace and we will
see what needs to be done.'

He waited to see them go before he moved. Mergus,
Estaph, Kleopatra; those three turned back towards the
city, to the baths, and the markets and the clamour of
celebration.

Hypatia turned away from the city and Iksahra with
her in a swirl of white linen, her cat a smear of gold-
black pelt and muscle at her heels; they three, two

women and their beast, with the hunting birds soaring above, walked back across the grasslands towards the hills.

Pantera stayed a while, watching them go, before he turned back to the city, to a man who must be both king and commander, and lead his army onward into war.

AUTHOR'S NOTE

While any historical novel must be broadly fictional in terms of character and motivation, the key events of this book – the sacrifice of the dove in Caesarea, the offer of eight talents to save the synagogue, the taking of Masada – are based around those outlined by Flavius Josephus in his *War of the Jews*, in which he relates the events leading up to the Hebrew rebellion that took place in AD 66, towards the end of Nero's reign.

Josephus was writing after the fact as a favoured historian in the house of the Emperor Vespasian, and later of his son Titus, but at the time he was Yusaf ben Matthias, by his own account, a man venerated for his wisdom, courage and foresight throughout Judaea and Galilee: certainly he was intimately involved in the Hebrew defences during the ensuing hostilities and he was a contemporary to most of the events in our time scale.

This notwithstanding, his recounting of the history is inevitably designed to show the Romans in their best light and he skips over some of the most momentous achievements of his people.

Most notable of these, in my opinion, was the taking of Masada by Menachem (or Menahem, or Menaheim), grandson of Judas the Galilean, the insurgent who had taunted Rome's power with his Sicari assassins for the first third of the century.

Those who wish to know the detail can do no better than to read *Wars of the Jews*, Book 2, chapters 14–18. For those of you who would rather not, there follows a list of the characters in this book who have a historical basis, bearing in mind that while Josephus was my primary source for the action, a multitude of other sources, both contemporary and modern, have informed the narrative.

In particular, I am indebted, as is any writer of this period, to Suetonius, Tacitus and Philo. In the modern period, I am indebted to Hyam Maccoby for *The Mythmaker*, his outline of Saul (Saulos), to Martin Goodman for his *Rome and Jerusalem*, to Daniel T. Unterbrink for his new synopsis of the possible historical versions of Christ, *The Three Messiahs: The Historical Judas the Galilean, the Revelatory Christ Jesus, and the Mythical Jesus of Nazareth* and to various authors for their insight into the archaeology of Masada.

Characters with a basis in historical fact

The Emperor Nero (AD 37–68) Although he is never centre stage in this novel, Nero's presence underpins the narrative. In AD 66, he was nearing the end of his reign – and his life – and becoming increasingly paranoid. In addition to the Pisoan conspiracy of which Seneca was a part, a number of other attempts had been made on his life and a great deal of his energy was spent in removing opponents. The intelligent, resourceful and highly popular general, Corbulo, who was in control of most of the eastern legions and had led a successful campaign against the Parthian empire, was summoned to Greece and then ordered to commit suicide around the time of the events related here. Had he not been, he would undoubtedly have had command of the legions which in AD 70 eventually razed Jerusalem to the ground. Nero, meanwhile, clung on only until AD 68, when the infamous 'Year of the Four Emperors' wrought havoc on Rome and the empire.

All that said, Nero was not quite the maniac that later history has made out. The early years of his reign, when he allowed Seneca to rule through him, were considered by many to be a golden period of the empire and even as late as the fire of AD 64 he was beloved of the proletariat, if not, by then, of the Senate. On the night of the fire, he was in Antium, a good eleven miles from Rome. He could have remained there in safety, but, according to Tacitus, chose instead to ride back into the flames, and threw open his palace to the people. The architectural changes he made later were sane and went a long way to preventing a future fire. The fact that he bankrupted the treasury in doing so is not entirely his fault: it had been strained to destitution by wars in Britain and Corbulo's venture against Vologases of Parthia, neither of which was entirely of Nero's making: war is ever a powerful eater of money. His attempts to gain gold from the provinces, while appalling in our eyes, were hardly so to the ancient mind-set: from Rome's perspective, provinces existed in order that Rome might drain their wealth; it was the reason they had been conquered in the first place.

It remains to be said that his wife, Poppaea, died in suspicious circumstances in AD 65. Later sources claim that Nero killed her, either accidentally or deliberately, but the fact that she was carrying his only child makes this seem immensely unlikely.

Yusaf ben Matthias, later Titus Flavius Josephus (AD 37–100) Josephus, known in our narrative as Yusaf, was the ultimate survivor. If his date of birth is accurate – we only have his word for it and he wouldn't be the last to pretend to be younger than his years – he was appointed young to the defence of Galilee when Vespasian's assault began. Later, as the city fell, he arranged for his co-defendants to commit mass suicide and, as the one man left alive, threw himself on the mercy of Vespasian, the commander of the Roman forces who had just successfully raised the siege of Jopata.

The fact that he got as far as Vespasian, and wasn't decorating a cross within hours of his surrender, suggests to me that he was already a Roman agent. But even if he were not, he threw himself on his face and publicly declared Vespasian to be the inheritor of the Star Prophecy, which had long ago declared that a king would come out of the east who would rule the whole world. This may not have pushed Vespasian to become emperor, but it certainly did his cause no harm.

In later years, having been adopted into Vespasian's family, Josephus wrote the books which are our only true history of Palestine under the Roman republic and early empires. Without them, the Christian gospels would be very much the poorer and there is a strong argument (see *Caesar's Messiah* by Joseph Atwill) that they are all written by the same man, or group of men, at the behest of the then-emperor Titus Vespasian, son of the Vespasian who took the Star Prophecy for himself. Josephus was a self-serving misogynist, but probably no worse than many men of his time, and his work is still well worth reading.

Governor Gessius Florus was governor of Judaea from AD 64 to 66 (his death in the beast garden is my fiction). Josephus is scathing in his account of this man, who achieved the rare notoriety of being more corrupt than his predecessor. It was common for men to use their rank as a means of enriching themselves – indeed, that was often the point – but some went about their assault on their unfortunate subject territories with more delicacy than others. What stands out about Florus is his singular insensitivity to the Hebrews. If he was not deliberately endeavouring to spark a rebellion in Jerusalem, then he was inordinately stupid. Apart from robbing the Temple, he taunted the people, publicly humiliated them when they became restive, and crucified individuals picked up at random, including, according to Josephus, Roman citizens. This latter was explicitly illegal. It's hard to put any other explanation on his behaviour than that he wished to spark a revolt.

Agrippa II, grandson of Herod the Great. Brought up in Rome, Agrippa was Roman to his core and was used as a client king by both Claudius and Nero. Josephus gives him an impassioned speech which 'proves' Rome's superiority to the Hebrews and is supposed to be an attempt to talk the rebelling zealots to peace. In reality, it was Roman propaganda, about as plausible as Boudica's speech to her warriors or Calgacus' famous speech before the battle of Mons Graupius, 'They wreak a desolation and call it peace', both of which were written by Tacitus as a way of speaking to his contemporaries without being charged with treason. Agrippa was weak, and achieved little with his reign. The rumours surrounding his sister were almost certainly false, but he died without issue, although even if he had sired a dozen sons the client kingships would still have been lost in the aftermath of the rebellion.

Berenice of Cilicia, Agrippa's much-married sister, sounds as if she was made of sterner stuff than her brother, for all that ancient historians give more weight to her fabled beauty and her many lovers than to her undoubted political acumen. Following her brother's failure to subdue the rebellion by speech, she is said to have walked barefoot with her head shorn in Jerusalem in 'fulfilment of a vow'. Historians are agreed that there was no known vow which required this, but it might well have been required as a penance. I have written it accordingly. Her son **Hyrcanus** is mentioned, but little else, and her sister **Drusilla** is important to us as being mother of Kleopatra, a fictional character (her real daughter was named Antonia Clementiana).

The Poet: Jocasta Papinius Statius is a fiction, but her brother **Publius Papinius Statius** was a well-known poet of the era. I have no evidence at all of a poetic sister, but it would not be the last time an accomplished woman had her work passed off as by a man.

The Teacher: Seneca the Younger, also known as Lucius Annaeus Seneca, died by his own hand at Nero's order in late AD 65 following the failure of the Pisoan conspiracy, which was aimed first at deposing Nero and then – possibly – at installing Seneca in his place. We have no record of his being a spymaster, but he was remarkably well informed throughout his life and it is improbable that he could have been so without a network of agents.

Jucundus, commander of the cavalry in Caesarea, is mentioned in the incident of the dove that was sacrificed on the upturned vessel. Josephus himself makes no mention of the meaning of this act, presuming that his listeners will know. I am indebted to the Whiston translation for its explanation of the act of desecration thereby symbolized.

Saulos (Saul of Tarsus, St Paul) is one of the most divisive figures in early first-century history. Depending on your viewpoint, he was either the vehicle by which Christianity was brought to the Gentiles, and a saint, or a charismatic egotist who believed he had a hotline to his own private deity and was prone to outbreaks of verbal violence to an extent that nowadays would be classified as psychologically unstable.

There are seven attested letters by someone who called himself Paul and who wrote first person, as if to congregations under his pastoral care. My thesis, explained in greater detail in the Author's Note following *Rome: The Emperor's Spy*, is that Saulos was a Roman agent, that he initially endeavoured to suppress by extreme violence the insurgency that was sweeping Judaea and Palestine and was named by Josephus the 'Fourth Philosophy', and when that failed, instead of trying to coerce the people of Israel into denying their god, he took that same god and changed it.

Inventing a messiah, based on the death of the insurgent leader Judas the Galilean, also known as Judas of the Sicarioi, he removed the conditions of the previous covenant: namely the table laws and the need to circumcise the boy children. He preached his new cult round the eastern Mediterranean in the face of considerable opposition from the Jerusalem Assembly. (See *James, the Brother of Christ* by Robert H. Eisenman for full details of the enmity between Paul and James.)

Those who had known the Galilean in life were, not surprisingly, unhappy about this development, and when Saulos was finally summoned to Jerusalem there were men among their number who took vows not to eat, drink or go near a woman until he was dead. The Romans, hearing this, sent in several brigades of men to get him out; not a likely act unless to rescue someone of high value.

Thereafter, Saulos vanishes from our historical record. He is conveniently absent by the time James, brother to the Galilean, was assassinated by the Sanhedrin for the crime of being too popular. James, the Nazarite, was a vegetarian, pacifist and celibate who kept order in Jerusalem for approximately thirty years. It was his death that set the War Party and the Peace Party at each other's throats, and led, ultimately – and with the help of Governor Florus' idiocy – to the war that destroyed their city.

And yet – the great fire of Rome began in AD 64 on the night the dog star rose over Rome and we know that there were at the time apocalyptic manuscripts declaring that the Kingdom of Heaven could not arise unless or until Rome had burned under the eye of that star. Somebody, in my view, lit the fire in an effort to bring about the prophecy. I believe that person to have been Saulos, or his agents.

Although I have no proof, it seems to me also likely that someone was acting to push Gessius Florus to his acts of overt insanity in Jerusalem: there is no other reason for him to have behaved as he did, except to instigate the ultimate riot that would see the destruction of that city, and therefore of Judaea as a semi-independent province.

And so I have built my fiction around this supposition: that Saulos required Jerusalem to fall in order to fulfil a prophecy. Or at least, to tell his followers that he had fulfilled the prophecy. He himself, I imagine, would have been very happy to rule a client kingdom under Rome, where his cut of the taxes would have left him a wealthy man, ruling at last over people he had failed otherwise to subdue.

Menachem, grandson of Judas the Galilean, also known as Judas of the Sicarioi. Menachem was the hero-seed around which this book grew. His assault on Masada is written so simply in Josephus:

> In the mean time, one Menahem, the son of that Judas, who was called the Galilean (who was a very cunning sophister [sic] and had formerly reproached the Jews under Cyrenius, that after God, they were subject to the Romans), took some of the men of note with him, and retired to Masada, where he broke open King Herod's armoury, and gave arms not only to his own people, but to other robbers also. These he made use of for a guard, and returned in the state of a king to Jerusalem; he became the leader of the sedition.

> (Flavius Josephus, *Wars of the Jews* 2.7:18)

For nearly two thousand years, history has skipped past this passage, moving on to the more exciting moments of the siege, or the final assault by the Roman legions on Masada, five years later, when nine hundred Hebrews held off the might of Rome's army until, finally surrounded, they drew lots and killed themselves.

And yet Menachem, had he succeeded in creating of Judaea an independent nation and holding it against the might of Rome, would have been one of the great heroes of history. As it is, simply by scaling the rock at Masada in AD 66 and defeating the Roman garrison there, he achieved something almost miraculous that deserves recognition.

Masada

The image below is a modern one, but very little has changed in the past two thousand years except that the Romans built a vast ramp up the side to give their legions access when they retook the fortress in AD 70, and this can be seen today.

In Menachem's time, without the ramp, and with the Snake Path – visible here on the eastern slopes – as the only known entry, it was convincingly believed to be impregnable. Even today, it's still an imposing and awe-inspiring place. One look at the sheer drop on either side of the mountain of stone rising out of the desert would be enough to put off most assaulting armies.

Nevertheless, Menachem not only had the vision to attempt the assault but also the skill at arms to defeat the Roman garrison who held the fortress on top, and thereby arm his men in sufficient numbers to take Jerusalem and drive out the Roman garrison there.

Thereafter, as Josephus proclaims, Menachem 'returned in the state of a king' to Jerusalem, and became leader of the sedition, which makes him – in my opinion – the first likely contender for the title of Jewish messiah. If he had held the city and ushered in the theocracy his grandfather had fought and died for, he would have been the true King of Israel – and the history of the world would be different in so many ways.

This, therefore, is the heart of this book: the taking of Masada and the insurrection that could put a good king on the throne. It took place against a background of regional turmoil: Volgases, King of Kings of Parthia, had installed his own brother on the throne of Armenia and then effectively dared Nero to do something about it. The resulting war saw the humiliation of a Roman legion. An uprising in Judaea was the last thing anybody wanted or needed, but it was more easily dealt with than the giant empire to its east, which goes some way to explaining the Roman desire to keep Judaea secure throughout the first and second centuries.

Before that, though, the Hebrews had one more major triumph: the defeat of the Twelfth legion at the battle of Beth Horon, and the capture of its eagle. The next book in this series, *The Eagle of the Twelfth*, charts the fortunes of that legion and the efforts of some of the surviving legionaries to regain their standard, and their honour.

BOUDICA

DREAMING THE EAGLE
DREAMING THE BULL
DREAMING THE HOUND
DREAMING THE SERPENT SPEAR

Manda Scott

Boudica: at twelve, she killed her first warrior. At twenty-one, she defended her land against an invasion by the most powerful empire the world had ever seen. At forty, she led her people in a bloody revolt – and became a legend.

Set in a Britain before the Romans came, Manda Scott's thrillingly imagined novels bring the brutal world of druids, dreamers, warriors and their gods to vivid life in a story of passion, courage and spectacular heroism pitched against overwhelming odds...

'Alive with the love, deceit, wisdom and the heroics of humanity'
Jean M. Auel

'Manda Scott has created a fictional universe all her own, but close enough to our reality for it both to warm and break our hearts. Breathtakingly good, it reveals the best and worst in all of us'
Val McDermid

'Utterly convincing and compelling...
A stunning feat of the imagination and an absolute must-read'
Steven Pressfield

ROME

THE
EMPEROR'S SPY

—————— **M.C. Scott** ——————

'Stop this fire, whatever it takes. I, your Emperor, order it'

THE EMPEROR
Nero, Emperor of Rome and all her provinces, feared by his subjects
for his temper and cruelty, is in possession of an ancient document
predicting that Rome will burn.

THE SPY
Sebastos Pantera, assassin and spy for the Roman Legions, is ordered
to stop the impending cataclysm. He knows that if he does not, his life
– and those of thousands of others – is in terrible danger.

THE CHARIOT BOY
Math, a young charioteer, is a pawn drawn into the deadly game
between the Emperor and the Spy, where death stalks the drivers –
on the track and off it.

From the author of the bestselling *Boudica* series, **The Emperor's Spy**
begins a compelling new series of novels featuring **Sebastos Pantera**. Rich
characterisation and spine tingling adventure combine in a vividly realized
novel set amid the bloodshed and the chaos, the heroism and murderous
betrayal of ancient Rome.

'As exciting as Ben Hur, *and far more accurate'*
Independent

'A gripping tale, with more to come'
Daily Mail

ROME

THE
EAGLE OF THE TWELFTH

M.C. Scott

They are known as the Legion of the Damned . . .

Throughout the Roman Army, the Twelfth Legion is notorious for its ill fortune. It faces the harshest of postings, the toughest of campaigns, the most vicious of opponents. For one young man, Demalion of Macedon, joining it will be a baptism of fire. And yet, amid the violence and savagery of his life as a legionary, he realizes he has discovered a vocation – as a soldier and a leader of men. He has come to love the Twelfth and all the bloody-minded, dark-hearted soldiers he calls his brothers.

But just when he has found a place in the world, all that he cares about is ripped from him when, during the brutal Judaean campaign, the Hebrew army inflict a catastrophic defeat upon the legion – not only decimating their ranks, but taking away their soul, the eagle.

There is one final chance to save the legion's honour – to steal back the eagle. To do that, Demalion and his legionaries must go undercover into Jerusalem, into the very heart of their enemy, where discovery will mean the worst of deaths, if they are to recover their pride.

And that, in itself, is a task worthy only of heroes.

2012

EVERYTHING YOU NEED TO KNOW ABOUT THE APOCALYPSE

Manda Scott

The first thing you need to know about 2012 is
that it's just like any other year.

And the second thing you need to know . . . is
that it really isn't.

The Maya didn't make it their 'end date'
for nothing . . .